What readers are saying about Part One of Inklings

"...Enjoyed it immensely...It caught the mood of the city extremely well...Research was excellent and a good story line."

—G.J., Merton College, Oxford

"I bought this 'hidden treasure' after reading a glowing review in *World Magazine.* I thoroughly enjoyed every aspect of the book—history and personal tidbits about C.S. Lewis, J.R.R. Tolkien, and...the Inklings, the interwoven romance that shows the struggles of Christians desirous to remain pure in their devotion to God and to their future mate, and the importance of this—all told within the rich setting of Oxford.... The book delivers everything you could ask for from a Christian historical romance novel! You'll smile, you'll sigh, and you won't be able to put it down! You'll also want to read more of C.S. Lewis's writings *and* you'll want to take a trip to Oxford! I'm so looking forward to the rest of the series..."

—J.V., Deland, Florida, Christianbook.com

"...Wonderful book!...Visual imagery and character-building made everything as real to the reader as being there."

—S.H., former Oxford student

"I recently read the book *Inklings*....I thought it was fantastic and I'm looking forward to future tales of David and Kate."

—L.Q., Baton Rouge, Louisiana

"[My daughter] had a yearning to read *Inklings* yet again. I think this is number ten or eleven."

—C.P., Houston, Texas

"I couldn't put it down...Being a romantic myself, I enjoyed the book tremendously."

—E.B., missionary to Peru

"The book was a delight. I basked in an atmosphere still touched by the presence of C.S. Lewis and graced by the Inklings...Beautifully portrayed characters fit into these surroundings perfectly and together wove an engrossing story with an inspiring message."

—C.J., Sterling, Virginia

"I *loved* the book! I eagerly await the next one!"

—A.C., Christian counselor, Southwest Virginia

"....a great read that I found hard to put down... I got so involved in the story and identified so strongly with the characters...What surprised me most was that a good Kiwi bloke such as myself, identified so strongly with Kate. I felt her joy and her pain keenly, and I really felt I got inside her head and feelings. The characters are very believable and the situations real—something that is often missing from Christian fiction...."

—Kiwi in DC, Amazon.com

"...excellent atmospheric details transport t ... ing story. And the spirit of C.S. Lewis in delightf ...

... m

"I really enjoyed this book...Once I started re ...

... on.com

Praise for *Inklings* from the reviewers

"[This] novel is a warm tribute to Lewis' life and legacy. Her intimate knowledge of Oxford, and the Inklings' old haunts, make this an evocative read for Lewis lovers."

—Dr. J. Stanley Mattson, Ph.D. President and Founder of the C. S. Lewis Foundation

"*Inklings,* by first-time author Melanie Jeschke, is a novel set in Oxford in 1964. It combines romance, biography, and a love for C. S. Lewis. Although the book starts on the day of his funeral, Lewis is the central character, with his memory hovering over Oxford, drawing earnest admirers to the ancient university, and awakening in them a desire to follow in his Christian footsteps. Lewis inspires a young Oxford don to start a new Inklings group, where current students can come together for Christian community as they discuss literature, especially the works of the original Inklings. Of course, there is romance, but unlike a typical contemporary romance the characters are determined to seek God's will for their lives and maintain their purity. Educational side benefits of this engaging first novel, meant to be the first in a series: lots of details about Lewis's life and works, and even some intelligent discussion of Christian themes in Shakespeare."

—*World Magazine*

"Melanie has produced an evocative, romantic and charming novel. Familiar places and names are brought to life in this beautiful story about discovering oneself and discovering love amongst the dreaming spires of Oxford."

—Tiffany Ponsonby, wife of the Chaplain to the Oxford Pastorate and Assistant Minister, St. Aldate's Anglican Church, Oxford, England

"Melanie's book captures the spirit of Oxford, the spirit of Lewis, the spirit of the American studying abroad....an engaging read for anyone interested in any of these and a treasure for those like me who cherish all three."

—Jodi Johnson, Head Resident of *The Kilns,* C.S. Lewis' home in Oxford

"Fascinating! As a C.S. Lewis fan, I couldn't help but get involved...a great read!"

—Loree Lough, author of *Pocketful of Love* and *The Wedding Wish*

"*Inklings* is a delightful first novel....(it) evokes the charm and mystery of Oxford and its beautiful landscapes, as well as depicting the impact of C. S. Lewis and the other writers, including J.R.R. Tolkien, known as the Inklings, on Oxford literary culture and the lives of those who treasure their works."

—Dr. Bruce L. Edwards, Associate Dean and Professor of English at Bowling Green State University, international lecturer, seminar leader, and scholar on the Inklings, and web-master of the C.S. Lewis and Inklings web-site: http://personal.bgsu.edu/~edwards/lewis.html

"I very much enjoyed the unique combination of romance with the clear emphasis on purity and courtship...Great reading for busy home-school moms who would like a refreshing (and romantic!) escape from those schoolbooks!"

—Vickie Farris, author of *A Mom Just Like You*

"Great insight into the lives of C.S. Lewis and Tolkien. Five stars."

—Brandon D. Hill, *christianteens.about.com*

"[*Inklings*] weaves in the lives of C.S. Lewis and J.R.R. Tolkien...throughout a story focusing on a young Christian college girl from America, and a young... English Christian college man (professor) who both seek to serve God in the midst of longing for true love. With snares in both lives, a delicate story unfolds which shows the pitfalls of being 'unequally' yoked, and the grace of God who works all things together....This would be enjoyed by a high school student, or perhaps even more, by a mom who needs a bit of a holiday in a pleasant, sweet book, and to remember the joys of that 'first quickening of love' and the dreaded delight of waiting upon God for that precious 'one'. I enjoyed it, and am looking forward to more in this series!"

—Jenefer Igarashi, Senior Editor, *The Old Schoolhouse Magazine*

"Melanie Jeschke weaves a beautiful tale, certain to attract lovers of Oxford, C.S. Lewis, and English Literature. Amidst today's immoral romance novels, this book is a shining beacon of what true love should be."

—Rachel Haney, Eclectic Homeschool Association

INKLINGS

Melanie M. Jeschke

HARVEST HOUSE PUBLISHERS

EUGENE, OREGON

Cover by Left Coast Design, Portland, Oregon

Cover images © Adam Woolfitt/Corbis Stock; Sandra Ivany/Brand X Pictures/Getty Images; Max Dannenbaum/The Image Bank/Getty Images

Page 9: map of Oxford by Andrew White

INKLINGS

Published by Harvest House Publishers
Eugene, Oregon 97402
www.harvesthousepublishers.com

Part I of this edition of *Inklings* was originally published by Xulon Press in 2002.

Library of Congress Cataloging-in-Publication Data

Jeschke, Melanie M., 1942-
Inklings / Melanie Jeschke M.
p. cm. —(The Oxford chronicles; bk. 1)
Includes bibliographical references.
ISBN 0-7369-1436-6 (pbk.)
1. Triangles (Interpersonal relations)—Fiction. 2. Inklings (Group of writers)—Fiction. 3. Women college students—Fiction. 4. Americans—England—Fiction. 5. Oxford (England)—Fiction. I. Title. II. Series.
PS3610.E83I55 2004
813'.6—dc22 2004002115

Printed in the United States of America

04 05 06 07 08 09 10 11 / BC-KB / 10 9 8 7 6 5 4 3 2 1

To my parents, Betty and Earl Morey,
who instilled in me a love for learning, literature, history,
and above all—God.

A Note from the Author

This is a work of fiction, and the characters are entirely from my own imagination. Any mistakes I have made are my own. However, to the best of my knowledge, the historical details are accurate and the stories about the Inklings and C.S. Lewis are true, with the exception of their involvement with my fictional characters. Many of the stories about Lewis I heard firsthand at the Oxbridge '98 and 2002 conferences sponsored by the C.S. Lewis Foundation—from Lewis's stepson Douglas Gresham, his secretary Walter Hooper, and others who knew him. Others are taken from numerous books written about him (see my list of references on page 405).

J.R.R. Tolkien, Jacqueline du Pré, Stephen Bishop, the Millers, and Major Warren Lewis, who are mentioned in the book, are real people who were alive in 1964. However, the priest who married Jack and Joy was the Reverend Peter Bide, not my fictional Eric MacKenzie.

The descriptions of Oxford, Cambridge, the Kilns, and Blenheim Palace are as accurate as possible. On several trips to the UK and Oxford I was blessed to live "in college" at Christ Church, Jesus, and Merton Colleges in Oxford, and Magdalene College in Cambridge; visit the Kilns and Lewis's church at Headington; and attend a dinner–dance at Blenheim Palace. (The Oxford balls are generally given in the colleges during the Trinity or summer term, not in the autumn.) My fictional Clifton Manor, the Devereux country estate, is loosely based on Audley End in Essex as well as Knole in Kent.

St. Aldate's Anglican Church is a wonderful, vibrant fellowship of believers located across from Christ Church College in Oxford. My daughter Katherine attended this church when she studied at Oxford in the Michaelmas term of 1999. In 1964, St. Aldate's rectory was Number 40 Pembroke Street, which now serves as the Parish Centre, where they continue to serve Sunday luncheons to hungry students.

In the autumn of 1964, Jacqueline du Pré was on a concert tour, performing in small concert halls with pianist Stephen Bishop. I couldn't discover if she actually appeared in Oxford, but it's not unlikely since she did perform at Cambridge. The Custodian of the Sheldonian Theatre at Oxford, Sue Waldman, couldn't find any record. She actually attended a concert of Stephen Bishop (now known as Stephen Kovacevich) and personally asked him. He couldn't recollect such a concert but said it was certainly possible. I was intrigued by Miss du Pré's connection to Oxford when St. Hilda's College opened the Jacqueline du Pré Music Building. She was born in Oxford but never attended the University. However, she became an honorary Fellow of St. Hilda's and gave master classes there in the later years of her life.

Maggie Smith and Sir Laurence Olivier did perform in *Othello* at the Old Vic in 1964. This performance was videotaped and has been shown on public television.

Readers of Jane Austen will notice that most of the novel's minor characters have names taken from her novels. This was intentional and is my small tribute to this greatest of romance writers. Many of the principal characters' names are from my family. My grandmother's name was Katherine McKenzie Little, and my husband's grandmother was a Devereux.

Because some American readers may be unfamiliar with certain British words, phrases, and slang, I've included a glossary, which can be found on page 397.

As a devotee of English literature and history as well as of C.S. Lewis, I wrote this book as a labor of love. I hope it will inspire others to explore the lives and writings of the remarkable and creative authors known as the Inklings—as well as to seek to know the Divine Creator, Author of all Life and Love.

Soli Deo Gloria.

Melanie Morey Jeschke
Vienna, Virginia
February 2004

Map of Oxford

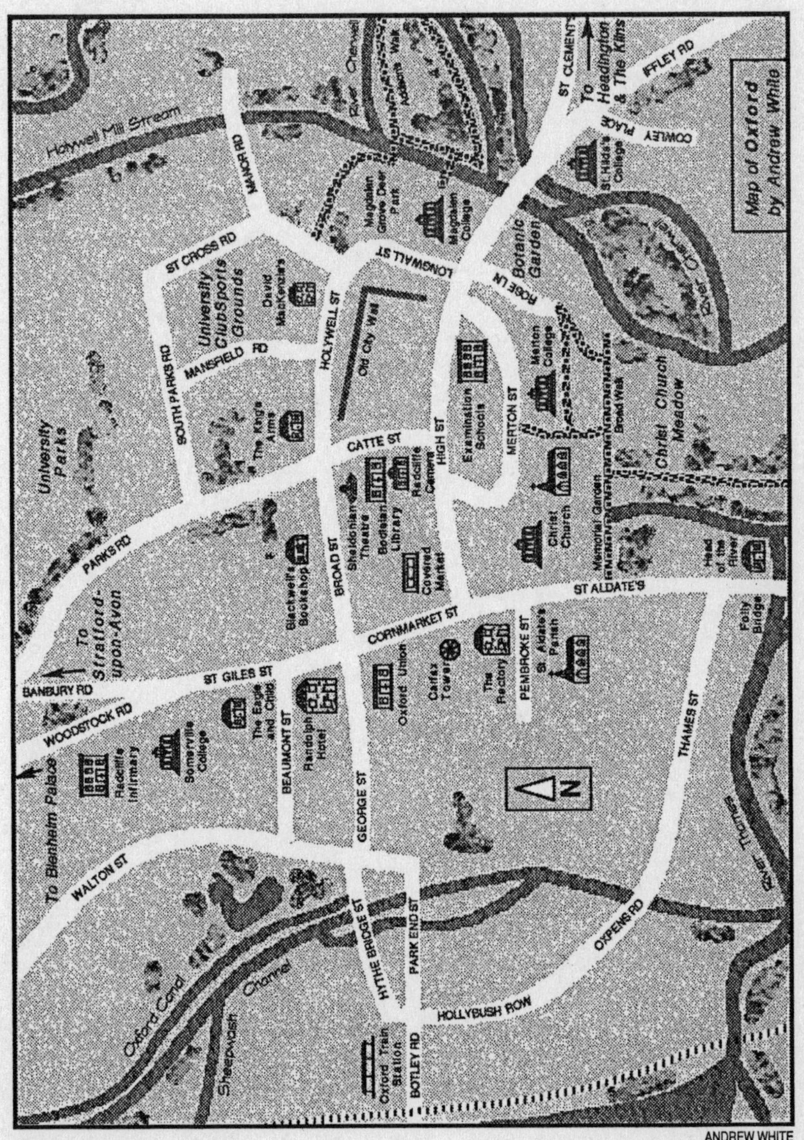

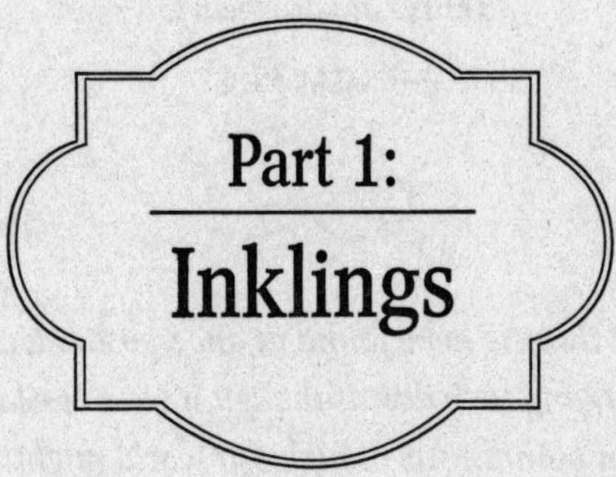

Part 1: Inklings

Take delight in the Lord, and he will give you the desires of your heart.

—PSALM 37:4

The great thing is to be found at one's post as a child of God, living each day as though it were our last, but planning as though our world might last a hundred years.

—C.S. LEWIS,
from *God in the Dock,* "Cross Examination" (1963)

Prologue

Oxford, England
November 26, 1963

David MacKenzie had made a decision. He just hadn't decided how to tell his fiancée.

For most of the day—after the funeral—he had walked around the parks of Oxford, thinking and praying. Now that he had reached his decision, he was sharing his thoughts with his friend and colleague, Austen Holmes, over dinner in the Eagle and Child pub. David wearily helped himself to shepherd's pie as he talked.

"Austen, I wish you could have been there. It's such a pity that Jack Lewis, *the* C.S. Lewis—one of Oxford's greatest writers and thinkers—should have had only a few friends and family at his funeral."

Austen replied quietly. "But really, David, don't you believe he would have preferred it that way? Besides, I don't think very many people even heard about it, what with the Kennedy assassination and all. Did his brother publish any notices?"

"I don't know." David thoughtfully set down his fork. "Poor old Major Lewis. He's quite beside himself and wasn't even able to get out of bed to attend the service. I don't know what he'll do without Jack. I don't know what any of us will do." David's young, winsome face clouded with grief. He took a deep breath and exhaled slowly.

"A lit candle was placed on top of the coffin as it was carried out to the churchyard," he said with more composure. "You know what the weather was like today: clear, cold, and crisp. One of those perfect autumn days that Jack absolutely loved. But what struck me most, Austen, was that the candle's flame burned so brightly and never wavered. Even outdoors, the flame held. I think everyone noticed. To me that brightly burning candle symbolized the man's very life."

Finishing his dinner, David poured himself a cup of tea. Austen waited without speaking, sensing his friend had more to share. Although both of the University tutors were considered handsome, they were a study in contrasts. Austen was the typical Anglo-Saxon: tall and lanky, blond hair, bluish-green eyes, fair skin, angular features. David had more of the Celt about him: muscular build, bright blue eyes, fair skin, but dark—almost black—wavy hair.

David broke their silence. "Austen, Jack Lewis *did* something with his life. He could have been just a quiet Oxford don, but he was compelled to share his faith—through stories, radio talks, lectures, and books. And everything he wrote or spoke had such excellence, such beauty. He made you want to believe as he did. That candle today—that would not be extinguished even with his death—challenged me and made me truly want to *do* something for God with my life. Maybe, in some small way, carry on the Lewis legacy, if you will."

"All right." Austen smiled. "I know you have a plan. What is it?"

David leaned forward eagerly. "I would like to organize a new Oxford student club, a sort of second-generation 'Inklings.' We could meet every week to read and discuss the writings of the original Inklings—Lewis, Tolkien, Williams, Barfield—right here in the Bird and Baby, just as they did. Maybe the students would be inspired to try their own hand at writing, and this could be the forum for it."

"And the 'we' means you want my help?"

"Of course!" David grinned. "You can be our resident Tolkien expert. And who knows? Maybe the venerable author himself may grace our presence now and then."

Austen considered the proposal briefly. "Well, I'm game. I think it's a grand idea."

"Excellent!" David happily leaned back in the booth. "We can do our part to keep the candle burning. I know God has called me here to Oxford to do more than teach, and that's what's been challenging me all day."

"Right." Austen glanced up. "And how are you going to square all this with Charlotte?"

David sighed heavily. "That's what I haven't figured out yet."

"Well, you'd best figure it out quickly." Austen motioned with his head. "Because she just came in."

Both men quickly stood to greet the striking young woman. The bangs of her shoulder length red hair stylishly fringed her blue eyes. A few freckles were sprinkled across her creamy skin. Under her black leather coat, she wore white boots and a short white sweater dress.

"Charlotte, darling!" David embraced her. "How good of you to come all the way from Cambridge."

She kissed him on the cheek in reply and greeted Austen.

"Well, good night," said Austen, moving aside for David's fiancée to take his place in the paneled booth. "This is my cue to exit and let you two lovebirds comfort one another." He put his hand on David's arm. "Ring me up and we'll talk about this some more."

David nodded in reply as the other man retrieved his jacket and slipped out.

"Talk about what?" Charlotte smiled across the table. David poured her some tea, took a deep breath, and then launched into a recitation of all he had shared earlier with his friend.

Charlotte listened intently until he paused long enough for her to ask, "David, just where do *I* fit into all of these grandiose plans for your being the next C.S. Lewis?"

"Charlotte, I don't intend to try to be the next C.S. Lewis. That isn't my point at all. And, of course, you will fit in as we've planned—as my wife."

Charlotte fumbled in her handbag for a cigarette. As she held one up for David to light, he noticed her hand was trembling. He knew that her smoking had begun as a showcase for her lovely slender hands, but it was now a necessity whenever she was nervous or aggravated. She took a deep drag and slowly blew out the smoke as she stared at the diamond on her ring finger.

"David, I know you're upset about Mr. Lewis. I know how much he meant to you and how much you miss him. I think you've had a hard day and the emotion has been too much for you." She took another long drag.

He watched her in exasperation. "You think I'm distraught—that I'm just raving or something."

"That's not what I said."

"But, that's what you meant."

When she didn't answer, David spoke again, more quietly. "Charlotte, I'm serious about this. I want to make a difference with my life, to really do something for God."

"And this—doing 'something for God' as you put it—means doing it here, in Oxford?"

"Well, yes." David sighed. "Look, I know our plan has always been for me to return to Cambridge as soon as something opened up there. I've been wrestling all afternoon with how to broach this with you. But, Charlotte, I feel quite strongly that God has called me here for a purpose. Now that Jack is gone, it seems even more important that I stay."

Charlotte flicked her cigarette ashes into the ashtray. After a moment, she said, "David, your religious beliefs are your own business. Frankly, I've never understood them. I'm a scientist, not a theologian. But now you're trying to tell me that 'God' wants you here in Oxford. Well, I don't want *your* God to interfere in *my* life."

David clenched his jaw and tried to speak calmly. "Charlotte, I'm sorry. I've sprung all this on you in my stream-of-consciousness mode. I know I haven't shared much of my spiritual side with you...well, frankly, because you didn't want to hear it. And I know we planned to live in Cambridge so you could continue your research there. But, Charlotte, couldn't you at least consider moving here with me? I really think I've got something important to do here."

"And what I'm doing isn't?" she asked, an edge to her voice.

"I didn't say that."

"You know, what you've really wanted all along is for me to be like your mother—a wife at home with a brood of obedient children in tow…but, David, that's not me. It never will be me."

"Charlotte…"

"David, your mother is a fine woman, but I will *never* be like her. You knew that when you met me. I'm a scientist, David. I'm doing important research at Cambridge. And if you think that I'm willing to give up my career to move to Oxford to become the mealy-mouthed wife of some dithering don…well…." She crushed her cigarette into the ashtray to finish her point.

Grief swept over him. "So," he sighed. "That's it, then."

"That's what?"

"That's it for us."

"No! That's not *it* for us!" Charlotte tried to lower her voice. "David, let's not get melodramatic here. Please, darling. Go get some drinks. Let's calm down and talk like the two intelligent adults that we are."

David pushed himself up from the table and headed to the bar. Taking out her compact, Charlotte reapplied her lipstick. She snapped the case shut and shoved it quickly back into her handbag when he returned with a pint of bitter, which he handed across the table.

"So, not drinking now either?" she asked archly, taking a sip.

He shrugged.

"David, darling." Her voice softened. "We're both tired. Maybe we've said things we shouldn't have or things we didn't mean. It's been a long, trying day." She reached across the table and took his hand.

"Maybe we should get a good night's sleep and talk about it in the morning."

He kept his hand in hers and smiled. "That sounds like a good idea. So where are you staying?"

She smiled back. "With you, of course."

David withdrew his hand and sadly shook his head. "Charlotte, not with me. Maybe you could stay with your mates at St. Hilda's or Somerville—or with my parents."

"Your parents?"

"Well, why not? They'd be glad to have you."

"David." Charlotte tried to keep her voice even, but the sharpness was unmistakable. "I did not come all the way from Cambridge to stay with your parents."

"Charlotte, you were wonderful to come and I'm so glad to see you, but you must understand that it just won't do to have you stay with me."

"Just won't *do?*" Charlotte's face flushed. "What is all this rot? Since when have you cared about what will *do?*"

David rubbed a hand across his forehead. "That's what I've been trying to tell you. I want to live my life differently now. Ever since I walked out of that churchyard this morning, I've felt like God has called me to live totally for Him. That I should do what pleases *Him*, not what pleases me."

"So, it doesn't please Him for you to spend time with your fiancée?"

"Charlotte, you know what I mean. And even if we didn't...and even if nothing...Charlotte, we should think of how it looks if nothing else."

"David, I don't believe I'm hearing this," Charlotte's voice rose. "Are you *daft?* You care what a bunch of pimply adolescents or doddering old men think? Who are you trying to impress with your newfound holiness? Them? God?" She stood up and leaned over the table, mocking him. "Or perhaps C.S. Lewis, your precious patron saint?"

Before he could defend himself, she shoved her ale across the table and into his lap.

Then she walked out.

October 1964

Michaelmas Term, Nought Week, Tuesday Evening

Katherine Lee Hughes was twenty years old and ripe for romance.

For as long as she could remember, Kate had longed to live and learn under the "dreaming spires" of Oxford. Finally all her youthful hopes and dreams, all her intellectual and spiritual aspirations, all her named and unnamed yearnings were coming to fruition.

Here she was sitting in the Eagle and Child—the 'Bird and Baby' as it was affectionately called—the very pub where C.S. Lewis, J.R.R. Tolkien, Charles Williams, and others had met weekly for so many years to read and discuss their writings in progress. She couldn't believe that she had found a meeting of "Inklings" here, and that other students shared her enthusiasm for these writers. With her heart full of awed joy, she uttered a silent prayer of gratitude for God's goodness in bringing her here—to Oxford.

Kate closed her eyes and leaned her head back against the wood-paneled wall. The heavy scents of tobacco and stale beer mixed with smoke drifting from the coal fire. The voices in the pub hushed as one young man earnestly began to read a passage from *The Fellowship of the Ring*. Kate let the rhythmic poetry of the hobbit's song wash over her, and her mind wandered in wonder.

Opening her eyes, she looked about the cozy room with its round, wooden tables and chairs huddled around the coal-burning fireplace. She couldn't decide if the walls above the dark wainscoting were yellow with paint or smoke stains. She studied the faces of the students in the hazy light as they listened intently to the reading. A small group to be sure. *"We few, we happy few, we band of brothers."* The line from *Henry V* came to her mind as Kate counted ten undergraduates and the two faculty advisors.

Several of the young men caught her eye and glanced away, embarrassed. Kate was used to men's admiring stares, but secretly it never failed to please her. Suddenly, she noticed David MacKenzie, one of the advisors, watching her. He held her gaze until *she* glanced away, embarrassed.

Her wandering attention was diverted back to the reader, Nigel, and she smiled in spite of herself. With his longish brown hair swept up in a pompadour style, a pair of spectacles perched on the tip of his nose, and the ever-present scarf flung around his neck, he epitomized the quintessential Oxford student. He read dramatically and well. The passage ended and was met with an appreciative silence, broken by David MacKenzie's sonorous voice.

"Thank you, Nigel. That was excellent. A fine choice and well done." He paused. "Well, now. At this point in the meeting, we open it up to those wanting to read other works or even original ones." He looked directly at Kate. "Would our friends from the other side of the pond have something to share with us?"

Kate blushed as she rapidly searched her mind for some memorized sonnet or passage. "No," she replied in a slight but charming southern drawl. "I'm afraid I've come unprepared." She looked anxiously at her suite-mate Connie, who simply shook her head.

"Sorry. My fault," David said gently. "This is your first meeting and I didn't give you any warning. But perhaps we should take this time to make some introductions. I'm David MacKenzie, a faculty sponsor, and this"—he indicated a lanky fair-haired man in his late twenties—"is my colleague, Austen Holmes."

Austen nodded and David turned to the others. "I'll let the rest of you gentlemen introduce yourselves."

The young men quickly went about the room giving their names, and Kate just as quickly forgot them, except for two: Nigel Elliot, the reader, and Colin Russell, a student with straight blond hair in a Beatles' cut. She had met them both the day before, manning a table for the Inklings Society at the university club orientation, dubbed the "Freshers' Fair."

"And you ladies are...?" asked David.

Kate spoke up first. "I'm Katherine Hughes, but I go by Kate." She turned to her suite-mate.

"I'm Connie Bennet," said her friend, somewhat shyly.

"Right. Glad you could join us. Now..." David looked around the room. "Who has something for us tonight?"

After an awkward silence and no volunteers, David grinned and said, "Guess you'll have to listen to me then—more from my Celtic epic." He pulled out a sheaf of papers, cleared his throat, and began reading in a deep, melodious voice. Soon the little group sat enthralled while he wove a magical tale of heroes and battles in a far away time.

The firelight flickered over his handsome face as he read, and Kate watched him intently. So this was David MacKenzie, her Shakespeare tutor. She couldn't believe how blessed she was—not only was she sitting in the Eagle and Child in Oxford, but her tutor obviously shared her passion for poetry. His bright blue eyes suddenly looked up at her and caught her gaze again. He had finished reading, and Kate realized she hadn't heard a word. She flushed and glanced quickly away as appreciative applause broke out.

"All right, all right." Laughing, David held up his hands. "I know half of you are applauding because you're my students. But I expect some of you to bring in readings next time. Now in a fortnight, we are in for a real treat. Professor Tolkien himself will be here to read to us from one of his books."

An excited buzz met this announcement as the group gathered up their belongings and began to file out of the pub.

"Ladies," David's commanding voice caught Kate and Connie's attention as they pulled on their coats. "Please permit Mr. Holmes and me to escort you home. If you're at St. Hilda's, we're going that way."

Kate smiled. "Why, thanks. Yes, we are, and we'd be much obliged as we're new here and just finding our bearings."

"Katherine Hughes, you said?" David looked thoughtful. "Wait… you're taking a tutorial with me, aren't you? Shakespeare?"

Kate nodded.

"Excellent! Well, I'm so glad you found out about our Inklings Society. We weren't sure how much of a following they have in the States." David glanced at Austen, who was wrapping a scarf around his neck. "I guess we'd better be off. You can tell us about it on the walk back." He pushed open the door of the pub and they stepped out into the brisk, dark night.

Kate looked up at the painted signboard hanging over the pub entrance. It depicted a cherubic infant riding on the back of a large eagle.

"What does it mean?" she asked as they began walking towards Carfax Tower.

"Sorry?"

Kate clarified her question. "The Eagle and Child. What does the pub's name mean?"

"Ah. Greek mythology," David answered. "The baby is Ganymede, cupbearer of the gods. The eagle is Zeus, who went looking for a new cupbearer and, spying this perfect little mortal specimen, scooped him up and took him to Mt. Olympus. Nobody really knows why the name was chosen. We had surmised that the pub owners were trying to entice the classically minded scholars to do their imbibing here. But there's been an inn here since the 1650s, and the original landlord was a retainer of the Earl of Derby, whose coat of arms had an eagle and child on it. The legend was that one of the Earl's ancestors found and adopted a child who had been nurtured by an eagle." David then turned the conversation back to the young women. "So anyway, where are you ladies from and what brings you to Oxford?"

The girls struggled to keep up with David, who walked with long strides. Austen, ahead by several paces, led the way down Cornmarket Street. Even at this time of night, people thronged the narrow sidewalks, making it difficult to walk side by side.

"Well," Kate began breathlessly, "we're both from the College of William and Mary in Virginia and are here for our junior year abroad."

Slowing his pace to match the girls', David dropped back beside them. "Ah, William and Mary...Thomas Jefferson's alma mater."

The girls nodded with pride. Connie spoke up. "It's one of the oldest colleges in the U.S." She smiled sheepishly as she looked up at the medieval tower of Carfax, which had guarded the central crossroads of the town for centuries. "But not very old by Oxford standards, I suppose."

David smiled. "No, it's hard to beat the twelfth century for age. But I've been to William and Mary. It's a beautiful school, and as with Oxford, you can credit much of your architecture to Sir Christopher Wren."

They turned and started down High Street, Oxford's main thoroughfare, which stretched from Carfax Tower to the River Cherwell and was lined with timber-framed shops and the stone walls of colleges. The crowds had thinned out.

"What were you doing in Williamsburg?" Kate ventured.

"Well, my mother is an American war bride—came over here before the war and stayed when she met and married my father. I've spent a few summers with my grandfather, who was a religion professor at the University of Virginia, and we always got in some sightseeing. Are you ladies from Virginia?"

Connie shook her head. "I'm from Bethesda, Maryland, near Washington, D.C., but Kate's from Richmond."

"Ah, the capital of the Confederacy. We Rebels will just have to stick together now, won't we?" David teased.

"My dad went to UVA," Kate replied thoughtfully. "I wonder if he knew your grandfather."

"Really?" David looked at her in surprise. "My word, it's a small world."

They had caught up with Austen, who had taken them down a side street and now waited politely for them outside a college gate near an imposing tower.

"This is Merton College," David explained as they approached. "And where we bid farewell to our friend, Mr. Holmes. He's a Fellow here."

"Good night, ladies." Austen smiled tiredly and nodded to them. "Lunch tomorrow, David?"

"Right. Cheerio."

"Merton College," Connie repeated excitedly as they walked on. "Isn't that where J.R.R. Tolkien taught?"

"Yes," David answered. "He retired about six years ago. Austen had the privilege of studying with him. Are you a Tolkien fan?"

"Oh, yes!" Connie gushed. "I love The Lord of the Rings. Kate and I were just thrilled to find out you had an Inklings club. I can't believe Tolkien himself will be coming!"

"So." David turned to Kate. "You're a big Tolkien fan too?"

Kate tilted up her head. A petite young woman, she was used to looking up to people, and she guessed David was nearly six feet tall.

"Yes. I am. But, I'm really more drawn to the writings of C.S. Lewis. I love The Chronicles of Narnia and *The Screwtape Letters,* and I like his science fiction trilogy too."

As the trio turned back on High Street, they walked past a massive Gothic bell tower brightly lit against the dark night.

"That's Magdalen Tower," David said as they began to cross the wide stone bridge that spanned the Cherwell. "Not pronounced the way it's spelled. More like 'maudlin.' You know, like the word for 'sentimentally sad.' The Old French 'maudelaine' is from the same Greek word as 'Magdalene'—as in Mary Magdalene. So it's actually a medieval pronunciation. Uh..."

He faltered self-consciously. "I guess I'm getting rather pedantic..." He drew in his breath and exhaled slowly. "Anyway, that's my college, and was Mr. Lewis's for many years."

Kate's dark eyes widened. "*The* Mr. Lewis? Did you really know C.S. Lewis?"

"Yes, I did. Quite well, really. My father was a friend of his. Then I went up to Magdalene College at Cambridge to study with him before he became ill."

Kate's mind reeled. Her tutor was tutored by C.S. Lewis. She was so close to the writer she admired so much.

The threesome turned down Cowley Place and walked along the yellow brick Georgian walls of St. Hilda's Hall.

"Yes, it was quite something. He was a remarkable man and mentor. Not only was he a great Christian writer, but he was also perhaps the finest man I've ever known. I always think of those words from *Hamlet: 'He was a man. Take him for all in all, I shall not look upon his like again.'"*

David paused, remembering. "He died almost a year ago—on November 22, the same day as your President Kennedy, actually. It's still hard to believe he's gone." He spoke very quietly. "We all miss him very much."

As they approached the front gate of St. Hilda's, his voice brightened. "Perhaps when you come for your tutorials, we can talk more about Mr. Lewis. We'll have plenty of time for Shakespeare too."

"I'd like that very much." Kate shook his extended hand. "And thank you for walking us back."

"My pleasure. Please come by this Thursday so we can get started. I'll look forward to seeing you."

He shook Connie's hand warmly. "Miss Bennet, nice to meet you as well. I hope you both enjoy your stay here in Oxford."

As Kate thoughtfully closed the gate behind him, she breathed another prayer of gratitude. She was certain she would enjoy her stay very much indeed.

David slowly walked back over Magdalen Bridge. He picked up some loose gravel and tossed the stones one at a time into the river. He knew it was a juvenile thing to do, but the boy in him had never ceased to relish the plopping sound as the water swallowed up the stones. He stared at the dark river flowing swiftly under the bridge and thought with amusement of how often such a scene had been used as a metaphor for the passage of life. He applied the metaphor to himself.

Since Jack's funeral, there had been a lot of water under the bridge. He had kept to his commitment to living his life for God and trying to make each day count. He had thrown himself into his studies and his work with the students as he and Austen had gotten the new Inklings Society off the ground. The long summer vacation had rushed by as he helped to sort through the massive piles of Lewis's notebooks and unpublished papers, which his American secretary had literally saved from the fire of Major Lewis's overzealous housecleaning.

But his work had come at a great personal price: Charlotte.

His hand went into his coat pocket and pulled out several sheets of stationery. It was a letter—yet another letter—to Charlotte, begging her to reconsider, to try to work things out, to see most of all the importance of a genuine faith in God. Most of the letters he had never sent, yet he found it cathartic to pour out his heart on paper.

When he could step back from himself, he knew that it was futile, that it was not meant to be, and that she was certainly not God's best for him. With deep repentance, he knew their relationship had been unholy, and he had determined he would conduct the next one in absolute purity. Yet if he allowed himself to think of Charlotte for too long, all those unholy yearnings would rush in on him again.

David balled the letter up in his fist. He was tempted to throw it in the river with the stones, but his reluctance to litter made him think the better of it. Shoving it back into his pocket, he leaned on the stone balustrade. David looked up at the magnificent spire of Magdalen towering above him, and his heart cried out to God.

Lord, You know how weak I am. You know I have the same temptations and longings as any other healthy young man. Lord, I really would like to find a wife—someone godly who shares the same values and interests I have...and it wouldn't hurt if she were pretty too. David grinned at his own thoughts. *Anyway, please bring this person into my life and help me to recognize her. And please take away my feelings for Charlotte. I know they are not of You. Please reveal Yourself to her, Lord. And help me to be a good example to the students You have given me. Bless the Inklings Society and use it to Your glory.*

David looked back down into the water. Like a bee searching flowers for nectar, he let his mind flit over the faces of women he knew, searching for one who might be *the one.* He thought of some of his colleagues, and girls he had met at church, and some of the students. His mind passed by Katherine Hughes and then reversed itself and paused. She was obviously interested in Shakespeare and the Inklings, C.S. Lewis in particular. Moreover, he had found it difficult to keep his eyes off her. He had a weakness for long hair, and hers was wonderfully thick and lustrously dark. He had noticed how the red highlights had shone in the firelight, setting off her large brown eyes, delicate features, and clear complexion...how she carried herself like a little gymnast with perfect posture...and that shapely little figure of hers—*Whoa, old chap. Don't go there. Change the focus—*

Well, maybe she's a believer too. He'd have to read over her tutorial profile more carefully. But he also warned himself to remember she was his student and he could not compromise their academic relationship.

David shoved his hand back into his pocket and pulled out his crumpled letter to Charlotte. He strode purposefully across the bridge and stopped a few feet from a large waste bin. Glancing both ways to make sure no one was watching, he took a jump shot and stuffed the letter into the garbage.

Nought Week, Thursday Morning

With her mouth full of toothpaste, Connie yelled something indecipherable from her room.

"Connie," Kate called back with some frustration, "please come in here if you want to talk to me." She pulled her brush through her long, dark hair, checked the mirror, and stuck her tongue out at her reflection. Kate knew she was pretty. Some would say beautiful. Like most young women, she would enter a room and size up her competition. She usually found little. But she disliked her vanity and struggled to be nonchalant about her appearance. Today she was irritated with herself for trying to look good for her tutorial with David MacKenzie.

Connie came into her room and sat on the bed. Their sleeping quarters each had a study area and washbasin and were joined by a shared sitting room. Connie was what some people would describe as 'mousy': of medium-height with medium brown eyes and medium brown chin-length hair. Men tended to overlook her, yet Kate knew that with a little attention to makeup, Connie could be quite attractive.

"I was saying," Connie complained, "that it's not fair you get a tutorial with Mr. Movie Star and I have to face that old dragon Mr. Croft at Christ Church."

"Oh, Connie." Kate sighed. "Don't be ridiculous. 'Mr. Movie Star,' as you call him, is old too."

Connie scoffed. "What? *Twenties* is old?"

"Well, certainly older than we are. He's my tutor for heaven's sake. I almost wish he weren't. It makes me nervous somehow. Anyway, I have Mr. Croft too, for Tudor History."

"Yeah, but I've got Norris for Medieval History. He's an old geezer who's practically deaf and probably drools. It's hardly fair." Connie pushed her glasses up on her nose. "Well, I guess I won't get distracted when I'm reading my papers to them. But next term, I'm gonna try to get Austen Holmes for something. He's cute too—and to think he studied with Tolkien himself!"

She looked up at Kate. "Hey, you look nice."

Kate blushed but tried to be gracious as she slipped into her black, sleeveless student's robe. "Thanks. Look, I'd better get going. It wouldn't do to be late for my first tutorial."

A burly porter in a black bowler stopped Kate at the narrow gate to Magdalen. After ascertaining that her business was valid, he gave her a small map of the college grounds and directions to New Building, where she would find David's rooms. She scarcely noticed the serene beauty of the cloistered quad as she hurried through. A massive stone Palladian building faced her. Kate checked her map and confirmed it to be the "New" Building. She guessed from the architecture that it was built in the eighteenth century. Shaking her head, she laughed to herself. These eccentricities were what charmed her most about Oxford.

Kate found her way up the wooden staircase to David's rooms and paused nervously at the open door. Her tutor was leaning against the windowsill, pensively staring out at the Deer Park. "Brooding" was the word that came to Kate's mind. She summoned her courage, cleared her throat, and knocked gently.

David turned around and his face lit up. "Ah, Miss Hughes, please come in and sit down—and you can leave the door open." He indicated a shabby green sofa in front of the fireplace. "Sorry, it's always rather chilly in here, even in the summer. Sometimes it's colder inside than out. Jack's rooms...um...that is...Mr. Lewis had his rooms one staircase over. He used to hold his tutorials wearing his dressing gown over his sweater and jacket."

They both smiled at the thought. Kate noted that David wore a navy blue Shetland wool sweater under his Harris Tweed sports coat—and she was surprised to see him wearing blue jeans and American penny loafers.

"Well, now." David sat down and leaned back in his chair, his hands clasped behind his head. "I've read over your profile for tutorials, but would you like to tell me what you're hoping to learn and what you'd like to work on?"

Kate hadn't expected this. She had been told that each week she would be handed a book list and would have to write an eight-page paper on the assigned reading. She would then meet with her tutor, and he would critique her essay as she read it aloud.

"Frankly, I thought you would tell me what I should do."

"Oh, don't worry," he assured her. "Soon enough you'll get sick of what your dons tell you to do. Obviously, you want to read Shakespeare, but unless you have some strong desire to read literary criticism as well, we won't concentrate too much on that."

Kate smiled agreeably. "That's fine with me."

"I do want you to start off with reading some theatre history and background on Shakespeare, the Globe Theatre, that sort of thing. To put things in their proper context."

David set his chair straight and handed her several typed pages. "Here's your basic reading list for the term. You'll find all of the books in the Bodleian Library, but I do suggest you buy the canon of Shakespeare's plays. I'm a big advocate of underlining and writing in margins, and you can't take books out of the Bod."

He stood up and, walking over to the windows, tried to speak nonchalantly. "If I read your file correctly, I would deduce from what you wrote that you're a Christian."

Kate was taken by surprise. "Why, yes, I am." She answered cautiously, not certain where this was going.

"Then, perhaps you would like to look at some of the plays in light of their references to biblical themes?"

"That's what I really was hoping to do," Kate replied, her unease somewhat assuaged. "So…yes…that would be just great!"

"Good!" David began to pace around the room. "Why don't we start with *Measure for Measure*? It has a lot of intriguing themes in it. You could explore the concepts of justice and mercy, or the biblical reference in the title. Let's do *All's Well that Ends Well* too. The women in both plays, Isabella and Helena, share many similar qualities. Two of Shakespeare's strongest heroines, I think. You could read *Two Gentlemen from Verona* too since there are plot similarities. I would like you to get Coleridge's commentary and look at that. You might find it gives you ideas. Then pick your thesis, write your paper, and we'll discuss it next time. Oh, and I would like for you to choose a soliloquy or a sonnet to memorize each week."

Kate wrote furiously as her tutor strode about enthusiastically. She was beginning to feel overwhelmed.

David stopped behind her and leaned over the back of the sofa to see what she was writing. She caught the scent of Old Spice as the sleeve of his wool jacket brushed her cheek. Losing her concentration, she stopped writing.

"No—I'm sorry," he said. "That's too much for your first essay. Stick to the background reading and the two plays, *Measure* and *All's Well*. We can do *Two Gentleman* and Coleridge later."

David sat on the edge of the desk and addressed her. "Here's the main thing. The usual requirement is eight pages double-spaced, or you can write it out in longhand. But I don't want eight pages of rubbish. If you have a good thesis and can explore it in fewer pages, that's fine with me. None of this rot of wide margins and nonsensical filler."

Then he looked at her sympathetically and said gently, "Look, if you get stuck, please ring me up. You have my number there and I don't mind, really. All right?"

Kate nodded.

"Good!" David ran his hands through his hair. His tone lightened. "I say, do you have some time for me to show you about? Magdalen is quite a beautiful college, and I like to give my new students a quick tour of the place. You are my last tutorial today, and if I have to stay inside another minute on such a splendid autumn day, I'll go absolutely batty."

"I'd love to," Kate replied, much more calmly than she felt.

True to his word, David made the tour very quick indeed. He rapidly showed Kate the Senior and Junior Common Rooms, the Chapel, the Hall, and the cloistered Great Quadrangle, talking all the while about the architecture and history of Magdalen College. Like a caged animal, he could barely wait to burst outdoors again.

It was indeed a splendid day—one of those rare warm, sunny Indian summer days. The bright blue October sky threw into relief the fall foliage surrounding the great meadow. Kate noticed that the autumn colors seemed somehow subdued and muted—faded green and ancient gold rather than the more vibrant scarlet and youthful orange she was used to in Virginia. They walked along a path that reminded her of a nave in a cathedral, the trees bending over like graceful vaulting. One thick, gnarled branch stretched directly across the path, supported by a metal rod. David stopped at this tree, leaning against the branch.

"This," he said, sweeping his arm to include the bowered walkway and the deer grazing quietly and unperturbed in the meadow, "is probably my favorite spot in Oxford. I come here to pray or just clear my head."

"So," Kate prodded, "you're a believer too?"

He smiled. "I am, indeed."

"I can't tell you how glad I am! It really helps when you're so far from home to know other people who share your faith are around for support and encouragement." She thought a minute. "Is Mr. Holmes a Christian?"

"Yes, Austen is. He's a Catholic like Mr. Tolkien, so he's a bit more mystical and private about his faith than an evangelical type like me."

Kate smiled. "Since you are an 'evangelical type,' as you say, would you mind telling me how you became one?"

"No, not at all. But may we please walk? I can't stand still on a day like this."

They turned down the wooded path and David began. "This, by the way is 'Addison's Walk.' The very place where Mr. Lewis walked until three A.M. one morning while Mr. Tolkien and Hugo Dyson tried to convince him that the 'myth' of Christianity was the only true one, and that all the other ancient myths were merely echoes of it. Shortly after that, Lewis wrote that he knelt down before God, perhaps 'the most dejected and reluctant convert in all England.'"

The path curved around to where they could see across the Cherwell River to the quaint Holywell Ford House bordered by weeping willows. David stopped and picked up a stone, then threw it, watching it skip over the quiet water.

"As for me," he said, "I don't really have a very exciting testimony. My father is the rector of St. Aldate's here in town, so I was raised in the church and in a loving, Christian home. When I was in senior school, I fancied I had intellectual doubts about the faith, and even refused to go up for communion for a time, to the great embarrassment of my parents. But my dad challenged me that if I had serious intellectual doubts then I should seriously study and address them, not just use my doubts as an excuse to sin." David skipped another stone across the water and then continued walking.

"My father gave me some books to read...several by Lewis, in fact. His spiritual autobiography *Surprised by Joy* and *Mere Christianity* were the principal ones. So I read them, and I couldn't escape their pure logic. It became harder for me to believe this whole universe was some cosmic accident than to believe there is a loving God who created us. Jack himself very patiently led me on the right path. I think he saw some of himself in me."

"Jack?" Kate was confused. "I thought his name was 'Clive Staples.' "

David laughed. "It is, but can you imagine being saddled with that name your whole life?"

Kate smiled and shook her head.

"Nor could he! When he was only four years old he announced to his parents that from then on he would be called 'Jacko, Jacksie, or Jack.' Never 'Clive' again. Of course, for most of my life, he was 'Mr. Lewis' to me. But when I went up to Cambridge, he treated me as an adult—and a friend—and asked me to call him Jack."

David paused and showed her the earthenworks that had been erected along the path in the seventeenth century, during the time of the English Civil War.

Kate, however, was interested in more recent history. "So, what was he really like as a teacher?"

David thought for a moment and his face brightened. "Brilliant. Absolutely brilliant. He was an extraordinary lecturer. There are two sides to teaching here: the tutorials and the lectures. You probably know you aren't required to go to any lectures while you are at Oxford, but you can and should afford yourself the opportunity to make the most of your education here by attending one or two each week. You can attend any lecture on any subject in any college—"

He stopped sheepishly and rubbed his jaw. "Sorry, I didn't mean to give a lecture myself—so back to Mr. Lewis. He was a superb lecturer.

The room was always packed with students. He was very popular with the students both here and at Cambridge. He was quite particular about time, hated wasting a minute, so his lectures were always forty-five minutes exactly. Sometimes he would bound up the stairs of the lecture hall, that deep voice of his booming out the beginning of the lecture before he even entered the room. At Cambridge, I always tried to get there early for a front row seat. He would see me, borrow my watch because he didn't have one of his own, and hand it back to me precisely when his time was up. Then he would stride out of the room, sometimes finishing on his way out."

David smiled at the memory. "Some of his books are taken right from lecture notes or speeches. *Mere Christianity* was taken from BBC radio broadcasts made during the war. He had such an incredible mind, but would explain things in such lucid terms that even a child could comprehend it. And that's certainly the kind of logic I needed."

"But," Kate asked, "what was he like as a tutor?"

"Well, to be perfectly honest, I never officially had him as a tutor. At Cambridge he no longer gave tutorials, which was a great relief to him. I think we undergrads must have bored him to tears with our sophomoric notions. You could ask my father more about that, because he studied some with him here in Oxford." David walked silently for a moment, thinking.

"But frankly," he said, "I probably had much the same experience as my dad. Even though Jack didn't give tutorials, he invited me to his rooms in Magdalene at Cambridge once or twice a week to talk about my studies or whatever I wanted. He could not brook illogical thinking and constantly challenged me about what I said or wrote. It was a style he learned from his beloved tutor William Kirkpatrick, 'the Great Knock,' as he called him—who, incidentally, is the model for Professor Kirke in *The Lion, the Witch and the Wardrobe*."

Kate was awestruck. "It must have been intimidating to be challenged by someone so brilliant."

"That's for sure," David agreed. "But when he was pleased with something I said, or when he broke into that great laugh of his—well, he always made me want to try my best."

They had come to the riverside part of Addison's Walk. A family of swans swam gracefully toward the fading sunlight as it flitted through the trees along the bank. Watching them, Kate stumbled over a rock in the path. David caught her by the arm to steady her. They walked for a few minutes in silence, his hand gently holding her elbow. Kate scarcely breathed, not wanting to break the spell of the moment.

"Well." David spoke first, glancing at his watch. "Looks like it's time to end the lesson. We'll both be late to hall, and I'd hate to miss my supper."

Kate was amazed at how quickly the afternoon had passed and was sorry to see it come to an end. She stalled just a little. "So, do you live in those rooms in the New Building?"

"No, thank God, not any more. I did last year, but they aren't the most comfortable and it's something of a fishbowl. This year I found some great digs a stone's throw away on Holywell Street. Nice widowed landlady upstairs to look after me. And I can easily walk over and eat in hall whenever I don't want to cook—which," he added with a grin, "is most of the time. You know, Lewis didn't live in college either. He owned a little cottage called 'The Kilns' up in Headington Quarry.

"Maybe..." he paused, considering. "Maybe I could take you up there sometime and show you the place, if you'd like—or no...well, maybe we could make it a field trip or something for the Inklings Society."

Kate couldn't help but feel somewhat less enthusiastic about the proposal of an entire group accompanying them—however, she tried to cover her disappointment.

"Sure, that sounds nice." They had reached Magdalen's front gate. "Thanks so much, Mr. MacKenzie. I really enjoyed my tutorial and appreciate you showing me around."

"My pleasure, Miss Hughes. I wish all my tutorials were so delightful. But please call me David."

She smiled. "Then please call me Kate." She looked up at him and said, "Well, good night. I guess I'll see you next Tuesday at the Bird and Baby for the Inklings Society."

"Right," he answered, holding her gaze with his bright blue eyes. "Right," he repeated slowly. "Well...good evening."

She turned to go when he hailed her back. "Ah, Kate! You might want to try our church on Sunday. It's St. Aldate's, right across from Christ Church. Half past ten. And afterwards we serve a luncheon to the students—free food, you know—it packs them in." He smiled. "No, really we do get a lot of students. My dad's a very fine preacher too, and I think you'd enjoy it."

"Well, thank you, I'd like that." Kate was pleased at this invitation. "I'll hope to see you then. Good night!"

David thoughtfully watched her go. "Good night, Kate." He spoke almost to himself.

Her heart full of joy, Kate had to restrain herself from skipping home across Magdalen Bridge. She recalled the entire afternoon: every word, every gesture, the way he had leaned over her as she wrote, and the way he had caught her elbow when she stumbled. She let her mind wander over all the possibilities of a romance in Oxford.

Yes, she would definitely be at St. Aldate's Sunday morning.

First Week

Kate did not go to St. Aldate's on Sunday morning. To her chagrin, she overslept. In penance, she attended the Evensong service at Magdalen College, which afforded her an opportunity to hear the world-renowned Boys' Choir. It also afforded her the opportunity of catching an unexpected glimpse of David MacKenzie, who read the New Testament lesson. He winked at her as he walked by to resume his seat. Afterwards when she looked for him, he was swallowed up in a knot of Fellows who, she presumed, went off together to supper.

The service at Magdalen had been lovely and uplifting. Kate found comfort in the purity of the boys' soprano voices and the ancient liturgy that had been written at the cost of Archbishop Cranmer's life. Yet despite the beauty of the service, Kate felt dissatisfied. She knew she needed the fellowship and the challenging sermon she would have enjoyed at St. Aldate's. As she walked back alone to St. Hilda's, Kate convinced herself that it was for these spiritual reasons—and not because of the missed occasion to talk to her handsome tutor—that she resolved not to oversleep again. The memory of that wink, however, kept intruding on her thoughts.

Now, on Monday, she was sitting at a table in the great Hall at Christ Church College. Her first, dreaded tutorial with her Tudor History don, Mr. Croft, had gone remarkably well. He was demanding, intimidating, and stern during their session together. Yet immediately afterwards, he turned from the "dragon" Connie had spoken of to a kindly fellow, who took her on a tour of the college—as David MacKenzie had—and then atypically invited her to lunch in hall.

She was in constant awe of the beauty she was encountering in these ancient colleges and the knowledge that there were at least thirty more to explore. Like many Americans, she had expected Oxford University to have a central campus similar to William and Mary's. Instead she had been surprised to discover that each college had its own unique architecture and traditions.

Mr. Croft and a colleague seated beside him were engaged in an animated discussion about the Anglo–Saxon burial site of Sutton Hoo. This gave her a moment to leisurely look around the vast Hall while she waited for lunch to be served. From the outside, she had mistaken this massive structure for the cathedral. From the inside, it reflected much of the soaring beauty of a church, with its high hammerbeam ceiling and stained-glass windows. She remembered to search for the window that depicted *Alice in Wonderland.* Its author, Charles Dodgson—writing under the pseudonym Lewis Carroll—had been a favorite son of Christ Church. Portraits of other august alumni and professors stared down at her. Henry VIII, in his famous Holbein stance, scowled at the High Table.

A conspiratorial whisper brought Kate back from her reverie. "Well, this is a delightful dish we should be served more often."

Then louder, "Pardon me, Gorgeous. Would you mind if we joined you?"

Kate looked up into the twinkling green eyes of a classically handsome student. His brown hair was clean-cut on the sides but very full on top, with a widow's peak, framing his heart-shaped face. She blushed involuntarily and fumbled for some clever retort.

Why can't I ever come up with anything? "Yes…I mean no…I wouldn't mind."

The attractive young man sat directly across from her and was joined by a group of other male students. With relief, she recognized Nigel Elliot from the Inklings Society as he sat down beside her. Before she could speak to him, the handsome one confidently made his introductions with the perfectly clipped pronunciation of a gentleman.

"I presume you are one of Mr. Croft's new protégés. He's a good egg for livening up our stuffy halls with such agreeable company." He reached across the table to take her hand. For a brief moment, Kate thought he would kiss it. Instead he gave her hand a gentle squeeze and then released it. "I'm Stuart Devereux and delighted to meet you."

"*Lord* Stuart Devereux," Nigel corrected. "Hello, Kate. Nice to see you again." He flashed a toothy smile at her. "Stu, this is Katherine, or Kate, Hughes. She's on a study-abroad program from the States. She came to our Inklings Society meeting last week."

"Ah, a Kate, and a lover of literature." Stuart sat up smartly, lifted his head, put his hand over his heart in a mocking tribute and quoted:

> *For you are called plain Kate,*
> *And bonny Kate, and sometimes Kate the curst;*
> *But Kate, the prettiest Kate in Christendom,*
> *Kate of Kate-Hall, my super-dainty Kate,*
> *For dainties are all cates; and therefore Kate,*
> *Take this of me, Kate of my consolation;—*
> *Hearing thy mildness praised in every town*
> *Thy virtues spoke of, and thy beauty sounded,*
> *(Yet not so deeply as to thee belongs),*
> *Myself am moved to woo thee for my wife.*

Nigel held up his finger. "*Taming of the Shrew.*"

Kate laughed. "So, are you a lover of literature too?" she asked Stuart.

"Naturally. I came to Oxford to read English, but, alas"—he put his hand to his forehead in melodramatic despair—"I had to change to something more practical like economics and management. Thought it would be useful to put Daddy's estate in the black." He dropped the teasing tone. "But, I do adore Shakespeare and have had a go at amateur theatricals."

"He was a marvelous Petruchio back at Eton," Nigel put in.

"You are as good as a chorus, my Lord," Stuart retorted.

Nigel held up his finger again, triumphantly. *"Hamlet!"*

"You are keen, my Lord, you are keen," Stuart said with a glint in his eye.

Kate recognized the lines and hoped they would not continue to the next double entendre. Her concerns were assuaged when everyone in the hall simultaneously hushed and stood as a blessing was invoked in Latin. They just as quickly sat down at the three long boards—planked tables—and began passing large platters of food brought in by the servants. The buzz of conversation again filled the hall.

"Ah, meat and potatoes! What a surprise. Well. Kate," Stuart said, handing her a platter, "have you grown tired yet of our endless variations on the potato?"

"No, I've really just arrived. So everything is still new for me. New and exciting," she said, gazing around the hall.

"Yes." Stuart looked up as if seeing it for the first time. "This is a splendid place." He turned back to her and their eyes met. "But please, tell us all about yourself."

Kate flushed and began self-consciously to talk. As Stuart asked her questions and showed a genuine interest in her, she soon relaxed and was chatting away comfortably with the entire group at her table.

"I say," said Stuart, "if you are a literature lover, why are you reading history with Croft here?"

"Well, I'm majoring in both English history and literature, so I'm also signed up for a tutorial on Shakespeare."

Stuart raised his eyebrow. "Who's the lucky don?"

"Mr. David MacKenzie at Magdalen."

"Ah, the Inklings connection." Stuart looked over his glass at her. "You know, MacKenzie is an excellent lecturer. Are you planning to take in any of his lectures?"

"Well, I don't know. I mean, I'd like to, but I haven't looked at the schedule yet."

"You simply must attend one. Don't you agree, Nigel?" Stuart turned to his friend, who had just taken a mouthful of potatoes and grunted in agreement.

"Yes, perhaps Nigel and I could accompany you. Where are you staying, by the way?" he asked smoothly.

"At St. Hilda's." Kate flushed again, flattered by his interest.

"Ah, St. Hilda's," Stuart repeated. "Excellent. Yes, we should definitely go to one of MacKenzie's Shakespeare lectures." He consulted his pocket calendar. "There's one Wednesday morning, ten o'clock, in the East School Hall. Shall we meet there at the Examination Schools at ten 'til?"

"Sure!" Kate swallowed hard, surprised by this invitation. "That would be great."

"It's a date then." Stuart smiled.

"What's this about MacKenzie's lecture?" asked Colin Russell, a fair-haired student, whom Kate also recognized from the Inklings Society.

"He's starting a new Shakespeare series on Wednesday," Stuart said. "Kate is going with us."

"Splendid lecturer, MacKenzie," Colin concurred. "But what's the matter with him? I always see him walking in the gardens or the meadow alone. Such a brooding fellow these days."

"Maybe he's still grieving over Lewis, his mentor," suggested Nigel.

"No, it's more than that," Colin mused aloud. "I never see him anymore at any parties or functions, at least not with any women. And it's odd. I mean he's a good-looking bloke. Why is he always alone?"

"Maybe he kicks with the other foot," Stuart replied with a raised eyebrow and a smirk which made Kate feel uneasy.

"Don't be absurd, Devereux." Mr. Croft had suddenly turned around, surprising the entire table, who had incorrectly assumed he had not heard a word of their conversation. "David MacKenzie is a straight arrow. Fine man, just like his father."

Chastened, Stuart gave a feeble smile. "Right, sir. Sorry, sir."

"Oh, that's right," said Nigel, remembering something. "Isn't he engaged to some brilliant bird he met at Cambridge?"

" 'Beautiful,' you mean," added Colin, "if she's the one he took last year to the Michaelmas Ball."

"Ah, yes." Stuart tried to make amends. "The stunning redhead. Well, then that explains his solitary walks and brooding. He's pining for his ladylove off at 'the other place.' "

Kate silently ate her dessert as her stomach knotted. *David MacKenzie engaged!* She berated herself for feeling shocked and then for caring at all. She felt foolish for flattering herself with the idea that his wink meant anything other than recognition or that his interest in her could possibly be more than that of a tutor in his student. Her thoughts were interrupted by Stuart's smooth voice.

"I'm afraid our gossip is bothering our American guest."

"Oh, no," Kate dissembled. "Your talk of Mr. MacKenzie made me realize how much work I have to do for my next tutorial."

Colin groaned. "That reminds me. I've got to go. I have three more pages to write. Excuse me." He pushed himself up from the table and hurried out.

His hasty exit seemed to cue everyone else to empty the hall. Mr. Croft cordially said his good-byes, and Kate followed the stream of students down the wide stone staircase out to the open grassy space of Tom Quad. It had begun to rain.

Nigel and Stuart hurried her past the fountain of Mercury to the cover of the main portal, under the imposing clock tower known as Old Tom. Nigel reminded her not to forget the next evening's meeting of the Inklings Society and urged her to bring her friend, Connie.

Stuart took her hand in both of his. Looking up, Kate realized how much he towered over her. The cliché "tall, dark, and handsome" flashed through her mind as an apt description of him.

"It's been a pleasure to meet you, Kate." His green eyes locked onto hers. "I'll look forward to seeing you again Wednesday morning."

"Yes." She gently pulled her hand away. "I'll see you then. Nice to meet you too. Good-bye...Bye, Nigel."

Kate walked quickly out of the portal of Tom Tower and started to cross the street to the crowded bus stop in front of St. Aldate's Church. She stopped herself just in time from stepping in front of a car. Catching her breath, she silently lectured herself about looking both ways carefully since traffic driving on the left was still foreign to her. As she climbed on the bus, she glanced back at the church and thought again, with a pang, of the opportunity she had missed there.

Then she remembered the gossip about David MacKenzie's engagement. Riding down High Street, she leaned against the windowpane, her thoughts tumbling about her head like loose laundry in a dryer. Why had she allowed herself to secretly entertain any fantasies about her tutor? But after all, it was natural to be attracted to him. Didn't he share her faith and her love for literature? Yet, how foolish of her! Why did she think he might be attracted to her? She chided herself for her vanity.

At Magdalen College, the bus lurched to a stop, and her stomach lurched with it. *David MacKenzie engaged!* She decided to get out and walk the rest of the way over the bridge. She needed more time to think before facing her curious suite-mate.

First Week, Saturday Afternoon

Kate stared out of the library window at Radcliffe Square, one of Europe's loveliest city plazas. Yet today it held no charms for her. It was raining, and she was miserably homesick.

She felt that her honeymoon with Oxford was over. The bleak reality of chilling rain and endless reading had overwhelmed her. She was sitting in the Radcliffe Camera, the neoclassical rotunda that housed one of the most beautiful reading rooms in the world, and all she could think of was her cozy family room back home in Virginia.

In reality, First Week in Oxford had gone remarkably well. She had attended the Inklings Society meeting with Connie and found the spirited discourse on Lewis's *Great Divorce* stimulating. Fewer students were there, and that allowed for a more relaxed discussion. The meeting seemed less intimidating now that Kate knew more people, and she felt brave enough in the open forum to contribute a Shakespearean sonnet she had hurriedly memorized.

Everyone applauded her rendition enthusiastically, yet it was David MacKenzie's approval she sought. Her eyes met his and he smiled warmly at her, seemingly pleased by her offering.

Kate purposely hung back after the meeting, hoping for another courteous escort home. Instead, David offered his apologies, saying he needed to head to the Bodleian Library to check some references for his upcoming lecture, and pressing Nigel Elliot into the service.

Chagrined, Kate chided herself for trying to repress the fact that David was engaged.

On Wednesday morning, she had met Stuart Devereux and Nigel at the Examination Schools, an imposing Victorian structure in the High Street, for David MacKenzie's lecture on Shakespeare. She was astounded to find the hall packed with students who evidently shared Stuart's opinion of her tutor's excellence as a speaker. They had to squeeze into the back, but had no difficulty hearing David's resonant voice.

She was surprised that the lecture was not on any particular play but on the identity of Shakespeare himself. David posed theories and presented evidence that challenged the traditional view that the author of the great plays was the man from Stratford-upon-Avon. The research and conjecture in this field was something Kate had never heard before, and it caused quite a stir among the students, who eagerly fired questions at the end of the lecture. David fielded the queries in a relaxed, confident manner. His arguments were compelling and were interspersed with wry wit, which often met with appreciative laughter. He concluded with the observation that the identity of the playwright did not affect the brilliance of the plays themselves one way or the other—however, the subject did make a good literary detective story.

As the lecture hour ended with spontaneous applause, Kate's estimation of her tutor rose even higher. Students immediately swamped him, and she left with her new friends without having an opportunity to speak to him herself.

Stuart tucked her hand into the crook of his arm and deftly guided her to a nearby shop for a cup of coffee. They spent a pleasant hour chatting together about the lecture, as well as commiserating about their tutorials, their hall mates, and of course, the weather. Stuart shared several deliciously gossipy and amusing stories about fellow students and dons at Christ Church that had Kate laughing in spite of herself. He was charming and solicitous, and Kate found him quite attractive.

After hearing David MacKenzie's erudite lecture on Shakespeare, she had been anxious about her Thursday tutorial with him and what he would think of her writing. However, David was reservedly complimentary of her essay and simply made suggestions to improve her writing style, not the substance. He challenged her on only a few points, and he was eager to discuss the biblical concepts she had introduced. She had hoped to have some time to talk more about C.S. Lewis or to ask him about the speculations he had raised in his lecture, but again was disappointed when he had to rush off to a meeting in the Senior Common Room.

On Friday morning, Kate had been surprised to discover a long-stemmed pink rose in her pigeonhole in St. Hilda's Porters' Lodge. Attached to it was an envelope of heavy vellum. The monogram on the inside note read 'SWD'. Boldly written in an elegant, elongated script were the words:

> *My dear Katherine,*
>
> *Please give me the honour of escorting you to a dance at the Oxford Student Union this evening at 8:00. Casual attire.*
>
> *Devotedly yours,*
>
> *Stuart W. Devereux*
>
> *P.S. Nothing fancy, but should be fun. Hope you aren't otherwise engaged or I shall be heartbroken. Ring me if you can't make it. (276150)*
>
> *SWD*

Kate reread the note and, tracing the monogram with her finger, mused over what name the initial "W" might stand for. She thought about the characters in Jane Austen's novels who had "W's" in their names. Would Stuart be like the honorable Captain Wentworth, or the agreeable but coldly scheming William Elliot in *Persuasion*? The charming but weak Lord Willoughby in *Sense and Sensibility,* or the affable but unscrupulous Wickham in *Pride and Prejudice*?

In any case, she was only too glad to put aside her studies and go out. She was happier still when Nigel and Connie joined their party. They did have great fun doing the twist and dancing to the beat of the Rolling Stones and the Beatles. During the slow dances, Stuart did not plod around in mindless circles—rather, holding her close, he skillfully wove her about the dance floor with spins and turns. She was glad now for her parents' insistence on dancing lessons at cotillion and her coming out as a debutante in Richmond society balls. She could hold her own with Lord Devereux. She was tiny next to his tall figure but enjoyed the sensation of being pressed close to his silk shirt and the smell of his rich cologne.

Later, at her door, Stuart had leaned over and given her a lingering good-night kiss before she had time to think or protest, if she had wanted to. She was not sure she would have. The whole evening had been delightful.

Yet on this Saturday afternoon she was stuck in the library reading boring books on Tudor history for Monday's tutorial. The reading list was extensive; the topic, uninteresting; her mood, that of feeling very sorry for herself. She sat slumped, leaning on her elbow, staring out at the dreary rain. Suddenly she sensed someone's presence. She looked up and her throat tightened. It was David MacKenzie.

"Hello, there." He smiled down at her and then squatted to eye level. "You're looking rather blue today," he whispered. "Hope it's not Shakespeare that's getting you down."

"No," Kate answered. "It's history. I have so much reading to do and I'll never get it all done. And it's all economics and government and I hate that. I like to read about people. It's the stories I like...not stuff about parliament. It's so boring. I just don't know if I can do all this." Tears of frustration welled up in her eyes.

He lightly touched her arm in sympathy. "You know what always helps in times like this?"

"What?" She sniffed.

"A 'cuppa' tea," he replied with a twinkle in his eye, handing her a tissue. "Why don't you take a break with me for a few minutes? Parliament is always easier to bear after a nice spot of Earl Grey."

They pulled on their mackintoshes and darted out into the rain, running through Radcliffe Square to the centuries-old King's Arms. A cheerful fire awaited them in the cozy front room of the pub, and Kate was soon warming up to a cup of hot tea.

"You know," she said, "I am beginning to understand your English penchant for tea. It does seem to take the chill out of you."

"Aye, it's the cure for what ails ye," David said, smiling. "So tell me, what ails ye besides a long reading list?"

Kate thoughtfully sipped her tea. "I guess I'm getting homesick. I never thought I would. When I was back home, all I could think of was leaving, but now..." Her voice trailed off.

"Well, nothing makes one appreciate home more than being away from it. Have you heard from your family?"

"Oh, yes. My parents have been great about writing. And so has my sister, Debbie. Even my brother has sent a note. I can't believe how much I look forward to checking my mailbox every day."

"Be sure to write your parents a nice, mushy letter about how much you appreciate them. I wrote my mum one when I went up to Cambridge, and I know she still treasures it."

Kate smiled over her teacup. "I've already written several."

David reached for a plate and held it out to her.

"Biscuit?" he offered.

"Biscuit?" Kate asked with amusement as she took one. "That's what we call a little roll or a treat you give your dog."

"Oh, sorry. You say 'cookie.' You Americans need to learn the proper appellations."

"I thought you said you were half American," Kate teased.

"I am, indeed, and proud of it. But this," he held up a cookie, "is a biscuit."

"Okay," Kate conceded. "Now, tell me about your American mom."

David shook his head. "First you tell me about your family. You're the one who's homesick."

"Well—I'm the oldest. My sister, Debbie, is two years younger and is a freshman at Mary Baldwin, a women's college in the Blue Ridge Mountains."

"I know of it. It's in Staunton. West of Charlottesville. So tell me—are you and your sister close?"

"Sometimes. We're very different, and we argued a lot in high school. But we've been writing a great deal since we've both been away and share a lot more in our letters."

"And your brother?"

"Scott. He's sixteen. He's a good kid. Into wrestling, youth group, that kind of thing."

"So, there are just three of you?"

Kate hesitated. "No, four. I have a six-year-old brother—Timmy. He's...special."

"Oh?"

"He's...retarded."

"Ah...right." David waited to see if Kate wanted to give any more explanation.

She did. "He was a surprise baby, and when the doctors determined he had mongolism, they recommended that my parents put him in an institution. But we couldn't bear that, and we were lucky enough to be able to afford a nanny for him. It's been hard, but we all love him so much. He's just the sweetest little boy in the whole world."

David smiled and poured Kate another cup of tea. "Your parents sound like great people. Tell me about them."

Kate stirred in her cream and sugar. "My mother's name is Helen. She's very pretty and talented. She's a violinist with the Richmond Symphony."

"So, do you like classical music?"

"Yes. I guess I had to in my house. I play a little piano and sing. But I like all kinds of music—you know, Bach to Beatles."

"Mmm." David bit into another cookie. "Me too. You know, Oxford has so much to offer musically. There are concerts every week at the Sheldonian Theatre. Since your mother is a violinist, I'd bet you'd really love to hear Jacqueline du Pré. She's an incredible cellist and was born here in Oxford. Have you heard of her?"

Kate thought for a minute. "No, I don't think so."

"Well, you must hear her play. Maybe we could go to her concert. She's giving one at the Sheldonian soon with an American pianist, Stephen Bishop."

Kate was puzzled. *Is this an invitation? Isn't he engaged? He certainly is being kind.* She tried not to get her hopes up. *Maybe "we" means a group of people again—like the Inklings.*

"Anyway," he was saying, "you didn't finish telling me about your family. What about your dad?"

"My father's name is Tom. He's a lawyer and also serves in the Virginia legislature, so he works a lot. But he's a good man, an elder in the church. He's strict with us, yet really very loving..." Kate's eyes filled up with tears again. "Gosh, this is ridiculous." She brushed at her eyes. "I'm sorry—I don't know why I'm being so emotional today."

"Hey." David reached across the table and gently placed his hand on her arm. "It's all right to be homesick. It's perfectly normal. Don't worry. You'll be fine."

"Thank you, doctor." Kate sniffed and sat up straight. "No, really. You've been very kind, and just talking helps." She looked down at her empty teacup and then up into his eyes. "That and the tea, of course."

They both smiled. David drew his hand away. "You know, I think you need to be adopted by another family while you're over here. My parents would love to add you to our clan. My mother especially would enjoy having a fellow Southerner around. Why don't you come over with me after church tomorrow? You can be a part of our family for a while." He looked at her teasingly. "You will be coming to church tomorrow at St. Aldate's?"

So he had noticed her absence. She blushed. "Yes, I'm so sorry about last week. I was up late studying for history and overslept."

"Well, then." He stood up. "We must get you back to the Rad Cam so you can get your work done."

He helped her into her coat and gently lifted her long, thick hair from the collar. She held still as he let it fall down over her back.

"My word, you've got gorgeous hair," he murmured almost to himself.

She turned around to face him. "Thank you." Kate met his eyes and smiled.

He took a deep breath and exhaled slowly.

"So, Kate, what do you say? Would you like to come over after church?"

She felt the fluttering of hope. "I would love to come. I'd love to be adopted by your family if they want me." She smiled again. "And I promise to set my alarm."

5

Second Week, Sunday

Kate did not oversleep on Sunday but awoke to the church bells pealing throughout the city of Oxford. It was a glorious autumn morning.

Resolving to dress conservatively, she chose a brown herringbone Villager suit and matching gloves. The skirt skimmed the top of her knees and her high heels set off her legs nicely. She wore her hair up in a French twist topped by a pillbox hat, the style popularized by Jackie Kennedy.

Kate decided to take a taxi and save herself a stuffy bus ride or an agonizingly long walk in heels. Even so, she arrived only shortly before the service at St. Aldate's. She was surprised to find the church already full. The welcoming ushers handed her a prayerbook and escorted her to an empty seat on a side aisle. The service followed the liturgy; yet instead of a clergyman chanting the litany, young people with guitars were leading the congregation in responses set to contemporary music. Kate had heard of these folk communions before and found this one very uplifting. Soon she caught on to the tunes, and her clear soprano voice joined the others in worship.

The Reverend Eric MacKenzie stood up to give the homily. Kate recognized him as a slightly taller, middle-aged portrait of David. The father and son shared many of the same striking features: the deep blue eyes, high cheekbones, and chiseled jawline. Eric MacKenzie's hair had turned gray and was thinner than his son's, but it enhanced his patrician and pastoral demeanor. When he spoke, it was with the same deep, sonorous voice but with a touch of a Scottish burr. His sermon text was Matthew 6:28-34, which concluded with the scripture,

Consider the lilies of the field, how they grow;
they neither toil nor spin; yet I tell you,
even Solomon in all his glory was not arrayed like one of these...
Therefore do not be anxious, saying,
"What shall we eat?" or "What shall we drink?"
Or "What shall we wear?" For the Gentiles seek all these things;
and your heavenly Father knows that you need them all.
But seek first his kingdom and his righteousness,
and all these things shall be yours as well.

His compelling and practical sermon on worry and anxiety, illustrated with personal and humorous anecdotes, was just what Kate needed to hear. She made a decision to live in the "now," enjoying God's presence and putting aside her worries about her studies.

During communion, Kate committed herself afresh to seeking the kingdom of God first in her life. She felt renewed and hopeful. Yet as the communicants streamed forward to the altar rail, she found herself trying to pick out David MacKenzie in the crowd. Finally, she spotted his dark wavy hair, just brushing the collar of his suit. He held a beautiful little blond girl in his arms. Several boys surrounded him as he took communion from his father, and she wondered if they were part of a Sunday school class.

When Kate returned from the communion rail, she glanced up and saw David sitting with the children near the front of the church. Just as she passed the pew, he caught her eye and winked. She blushed and hurried back to her seat, reproaching herself for so quickly shifting her focus from her heavenly Father to her handsome tutor.

After the service, Kate joined the surge of worshippers exiting the sanctuary. The Reverend Eric MacKenzie was greeting each of his parishioners at the front portal. As she started to shake his hand, David stepped up and introduced her.

"Dad, this is Kate Hughes, the American student I was telling you about. I'll be bringing her by the house after the luncheon."

Eric MacKenzie firmly shook her hand. "Nice to meet you, Kate. We look forward to seeing you this afternoon."

"Thank you, sir. And that was a wonderful message today. It really spoke to me."

"I'm glad. Thank you." He gave her a warm smile and then turned his attention to the next person in line.

David took her by the elbow and guided her through the crowd, stopping frequently to introduce her to the friendly parishioners. They threaded their way out to the sidewalk and followed the flow of young people past the St. Aldate's Coffee Shop, turning the corner at Pembroke Street and walking half a block to Number 40, the church rectory. It was a rather plain but large three-storied structure of yellow brick topped by gables. Kate could see through the wrought-iron railing along the sidewalk to the basement level below. Two Victorian-era covered porticoes bridged the deep cellar-window well between the sidewalk and the house.

They walked up the steps of the second portico, through a long narrow passageway, and into a large light-filled room. David explained that this, the Rectory Room or Hall, had been built over part of the rectory garden a hundred years earlier. They used the hall for dinners, receptions, and meetings. On this day, scores of students were being served a hot lunch by the women of the church. The number of students astonished Kate, who was used to denominational churches filled with elderly, pious people, not young adults—and certainly not young intellectuals. She sensed they were hungry for more than food, and evidently, they were being fed here spiritually as well as physically.

She felt warmly welcomed and aglow in the fellowship of this vibrant church family.

After lunch, David helped her from her chair and led her over to a set of French doors that opened into a walled garden—a small plot of lawn surrounded by flowerbeds with a profusion of late-blooming mums and roses. Kate never ceased to be delighted by the English gardens and their ordered creativity—such a riot of color and variety in small confined spaces.

"How pretty!" she cried. "I love flowers."

"My mum loves flowers too," replied David, closing the French doors behind them as they stepped out onto the lawn. "But she's never had much time for them. It's my dad that tends the flowers. I think he finds puttering about the garden a relaxing diversion from the stress of tending his parish."

"Please, tell me more about your family before I meet them."

"Well, you just met my dad, Eric MacKenzie. My mum's name is Annie."

"But what's she like?"

His blue eyes sparkled. "A lot like you."

She looked at him quizzically.

"Seriously. You remind me of her. She's very pretty and petite and has brown hair and eyes. Plus she's American, you remember."

Kate hadn't missed the "pretty" compliment but thought it best not to acknowledge it. "And do you have any brothers or sisters?"

He grinned. "Yes—I'm the oldest of seven."

"Seven!" Kate couldn't disguise her shock.

"Right. I have two sisters at university in London. Ginny, that's short for Virginia, and Natalie. Then three brothers at home who go to the Magdalen College School: William, who is fifteen; Richard, twelve; and Mark, ten. And then Hannah is the baby—she's three."

Kate tried to repeat all the names and shook her head in disbelief. "Seven kids. Three girls and four boys. How does your mother do it?"

David smiled. "She always says she did it one at a time. It's not like she had us all at once. Though in truth, I think my mum is a remarkable woman."

"But your father is a rector. How can they afford such a big family?" Kate knew she was bordering on rudeness, but her curiosity got the better of her good manners.

"They can't. My father says if they had waited until they could afford children, they would never have had any of us. I was born during the war, you know. I wasn't convenient, but I know I was loved."

It had grown quite warm. David removed his coat and tie and flung them over his shoulder while they talked. "Now, don't think my parents have been irresponsible. My father works very hard to provide for his family. And we may not have gotten all our 'wants,' but we've certainly had all our needs met. We've been dependent on the Lord's provision all our lives, and that's not such a bad thing."

He looked into her eyes and said teasingly, "Besides, didn't you hear the sermon today? About not being anxious for food and clothes? Frankly, we've had some tough times. But we've also seen God's hand in miraculous ways."

Kate had never thought much about God's provision for her, other than her gratitude for being able to come to Oxford. Since her father had been a successful lawyer, her family had never lacked for anything.

David resumed walking. "Well, now you know about my family. So let's go meet them."

Three boys were skirmishing with a soccer ball in the paved courtyard that separated the Rectory Room from the rectory itself.

"Pardon me," David said to Kate, dropping his jacket on a garden bench. Then he ran up to the boys, stole the ball, and deftly scored a goal between the two designated flowerpots against the brick wall.

"Cheater!" yelled the boys, trying to jump on his back.

"Whoa, gentlemen." He laughed and grabbed the youngest in a wrestling hold. "I want you to meet one of my new students, Kate Hughes. She's from the States."

The boys straightened up and took turns awkwardly shaking her hand and murmuring, "How d'you do?"

Kate could see a family resemblance among them, and yet each was unique. William, the fifteen-year-old, looked most like David, but with fair hair. He was stocky and muscular. Richard, the twelve-year-old, retained a slender boyish look. He had David's dark hair, yet had dark eyes as well. Ten-year-old Mark was a composite: sturdy, with light brown hair and large brown eyes.

"And this is our baby, Hannah," David said, hoisting up a young girl who had run out of the house to greet him. She was the child Kate had seen in church. Hannah looked like a little angel: blond ringlets, huge blue eyes, fair porcelain skin. She planted a sloppy kiss on David's cheek.

"Hannah, say hello to Kate," David coaxed his little sister.

Hannah stared at her openly and without inhibition. "You're pretty," she declared with stark honesty.

"Thank you, so are you."

Hannah continued to appraise her. "Are you going to marry David, like Charlotte?"

David laughed uneasily. "No, Hannah. Kate's a student of mine." He put her down to cover his embarrassment. Then running his hands through his hair, he turned to Kate and motioned for her to precede him. "Let's go inside."

Kate felt her heart sink at the mention of David's engagement. *Charlotte—so that's her name. And I am just a student to him.* She was distracted from further thought, however, as soon as she stepped through the back door of the house into a long central hallway. On the opposite side, she could see the front door.

"Sorry to bring you in the back way," David said, "but I wanted to avoid the crowd leaving the luncheon. Here, I'll take you on a quick tour of the ground floor."

He pointed out the location of a powder room and cloakroom on their right and told her that the room closest to the front door was used as an office by the church secretary. Then he led her into a large formal parlor, filled with light from the front bay window and the two artificially lit wall recesses on either side of a dark marble fireplace.

"This room is used for meetings or parties, but not often by our family," he explained as he guided her through a back passage, past the stairwell, and through a large dining room.

The rectory had the air of a shabby gentleman whose once fine clothes had been worn far too long. But everything was sparkling clean and cheerful. Kate had the sense that the house held a long legacy of love.

They came into a spacious kitchen and saw a small, pretty woman busily wiping counters and putting away dishes. Kate's first thought was that this must be one of David's sisters. She was stunned when David introduced his mother. Annie MacKenzie looked remarkably young. She wore her shoulder-length golden brown hair in the sleek style of Diana Rigg as Mrs. Emma Peel from the popular *Avengers* television show. Her warm smile and big brown eyes welcomed Kate, whose preconception of a portly faded beauty could not have been more wrong.

David gave his mother a big hug and kissed her on the cheek.

"Isn't she beautiful?" he asked Kate. "And don't tell her she looks great for having seven kids," he warned. "She just looks great. Period." David proudly put his arm around his mother's shoulders.

"Mrs. MacKenzie," Kate said, "I must say I don't know how you do it. You could convince me to have a large family."

Annie MacKenzie looked pleased but dismissed the compliments. "Oh, you all are being too kind. David, get Kate some ginger beer or some tea, and Kate, feel free to make yourself comfortable." She pointed to her own feet, which were clad in bedroom slippers.

Kate stepped into the hallway, took off her suit jacket, and placed it with her purse on a bench. Glancing into a mirror, she realized she was still wearing the little pillbox hat. As she removed the hatpin and hat, her thick dark hair came tumbling down her back. She turned around to see David leaning against the doorjamb, admiring her.

"You certainly have been blessed with lovely hair."

"Thanks," she replied, slightly embarrassed. "Sometimes I think about cutting it all off. It would be a lot easier to take care of."

"Oh, no." He looked alarmed. "Don't ever cut it. The Bible says a woman's hair is her glory. And yours is particularly glorious."

She suddenly felt a little shy. "Don't worry. I'm not going to. Anyway, my dad would kill me."

"Ah." David grinned and held up a glass as if in a toast. "I like your dad. Great minds think alike." He handed her a glass of ginger beer. "Try this—it's nonalcoholic. American ginger ale is its weak cousin."

The beverage bore slight semblance to the American soft drink. It tasted strongly of ginger spice, very pungent yet refreshing.

She and David walked out to the garden, where his parents sat watching the boys play soccer in the adjoining courtyard. Hannah had crawled into her father's lap and gone to sleep.

While David took part in his brothers' game, Kate chatted comfortably with the MacKenzies. They asked her about Virginia, her family, her church, and her studies. Kate wondered why she often found it easier to talk with her parents' peers than with her parents themselves. She noticed that Annie MacKenzie had picked up the singsong inflection of the British, yet still retained a hint of the American flat vowels. When she made this observation, they began comparing the speech of the two countries. They laughed together about some of the peculiarities of British versus American English.

Kate discovered that Eric MacKenzie was originally from St. Andrews, Scotland. At the outbreak of World War II, he had joined the

RAF, and he had met and married Annie, in England where she was serving as a nurse. When she became pregnant with David, Annie moved from London—away from the bombing blitz—to Oxford. After the war, Eric joined her and worked his way through divinity school.

Kate felt this was the perfect opener for her question. "Your son tells me you were a good friend and student of C.S. Lewis. I'm a great admirer of his and would like to know more about him. What was he like as a teacher?"

"Wonderful," Eric MacKenzie quickly replied. "He had such a brilliant mind. I've known many learned men, yet he seemed to surpass them all. His memory was prodigious. You know, I think he truly had a photographic memory."

"Really?"

"Once he read something, it always seemed to stick with him. He loved books, but he didn't buy very many, I think, because they were all in his head and he had some scruples about spending money on luxuries. He loved to play a game with his students. Sometimes he would ask us to choose a book—any book—from off his study shelves. We would try to find one way up high that had a lot of dust on it and looked like it had never been opened. Then he would say, 'Choose a page, any page.' We would, and he would tell us to read a line. Then he would pick up and recite the rest of the passage from memory."

"No." Kate found this difficult to believe.

"I'm absolutely serious. It never ceased to amaze us—and delight him."

David took a breather from the game and refilled everyone's glasses with ginger beer. He gulped down a glassful.

"What tales is he filling you with?" he asked Kate.

"I was telling her about Jack's game of having us pick random passages and his reciting them from memory."

David poured himself another glass. "It's true. I would always try to find some obscure volume on his shelf, but he never failed to know the passage by heart. It was incredible."

"Tell her about the Scrabble games," Annie prodded.

"Oh, yes." Eric chuckled at the memory. "He and Warnie, his brother, loved to play Scrabble, and when he married, his wife, Joy, loved it too. Well, we were invited to join them after dinner sometimes, but you would never want to be on the opposing team. Their rule was that they could use any word in any known language—and they could read and speak quite a few: Latin, Greek, Hebrew, French, Italian, German, and"—he started laughing and wiped his eyes—"even the languages Tolkien had invented for Middle Earth."

"But, they had to prove they were actual words," interjected Annie.

"Yes, the rule was, you know, that if a word was disputed they would have to prove its existence by finding it in a book. They would send their boys scurrying around the house to fetch the books. You would never believe Scrabble could be so hotly contested or so much fun."

Kate was amazed at what she was hearing. However, something he had said in passing had caught her attention. "I didn't know Mr. Lewis had a wife and children. I had always assumed he was just an old bachelor."

"Quite right, he was an old bachelor for many years. Then he met and married an American woman, Joy Gresham. She had two sons from a previous but unfortunate marriage. Jack and Joy were only married a few years and then, tragically, she died of cancer."

"Oh my, how sad," murmured Kate.

"Yes—well, I'd love to tell you more about it, but I must be getting ready for Evensong." Eric MacKenzie stood up to leave, shifting Hannah to his shoulder.

"Dad." David stopped him. "I was thinking of taking Kate up to Headington to see the church and the Kilns. Is Major Lewis there now?"

Eric looked at Annie questioningly. "I think Warnie is in Ireland now," Annie answered. "We've tried to ring him regularly to see how he's faring. He's taken Jack's death hard, as you know, and—well, I won't say more. Just keep him in your prayers. The Millers still keep the place, so you could phone to see if anyone is there to let you in."

"We'd probably just look at the outside of the cottage. I don't want to disturb anyone. I just thought Kate might enjoy seeing where Jack lived. Anyway, you've got to get going, Dad. I didn't mean to keep you."

Kate stood and thanked the MacKenzies as they carried Hannah back into the house.

David lightly put his hand on Kate's shoulder. "I have to read at Magdalen's Evensong," he said. "Would you like to come with me and then join me afterwards for supper?"

"I'd love to," was Kate's quick and heartfelt response. Then she remembered something with a sinking feeling. "Oh, no."

"What is it?"

"I would really like to go with you, but I forgot I promised to meet someone for the Evensong service at Christ Church."

The disappointment in David's face was unmistakable. "Oh, right. No problem."

He made an effort to brighten his voice. "You know, Christ Church has a wonderful men's choir as well, and the chapel is actually the cathedral for Oxford. Extraordinarily beautiful. Quite right, you should go there. Why don't you go get yourself ready and I'll walk you over?"

"Okay." Kate went inside to retrieve her belongings. She felt miserable. After such a pleasant afternoon with David and his family—well, there was nothing to be done.

Annie saw them to the door and told Kate to consider their family as hers while she was in Oxford and to feel welcome to come by anytime—even without David. He thanked his mother and affectionately kissed her good-bye.

"You are very blessed to have such a wonderful family," Kate said as they walked down the steps of the portico. "Thanks for sharing them with me."

"You're welcome. Feel a little less homesick now?"

"Yes—and no. While I was with them, I didn't feel homesick at all. But now I'm afraid I'll think of your family, as well as mine, when I should be studying. You know, I almost felt like I had stepped into a Dickens novel, with this perfectly happy, idyllic family around the hearth."

"Hmm. I shouldn't carry that idea too far. Once you get to know us, we aren't so idyllic or always so happy. We argue and complain, and are annoyingly sinful just like everybody else." He smiled down at her. "But there is a lot of love in our home."

"I could tell. And also love for others. I felt perfectly at home with your parents. More so, even than with my own parents, in a strange way."

"Well, that changes. After we grow up and away from our parents, then we're able to go back home and be friends with them. Although there are some things I may never tell them about myself. I guess, in that respect they will always be my parents, regardless of how much I enjoy their company now as an adult."

They had reached St. Aldate's Street, which lay between the church and Christ Church College.

"Be careful, now," David warned. "The traffic is wicked. Nobody stops for pedestrians like they do in the States." He waited until there was a break, then quickly led her across the street and under the portal of Old Tom.

"Are you meeting your friends here or in the church? Would you like for me to wait until they get here?" he asked.

Kate was uncertain how to answer. Even though she hated to leave his company, she thought it best for him to go. While she deliberated on what to say, a smooth, mocking voice broke in on her thoughts.

"Hello, Gorgeous. You're here early. Lucky I was in the Porters' Lodge checking my pigeonhole, or you would have been left waiting."

It was Stuart Devereux.

Second Week, Sunday Evening

"Why, Mr. MacKenzie, what brings you here to Christ Church?"

Before David or Kate could reply, Stuart went on. "Sorry, sir, we haven't been properly introduced. I'm Stuart Devereux, a friend of Miss Hughes." He offered his hand. "I've been a great admirer of your lectures, Mr. MacKenzie. In fact, I took Miss Hughes to your last lecture on the mystery of Shakespeare's true identity. Fascinating."

"Really?" David looked perplexed. "I'm glad you enjoyed it. Well, uh...I really need to get back to Magdalen now. Nice to meet you, Devereux." He turned to Kate and their eyes briefly met—his filled with unspoken questions. "Miss Hughes." He gave her a nod. "Good night. Uh—I hope I'll see you Tuesday at the Inklings Society." Then he dashed off.

Stuart watched him with a bemused expression. "Rather odd chap, what?" He smiled at Kate, cheerfully oblivious to her discomfort at the turn of events. "I say, my dear, I'm absolutely famished, and since you're here early, would you mind if we popped across the street to get a bite to eat?"

Kate acquiesced and crossed the busy street with him to the St. Aldate's Coffee Shop. The little café did a brisk business selling sandwiches and beverages to hungry students and used the proceeds for the church's ministries. Kate felt ambivalent about eating there with

Stuart after spending all afternoon with the MacKenzie clan, yet soon forgot all her discomfort as they shared good food and easy conversation.

After polishing off a sandwich, Stuart looked at her with the self-satisfied grin of the Cheshire cat. "So, guess what I've got."

"Oh, I hate guessing. Just tell me." Kate waited, smiling. Reaching into his coat, he removed his wallet from the breast pocket and triumphantly produced two tickets. "We've got tickets for the Old Vic."

"Old Vic?"

"National Theatre in London. *Othello* with Sir Laurence Olivier and Maggie Smith. Rave reviews. So..." He raised an eyebrow. "May I please escort you to the performance?"

"Of course! I'd love to go. And I'll be reading *Othello* for my tutorial."

"Excellent. Then during the interval, you can fill me in on all the deeper meanings. The show's a week from Tuesday. I'll drive you down after lunch, we'll change at my house in Mayfair, take in dinner and the show, and drive back afterwards."

Kate's face fell. "Did you say Tuesday?"

"Yes. Is that a problem?"

"Well, it's just that I go to the Inklings Society meetings on Tuesdays."

"Surely, your dear tutor, Mr. MacKenzie, would not begrudge you going to see the great Shakespearean actor Sir Laurence Olivier?"

Kate felt a rush of guilt and then dismissed it. "No. I suppose not."

"I'll tell you what," Stuart said soothingly. "What if we strike a deal? You come to the play with me, and I'll go to an Inklings meeting with you."

"Okay." Kate smiled. She considered she was probably getting the better end of this deal. She would love to see Olivier, and the Inklings might have a very positive influence on Stuart.

"So, what's going on there this week?" he asked.

Kate answered enthusiastically. "This would be a great week for you to come. Professor Tolkien will be there!"

"The author of The Lord of the Rings?" Stuart shrugged nonchalantly. "That could be interesting. All right, I'll come to that one then." Taking a silver cigarette case from his pocket, he snapped it open and held it out to Kate. "Cigarette?"

She shook her head.

Lighting one, he inhaled deeply, leaned back in his chair, and blew the smoke out in perfect rings. "So, do you still want to go to Evensong?"

"Yes!" cried Kate, anxiously looking at her watch.

Stuart chuckled. "Take it easy. We still have time. Tell me—is attending the service important to you, or do you just want to see the cathedral?"

"Well, of course I want to see the cathedral and hear the choir. But attending church is very important to me."

"Why?" he asked laconically.

Kate wasn't sure of his reason for asking. Was he a believer trying to ferret her out? Was he just curious, or was he seeking for himself?

"Church is important to me because my faith is a very important part of my life—and I know that for my faith to grow, I need to go to church." Kate turned the tables with her own question. "And, what about you, Stuart? Is church important to you?"

He took another drag on his cigarette. "Important? Oh, I'm not sure that's quite the word. I do attend a service most Sundays and sometimes go to chapel during the week."

She decided she needed to be even more direct. "But what I mean is, is your *faith* important to you? Are you a Christian?"

He looked at her, seeming almost surprised by the question. "My dear Kate, my forebears built our village church. And I was baptized into the Church of England when I was still in nappies. So I suppose you could say, I've been a Christian all my life."

"Stuart." Kate persisted. "You should know as well as anyone that just belonging to a church doesn't mean one believes it for oneself. Someone once said that being in a church doesn't make one a Christian any more than being in a cookie...er, biscuit tin makes a rat, a biscuit."

"That's good. I'll have to remember that." Stuart laughed and extinguished his cigarette. "However, if we don't suspend this conversation, we shall be late for the very cause of the discussion." With that he abruptly closed the matter and escorted her to Evensong at Christ Church Cathedral.

~

David sighed and shoved away his empty plate. Austen calmly continued to finish his supper. After Magdalen's Evensong service, they had settled into one of the booths in the King's Arms for a few minutes of relaxation before facing student essays.

"What gives with you?" Austen asked.

"Nothing."

"Right." Austen frowned in disbelief.

"Well, all right." David rubbed his forehead. "There's this girl."

"We're not talking about Charlotte again, are we?"

"No. Not Charlotte. I'm trying not to think of her."

"Trying?" Austen looked amused.

"She's hard to forget."

"Evidently."

"Anyway," David started again, "do you remember Kate Hughes, the little American girl who's come to the Inklings?"

"Pretty? Long dark hair?"

"Yes—that's the one."

"Well, what of her?"

"She came to St. Aldate's today. And after the luncheon, I invited her over to the rectory. She was rather homesick, and I thought she'd like to be around a family."

"And?"

"And—I don't know. She's quite attractive and she's a believer. I really enjoyed being with her. But..."

"But, what?"

David set his jaw. "Well, for one thing, I invited her to Magdalen's Evensong and then to supper."

Austen chuckled. "Obviously that didn't work out, or you wouldn't be here with me."

"Right. She said she had promised someone she would meet him at Christ Church. It was Stuart Devereux, one of the toffs in the House."

"Do I detect a note of jealousy, Mr. MacKenzie?"

"Maybe. I don't know. Well, yes. I guess so. The sticky thing is she's taking her Shakespeare tutorial from me, so I feel obligated to maintain some professional decorum in the relationship."

"And so you should."

"Right." David sighed. "But Austen, I really like her. She's a believer, she likes the same things I do, and she's full of life and is very sweet. And she got on very well with my parents."

"Everybody gets on well with your parents," Austen observed dryly.

"Charlotte didn't."

"That's because Charlotte couldn't abide the fact that your mother gave up her nursing career to have you and the rest of your brood."

"Yeah." David agreed. "But you know, Kate seemed to like her for that. She said my mum inspired her to consider having a big family."

"All right, David." Austen looked at his friend with concern. "You've met a pretty little American whom you find very attractive and who shares some of your interests and values, but who happens to be one of your students. So what are you going to do?"

"That's what I was hoping you'd tell me."

"What can you do?" Austen pushed his plate aside. "Seems to me you have to be very careful to be above board and not take advantage of the fact that you're her tutor. Maybe you could spend time with her doing things in groups—like church stuff, the Inklings, and so on. Just be sure you don't lay a hand on her."

"I wouldn't anyway. When Charlotte and I broke up, I decided from then on to follow the biblical injunction in Timothy to treat the 'younger women as sisters, in all purity.' "

Austen raised his eyebrow. "I'm glad to hear it, old boy. I hope you will."

"With God's help, I will," David said resolutely. "So then, would you mind playing chaperone for me? Come with us if I invite her somewhere, or walk back with us from the Inklings?"

"Of course, I will," Austen answered. "However, if I have to play your nursemaid, it would help if you invited some other pretty girls along as well. Being a third wheel gets rather awkward."

"All right. I'll do what I can," David replied. Since Austen had shown little inclination to socialize since his wife Marianne's death two years before, David was doubly pleased at his response. He thought for a minute. "Ah! I've got a brilliant idea. Suppose we get a block of tickets for the Inklings to go up to London to see Olivier at the Old Vic."

Austen nodded his approval.

"Excellent! She'll definitely go for Shakespeare, and she'll be reading *Othello*. We'll announce it at Tuesday's meeting." David stood up from the table and smiled cheerfully. "See you then."

Second Week, Tuesday

Students eager to hear J.R.R. Tolkien crammed into the Eagle and Child that Tuesday evening. Many stood along the walls, and some overflowed into the bar area and adjoining rooms. Stuart managed to secure a chair for Kate and stood behind her as they listened to the famous author speak.

Kate had expected a tall figure like the magician Gandalf in The Lord of the Rings; however, Mr. Tolkien was of average height and slight build. Gray hair and bushy gray eyebrows framed his long, almost elflike face. He wore ordinary flannel trousers, a tweed jacket, and sturdy brown shoes. The only hint of his penchant for the whimsical or fantastic was his brightly colored vest. He seemed rather shy and embarrassed by all the attention, but once he began warming up to his subject, he spoke with great animation—and so rapidly and almost unintelligibly that Kate had a difficult time following him. She thought she understood him to say he would be reading from *The Silmarillion,* his unfinished and unpublished history of the elves, which formed the mythology of his popular trilogy. Many of these stories, he explained, had actually been written prior to *The Hobbit.* The one he had chosen to read to them was the love story of Beren and Lúthien.

A hush fell over the crowded pub as the elderly man began to read. No longer mumbling, he thundered the text with the aura of a bard in an ancient Anglo-Saxon mead hall. He held the group spellbound.

Kate recalled W.H. Auden's description of Tolkien's readings of *Beowulf*: "The voice was the voice of Gandalf."

His intonation grew softer as he read of Beren's first glimpse of Lúthien, as she danced in a moonlit glade:

> *Then all memory of his pain departed from him, and he fell into an enchantment; for Lúthien was the most beautiful of the Children of Ilúvatar. Blue was her raiment as the unclouded heaven, but her eyes were grey as the starlit evening; her mantle was sewn with golden flowers, but her hair was dark as the shadows of twilight. As the light upon the leaves of trees, as the voice of clear waters, as the stars above the mists of the world, such was her glory and her loveliness; and in her face was a shining light.*

At times during the reading, Stuart gently massaged Kate's shoulders or leaned over her and whispered something in her ear. Kate enjoyed the attention but felt uneasy about receiving his favors in front of the others, especially David MacKenzie. Once she caught David frowning at them, his jaw set. Their eyes met, and he abruptly changed his demeanor, giving her a rather sheepish smile.

Professor Tolkien stopped reading, and after a brief moment of appreciative silence, the little pub erupted with the din of enthusiastic cheering and applause. David and Austen exchanged pleased glances.

When the applause died down, David opened the forum to questions. Many of the students were eager to ask about the intricacies of Elven-lore, and the professor was most gratified to oblige them. Soon he was wreathed in smoke as he puffed away on his pipe, talking all the while. *He looks almost like a hobbit himself,* Kate thought as she tried to decipher his rapid speech, garbled all the more by the pipe.

When Tolkien eventually appeared to tire, David graciously resumed control of the meeting. "I know that we are all most grateful to Mr. Tolkien for joining us tonight, and perhaps we can convince him to return at another date." The professor smiled and nodded to another burst of applause.

"Meanwhile," David continued, "we'd like to welcome all the first-timers to the Inklings Society and invite you back for more readings and discussions on the works of the original Inklings, as well as other favorite writers—or even your own works in progress. Please feel free to join us every Tuesday evening right here in the Bird and Baby. Also, Mr. Holmes and I will be getting a block of tickets for the National Theatre performance of *Othello* with Sir Laurence Olivier and Maggie Smith in London for Thursday next. We'll ride up on the Oxford Link together, so you will need money for the coach and Tube. Anyone wanting to reserve a ticket—" he paused for effect—"and willing to pay, please see me in the front left alcove on your way out."

The meeting broke up with good-natured banter and laughter. David pushed his way to the front of the pub, where several students had already formed a queue to sign up for the play. He could hear the groans of those heading out as they opened the front door to a torrent of rain.

In the narrow hallway, Stuart helped Kate into her raincoat. "Wait here, Beautiful. I'll go fetch my car and bring it up for you." Stuart pulled on his London Fog trench coat, grabbed his umbrella, and dashed out the door.

Kate stood waiting in the hallway, saying good night to those leaving. David looked up from the booth where he was taking ticket requests and called out to her. "Kate, would you like for me to reserve a spot for you?"

She blushed and shook her head. "No, thank you. I'm already going." She was saved from any further embarrassing explanations when Stuart came in to retrieve her. She called out her good-byes as they ran out to his idling black Jaguar.

Austen poked his head into the alcove doorway. "David, I'm going to take Professor Tolkien home now. Do you need a lift?"

David shook his head. "No, my car's parked up the street. Thanks though. Good show, eh?"

"Splendid!" Austen was quite pleased with the success of the evening. "I hope some of these newcomers will come back. By the way, how are the Shakespeare tickets going?"

"Good, I should say. Fourteen signed up."

Austen lowered his voice. "And the little American?"

"Already had a ticket." David shrugged. "Maybe Lord Devereux beat us to the punch."

Austen looked sympathetic. "Sorry, old boy. Lunch tomorrow?"

"Righto. See you then. Thanks for all your help, Austen."

~

David drove back slowly to Magdalen in his hunter-green MG Midget. He parked in the Fellows' car park and walked the two blocks to his flat on Holywell Street. The pelting rain matched his mood. He didn't bother to put up his umbrella.

A chorus of barking dogs met him as he unlocked the front door and stepped into the narrow foyer. A stout, elderly woman stood on the stairs trying to quiet them. Mrs. Bingley, his landlady, was a good-hearted widow. Her large features were plain, even ugly, but she always had a kind word or a sympathetic ear for her neighbors. *Too* sympathetic, perhaps, as one of her chief pleasures in life was garnering the latest gossip. Her other chief pleasures were her dogs—all four of them. Like the queen, she had Welsh Corgis. Unlike the queen, however, she had no children, and so her pets filled that void—her pets and David MacKenzie. She relished the maternal role she had assumed since he had leased the ground-floor flat.

"Oh, David, dearie, look at you, soaked to the bone! Why for goodness sake, you look like something the cat dragged in. Shush, dears." She silenced the dogs. "Don't you know your big brother David? Come in, lad. Go take those wet things off and I'll put the kettle on so you can 'ave a nice 'ot cuppa."

David smiled graciously as he stepped over the dogs, opened his apartment door, and let her in. "Thanks, mum. 'Tis kind of you."

He walked through his little sitting room lined with bookshelves, past the galley kitchen, and into his bedroom, where he exchanged his wet clothes for dry. Mrs. Bingley squeezed her portly figure into the tiny kitchen to heat some water. She whistled under her breath as she lit the gas and busied herself with getting out a cup and saucer and finding the tin of Earl Grey tea while the water boiled.

" 'Tisna fit night for you to be out walking with no umbrella," she called out from her spot by the stove. "You like milk and sugar, now, don't you?"

David walked in, pushing his wet hair back off his forehead. "Yes, mum."

"What were you thinking, lad?" She continued her lecturing. "I always says you scholars 'ave your 'eads in the ivory towers. No common sense, I says. 'Ere's your cuppa, dearie." She handed him the tea, and since there was not room enough for him to let her past, she waddled behind him into the sitting room.

"Thanks, mum. This is just the thing. Will you sit with me?" he asked as he lowered himself into a worn, overstuffed armchair.

"No, dearie, thank ye kindly. I know you like your privacy and I must put my little darlin's to bed." Then her small eyes, nearly engulfed by her plump, over-rouged cheeks, lit up. "I just remembered that your lady friend rang you up tonight while you was out."

"Lady friend?" David asked blankly. Mrs. Bingley looked coy. "Oh, I know. You must 'ave heaps of lady friends. I mean the one from Cambridge."

David felt his stomach tighten. "Charlotte?" He tried to keep his tone light. "Did she leave a message?"

"She says she's coming up to Oxford in a week for a symposium or the like. Wants to get together with you. Says she'll ring you again later."

"Right. Well, thank you, Mrs. Bingley. You've been most kind." He stood to see her out. "I know my mother is pleased that you look out for me so well."

"Oh. 'Tis nothin,' dearie. The pleasure's all mine. Good night, David, dear."

"Good night, mum." Thoughtfully, he shut the door behind her and sank back into his chair.

Now, what's this supposed to mean? Charlotte wanting to get together?

He wished he had gotten her call so he could have heard her voice and been able to talk to her himself. Perhaps he would have been able to discern her true feelings and reasons for wanting to see him. But now, if he dwelled on it too long, he would start to fret over it. And he had enough to fret over.

There was Katherine Hughes and that sycophantic Stuart Devereux hanging about her constantly. He wasn't one to be trusted. An inner voice chided David and reminded him that he had been called to minister to the Stuart Devereuxes of this university. David groaned and, reluctantly yet obediently, prayed for the students who had attended the evening's meeting.

He began with Stuart.

8

Second Week, Wednesday

Kate curled up on the wooden bench in the warm afternoon sun. She hadn't expected such glorious autumn weather, but she'd come to learn that although it rained often in England, it did not rain constantly. In Oxford, in the "heart of England," far inland from the sea, the weather was especially temperate, and the showers, brief. Still, she had heard that, come November, things would turn decidedly more chilly and rainy. She determined to follow the maxim *carpe diem*—seize the day—and enjoy the outdoors as much as possible. That was why she was sitting in the Botanic Gardens on Wednesday afternoon, writing furiously for her Shakespeare tutorial.

"Hello, Katherine Hughes. What brings you here?" Her thoughts were interrupted by a deep voice. She looked up to see David MacKenzie smiling down at her, and her breath caught in her throat.

"Same as you, I suppose," she answered, smiling back. "Can't stay indoors on such a beautiful day."

"What are you working on?"

"My paper for you. I thought if I sat where I could see Magdalen Tower, I might be more inspired." She pointed behind David to the elegant bell tower just in view past the fountain and through the tall, golden trees of the garden. She had a lovely vantage.

David glanced back. "I'm surprised you can concentrate surrounded by all this beauty. How's it coming along?"

"Fine. Except for people stopping to interrupt me." She was joking, but he did not interpret it that way.

"Oh, I'm sorry. Please don't let me disturb you…I'll see you tomorrow."

"No, don't go. I was just kidding. I'm really ready for a little break. Please sit down." She moved her books to make room for him on the bench. "I wanted to thank you again for inviting me to St. Aldate's and over to the rectory. I really enjoyed it so much."

"I'm glad. How's the homesickness?"

"Better. I loved your family. And your mom was just great to me. She invited Connie and me to come over to celebrate your family's American Thanksgiving dinner."

"Did she now?" David looked pleased.

"Yes, and that's something we were already worried about missing, since Thanksgiving is not celebrated here. By the way, your sister Hannah is so adorable."

"Aye, she is," David replied smiling, "and in great danger of being terribly spoiled by us all."

"How can you help it? And your father was so easy to talk to. You were right—he is such a good preacher. His sermon really spoke to me."

"Did you like the service, then?"

"Very much. Y'all are so wise to make it contemporary to attract the students, and having the lunch afterwards is a great idea."

"Y'all?" David mimicked her drawl.

"Aye!" Kate teased back.

They both laughed, then sat for a minute just looking at each other and grinning.

David broke the silence. "So, what did you think of Professor Tolkien?"

"Wasn't he terrific? I wish I had had the nerve to ask him for his autograph. Connie was just dying to, but we thought it probably wasn't kosher, or cricket, as you would say. Will you have him back again?"

"I hope so. And I don't think he'd mind signing a book for you. What did your friend Stuart Devereux think of him?"

Kate blushed. "Umm...well, he was impressed and enjoyed the readings, but he's really not a big Tolkien fan."

"Then how did you manage to get him to the meeting?"

"Well—you see, we made a deal. He would come with me to the Inklings this time if I would go with him somewhere next time."

"You mean on a Tuesday night?"

Kate nodded, unhappy with this line of questioning.

"It wouldn't be to the Old Vic, would it?"

Kate nodded again, avoiding his eyes.

"Ah, I see. Pity. You both could have come with us on Thursday." David decided to drop the matter. "Well, now, how did you find Evensong at Christ Church?"

"Very nice." Kate was glad at the change in subject. "The men's choir is wonderful. I think I should go back and see the cathedral during the day though. It's a little spooky sitting in the choir stalls with the cavernous dark all around. The service is beautiful, but I'm not sure how much is spiritual and how much is show."

"That may be a little harsh, but I know what you mean. Still, I enjoy Evensong at Magdalen. And you know, St. Aldate's has a traditional Evensong service since many people, especially the older folks, find great comfort in the ancient liturgy. I suppose it depends on the heart of the individual how much one gets out of any service."

He couldn't resist the temptation to pry a little. "And what about Stuart Devereux? Is he a believer too?"

"I'm not really sure," Kate replied. "I try to ask him about his beliefs but he changes the subject. Anyway, he said he's gone to church all his life and his family built their parish church, so of course he's a Christian."

"Hmm," David grunted.

Kate rushed on, suddenly feeling defensive. "You might call him a nominal Christian, or maybe even an unbeliever. But he seems very interested in spiritual things and going to church and meetings, so if he is not a believer yet, he seems very close to it and is definitely seeking."

"I see." What David really saw was that Stuart Devereux was most likely seeking *her* companionship, not God's; however, he did not feel it was his place to tell her that.

"Well, that's great. That's what we're about: reaching those students who are seeking. So, have you invited him to St. Aldate's?"

"He prefers going to Christ Church's Evensong for now. It's hard for some people to get up on Sunday mornings, you know."

He remembered her oversleeping the week before and smiled. "Yes, I know."

Kate felt uncomfortable with his allusion and all these questions about Stuart Devereux. "Could we change the channel for a minute?" she asked.

"Sorry?"

"Change the channel? Like on television? Switch stations? You know, could I ask you about something on another subject?"

David nodded. "Of course. What do you want to know?"

"When I was talking with your parents, they mentioned C.S. Lewis had been married for a few years and his wife died of cancer. Would you please tell me more about that?"

"Sure. I'd be glad to." He looked back towards the river. "But let me 'change channels' first. Have you been punting yet?"

"No."

"What if I tell you the story while I take you punting? I can't sit still for long, and there won't be too many more days for punting. You can't go back to the States without being out on the river at least once."

"Well, all right. That sounds great." Kate's philosophy of *carpe diem* couldn't let her pass up such an opportunity. "I've been wanting to go; it looks like such fun. But I knew Connie and I would make idiots of ourselves if we tried." She stood and gathered up her books.

"It does look easier than it is," David said as they walked towards the great arch over the entrance to the gardens. "In the summer, I've seen so many tourists spin round and round in circles or crash into other punts. Some even get their poles stuck in the mud and, if they hang on too long, get pulled into the river." He chuckled. "It's jolly good amusement for the locals to sit on the riverbank and watch them. But 'don't worry your pretty little head,' " he added in a mock southern drawl. "I've had lots of practice. I've earned a lot of pocket money punting for the tourists."

He led her down below Magdalen Bridge and signed out the punt. Taking her hand, he helped her step into the flat-bottomed rectangular boat and called to the student attendant to bring her some cushions. When he was satisfied she was comfortable, he stuck the pole into the water and shoved away from shore. Soon they were gliding under the bridge—by the very gardens where they had been sitting. They slid past weeping willows bending over the river and emerald carpets of playing fields. It delighted Kate to see St. Hilda's from this vantage—the familiar span of dining-hall windows opening to the gently sloped lawn and paths bordered by flowers. She contentedly leaned back against the cushions, the warm sunshine on her face, her hand trailing in the water.

Ah, Oxford! she thought. *This is the life.*

"Shall I spoil your reverie by talking, or do you want to enjoy this in peace and quiet?" David smiled down at her from the stern of the punt.

"This is so lovely, David. Thank you so much. I can't believe how beautiful Oxford is, or that I'm really here." She suddenly laughed. "You know, you remind me of a Venetian gondolier, standing there with that pole. I almost expect you to burst out singing."

"'*O sole mio...*" David's rich baritone began the aria. After a few obligatory phrases he stopped. "Hey, let's sing together...*Row, row, row your boat, gently down the stream...*"

Kate joined the round in her clear soprano. Their voices blended well, and the duet won appreciative and indulgent smiles from other boaters. Some stopped their punts and joined in exuberantly until the round got hopelessly confused—and laughing, they had to quit.

"Oh, gosh, that was fun." Kate wiped tears of laughter from her eyes. "Now, David. Please tell me about Mr. Lewis and his wife."

"It's a bittersweet story," he warned. "Very sad."

"Yes, I know, but I do want to hear it."

"All right," he said. As he poled the punt along and began to tell the tale, he took on the air of a bard.

"Joy Davidman Gresham was the last person many people would have chosen for C.S. Lewis. She was a Jewish American, had been a communist and an atheist, and was divorced with two young sons. When she and Mr. Lewis first met, she was thirty-seven and he was fifty-five.

"She had come to England to research a book, but in fact, she was escaping a very unhappy marriage to a man who was a brilliant and promising writer, but an abusive alcoholic. He was said to have broken a bottle over the head of one of his sons. There is no doubt that she made the trip hoping to meet Jack, a writer she greatly admired. They had been corresponding for some time, and she wanted to seek his advice about her marriage.

"She made the incalculable error of leaving her sons at home under the care of her cousin. While she was abroad, she received word from her husband that he wanted a divorce because he had fallen in love with her cousin and wanted to marry her. Joy returned to the States to settle her affairs, grant the divorce, and get custody of the boys. She decided that as a single mother she could live more cheaply in England and so sailed back a year later. Some believe she knew all along she wanted to be with Jack; however, she first lived in London and then, after renewing her acquaintance with him, moved to Oxford a year later."

"Was she still an atheist? And how did she meet him?" Kate interrupted.

"Joy was a writer also and quite an intellectual. She became a Christian partly through Jack's books, and she felt compelled to write to him. He was very dedicated to answering all his mail, either personally or through Major Lewis, his brother. Something about her letter really caught his fancy, and they struck up a lively correspondence. So when she decided to come to England the first time, she wrote and asked if they could meet somewhere. Jack invited her and a friend to lunch in his rooms at Magdalen. Major Lewis was supposed to be Jack's support, but he backed out and was replaced by George Sayers, a friend and former student.

"Anyway, they hit it off quite well. I'm sure Jack had never met anyone like her before. She was a New Yorker, much more bold and assertive in her opinions than a reserved British gentleman would be used to. But the great thing was that she was absolutely brilliant and, like Jack, had a photographic memory. My mother tells about seeing her look over a sheet of music, perhaps a sonata by Mozart. Then she would close the music and play the entire piece by memory."

"That's incredible!"

David shrugged. "I know it sounds implausible, but it's like the stories about Jack remembering whole passages of books. I know a number of people who can attest to it. They both had prodigious photographic memories. And that, I think, was his main attraction to Joy. He had finally found a woman who was his intellectual equal and who could make him laugh. And best of all, she was also a Christian by that time.

"When he took the Chair at Cambridge in 1954, she had just come over to live in England. But when asked how he could give up Oxford after so many years, his answer disclosed that even at that time he was contemplating a lasting relationship with her. He said to some that he needed to make more money to support a family. Now on the face of it, no one except those closest to him suspected that he and Joy were anything but good friends. However, he did urge her to move to Oxford, and he began to help financially with the boys' schooling.

"The next year, Joy was threatened with deportation. To prevent that, Jack agreed to secretly marry her so she could legally stay on as the wife of a British citizen. However, no one knew about the marriage except for the judge, Jack's lawyer, and Major Lewis. At that time, Joy didn't take Jack's name, and she lived in a separate house. They were married in law only, but their relationship continued to grow—Jack would race home weekends from Cambridge to spend time with her.

"Then a year later, tragedy struck. Joy had been complaining about pains in her leg. One night she got up from her desk to answer the phone—and fell in great pain. Her femur snapped like a twig. After rushing her to Churchill Hospital, they discovered she had very advanced bone cancer and the prognosis was poor for her recovery. Joy was only about forty-two by then, and Jack would have been close to sixty.

"When he realized he might lose her, Jack recognized how much he really did love her and decided he wanted to marry her before God and publicly declare her his beloved wife. Even though Joy's husband had been abusive and an adulterer, because she had been divorced, the bishop of Oxford would not agree to marry them. Jack finally found an Anglican priest, one of his former students, to perform the ceremony right there by Joy's hospital bed. The priest asked if he could lay his hands on Joy and pray for healing—and when they agreed, he did so."

David broke off and began to turn the punt around for the return trip up the river. He said very quietly, "The priest was my father.

"Then Jack took Joy home to die at the Kilns. However, many people besides my father were praying for her. Rather than dying, she very slowly began to recover. She had a gradual but very definite remission. Everyone, including the doctors, saw it as miraculous. A year after their bedside wedding, Joy was up and around and transforming the Kilns from a dirty, rundown bachelor quarters to a lovely home. They began having friends over for dinner parties and even took a belated honeymoon to Ireland, Jack's birthplace and childhood home.

"They had three-and-a-half years together. It was the happiest time of Jack's life. He once said, 'I never expected to have in my sixties the happiness that passed me by in my twenties.'

"But the cancer returned in the autumn of 1959, and Jack did not feel that they could ask for another miracle. They had enjoyed what one poet has coined a 'stolen season.' In April, although she was in tremendous pain, Joy was determined to take a trip with Jack and their friends, the writer Roger Lancelyn Green and his wife. They went to Greece and saw all the sites of those wonderful myths and histories Jack loved so much. It was a marvelous trip for both of them. But when they returned, her health continued to decline, and in July of that year—1960—Joy went to be with the Lord. Two of the last things she said were 'You have made me happy' and 'I am at peace with God.'"

David fell silent as he poled the punt up the river.

Finally, Kate asked, "How did he deal with her loss?"

"He took her death very hard. He had a crisis of faith, yet he came through it. Some people allege that he lost his faith, but that's not true. He kept a journal during that time to chronicle his grief and then later adapted it as a little book to help others, which he published under a pseudonym. The book is called *A Grief Observed*, and it clearly shows his journey through doubt to a renewed and hope-filled faith.

"Besides, I knew him during that time at Cambridge. He poured himself into his work and other people. He always had time to see people and kept up a voluminous correspondence. He even continued to have friends over for dinner parties at the Kilns. But, I think, he never quite got over losing her. He didn't take very good care of himself. It was as if he were tired and ready to go home to be with the Lord and with Joy. His stepson Douglas once said that the end of Jack's life was 'an exercise in patience and obedience'...and I think he was right."

"What happened to the boys?"

"Well, after Joy died, Jack continued to care for them and support them. They were teens by then and off at boarding school, but came back to the Kilns for the holidays. Douglas was living there the summer before Jack died. Jack left his estate to them in trust for schooling and in entirety after Major Lewis dies. Now they live with friends between school terms. But it's been very tough for them. They lost their mother, then their natural father committed suicide after learning he had cancer, and within three years, their stepfather Jack died also."

"Oh my. How sad. Sometimes we don't realize how blessed we are."

"You're right. But you know, they were very blessed as well. Even though they've had so much hardship, they had a remarkable upbringing."

They said nothing futhur as they glided back by the Botanic Gardens, under the bridge, and returned to the dock. The silence was not an uncomfortable one. They both respected the other's desire for quiet reflection.

David helped Kate out of the punt and onto the landing.

"Thank you for the lovely ride and the lovely story."

"My pleasure," David replied. I'm glad to have had an excuse to get out on the river before the end of the season."

They climbed the stone steps to the top of Magdalen Bridge.

"I guess I'd better finish this paper or my tutor will be furious with me," Kate teased.

"Good idea. Sorry to take you away from your work for so long. Maybe your tutor will have a little grace for you," he said, grinning. "I'll see you tomorrow." He started to turn and then stopped, remembering something. "Would you still be interested in that visit out to Headington to see the Kilns and Jack's grave?"

"Why, yes, I'd like that very much."

"Right. How about after church and the student luncheon on Sunday?"

"Sounds good to me."

"Excellent! We'll plan on it. Till tomorrow then for the tutorial. And don't get under stress about that. Please call if you have any trouble." David gave her a little salute with two fingers. "Cheers."

"Cheers! I'll see you tomorrow." Smiling, Kate turned and walked across the bridge to St. Hilda's, softly singing, *"Row, row, row your boat..."*

Second Week, Thursday Through Sunday

Kate had no trouble finishing her paper for the tutorial with David MacKenzie. She had chosen to write about Shakespeare's portrayal of love, courtship, and marriage in the plays *Romeo and Juliet* and *Much Ado About Nothing.* After the romantic ride in the punt listening to the poignant tale of C.S. Lewis's marriage to Joy Davidman, she immersed herself in her topic with great enthusiasm.

David paced about the room listening carefully as she read her paper to him. Occasionally, he would stop to clarify a point or to challenge her on an assertion. Once he leaned over the back of the sofa to look closely at what she had written. She again caught the scent of Old Spice. With his cheek close to hers, he became aware of the fragrance of her shampoo. Utterly distracted, he could scarcely breathe. He abruptly stood up, walked across the room from her, and sat leaning against his desk.

"So, did you have a chance to memorize any speech from the plays?"

"Yes, I learned a speech of Juliet's from the balcony scene." Kate tried to keep from blushing, which made her blush charmingly all the more.

"Excellent. Let's hear it."

Kate sat up straight and tried to look beyond her tutor, out the windows overlooking the Deer Park. It was overcast and raining outside so that her face reflected the glow of the lamplight.

Thou knowest the mask of night is on my face;
Else would a maiden blush bepaint my cheek
For that which thou hast heard me speak tonight.
Fain would I dwell on form—fain, fain deny
What I have spoke; but farewell compliment!
Dost thou love me?

She glanced at him then, and he was staring at her intently. She quickly looked away.

I know thou wilt say 'Aye';
And I will take thy word. Yet if thou swear'st,
Thou mayst prove false. At lovers' perjuries,
They say Jove laughs. O gentle Romeo,
If thou dost love, pronounce it faithfully.
Or if thou thinkest I am too quickly won,
I'll frown and be perverse and say thee nay,
So thou wilt woo; but else, not for the world.
In truth, fair Montague, I am too fond,
And therefore thou mayst think my 'havior light;
But trust me, gentleman, I'll prove more true
Than those that have more cunning to be strange.
I should have been more strange, I must confess,
But that thou overheard'st, ere I was 'ware,
My true love's passion. Therefore pardon me,
And not impute this yielding to light love,
Which the dark night hath so discovered.

Mesmerized, David watched her. As she spoke the words so earnestly and passionately, he held his breath and felt his chest tighten.

He ached for her. She was so exquisitely lovely. The poetry sounded like a personal declaration of love. He yearned to take her in his arms and answer "Aye" to "Dost thou love me?"

She finished, gripping the arm of the sofa to stop herself from trembling. Their eyes met; the silence was charged with unspoken emotion.

David opened his mouth to speak and then hesitated. Rubbing his jaw, he looked away. *I must be going mad,* he thought to himself. *She was just quoting a speech. Steady, old boy.*

"That was..." he paused, "wonderful! Have you been in the theatre? I mean, you quoted those lines so believably and with such passion. It was just splendid."

Kate blushed again and looked down.

"Well, now," he rushed on to cover his confusion. "What would you like to write about next time?"

"Um...I thought I could look at the same themes in some of the other romantic comedies."

"Love and marriage again?" David looked doubtful, then sighed with resignation. "Well, all right. Pick two of these: *Taming of the Shrew, Twelfth Night, All's Well That Ends Well.* I guess just about any of the romances would suit your theme. And you should read *Othello* since you'll be seeing it. That should be a nice contrast to the romance. Jealousy, a marriage destroyed by distrust, and all that."

She started to quickly gather up her books and papers.

"Are you busy tomorrow night?" he blurted out, then instantly regretted it. "No, sorry. I...I didn't ask that right...Look...I was thinking of going with Austen Holmes to the Sheldonian tomorrow night for a concert. It's to hear the cellist I told you about, Jacqueline du Pré. And maybe we'll go to a pub or coffee shop after. Would you—and, uh...some of your friends like to join us?"

"Why, yes. That sounds very nice. I know my mother would love for me to hear her."

"Right. Great! Should we just meet you there at the door?"

"Yes. I have to put some time in reading at the Bod. So that would be a nice break. What time?"

"The concert starts at eight, but it will be crowded, so you should get there at half past seven."

"Okay." She smiled at him. "I'll see you then. Oh, I almost forgot. Here's my paper." She handed it to him, feeling very awkward. Their fingers brushed each other as he took it from her. Their eyes met again, but neither spoke.

Finally he said, "Right. Tomorrow then."

And she left.

~

David lightly knocked on the outer door to Austen's rooms at Merton College, then pushed the door open, strode in, and flung himself into an overstuffed chair. Austen, not looking up, continued to write.

"Hello, David, what is it?"

David groaned, "Austen, this is bloody awful."

Concerned by his friend's uncharacteristic word choice, Austen put his pen down and looked up. "What?"

"This girl. I'm utterly captivated by her."

"Who? Charlotte?"

David rolled his eyes in exasperation. "No, not Charlotte. Kate! I told you about her."

"The pretty little American?"

David sighed and put his head in his hands. "Yes, the pretty little American."

"Well, what of her? You aren't behaving inappropriately, are you?"

"No! Well, at least I don't think so. I went walking in the Botanic Gardens yesterday. You remember the incredible weather?"

Austen nodded.

"Well, I saw her and we started talking. She asked me to tell her about Jack and Joy Lewis—their courtship, marriage, Joy's death, and so forth. So I asked her to go punting with me while I talked."

"Uh-oh. Punting, eh? Rather romantic, what?" Austen looked skeptically at David over the top of his wire-rimmed reading glasses.

"Well, that wasn't my intention. I just thought it would be fun. And it was. We sang and laughed, and it was after all in broad daylight in a very public place, so I thought there would be no harm done."

"And was there?"

"Well, today she came for her tutorial. She's my last student for the day. Her topic was love, courtship, and marriage in *Much Ado* and *Romeo and Juliet*."

Austen sighed. "Right."

"So, she memorized a speech from the balcony scene. And she sat there in the lamplight and quoted this lovely poetry with this innocent fervor." He put his head in his hands again and groaned. "Oh, God help me, she is so beautiful."

"Poor David. Undone by a beautiful girl spouting Shakespeare," Austen commented wryly.

"It was all I could do not to take the part of Romeo and cry, 'O, wilt thou leave me so unsatisfied?'"

Austen looked concerned. "You didn't do anything improper, did you? You had the door open?"

"Yes, I had the door open," David answered tiredly. "I follow all the protocol for being with young ladies. And I was most unfailingly proper. But the point is, I was so tempted *not* to be."

"Not good, old boy. You *are* rather smitten, aren't you? Perhaps you should avoid seeing her, give yourself a cooling-off period."

"Too late." David rubbed his forehead. "We're meeting her tomorrow night at the Sheldonian for the du Pré and Bishop concert."

"We?"

"You promised to be my chaperone, remember? Anyway, I blurted out the invitation before even thinking. So I included you and asked her to bring along some girlfriends."

"Should be reasonably safe. Anyway, I do want to hear Jacqueline du Pré. Everyone says she's an amazing artist."

"Yes, well then, you'll meet us before eight at the door?"

"Righto. Any other engagements I should know about?"

"I did ask her if she wanted to go to Headington on Sunday after church to see the Kilns and Jack's grave."

"David!"

"Well, we had talked about it at her first tutorial when she showed such an interest in him," David explained lamely. "So anyway, it'll be during the day and maybe I'll drag one of my brothers along. Besides, how romantic can a cemetery be?"

"Fine." Austen picked up his papers again. "Now, please go. Leave me to my work and I'll leave you to your lovesick misery."

Kate asked Connie and Twila Hurst, another girl in their college, to meet her at the Sheldonian on Friday night. Connie was more than happy to comply with an outing that included Austen Holmes.

Kate knew she had a hopeless crush on her tutor, and his interest in her seemed genuine enough that she allowed herself to fantasize about the possibilities. She felt that something had happened between them. At times, she was certain of it. The way he looked at her. The way he acted after she had quoted Juliet's speech. Yet, at the same time, she reminded herself to be realistic and acknowledge the fact that, as far as she knew, he was still engaged and was merely being kind or, at most, attentive.

A huge crowd had shown up for the concert. David managed to find their party, and having gotten tickets in advance, they proceeded to climb the narrow twisting stairs to the top balcony of the hall, where they had an excellent view. The Sheldonian, designed by Sir Christopher Wren, was a lovely baroque hall with gilt trim and grand chandeliers.

Kate peered up at the giant mural painted on the ceiling. She soon discovered that the hall had been built for beauty, not for comfort. Like most of the benches, theirs was backless and was so high that Kate's short legs dangled uncomfortably. David quickly discerned her difficulty and moved their group to the very top of the theatre, where they could lean back against the wall. From this crow's nest vantage, they could still see and hear everything quite well.

The crowd broke into applause as Stephen Bishop and Jacqueline du Pré strode onto the stage. The young duo seemed an unlikely pair. Bishop, the American pianist, was medium height with dark hair. Du Pré, the English cellist, was very tall and statuesque, with long, straight blonde hair. She looked almost ungainly as she carried her cello to her chair and placed it between her knees, and Kate thought—as she had many times—that playing a cello initially appeared so extremely awkward. Yet as the cellist confidently readied her instrument and the yards of shiny silk fabric from her evening gown gracefully enveloped it, Kate quickly forgot these first impressions.

They began with Bach's *Second Sonata for Viola da Gamba,* which was followed by Schumann's *Fantasiestücke,* and the pair concluded with Beethoven's *Cello Sonata in A Major.* Bishop played with classic expertise and a cool passion. At times his piano threatened to overpower the more subtle nuances of the cello, but nonetheless it was the cellist who captivated everyone's attention. Du Pré played with an intensity and exuberance that astonished the audience. The gawky girl who had walked onstage had been transformed suddenly into a graceful swan. As she swayed with the music and tossed her long hair about, she drew the audience into the changing moods and fervor of each piece. She played simultaneously with utter concentration and total abandonment. Several times after she had completed a particularly difficult passage, she would look up and flash a smile at her partner, as if to say, "There, I did it and it was such fun!"

As the concert ended, the audience jumped spontaneously to its feet with thunderous applause for the performance of this exciting young duo—and it was rewarded with an encore: Debussy's *The Girl with the Flaxen Hair*. The lush, romantic melodies of that composer never failed to move Kate, and this one in particular evoked a poignant sense of yearning.

As the musicians took their bows, shouts of "bravo" for du Pré filled the theatre. No one in the audience that night doubted they had heard a blossoming musical genius...and certainly no one had any way of knowing she would be struck down with multiple sclerosis in only a few short years.

Afterwards, they followed the throng out into Broad Street and walked across to the King's Arms, but the crowd was so thick they decided to go to the Eagle and Child instead. They settled into the quiet back room where the Inklings had met and a coal fire was blazing cheerfully, separated from the boisterous camaraderie of the bar. At first they quietly discussed the concert and the amazing artistry of Jacqueline du Pré. But they quickly shed the mood of thoughtful poignancy left by the cello in exchange for witty conversation and warm laughter.

Nigel Elliot and Colin Russell joined their group, and the two students soon diverted the conversation to sports. Austen deftly brought things around to football, or "soccer, as you Americans would have it"—and specifically the Merton–Magdalen friendly match held that afternoon.

"I like to flatter myself that I'm still a decent defender," Austen said, "but MacKenzie here glories in humiliating me. What was the score, David? Five to one?"

"Six." David grinned. "But who's counting?"

"See what I mean? They crushed us. And most of those were either his goals or assists. You know he plays for Mansfield Road, our University staff team, and we've got one of the top sides in the premier league. Actually, David, you really shouldn't be allowed to play in the college friendlies. It's not quite fair to the rest of us."

The students, and particularly Kate, were suitably impressed with Austen's glowing account, while David looked modestly pleased at his friend's praise. He knew Austen was purposely trying to raise his estimation in Kate's eyes. He was grateful, but was growing slightly embarrassed at the attention.

"Mr. MacKenzie, is it true you were recruited by Oxford United?" asked Nigel. When David nodded affirmatively, Nigel shook his head. "Why didn't you sign with them?"

"And miss out on the pleasure of teaching you lads? They couldn't offer me enough to do that." His eyes twinkled mischievously. "Now if it had been Arsensal…"

The students laughed. But Nigel persisted. "Seriously, wouldn't you rather be playing football and making a heap of quid?"

"Well, perhaps on days when I'm staring at a heap of essays," David quipped. "Really, I do love football, but it's only one part of my life—and I honestly felt I was called to teach."

"Called? By what?"

David paused, measuring the openness of the group. "By 'whom'—not by 'what.' I believe I was called by God."

"But how, as a man of letters, can you be intellectually certain there is a God?" broke in Colin.

"Do you really want to know what I believe and why?"

"Of course. I'm here to read philosophy after all. And what's our University motto? *Dominus illuminatio mea.* 'The Lord is my light.'"

Kate watched David and Austen exchange glances. They obviously relish the opportunity to share with these students, who seemed to be serious seekers of truth, so they seized the invitation to engage in what quickly became a lively but amicable discussion about God and Christianity. Kate recognized that some of the logical arguments being proffered by the dons were from Lewis's writings. The points from

Augustine and Aquinas, however, she did not follow as well. Although she understood the necessity for an intellectual basis for one's beliefs, her own relationship with God had come from a nurtured childhood faith.

Connie and Twila actively joined the discussion as Kate sat listening in silence. Some of the philosophical arguments were over her head, yet she had an intense desire to learn and grow. This kind of interchange of ideas seemed to her one of the most stimulating benefits of a term at Oxford.

As the two Fellows offered to loan the students some of their books by Lewis and invited more discussion at the next Inklings Society meeting, Kate remembered with a pang of regret that she would be missing it because of her date with Stuart. She enjoyed just listening to the apologetics and found her own faith bolstered. It impressed her that David and Austen could present their beliefs in such clear, logical terms and with such a winsome ease that no one felt threatened or judged. They made the listeners hungry to know more, and the discussion continued even as they escorted the girls home. The younger men expressed their interest in attending St. Aldate's and the student luncheon on Sunday.

Kate was really looking forward to returning to St. Aldate's herself, especially after spending a grueling Saturday in the Radcliffe Camera toiling over her research for Tudor History. David had offered to pick her up and drive her over to save her the taxi fare or a long walk, and she had been only too happy to accept.

They arrived early. David's family warmly welcomed her, and little Hannah begged her to sit with them. Kate found the upbeat music and message of the service refreshing. The Reverend MacKenzie preached on the importance of forgiveness. Kate glanced at David during the sermon and was surprised to see his jaw set and his face hard. During the communion prayers he knelt, his head in his hands. The thought crossed Kate's mind that this message had pierced something in his soul—and that perhaps he had business with God over some bitterness or unforgiveness. When he returned from taking communion, however, the cloud had lifted from his countenance, and he smiled at her and winked.

Kate enjoyed the friendly fellowship of the student luncheon and was pleased to see that Nigel and Colin had come. David himself gave a short and practical teaching to the group on dealing with the stress of university life. The students clearly admired his delivery and wit. Kate felt proud of him and the fact that he was her tutor. She knew it was rather silly of her, yet she could not help but feel important through her association with him and the attention he had shown her.

David took her into the rectory to say hello to his family and prevailed upon his youngest brother, Mark, to accompany them out to Headington and the Kilns. Mark had to sit scrunched up behind the two seats of David's MG convertible, and Annie MacKenzie put an apple pie in his lap to take to the Kilns if Major Lewis had returned from Ireland. They stopped by St. Hilda's long enough for Kate to change into slacks and a sweater; and putting the top down on the car to enjoy the sunny weather, they drove up the long hill to Headington Quarry.

Third Week, Sunday Afternoon

The little MG bumped over the long rutted gravel driveway that led to the Kilns. David yelled over the racket that the name came from the two towering brick kilns that leaned hazardously over the property. They had been used by the Lewises to store their coal but were soon to be torn down for safety. He explained that the property covered several acres, and that behind the house and through the woods was a little pond that had been dug out as a clay pit for the former kilns. Legend had it that the poet Percy Bysshe Shelley had wandered these woods and sat in meditation at this very pond, which was now called "Shelley's Pond." David pulled the car around the house to the garage, hopped out, and opened the door for Kate.

The house, a charming brick cottage with a tiled roof, was in a state of decided disrepair and neglect. Roses still bloomed in the large overgrown garden. Followed by Kate and Mark, David walked to the door, called out loudly, and knocked. After a long wait, a very short, plump woman, who was wearing a wig, appeared at the door. She barely cracked it open and looked suspiciously out at the trio.

"Hello, Mrs. Miller." David tried to sound cheerful and reassuring. "It's David MacKenzie here with my brother Mark and my friend Katherine Hughes. My mother sent a pie up for Major Lewis. Is he at home, or is he still in Ireland?"

" 'E's 'ere. But 'e ain't seein' anybody. 'E's restin.' "

"I see. Well, will you please give him this pie and this note from my mother? And please give him our regards."

"All right." She opened the door wider to take the pie and then started to close it again.

"Thank you, Mrs. Miller," David said quickly. "I hope the Major is well, and that you and Mr. Miller are well too?"

"Well enou', thank you. I'll give 'im your regards." She shut the door.

"What's wrong with her?" Mark asked as they headed back to the car.

"I don't know," answered David. "I hope they're taking decent care of Major Lewis. He's a good, kind man, but he's always struggled with controlling his liquor, and probably now more than ever with Jack gone. I don't like the looks of this, but I don't think there's much to be done about it."

They climbed back in the little sports car and drove slowly down the drive.

"It's sad." David sighed. "This used to be a place of such joy."

"I'm surprised at how small it is," Kate said. "I guess I expected a famous author like C.S. Lewis to own a bigger house."

"Well, he bought it when he was just a Junior Fellow like myself. But Jack was never one for possessions. In some ways he led a very ascetic life. His bedroom just contained a bed, a desk, a chair, and some bookshelves."

"So, what do you think he used his money for?"

"I'm sure he gave generously to the church and charities. But, you know, most of his royalties went into a trust for helping young men with their education. He not only supported his stepsons, but I believe that our family—among others—benefited from his generosity. My father has never said so, but I know he couldn't have afforded to put me through Cambridge or any of us through the Magdalen College School without help. I suspect that Jack was more than just my mentor."

A few moments later, David pulled up to the Church of the Holy Trinity in Headington Quarry.

"This is the church Jack and Warnie—that is, Major Lewis—attended every Sunday while they lived at the Kilns," David explained as he helped Kate out of the car. Finding the door to the small stone church unlocked, they stepped inside. Although the interior air felt chilly, a sense of peace and warmth pervaded the sanctuary, which was filled with light streaming through the stained-glass windows.

Mark looked around briefly and then headed back outdoors to explore the cemetery. David led Kate to the far-left aisle and indicated a pew near a back pillar.

"This is where Jack and Warnie sat. They wanted to be unobtrusive and usually slipped out during the final hymn." He sat down, and Kate sat beside him.

"It's so pretty," she said in hushed awe as she looked around the church. "Did he really sit here? I can't believe it. It would be so neat to pray where he did every week. Would you mind if we prayed?"

David answered by lowering the wooden kneeler and dropping to his knees. Kate quickly joined him, and they lifted their hearts silently to God.

Father, David prayed, *thank You so much for Jack's life and the friend and example he was to me. Help me to be more like him and more like Your son, Jesus. Please forgive me for all the times I have failed You, for my anger and lust and impatience and pride. And for not loving others as I should. Forgive me for not always putting You first in my life. Help me to be a better example to the students You have given me.*

And for this dear girl beside me...encourage her, bless and strengthen her...Father, You know I want to be married, that I've asked You for a godly woman to share my life with. Is she the one? Please show me clearly Your perfect will for my life. And help me to treat her as a sister in all purity as You have commanded. In Jesus' name. Amen.

He sat back in the pew and watched Kate, her head bowed over her pretty hands, her thick dark hair streaming down her back. Her exquisite face glowed with rapt fervor. She looked like a Madonna.

Dear Lord, she was praying, *thank You so much for bringing me here to Oxford and to this place. Oh, God, I know I am so blessed. Help me to be ever mindful of Your blessings. Please help me not to be homesick, and to learn everything I should. And thank You for David, for giving me a Christian tutor and friend. He is such a special person. You know I really like him a lot. I just don't know what to do about it or if I should even think this way. Well, I guess I shouldn't since he's engaged but…are You in this somehow, Lord? Please help me know what to do, and bless David and his family. In Jesus' name I pray. Amen.*

She finished praying and started to pull herself up by the pew in front of her. He took her hand to help her. She sat beside him and squeezed his hand. "Thank you for bringing me here," she whispered. "This is so special."

He smiled at her and stood up. "Let's go out and I'll show you where Jack is buried. My brother must be out there playing around somewhere."

They walked outside to the churchyard. The gravestones stood like silent sentinels. The sky was overcast now, and a chilly wind signaled colder weather moving in. David recounted to Kate the same details of Jack's funeral that he had shared with Austen the year before. He spoke of the candle burning without wavering on that crisp, cold November morning. He explained to her how that image had burned in his heart and had been the impetus for beginning the Inklings Society and for his own new beginning of living his life truly for God. However, he stopped short of telling her about Charlotte.

They stood over a large, flat granite stone that marked the grave. The words "Men shall endure their going hence" were inscribed in the epitaph.

"It's from *King Lear,*" David said in answer to her unasked question. "Major Lewis chose it. The quote was on a calendar hanging in their house when they were little boys and their mother died of cancer. Neither of them ever forgot it, and it seemed appropriate for Jack."

A gust of wind caught them and Kate shivered.

"Here, you're cold." David took off the leather RAF jacket that had been his father's and placed it over her shoulders. He carefully pulled her long hair out of the collar. For a brief moment, he put his face close to her hair and breathed deeply of its fragrance. She turned around and, impulsively, he pulled her protectively to him. She lifted her face up to him, and their eyes met. Gently pushing her hair back off her face, he softly stroked her cheek. She held her breath, certain he was going to kiss her.

"Hey! Come on, David!" Mark's childish voice carried over the cemetery in the wind. "It's getting cold. Let's go!"

"I'm sorry," David said, releasing her and backing away. "I...I shouldn't have done that. Please—I'm sorry." Looking disconcerted, he turned to follow Mark out to the car.

For a minute, Kate stood still as if she had been slapped. She felt deflated like a balloon that had just popped, her hopes seeping away like escaping air. She dully followed the others out of the churchyard.

The ride back to Oxford seemed interminable. They put up the car top because it had begun to rain. An awkward silence hung between them. David began talking to his brother about sports, and Kate miserably tuned out their banter about English football and American basketball.

Pulling up to St. Hilda's, David left the car running as he escorted her up to the front gate. She thanked him for the afternoon, returned his jacket, and started to step inside. He could tell that she was upset but misinterpreted the cause. He worried that she felt he had taken advantage of his position as her tutor.

"Kate." He stopped her with his voice. "I am sorry for what happened up there. I promise it won't happen again."

Nodding, she closed the gate behind her, hot tears springing from her eyes.

11

Third Week

Kate didn't have an opportunity to talk to David either Monday or Tuesday. First, she had to finish her paper for her Tudor History tutorial. Then she had to read and take notes on *Othello* before attending the performance at the Old Vic.

Stuart picked her up after lunch on Tuesday in his sleek black Jaguar and sped up Headington Hill to the London road. Kate tried to pick out the lane that led to the Kilns, but everything flashed by too quickly. She leaned her head back against the seat and let the onerous burden of essays and her complicated feelings towards David MacKenzie slip away with the miles. Stuart was in high spirits—and as they headed into London, hers rose as well.

She had been to London only once, with Connie when they first arrived in England. Although they had taken a whirlwind tour, she knew this exciting city would require multiple visits to experience all it had to offer. Stuart pointed out some interesting sights as he confidently wended his way through the busy streets to the posh section of Mayfair. There on a quiet residential street, he pulled up to an elegant Palladian mansion.

"Here we are, Gorgeous. Our townhouse."

To Kate, a townhouse meant a narrow row house, but anxious not to appear like an American tourist, she refrained from commenting.

"Are your parents at home?" The thought of a formal introduction to nobility hit her with sudden panic.

"I hope not," Stuart muttered. "Don't fret, Gorgeous," he said cheerfully. "My father is usually out and about at his clubs or snoring through a session of the House of Lords. Mother, if she's in town, is usually indisposed. So you shan't have to meet the family."

Leaving the car running, he opened her door and escorted her up the steps to the imposing house. A servant greeted them at the front door and took their bags and coats. Stuart gave directions for the car to be parked and orders that they be served refreshments in the small salon. She followed him through the vast marble foyer, past cavernous darkened rooms that must have been the formal salon and dining room. They passed a large portrait of a handsome man in Elizabethan dress, and Kate stopped to read the inscription: *Robert Devereux, Second Earl of Essex.*

"So, are you related to the same Robert Devereux who was Elizabeth the First's favorite and was later executed?" she asked in awed excitement.

"Yes. He's the first and last Devereux who completely lost his head over a woman," he joked. "Didn't much help the family fortune. The third Earl," he said, pointing to the next portrait, "also rebelled against the crown and led some of Cromwell's troops against Charles I in our Civil War. The fourth committed suicide when the monarchy was restored under Charles II. The fifth finally got our family back into good graces with the last of the Stuarts, Queen Anne, which is why we have this lovely house and our country estate today. But," he placed her hand in the crook of his arm and whispered sardonically, "you can see that I come from a long line of rebels and rogues."

The small salon was a comfortable room furnished in contemporary style. Stuart invited her to be seated, and a servant promptly appeared with a tray of drinks and snacks.

"Thank you, Crawford," Stuart said. "By the way, is my mother at home?"

"No, my lord. The Lady Devereux is visiting your sister, Lady FitzWilliam."

"And my father?"

"The Lord Devereux is in town attending to business, my lord."

"Lovely." Stuart sighed and stretched out his long legs. "A lager for me, Crawford, and for Miss Hughes?" He looked at Kate.

"A Coca-Cola would be fine, thank you."

"Very good. And where would you like the lady's things to be put, my lord?"

"Oh, put them in the Queen Anne bedroom. And bring the car around at half past five. I want to stop in Chinatown for a light dinner before going to the theatre. And have a box of cold supper for us after the play."

"Very good, my lord." Crawford poured the drinks and shut the door behind him.

"Sorry about the early dinner. But I know you need to get back to Oxford tonight after the show, and I thought we could take some food on the road."

"Oh, that sounds like a good idea." Kate took a swallow of soda. "So, are you an earl too?"

"Over my father's dead body." He chuckled. "That's literally true. When he dies, I become the next earl."

"Are you called anything, then?"

He looked at her with a twinkle in his eye. "I'm called a lot of things, but I wouldn't repeat them to a lady."

"Stuart!" she cried in exasperation.

"Yes. I'm called that too. No, seriously, as his heir, I'm allowed to take one of my father's lesser titles as a courtesy title. Which means that officially I am a viscount, and my wife, when I marry, would be a viscountess until I become the next Earl of Essex. Now," he asked with a sly smile, "are you suitably impressed?"

"Yes, I am," Kate said honestly. "One more question, if you don't mind. What does the initial 'W' in your name stand for? I've wondered if it could be for Willoughby or Wentworth or Wickham."

He looked at her in puzzlement for a moment and then laughed. "Ah, I get it. Jane Austen characters. You want to know if I'm a rogue or a gentleman, don't you?" He arched his eyebrow. "Well, I'm both, my dear. Seriously, the 'W' is for Winston. We're distant cousins of the Spencers and Churchills, and my father is a big admirer of Sir Winston and asked him to be my godfather. So I am named for a modern hero, but I don't expect I shall live up to it." He grabbed a handful of peanuts and stood up. "Now, I suppose you want a tour of the old place?"

"Oh, could we? I love historic homes."

"Ah, yes, I forgot you are reading history as well as English. Well, come along then."

They carried their drinks with them, and he showed her the formal reception rooms they had passed on their way in. The decor of the Grand Salon had an Oriental motif with rich silken fabrics and latticed Chippendale chairs. Kate remembered that this style of chinoiserie had been the rage in American colonial homes of the same era. Stuart politely answered her eager questions, but she could tell he was rather bored with these familiar furnishings, as fantastic as they were to her. Kate was related through her mother to the Lees, an "FFV," or First Family of Virginia, yet it amazed her to consider that Stuart's family had an even older and more illustrious heritage. She could have spent the rest of the afternoon exploring, but he suggested they both retire to change their clothes.

A maidservant accompanied her up the wide staircase to the formal Queen Anne bedroom. Although the queen had never actually stayed there, Stuart had explained that it always remained ready for the possible arrival of the family's benefactress. He thought Kate would enjoy seeing it, and he was right. The huge oak canopied bed, the sculpted marble mantelpiece, and the elegant fabrics and furnishings all fascinated Kate, who had to force herself to get down to the business of dressing for dinner.

She had chosen a simple but chic short black cocktail dress set off by a pearl necklace and stiletto heels. She decided to wear her thick hair up in the popular beehive style. Surveying herself in the huge gilt mirror, she knew she looked lovely.

Stuart concurred. As he watched her come down the stairs, he gave a low whistle. He scanned her from head to foot and back again until she blushed, and she hurriedly threw on her wrap. However, he behaved like a perfect gentleman, and Kate thoroughly enjoyed the novel experience of being squired around town by a handsome and attentive nobleman.

Sir Laurence Olivier lived up to his reputation as a theatre icon, and his performance of *Othello* completely swept them both away. They discussed the play excitedly during the return trip to Oxford. The entire evening had seemed like a fairy-tale dream, and Kate returned exhausted but happy.

The next morning she discovered a long-stemmed red rose in her pigeonhole, along with a note in elegant script on the monogrammed stationery she recognized as Stuart's.

My dearest Katherine,

Please give me the honour of escorting you to the Michaelmas Ball to be held at Blenheim Palace on Saturday, the seventh of November. You may give me the favour of your reply when next we meet, or ring me up at your convenience. (276150)

Yours devotedly,

Lord Stuart Winston Spencer Devereux
The Right Honourable Viscount Devereux

P.S.—I hope you are sufficiently impressed by my title that you wouldn't dare to break my heart by refusing me.

SWD

Kate was more than impressed. She breathed in the fragrance of the rose deeply and thought with glee, *Wait till I write my sister about this. She'll be so jealous when I tell her an English lord has invited me to a ball at Blenheim Palace!* She suspected that, like herself, Stuart viewed their relationship as merely a fun flirtation. Yet fun it was indeed, and this would be an experience to savor.

Then her thoughts were quickly drawn to David MacKenzie. Her feelings of affection and hope conflicted with disappointment and doubt, making a knot in her stomach. She decided she would try to go by his rooms in the New Building under the guise of needing help on her essay. Perhaps then she could sort through her confusion and lay to rest any possibility of a romance. As far as she knew, David was still spoken for by another.

David sighed and pulled out yet another student essay from the large pile on his desk. He was trying to get ahead in his work, so that tomorrow he could spend a worry-free evening with the Inklings Society at the National Theatre. Now he was beginning to understand C.S. Lewis's aversion to tutorials. Teaching and lecturing gave him great personal satisfaction, but marking papers was a loathsome chore.

He had only just begun reading the new essay when a familiar, smoky voice interrupted him.

"Well, aren't you just the picture of the dedicated don?"

He looked up to see a striking redhead dressed in a Mary Quant minidress and high boots. He silently thought, *And aren't you just the picture of the sexy siren?*

He said simply, "Hello, Charlotte."

"Your door was open, so I hope you don't mind if I come in?"

"Of course not. What brings you here to Oxford?"

"Didn't your landlady give you the message that I was coming up for a symposium?"

"Yes, she did. I just wasn't clear on the dates. Please come in. Sit down."

He stood up to offer her a seat—but moving some papers aside, she sat on his desk. David averted his eyes from her legs, which she was clearly displaying to their best advantage.

"I wanted to talk to you, David," she said as she pulled out her cigarette case and lighter. David dutifully lit her cigarette, and she took a long drag, blowing the smoke out slowly.

"This is a new development," he observed dryly.

Her long fingers reached out and toyed with his hair. "My dear, I'd forgotten how handsome you are. I've really missed you."

He gently pulled her hand away. "Charlotte, what did you want to see me about?"

"We never really talked, did we? After that night in the pub?"

"No, we didn't."

"Well." She dragged more nervously on the cigarette and then rushed on. "I want you to know, David, that I am sorry about what happened. I behaved very badly, and I know I really hurt you. For some time now, I've wanted to apologize. I really am sorry."

David was stunned. Charlotte wasn't the type to admit when she had been wrong. A month before he would have been thrilled at such an admission and would have taken it as an invitation to renew their relationship. Now, not only had he turned a corner in his desire for her, but just this past Sunday, he finally had been able to forgive her. At last, her hold on him had been broken.

He looked her in the eyes. "Charlotte, I really appreciate your saying that. It means a lot to me. And I want you to know I have forgiven you. But I need to ask you to forgive me as well for not being more considerate to you and for not treating you with the respect that you deserve. I wasn't much of an example to you as far as being a Christian goes, and I'm sorry for that."

Charlotte smiled and said, "Of course I forgive you, darling. But our views on religion aren't that important. You can believe whatever you want. It really doesn't matter."

But it matters a great deal, David thought. *It matters most of all.*

"Well, can you leave your work for a while?" she was asking. "And take me out for a drink?"

David paused before speaking. "Look, Charlotte, maybe we need to clear up some more things. Are you suggesting that we go out as friends, or is there something else you want?"

In answer, she snuffed out her cigarette and hopped down from the desk. Leaning against him, she reached up to push his hair back from his face. Then putting her arms around his neck, she pulled his head towards her and began to kiss him eagerly on the mouth.

Just as suddenly, she stopped. He wasn't returning her kiss.

A noise at the door caught their attention.

It was Kate.

12

Third Week, Wednesday Afternoon and Thursday

Kate had found the door to David's rooms in the New Building slightly ajar. Knocking softly, she pushed the door open. To her astonishment, she saw a leggy redhead kissing David. Hearing her, the woman abruptly broke off. Kate felt ill.

"I…I…I'm so sorry," she stuttered, backing out of the door. The woman, with her arms entwined around David's neck, eyed her with interest. David sprang for the door.

"No, Kate! Don't go! Please, come in." He coaxed her inside. "Please. What can I do for you?"

Kate hesitated. "Um…I just had a question about my essay, but it can wait. I didn't mean to interrupt you."

"It's not a problem, really." The redhead cleared her throat. "Uh…Charlotte, this is Kate Hughes, one of my students. Kate, this is Charlotte Mansfield. She's a research Fellow at Cambridge." David spoke rapidly, as if speed alone could cover his mortification at the scene that had just transpired. "So, Kate. What was your question?"

Charlotte. So this is Charlotte. I am such a little fool! Kate glanced back and forth between them and finally answered. "You know, I can see you're busy. I think I can figure this out on my own. I'm sorry to have troubled you. I'll see you tomorrow." She headed for the door.

"Kate!" He followed her. "I'll be at home tonight after supper, so please ring me if you still have a question."

"Okay," she said and then glanced back at Charlotte. "Nice meeting you." She slipped out the door and forced herself not to run down the stairs.

David strode across the room and flung himself down on the sofa. He was seething with anger, embarrassment, and frustration. Charlotte had carefully observed their exchange. She walked around and stood close to him.

"You like her, don't you?"

He looked at her with exasperation. "What?"

"The girl. You're quite taken with her." Charlotte spoke as if certain of her conclusions.

David rubbed his forehead. He didn't reply.

"Well, now," she said. "I can't say I'm sorry to have dashed her hopes. When you get over your infatuation—and you will—you know where to reach me." Then she bent over and gave him another lingering kiss on the mouth.

"I know you still want me," she whispered. "Good-bye, darling."

Then she was gone.

Kate absentmindedly picked at her dinner while the chatter of female voices swirled around her in the spacious dining hall at St. Hilda's.

"Kate!" Connie repeated her name. "Quit daydreaming and tell us who gave you that beautiful red rose. Is it from David MacKenzie?"

"David MacKenzie? That gorgeous Fellow from Magdalen?" Another voice piped up across the table. "Did you say he gave Kate a rose?"

"No, no." Kate started to protest but Connie cut her off and leaned over the table to be heard.

"He's Kate's tutor, but she's seen him quite a bit outside tutorials. He's even invited her over to meet his family."

"I thought David MacKenzie was engaged to a Fellow at Cambridge," someone spoke up.

"He is—" Kate began but was interrupted again.

"He *was.* But they broke up," Twila corrected. "I have a friend in the biology lab who knows her. Charlotte Mansfield is her name. She's in biochemical research. My friend couldn't really see them together anyway."

"Well, they're together now," Kate said flatly. "I just saw them."

"Ooh." Connie realized she had made a huge blunder in bringing this subject up for discussion. "So, Kate, um...who did send you the rose?"

"Stuart Devereux."

"Lord Stuart Devereux?" The girls were impressed.

"So," prodded Connie, "did he ask you to the Michaelmas Ball?"

Kate nodded.

"Great! Because Nigel asked me today, and Colin called Twila. Maybe we can go together. Isn't this exciting?" Connie bubbled. "A ball at Blenheim Palace!"

The other young women took up the conversation again, talking animatedly about the approaching dance and who was going with whom. Kate tuned them out. She couldn't erase the mental picture of David embracing that woman.

How ironic. My essay is on jealousy in Othello, *and now the "green-eyed monster" strikes me. Well, maybe I'll be able to write with compassion about Othello's plight. Anyway, I need to get to work on that paper and get over this. Besides, I do have Lord Devereux at my service and the ball coming up, so I should think about that and stop dwelling on this hopeless relationship. It just confuses me. Yes, I will phone Stuart after dinner and thank him for the rose and accept his invitation.*

She did just that—and did not call David MacKenzie for help with her essay.

~

The next afternoon, their tutorial began awkwardly. Kate hesitated at first to read aloud a paper on jealousy, but gained confidence as David encouraged her and behaved in a professional manner. Although David retained an outward composure, inwardly he was anxious to complete the tutorial and get to a more personal level. His strict policy with female students was to discuss only literature in his rooms and to go to a public place to discuss private or spiritual matters. However, because the Inklings Society was going into London that evening to see *Othello,* he knew his time was short and he would have to bend his own rules to make some explanations to Kate.

"Well done," he said when she finished reading. "Very thorough and insightful. You know, perhaps next week you should look at the theme of appearance versus reality." He tried to give her a significant look, but she was busily writing with her head down.

"Take Hero, for instance, in *Much Ado,* or Desdemona in *Othello.* They are both falsely accused of impurity and infidelity, and—in contrast—the Prince's brother and Iago are most trusted advisors when they are, in reality, treacherous. Shakespeare frequently uses this theme that things are not always what they seem. You should use one other play to expand the point. Perhaps *Twelfth Night* or *King Lear.*"

"Okay." Kate looked up. "I'm sorry, but I didn't have a chance to memorize anything this week because I went to see the play."

"That's fine. I have to be leaving soon anyway. So how was it?"

"Wonderful! Olivier was incredible, and Maggie Smith was great too. I know everyone will enjoy it—well, enjoy is not quite the right word, because it is such a bleak play."

"Yes, well..." David came around to sit in the chair next to the sofa. "Kate, I've wanted to talk to you about—"

He was interrupted mid-sentence by Austen, who popped his head in the door and called out, "Come on, old boy! We're going to miss the coach if we don't leave now." He saw Kate. "Oh, sorry, Miss Hughes. Didn't know you were still here."

Kate rapidly gathered her things. "I was just leaving. Please don't let me hold you up. Enjoy the show!" Then she scurried out.

David's frustration at not being able to talk to Kate only increased over the next week. She declined his offer for a ride to church, saying she would be coming with her friends Connie and Twila. At the next Inklings Society meeting, she brought Stuart Devereux along and left immediately afterwards with him. Then David had to hurry to a faculty meeting after their next tutorial. He agonized over whether or not to call her, yet felt a telephone conversation would not only be awkward, but would also put things in too serious a light. Finally, when he heard through the dining-hall gossip that she was going with Lord Devereux to the Michaelmas Ball, he decided that he and Austen would just have to make an appearance as chaperones.

13

End of Fourth Week, Saturday,
The Blenheim Ball

Stuart hired a chauffeur and Rolls Royce for the ball. Their group, decked out in tuxedos and evening gowns, drove in high style as their host merrily passed out cocktails from the car's pullout bar. Kate felt like Cinderella riding in her coach. Her gown was a shimmering white sheath that flared in a swirl at her feet. Daringly strapless on one shoulder, the dress set off her dark hair, which she wore up in an elegant French twist.

They drove over the stone bridge that led to the expansive courtyard of Blenheim Palace, home to the Dukes of Marlborough since the eighteenth century, birthplace of Sir Winston Churchill, and England's answer to Versailles. The yellow stones of the massive Baroque palace were awash with bright lights. As they walked up the broad steps leading to the hall, the strains of a Scottish bagpiper greeted them.

When they entered the vast, three-storied marble hall, servants in livery checked their wraps and offered glasses of wine and hors d'oeuvres from silver trays. A string quartet played softly under the vaulted arcade running along the side of the hall. Kate tried not to gape at the nearly seventy-foot-high painted ceiling as Stuart guided her into the Saloon, or State Dining Room, where a long table groaned under the weight of assorted delicacies. Fires blazed hospitably in the marble fireplaces on either side of the great doors, where they stopped to pose for photographs. Kate was grateful they would have some tangible remembrance of this magical evening.

After chatting with friends and indulging in refreshments, they strolled through three staterooms heavily adorned with priceless tapestries and gilded furniture. Over the fireplace in the First State-room, Stuart pointed out the large portrait of Consuela Vanderbilt, who, against her will, married the ninth Duke of Marlborough, cousin and friend of Sir Winston Churchill. Stuart explained that the unhappy marriage ended in divorce.

"A cautionary tale for noblemen who marry rich American women for their money," he quipped.

As they walked into the Queen Anne, or Long, Library that served as the evening's ballroom, Kate gasped in delight. The gallery, a peach and cream Baroque confection, stretched for a hundred-and-eighty feet to a massive pipe organ at the opposite end. Kate and Stuart stood in a two-story domed section with floor-to-ceiling bookcases set into the walls behind gilt screened doors. The recessed bookcases and portraits lined both sides of the vast room. Kate looked at the rare and beautifully bound books with undisguised longing. She had never been in such a lovely room, and she fervently hoped that her heavenly mansion would have such a library.

Stuart chuckled as he took her elbow and drew her away from the books.

"Come along, Gorgeous. We're here to dance, not read." Under the silent organ, the rock band Gerry and the Pacemakers blared out their hit song "I Like It," and soon Kate and Stuart had joined the throng of students, laughing and dancing to the beat.

After several dances, they stumbled out the main doors and into the Great Hall for cooler air and drinks. Kate casually looked about while she talked to friends and waited for Stuart to return with her punch. Suddenly, she spied David MacKenzie talking with a group of students, and she caught her breath. He looked up at the same instant, and their eyes met across the crowded hall. Smiling, he gave her a little nod of acknowledgment.

Stuart reappeared at her side with the punch. "Here, my dear—would you mind terribly if I retire with some of the gents for a bit of a smoke?"

"No. Go ahead. I'll be fine."

Stuart put his arm around Kate and nuzzled her neck. "Just don't let too many chaps dance with you while I'm gone. You may be the belle of the ball, but you are mine tonight."

Stuart excused himself and Kate sipped her punch, gaily resuming her chitchat. But the girls abruptly stopped talking as David MacKenzie entered their circle.

"Good evening, ladies. Everyone looks simply smashing tonight."

The girls giggled. They thought David looked simply smashing as well.

He moved towards Kate and made a little bow. "Miss Hughes, may I have the honor of this dance?"

Kate blushed. "I'd be delighted."

David placed her punch cup on the tray of a passing waiter. Taking her hand and putting it in the crook of his arm, he led her back down the hallway to the Long Library.

"I would prefer ballroom dancing with a string quartet, but we don't seem to have that option." He bent his head down close to her ear and whispered, "By the way, you are absolutely dazzling tonight."

When they entered the ballroom, the band was playing their hit ballad "Don't Let the Sun Catch You Crying." Holding her very close, David skillfully swept her around the dance floor. With her head against his chest, she could hear his heart beating. At the end of the dance, he playfully twirled her out in a spinning turn and caught her up again in his arms. For a brief moment he held her tightly and then released her. She felt breathless.

The band struck up a loud rock number, and he offered his arm to escort her back to the foyer.

"You are full of surprises," she laughed. "I didn't expect you to be able to dance like that."

"So, you think only the toffs can?"

She looked up at him quizzically. "The toffs?"

"The rich boys. The privileged class."

"Well, back home, for the most part only the kids who go to cotillion learn to ballroom dance. And that's mostly the socialite types."

"Hmm, I see." He mockingly assumed a cockney accent. "Well, some of us 'ere workin' class blokes gets to go to them 'ighfalutin schools loike Magdalen where we learns to be loike 'igh society."

Kate felt chagrined. "I'm sorry. It was wrong of me to presume you weren't a good dancer." She was eager to change the subject. "Are you here with anyone?"

"Right now, I'm with you." She frowned at him, and he breezed on to explain. "No, I'm not here with anyone. Unless you count Austen. Since Magdalen is sponsoring the ball, I came as a chaperone and I dragged him along."

She blurted out the question that had been nagging her since she had first seen him across the Great Hall. "Why didn't you bring Charlotte?"

He looked pained and said seriously, "Look, Kate, I've wanted to talk to you about—"

"Well, now, Mr. MacKenzie," Stuart interrupted him, "how kind of you to keep my lovely date entertained while I was in the gentlemen's smoking lounge. Now if you'll excuse us, I'd like to dance with her."

David set his jaw and slightly bowed his head. "Good evening, Lord Devereux." He nodded to Kate. "Miss Hughes." He walked off to console himself at the refreshment table before making the rounds to ensure the young men were behaving themselves in a gentlemanly fashion.

Stuart smelled not only of cigar smoke but also of liquor, and Kate assumed the gentlemen were doing as much drinking as smoking in their lounge. However, she reassured herself with the knowledge that they had a chauffeur to take them home.

Stuart swayed slightly as they walked back to the ballroom, yet he still danced superbly. After three fast numbers, Kate was gasping for breath.

Over the din, Stuart yelled, "Would you like some fresh air?"

Kate nodded. Stuart led her by the hand, skirting around the band and slipping out a side door behind the organ to the terrace. Grateful for the refreshing cool night air, they looked out over the immense arms of the palace that embraced the courtyard and extended out to the grounds. Moonlight made a path across the lake to illuminate the Column of Victory and the park beyond. Laughter and boisterous conversations, punctuated by the driving throb of the band's bass guitar, drifted out of the brightly lit windows. The stars hung low and luminous in the midnight-blue sky. It was a perfect evening. Kate felt like a princess in a fairytale. She wanted to hold the moment locked in her memory forever.

Stuart pulled her behind one of the giant pillars and placed her back against it. With one hand on the pillar, he leaned over her.

"Katherine Hughes, you are without doubt the most ravishing woman I have ever laid eyes on. And if I were any more drunk, I would propose to you on the spot." He bent down and began kissing her slowly, then more urgently. Kate felt herself yielding to the pleasure of being kissed. He pulled her close.

"No, Stuart," she murmured. "Please stop." His kisses became more insistent, and he leaned against her, pressing her into the hard pillar. A warning signal went off inside Kate. She tried to push him away.

"Stuart, stop, please," she gasped. He covered her mouth with his own, demanding more. Kate suddenly panicked, and struggling, pulled away with a cry.

"Anything wrong?" Kate recognized the deep voice as David MacKenzie's. Relief followed by shame flooded over her.

Stuart straightened up, his face flushed with anger.

"Are you all right, miss?" David asked her gently. Then realizing who she was, he took a step back in shock.

"She's quite all right, *sir.*" Stuart almost spat out the last word. "We're just out here getting some fresh air and enjoying the moonlight. And don't need any chaperoning." With that, he jabbed David's shoulder.

"Take it easy, Lord Devereux. I didn't mean to disturb you. I just thought I heard the lady cry out."

"Well, you thought wrong, Mr. MacKenzie. So you can go along now."

David turned to Kate. "Are you all right?" he repeated. Before she could nod, Stuart shoved him away. "Stay away from her!" he growled.

David grabbed the front of Stuart's shirt and pinned him against the pillar.

"Look, Devereux. You've had too much to drink. I'll stay away from the young lady when you start behaving like a gentleman. Understand?" Stuart nodded, and David released him. "The band is playing the end of their gig. Why don't you two go in and dance?"

Stuart smoothed out his shirt and straightened his tie. Without saying a word to David, he offered his arm to Kate and took her back in for the last dance.

14

Fifth Through Seventh Weeks

For the rest of the Michaelmas Ball, Stuart behaved like a perfect gentleman, and no further mention was made of the incident outside the palace. Their crowd ended up at someone's flat for a champagne breakfast, and the girls were escorted home in the wee hours of the morning. Kate slept in, missing church, and skipping Evensong as well to complete her Tudor History essay on time.

To the delight of the other young women in hall, at dinner one of the waiters surprised Kate with a delivery of a dozen long-stemmed red roses. Inside the box was a note from Stuart, on the now familiar monogrammed stationery. He begged her forgiveness for his unchivalrous behavior the night before.

Although the entire episode had been distasteful to Kate, this romantic overture of remorse did much to restore Stuart to her good favor. In the weeks that followed, she found herself drawn more and more into his orbit. He attended the next Inklings Society meeting with her, but seemed uninterested in their discussion of Charles Williams and his novel *The Place of the Lion.* Christian fantasy had no special appeal to him, he explained. He politely declined to go to the next two meetings and asked her to go with him instead to debates at the Oxford Student Union. The debates were intellectually interesting but not soul-satisfying to Kate, yet she went along anyway.

She spent the next two Saturdays with Stuart, as well. On one, he drove her into London to visit the National Portrait Gallery, have dinner in Covent Garden, and attend a play in the West End. The following Saturday, he took her to a polo match at Windsor Castle. The excitement of the game, in which Stuart acquitted himself well, was surpassed by the thrill of being introduced to the Prince of Wales. Kate felt herself sweetly seduced by the glamour of this privileged set. The pull of Stuart's world was difficult to resist, and she convinced herself that there was no need to.

Although Stuart was becoming almost possessive in his public demonstrations of affection, he had not tried again to take advantage of her. He was always the courteous gentleman: charming, affable, and endlessly amusing. He would regale her with humorous anecdotes or his opinions on various and sundry topics, yet it troubled her that he avoided any discussion about his personal or family life. As much as she enjoyed his company, she felt deep down that she really did not know him at all.

Certainly, he assiduously dodged any further discussion of his religious beliefs. He found excuses not to attend St. Aldate's, and she contented herself with his presence at Christ Church's Evensong.

She missed the vibrant worship and warm fellowship of St. Aldate's, but to a large extent was hoping to avoid David MacKenzie as much as possible. Ironically, Stuart still wanted to attend David's lectures. Either he had forgotten the incident at Blenheim, or else he had been chastened by it.

Being around David aroused a host of conflicting emotions that Kate would rather suppress. She admired him, but she did not want to adore him. She certainly did not want to nurse a crush that would only leave her disappointed and frustrated. Despite this and her regular apprehensions beforehand, she always thoroughly enjoyed her tutorials with him. His method of teaching challenged and engaged her, and they both shared a passion for their subject. He had twice offered to walk her home after the tutorial, and twice she had excused herself.

However, on this day of Seventh Week, she could not refuse his company again. It was Thanksgiving, and she had long before accepted the invitation to dinner with his family.

A chilling misty rain was falling. Kate had dressed up in the black cocktail dress she had worn to the theatre in London, and David gallantly suggested that he drive her over to the rectory. Connie, coming from her tutorial with Mr. Croft at Christ Church, planned to meet her there—and so Kate felt obliged to accept David's offer.

Once they were away from the familiar comfort of the tutorial, an awkwardness crept between them. Both remembered their last ride together out to Headington Quarry in the little MG, and the memories tugged at their hearts and threatened to wrap them in silence. David longed to explain away the scene with Charlotte that Kate had stumbled on, or quiz her about her relationship with Stuart; yet somehow it didn't seem the right time or place. Instead, his thoughts on their outing to Headington led him to talk of Jack Lewis.

David spoke rapidly, as if his rush of words could rip through the screen of silence.

"You know, driving with you in the car again reminds me of our trip out to Headington and the churchyard. It's almost been a year to the day since Jack's funeral. Our last Thanksgiving dinner was a sad affair. The whole family was quite devastated. We had taken to inviting him over for Thanksgiving after he married Joy, since she was American. And he continued to come after she died. He would return on the train from Cambridge with me. It was so strange not to have him with us last year. It was most dreadful. I wonder what it will be like this year."

Kate didn't know how to respond, but David kept up the stream of conversation as he pulled up to the rectory and hopped out to open her door.

"My sisters will be here tonight. They're home from university for the weekend." He reached into the back of the car and pulled out a large laundry bag. She raised her eyebrow and tried in vain to stifle a smile. The awkwardness was gone.

"Ah, I know what you're thinking." He chuckled. "I'm bringing the laundry for my mother to do. And if you say you don't bring all your laundry with you when you go home for the holidays, well, I won't believe you. No, I do the laundry and don't expect Mum to. It's just that they have a washer here and the prices at the laundries are so dear. But I'm staying here over the weekend. We make Thanksgiving a family holiday weekend, just like in the States. My American grandparents send over parcels of special food like jellied cranberry sauce, pecans, and pumpkin—that sort of thing—which we can't easily find here. So we really try to do things properly."

They walked through the little white Victorian portico, and David opened the front door of the rectory for her. He stowed the laundry bag in the cloakroom out of sight, took her coat, and showed her into the front parlor. A crowd of people had already gathered around the fireplace. Kate spied Connie on the settee in front of the large bay window, but the Reverend Eric MacKenzie intercepted her with a cup of hot mulled cider and began introducing her to the other guests. Kate estimated that, in addition to the MacKenzie family, there were about a dozen American students present, a few of whom she had met before at the St. Aldate's luncheons.

After a few minutes of politely greeting the guests, David excused himself and Kate. He led her down the long hallway, through the family dining room, and into the big kitchen, where his mother was handing trays of hors d'oeuvres to his younger brothers.

"Hullo, Mum. Happy Thanksgiving!" David sang out as he strode over to give his mother a peck on the cheek. "Hullo, lads. Do you remember Kate?" He grabbed some ham biscuits from a tray and popped them into his mouth.

The boys smiled shyly and nodded their greetings to Kate as they carried their trays out to the parlor. Annie wiped her hands on the hostess apron she wore over a sapphire-blue cocktail dress. Her beauty and youthful appearance once again astounded Kate. How could this lovely woman be the mother of an Oxford Fellow and six other children as well?

"Hello, dear," Annie said as she graciously extended her hand. "So glad you could be with us tonight. We've missed seeing you at church lately. Are you doing all right?"

Kate shook her hand and smiled sheepishly. "Yes, ma'am, thank you. This is really wonderful of you. Otherwise, it wouldn't seem like Thanksgiving at all. Is there anything I can do to help?"

"No, that's okay. I think we have it under control. I just want you to relax and enjoy yourself. I dare say David and Mr. Croft keep you very busy with all those essays, and you must be tired. Anyway, I have his two sisters here to help. David, the girls are over in the Hall kitchen if you want to see them."

"Great. I will shortly." He looked at Kate. "Will you excuse us for just a moment?" Then putting his arm around his mother, he drew her to the other side of the kitchen and talked to her in a low voice. When Annie nodded, he turned back to Kate.

"Would you like to see the rest of the rectory? I've just been given permission for a grand tour. Mum is usually reluctant to take people upstairs because she fears her children have left it in some unpresentable state. But it should be decent at the moment, if you'd like to see it."

"Oh, I'd love to!" exclaimed Kate. "I must say, I am fascinated by old houses and am always tempted to explore all the places that are off-limits. But don't worry, Mrs. MacKenzie. I have two younger brothers and I know how messy boys can be."

"Sometimes the girls can be worse with all their clothes," muttered David as he led her back through the dining room, down the corridor, and up a half flight of stairs. "Here is the master bedroom, which opens out onto a roof terrace overlooking the garden. And up here on the first floor, or second floor as the Americans would have it, we have a guest bedroom in the back—and here's our sitting room."

He opened a door to a room identical in size to the formal parlor directly below it, with a similar bay window, and a fireplace set between lighted recessed alcoves. This room lacked the formality of its counterpart and seemed cozier, with its well-worn furniture, shelves of books, and television in the corner.

"This is where we really live. Well, here and in the kitchen. And this is where my father spends most of his time." He slid open a set of wooden pocket doors to a spacious study lined with floor-to-ceiling bookcases.

"Oh, my!" exclaimed Kate as she walked up to a shelf and reverently touched the spines of some beautifully bound leather volumes. "This is where I would spend all my time too. What a wonderful room."

"Yes. I quite envy him. Although I do enjoy my rooms in the New Building."

Kate looked around in puzzlement. "So where do all the kids sleep?"

David laughed. "Upstairs. And there's even a garret room on the next level that is mine. Come on, I'll show you." He took her back to the landing and bounded up the flight of stairs to a third sitting room with a fireplace, but with a smaller window than its downstairs counterparts. Shelves and cupboards around the room fairly groaned under the weight of children's books and toys. Some constructions of Tinkertoys and Lincoln Logs had been left standing. A large dollhouse stood in the corner. Adjacent to this playroom lay a small bedroom decorated in pink rosebuds. Dolls and stuffed animals vied for pillow space on the bed.

"Hannah's room." David's identification was unnecessary. "After three boys, Mum couldn't resist pink."

They peeked into side-by-side rooms with a decidedly boyish décor. "Will has his own room, and Richard and Mark share. Then back on the half-landing is Ginny and Natalie's room, which is similar to my parents.' "

"Gosh, this place is huge!"

"Isn't it wonderful? Perfect for a big family. I guess in Victorian times, they expected the rector to have lots of children. I suppose if the next rector has his one-point-five average of children, they'll turn this into several apartments or offices or something. Anyway, we've been enormously blessed. But come up one more flight and you can see my old room."

They climbed steep stairs up to the attic and entered a narrow room with a sloped ceiling. Bookshelves also lined the walls of this room. One of the shelves held a large display of trophies.

"What are all these for?" Kate asked as she walked over to examine them.

"Football...well...soccer, you'd say."

"So, Austen wasn't exaggerating when he bragged about your playing?"

"Hmm. I've played a bit."

Kate looked at him, and his eyes were laughing. She read the inscriptions. Some were for Magdalen College School, but many were for Cambridge University.

"So, you beat Oxford, did you?"

"Just all three years I played for Cambridge."

"Wait a minute." She had come across two other trophies. "What are these, Oxford over Cambridge?"

"Graduate school, here." He grinned. "There are no eligibility limits as long as you're a student."

"But Austen said you're still playing."

"Yes, I play for Mansfield Road—that's the University staff squad—and friendly matches, like the one at the beginning of the term with Merton. I also help train the University team. I say, have you seen any football matches?"

"No. They're just starting to play it in the States. I wonder if it will catch on there."

"Oh, it will. I've helped coach some summer camps when I've been over to visit my grandparents. It's a great sport for kids of all sizes, and not one that requires money like polo or tennis, which are played more by the upper class here. Soccer is a much more democratic sport, which is why I think it will be big someday in the States. But," he said, offering her his arm, "we'd better get back downstairs to the other guests. And I'd like you to meet my sisters."

Since she was wearing high heels, Kate gratefully took his proffered arm as they walked back down the flights of steps. Yet feeling the scratchy wool of his tweed jacket and being so close to him, who seemed so unattainable, made her heart ache with mingled joy and sadness.

The ache remained as she witnessed the poignant reunion of brother and sisters in the rectory room kitchen. The girls lovingly embraced David, and Kate was struck with envy for their having such a brother and for their right to embrace him freely. Standing at the door, she felt like an outsider observing an intimate scene, and profound homesickness engulfed her.

Sensing some of her feelings, David hastened to draw her into the family circle and introduce her to his sisters.

"Girls, you must meet Kate Hughes. She's an American and taking a Shakespeare tutorial with me this term. Kate, this is Ginny." He put his hands on the shoulders of a slender girl about her own age with long, wavy fair hair and wide blue-green eyes. "Ginny is a third-year nursing student in London." The young women smiled at each other and shook hands. "And this is Natalie," he said putting his arm around a diminutive brunette. "She's in her first year at London University."

As Kate shook hands, she realized that she and Natalie were similar in height and coloring, although Natalie's dark hair just swept her shoulders. Kate could see in the sisters a resemblance to David, as well as to both of their parents. The girls, like their mother, were certainly pretty. Each wore cocktail dresses similar to her own, but covered by hostess aprons.

Little Hannah came running up in a smocked blue dress with a crinoline petticoat. Her golden curls tumbled down her back and her face glistened with perspiration. She lifted her chubby arms, and David scooped her up.

"Hello, angel. How's my little girl?" Her answer was a tender kiss on his cheek. She nestled her head on his chest and looked shyly at Kate.

"Don't you remember my friend Kate? Why don't you say hello?" Hannah just sucked on her finger and then buried her head deeper into his chest.

"That's okay, Hannah. You haven't seen me for a while." Kate felt remorse even as she explained away Hannah's shyness. Turning to Ginny and Natalie, she asked if she could help, and they gave her a pitcher to fill the water goblets. Then Annie MacKenzie rushed in with her three younger sons carrying platters of food.

"David," she said breathlessly, "would you please take out the turkey and bring it in when the others come? And Hannah, run back over to the house and ring the dinner bell. Make sure Daddy hears you, okay? Now, let's put this food out before they all get here."

Kate looked about the rectory room as she poured the water. Two long tables were set with gleaming silver and china. Crystal goblets sparkled in the candlelight, reflecting the rich autumn colors of chrysanthemums and horns-of-plenty between the rows of settings. A third table, connecting the others in a U shape, held the various serving dishes and platters, from which were wafting the savory scents of sweet potatoes and freshly baked bread.

The other guests filed in and found their place cards. They cheered and applauded as David triumphantly bore a huge golden roasted turkey to its place of honor in the center of the buffet.

Kate was pleased to be seated between David and Ginny, with Natalie and Connie across from her. As she looked around the room, it suddenly occurred to her that Charlotte, David's fiancée, wasn't there. All week she had dreaded seeing Charlotte with David; but since arriving, Kate had forgotten all about her. She wondered at her absence, and then realized that this was a weeknight, not a British holiday. No doubt, Charlotte couldn't be expected to leave Cambridge for an American celebration. Suddenly, everyone hushed as Eric MacKenzie stood over the turkey to give thanks.

"Before we pray, I would like to thank each of you for coming tonight and making this Thanksgiving celebration even more special. And I would also like to thank my wonderful wife, Annie, for preparing this splendid feast."

Annie's eyes shone as she accepted her guests' grateful applause. Smiling, Eric waited and then continued. "I would also like to take a few moments to remember our dear friend and mentor, Jack Lewis, who went to be with the Lord at this time last year." His voice grew husky. "We miss him immensely, but are deeply grateful for his life and example to us all."

He held up a piece of paper and put on his reading glasses. "Jack wrote this about thankfulness: 'We ought to give thanks for all fortune: If it is 'good' because it is good, if 'bad' because it works in us patience, humility and the contempt of this world and the hope of our eternal country.' "

He paused, putting down the paper. "Let us bow our heads to pray...Heavenly Father, we come to You in humble thanksgiving for all Your manifold blessings to us—for this food we are about to eat, for

Your provision, for our families present and far away in America, for our friend Jack and the fact that one day we can be with him again for all eternity. We thank You most of all for the gift of your precious Son, Jesus the Christ, whom to know is life everlasting. Bless each family represented here, bless this time of fellowship together, and bless this food to our nourishment so that we can better serve You and one another. In Jesus' name. Amen."

Everyone repeated "Amen." Then the Reverend MacKenzie began to carve the turkey, singing as he did so, "We gather together to ask the Lord's blessing..." The entire group joined in, and the sound of the hymn reverberated off the rafters of the hall and enveloped them. Singing along in her clear soprano, Kate felt a thrill of joy. Her homesickness faded as she sensed the presence of God's Holy Spirit and her unity with His family throughout the world. She knew she had so much to be thankful for: not only her own family, but also this one in Oxford, the MacKenzies and the church family of St. Aldate's. She wondered why she had let herself stay away for so long.

Soon Kate took her turn at the buffet table, loading her plate with turkey, stuffing, cranberry sauce, sweet potatoes, hot rolls, and vegetables. The laughter and conversation flowed as richly as the food and drink, and her heart was warmed.

After David and others had returned for second and even third helpings, Ginny and Natalie hopped up to assist their younger brothers in bringing out apple, pumpkin, and pecan pies, as well as coffee and tea to the dessert table. Everyone nearly moaned from fullness, but managed to help themselves to the desserts anyway. When the dishes had been cleared away, Eric MacKenzie stood and asked his guests to join him in singing another hymn, "We Plow the Fields, and Scatter the Good Seed on the Land."

Then William, Richard, Mark, and Hannah came into the hall carrying boxes of board games, which they handed out around the tables. The guests divided into smaller groups according to their interests. Some milled around drinking coffee and talking, and some enthusiastically joined in the games. Laughter filled the room. Kate and Connie played the game of "Life" with David and his sisters. David was quite pleased to fill up his little game car with children, even when he wound up at the "Poor Farm" rather than "Millionaire Acres."

"I wonder if this game is at all prophetic," he laughingly mused. "I do want a boatload of kids, but would rather not be a pauper."

The party began to break up around ten o'clock as the students reluctantly remembered their need to get back to their books and beds. David accompanied Kate and Connie back to the main house and brought them their coats.

"You're sure you don't want a lift?" he asked, holding Kate's coat for her. She slipped into it, and he once again gently lifted out her long, thick hair and let it fall down her back. She heard him take a deep breath and slowly exhale.

She turned and smiled up at him. "No, thanks, really. We'll just catch the bus back. You should be here with your family. And thank you so much for inviting us. It was absolutely wonderful. We're going to go back and call our folks now."

"Excellent. I'm sure they'll be happy to hear from you. Please send along my regards. And do you think we'll see you ladies at St. Aldate's this Sunday?" He looked at Kate expectantly, but Connie answered.

"I'm coming. And Nigel Elliot plans to come too."

"Splendid!" He still had his eyes on Kate.

"I plan to," she said with some hesitation. "I've just got to get more work done on my essays. It's almost Eighth Week, you know. Can you believe it? The term is going by so fast! Well, good night, everyone, and Happy Thanksgiving!"

Kate and Connie stepped out into the street amidst a chorus of "Happy Thanksgiving!" from departing guests, whose stomachs and souls had much for which to be thankful.

15

Seventh and Eighth Weeks

David closed the door after the guests departed and, picking up some discarded trash and glasses from the parlor, walked back to the kitchen. His mother stood at the sink washing dishes while Natalie dried. Eric MacKenzie brought in the last of the plates from the rectory room, placed them on the counter, and gave his wife a kiss on the cheek.

"A splendid dinner, Annie. Perfectly lovely."

Annie pushed a loose strand of hair off her forehead with her wrist, trying to avoid the soapsuds on her hand. "Thanks, honey. Everyone seemed to have a good time, don't you think?"

"It was great, Mum," David chimed in, grabbing a towel to help. "Thanks so much for hosting it. I know it means a lot to these American kids who are away from their families."

"Yes—well, it is a lot of work, but I'm always glad we've done it after it's over."

Ginny came in. "I've put the baby down, but the boys are starting to get into it."

Annie looked at her husband.

"Don't worry, darling." He headed for the stairs. "I'll take care of the lads."

Ginny pulled her mother away from the sink. "Let me wash for a while, Mum. You sit down. You've been on your feet all day."

Annie didn't protest. She sat down and picked up a tea towel. "I can dry silver. Just pass it over here."

"Okay, David. What's the story on you and Kate?" Ginny asked as she plunged her hands into the soapy water."

"What do you mean?" David replied hastily. "Nothing!"

"Oh, right!" Ginny exchanged knowing glances with Natalie.

"Gin and I think you're in love with her," Natalie teased.

"Don't be ridiculous!" David exclaimed, angrily rising to the bait. "Where did you get such an idea? She's a student of mine!"

"Uh, huh…we watched you practically devour her with your eyes," Natalie retorted.

"Oh, please. Don't be absurd."

"The gentleman doth protest too much, methinks," Ginny whispered loudly.

"And did you notice how adoringly she looked at him?" Natalie continued her teasing. "With those huge brown eyes of hers? And how she blushed at everything he said? Yep, she's definitely batty over him."

"Do you really think so?" David asked eagerly.

"Gotcha!" both girls yelled in triumph.

David sheepishly grinned. "Touché."

"You *do* really like her, don't you, David?" Annie asked.

"Yes, Mum," David answered truthfully as he pulled up a chair beside her. "I do. Very much."

"Well, she seems like a very dear girl, honey. And a true believer, which is most important."

"She's very pretty and nice too," added Natalie. "And she's American. That's a plus, wouldn't you say, Mummy?" Ginny asked.

"Well, I should hope so." Annie smiled.

"We like her, David," Ginny confirmed. "Nat and I give our approval. She's much better for you than Charlotte. What did you ever see in her anyway?"

"Now, really! How about beauty and brains?" Natalie quipped sardonically.

"Charlotte is an attractive girl," said Annie. "But she is not a believer, and your father and I would never have been happy with you marrying someone who does not share your faith."

"Yes, well...I'm glad you all like Kate," David said as he dried a pile of silver Natalie had placed in front of him. "But there are just a few obstacles to overcome before you can marry us off."

"Such as?" All three women looked at him.

"Such as the fact we don't know what her feelings really are towards me. Such as the fact I'm her tutor and so must respect the teacher–student relationship and not jeopardize her studies or my job. Such as the fact she has been seriously dating Lord Stuart Devereux, Viscount of Essex. Such as the fact she stumbled in on Charlotte trying to kiss and make up with me a couple of weeks ago and I still haven't been able to explain it to her."

Ginny gave a low whistle. Natalie looked deflated. For a moment the women were speechless.

"And what of Charlotte, David?" Annie asked gently.

"It's over, Mum. For me, it's finally over. I know now that God doesn't want me to be unequally yoked with an unbeliever. I made that decision at the beginning of the term and have been praying since for a wife who shares my beliefs."

"I'm glad, honey. Your father and I have been praying for that too."

"For what?" Eric MacKenzie asked as he strode into the kitchen.

"For David to find the right wife."

"What about Kate, that little American girl?"

Everyone groaned. Eric looked around, perplexed. "What did I say?"

"Nothing, dear. We all like Kate too. And so does David. He just finished explaining some difficulties with—" The jangle of the telephone interrupted her. They all groaned again. "Who on earth can be calling at this time of night?" Annie sighed.

"I'll get it." Eric answered the phone, talking quietly into the receiver.

"Well, anyway, David," Annie resumed, "we are praying for you. You know that if Kate is the one for you, the Lord will work it out and make it clear to you both. And if not, she'll go back to the States and He'll bring someone else along. Just trust in Him to work out His plan for your life."

"Yes, Mum. I will."

"But don't sit around on your derrière and do nothing!" Ginny spoke up. "At the end of term, you should talk to her so she doesn't go home without a clue about how you feel."

"Definitely," Natalie concurred. "You need to declare yourself, like one of the heroes in your Shakespeare plays."

David chuckled. "Should I spout poetry?"

"Why not? I think it's romantic, and she likes Shakespeare, doesn't she?" Ginny smiled at the idea. "Then, if she doesn't like you after all, she can feign ignorance of what you're doing. And you can save face by pretending you were just quoting the bard!"

Their banter abruptly stopped as their father somberly hung up the phone.

"What is it, Eric?" Annie asked anxiously.

"That was Henry Lucas. Poor Mrs. Lucas fell and broke her hip. So, I'm afraid I should go over to the Radcliffe Infirmary to see her. She was just admitted." He came over and kissed the top of Annie's head. "I'm sorry, darling."

Annie leaned back against her husband and took his hand. "It can't be helped. Of course, you should go. I'm just sorry for Clara Lucas and you, after such a long day."

David put his towel down. "I'll come with you, Dad. We can take my car."

"That's very kind of you, lad. I'd appreciate your company, if you really don't mind." He smiled ruefully at his family. "Never a dull moment, eh? Well, we'd best go, David. The sooner there, the sooner home."

Kate and Connie did attend the Sunday morning service at St. Aldate's, along with Nigel and Colin. Ginny and Natalie sought out Kate after the service, and even little Hannah seemed less shy around her. The friendliness of David's family delighted Kate, but under pressure to complete her last history essay, she declined their pleas to stay for the student luncheon.

All that week, she worked diligently to complete her final Shakespeare paper on *Hamlet.* She wanted it to be absolutely brilliant. David had suggested that she write again on "appearance versus reality." She wondered why he seemed to be harping on this theme, but found so many examples in the text that the essay flowed easily out of her. Indeed, David complimented her highly on her work, and their earnest discussion of this greatest of plays gratified them both.

An awareness that this was their last official tutorial stole sadly over them. Kate wanted to linger, but could not. Stuart had arranged that all their set would be leaving for a long weekend to celebrate the end of the term with a house party at his country estate. When David invited her to dinner, she awkwardly explained why she couldn't stay. He replied with some irritation that he would at least escort her down to the front gate. They walked down the stairs in silence.

When they reached the entrance of the New Building, David ventured to speak.

"Uh, Kate, perhaps you will think this is none of my business, but I'm...concerned about you and this weekend, especially after...well, especially after what happened at the Blenheim Ball."

Kate blushed. "You know, it really isn't your business, but since you've been my tutor and friend, I'll just say that you don't need to worry about me. Stuart was very contrite about what happened and has behaved perfectly since."

David rubbed his jaw thoughtfully as they walked along. "Well. I'm glad to hear that, but I also have to tell you I'm concerned about you getting so involved with someone who is not a believer."

"How can you judge that?" Kate grew defensive. "You don't know that he isn't! He's been going to Evensong with me and some of the Inklings meetings as well."

"Yes, but you yourself said that you weren't really sure what he believed. That he always changes the subject when you bring it up."

Kate was angry now. She didn't like to have her judgment questioned. "Mr. MacKenzie, Lord Devereux says he's a Christian. He has been very kind to me and, except for that one incident, has always acted like the gentleman he is. And I don't appreciate your criticizing him or me."

David felt his temper rising but tried to hold it in check. "Right," he said curtly. "I'm sorry I said something. I am just concerned for you, that's all."

Again, they fell into silence. Then abruptly, Kate spoke up. "I didn't quote my speech for you."

"Sorry?"

"My speech from *Hamlet.* I learned one of Ophelia's that, I think, would be appropriate now."

They were standing by the Porters' Lodge. "You want to recite a speech of Ophelia's *now?*" David asked incredulously.

"Yes. I do." She defiantly met his eyes and then began:

I shall th'effect of this good lesson keep
As watchman to my heart; but good my brother,
Do not, as some ungracious pastors do,
Show me the steep and thorny way to heaven
Whilst like a puffed and reckless libertine
Himself the primrose path of dalliance treads
And recks not his own rede.

She glared at him. "I believe that last line means 'and heeds not his own advice.'"

David blanched as her meaning dawned on him. He started to protest his innocence, but she had gone.

End of Term

Kate was seething as she packed her suitcase for the weekend house party.

Of all the nerve! Who does he think he is? Telling me to be careful! And that fiancée of his was all over him and she wasn't exactly modestly dressed. She's supposed to be a believer? Right! Well, I've worked hard all term, especially for his tutorials, and I deserve to have a nice break. What can a weekend in the country hurt? It's not like I'm going off alone with Stuart. Plenty of our friends will be there. And probably his parents too. Besides, it will be so nice to be treated like a lady and stay in a huge mansion and be pampered by servants.

"Kate!" Connie shouted from the adjoining room. "Are you packed yet? Are you taking your evening gown?"

"Yes!" Kate called back. "We're supposed to dress up both Friday and Saturday for dinner. But tonight, Stuart said to wear slacks. Hey, have you seen my brush?"

Both girls managed to finish packing before Stuart pulled up with Nigel in his Jaguar. Colin and Twila were driving down separately, as were some other friends of Stuart's from "The House," as they called Christ Church.

The drive to the Devereux estate of Clifton Manor in Essex took well over two hours, but the excited young couples hardly noticed the time. The term was essentially over. The stress of Oxford's grueling tutorials rolled away, and their spirits rose at the prospect of escaping to the country for a weekend of relaxation and fun.

Although it was late when they arrived, bright lights beckoned to them from the large mullioned windows of the three-storied mansion. The yellow stone walls rose almost castle like before them, but the stone tracery along the roof and the cupolas that capped the eight turrets made the multiwindowed facade appear more like a palace. Kate had never seen such architecture before and asked Stuart about it.

"Jacobean," he replied. "This wing was built in the time of James I over the old Elizabethan manor house. The third earl got carried away and built the largest Jacobean building ever. The original gallery was nearly half again as large as the one at Blenheim, to give you an idea. But the old boy outspent himself and much of it had to be torn down. And then when we backed the wrong side in the Civil War, Charles II confiscated the property during the Restoration and everything but this wing was demolished. Nice though, isn't it? Quite unique."

"And didn't Queen Anne give it back to you?" Kate broke in. "I remember you telling me about it when we visited your London townhouse."

Stuart raised his eyebrows and gave a half-smile to show he was impressed. "Quite right. So the other wing dates from that eighteenth century neoclassical period, like Blenheim. But you'll see all that tomorrow. Inside it's a hodgepodge of styles."

He drove right up to the front portico, where a servant came out to greet them and take their bags. Stuart led them into a high wood-beamed entrance hall and spoke to his butler.

Then he turned to his guests. "Collins will show you to your rooms. Just take your time freshening up, and please dress casually or don't bother to change. We'll have a cold supper and drinks tonight in the family dining room when you find your way down. The others should be here soon. Now, if you'll excuse me. I'd like to speak to the cook about tomorrow's meals."

Kate and Connie couldn't suppress their grins as they exchanged glances. Connie mouthed one word. "Wow!"

The next morning Kate yawned and stretched luxuriously on her bed of satin sheets. A soft quilted duvet covered her. Gray daylight peeked through the thick drapes as Kate happily looked around her room. Swags of a pretty floral fabric hung from her cherrywood four-poster. A fire still glowed in the gleaming white marble fireplace, its warmth augmented by an electric heater. As soon as she began to stir, a gentle rap at the door announced a perky but polite serving girl with a tea tray.

"Good morning, miss. Would you like some tea or should I return later?"

"Oh, no. Please. The tea would be just fine. Thank you."

"Shall I open the curtains for you, miss?"

"Yes. Thank you."

The maid pulled back the drapes to reveal an overcast sky. "Looks like rain today, miss. But I don't suppose the gentlemen will mind staying in. I hear, after you ladies retired, they were up most of the night, playing cards and all."

"Have they come down for breakfast, yet?"

"Oh, no, miss. But the buffet is all ready, whenever you wish to come down. Will that be all, miss?"

"Yes. Thank you." The maid quietly closed the door, and Kate slipped into her robe and sat down in a large wing chair by the fire to sip her tea.

Now this is the life. I feel quite the grand lady. I could be happy just to curl up in a chair with a pot of tea and read the day away.

Kate reminded herself that she should begin her day with devotions, and she pulled out her Bible. As she randomly flipped open to Proverbs, her eyes fell on chapter three, verses five and six.

> *Trust in the Lord with all your heart, and do not rely on your own insight. In all your ways acknowledge him, and he will make straight your paths. Be not wise in your own eyes; fear the Lord, and turn away from evil. It will be healing to your flesh and refreshment to your bones.*

She said a quick prayer to commit the day to the Lord, her mind already wandering over the possibilities that lay before her. After dressing in slacks and a sweater, she went down for breakfast.

It was well past eleven, and the young ladies of their party had gathered in the dining room to help themselves to the "brunch" spread out in silver chafing dishes on the sideboard.

Kate found the usual English breakfast of eggs, bacon, sausage, baked beans, tomatoes, mushrooms, and buttered toast, with the pleasant additions of fresh fruit, scones, and muffins. Ravenously hungry, she generously piled the food on her plate and sat down beside Connie. Nigel, the only male present, flashed his toothy grin.

"Good morning, luv! You slept well, I trust?" he asked cheerily.

"Divinely," Kate murmured. "How about you?"

"Short night. But good. I turned in before most of the blokes. I doubt we'll see them this morning. Some of them had a bit too much to drink last night."

Kate frowned. "What were y'all up to anyway?"

Nigel smiled amiably and mimicked her drawl. "Well, when 'y'all' ladies went to bed, some of the gents were playing cards and got a bit rowdy. But nothing too untoward. Everyone was just feeling like celebrating the end of term."

"And Stuart?" She raised her eyebrow.

Nigel shook his head, grinning. "Don't expect to see him for a while. He celebrated a wee bit much."

"Oh, I see." Kate decided to change the subject. "Well, Connie, how is your room?"

"It's so neat, Kate!" her friend enthused. "I feel just like a princess, staying in this grand house, don't you?"

"Yes. It's fabulous. Would you like to explore with me after breakfast?"

So they wandered through staterooms and galleries from various centuries, exclaiming over the fine collections of furniture, portraits, and porcelain. Inevitably, Kate found herself drawn to the great library with its paneled ceiling and impressive array of beautifully bound volumes. She spent the afternoon as she had most desired, curled up on a huge sofa happily re-reading Jane Austen's *Sense and Sensibility.*

Suddenly, she sensed someone leaning over the back of her couch. She looked up to see Stuart.

"Hello, Gorgeous. I thought I'd find you here." He smiled wanly. "I'm sorry I've neglected you so shamefully today. But I see you're well occupied." He came around and sat beside her. "So, which are you—sense or sensibility?"

She smiled at him. "Both, I hope…I heard you had a rough night." She wanted to reproach him, but could not. Her day had been too delightful.

He rubbed his temples ruefully. "The night was fun. It's today that's been bloody awful. Well, I shall try to be better behaved. Tonight we'll have a proper dinner in the grand saloon, so we should be more civilized. Have you found everything to your liking?"

"Everything's been wonderful, but I should like it even better if you would show me around. And I do hope the weather clears so we can see the gardens tomorrow."

"Yes—well, the weather here is much more unpredictable than it is in Oxford. Except that it will rain every day at sometime or other. The land here is so flat that everything from the sea just sweeps across the fens unhindered. It can be rather dreary. That's one reason I picked Oxford over Cambridge. Anyway, it's already time for tea. Would you like to have yours brought in here, or would you prefer to join us in the sitting room?"

She chose to take tea with the others, and then they retired to dress for dinner. The long table in the grand saloon easily sat their group of ten, and they dined by candlelight on smoked salmon and chicken cordon bleu. Strands of classical music, piped in from the drawing room, wove through their witty conversation and laughter. Kate felt as if she had wandered onto a movie set or was living a fantasy.

Boy, wouldn't my sister just love to be here? She'll just turn green when she reads my next letter. I wonder what it would be like to own all this, to be the Lady of Clifton Manor? To be the Viscountess of Essex? What if Stuart proposed to me and all this would be mine someday? Then, as many girls do, Kate "tried on" some married names in her imagination. *Katherine Devereux...Lady Katherine Devereux. Definitely had a nice aristocratic ring to it. Katherine MacKenzie...Kate MacKenzie...rather plebeian...*

"Hello, Kate!" Stuart was whispering to her. "Where are you? Lost in one of your Jane Austen novels? You missed my entire spoof of Mr. Croft."

"Oh, I'm sorry, Stuart," she replied, slightly blushing. "I was just thinking about how wonderful all of this is. Thank you so much for having us and planning this lovely party."

He took her hand and kissed it. "All for you, my darling. It's just a ruse to seduce you." His tone was lightly sarcastic, and she laughed uneasily. He then tapped his knife against his crystal goblet to gain everyone's attention.

"Ladies and gentlemen, I am pleased that you could all join me at Clifton Manor to celebrate the end of the Michaelmas term. After an arduous eight weeks of essays and tutorials, we all deserve a little R & R."

A chorus of "Hear, hear," echoed from his guests.

"I hope you have found your rooms satisfactory, and if there is anything you need to make your stay here more comfortable, please speak to me or my man, Collins. Now, I apologize to the ladies for our rather boisterous first night, but want to assure you that we gentlemen intend to turn in at a decent hour tonight to be up for breakfast and a morning horseback ride. So, please join me now in the game room for after-dinner drinks and cards."

With an excited buzz of conversation, everyone adjourned to a room set with three card tables. As Collins rolled in a beverage cart, the couples chose to play canasta or bridge. Kate's parents had taught her bridge the summer before she had left for college, and she reveled in playing the role of savvy partner to Stuart. Cigarette smoke soon filled the air. The clink of cocktail glasses and the shuffling of cards were punctuated by the whoops of victory and the groans of defeat.

Suddenly, everyone fell silent. Collins had entered the room and announced in a commanding voice, "Lady Devereux, Countess of Essex!" Stuart looked completely shocked but rose slowly to his feet, followed by the others. A tall, slender woman with frosted hair nodded at the young people standing around the tables, until she spied her son.

"Stuart, darling!" She approached him, swaying slightly. "I hadn't remembered you were having a party." She tilted her head, and he dutifully kissed her cheek.

"Hello, mother." Stuart maintained proper decorum but was obviously unnerved by her arrival.

"Please, everyone, be seated. Don't let me interrupt your soirée. Please, play on." Lady Devereux waved her hand and wandered over to the beverage cart. Kate noticed that, although she was still an attractive woman, her face had a hardness that belied her faded beauty.

Lady Devereux sloshed Scotch into a glass tumbler. Stuart quickly rescued the whiskey decanter from her.

"Here, mother. Let me do that. Would you like to join us for bridge? You can take my place." His politeness held an edge of irritation.

"Oh, no, dear—I don't want to spoil anyone's fun." She spoke slowly, with a slight slur. "I'll just sit here on the sofa for a while and watch you play." Stuart helped her to a seat and then resumed his place at the card table. But the gaiety of the evening had vanished. The group half heartedly played a few more rounds and then began to retire for the night.

"Good night, everyone!" Lady Devereux called. "Stuart, dear, fix me a drink and then ring Fanny to attend me."

Stuart signaled to Kate to wait while he poured his mother another Scotch, filling the tumbler halfway with water. Then he brought it to her and spoke. "Mother, I would like to introduce you to my friend, Miss Katherine Hughes. Kate, this is my mother, Lady Devereux."

Kate took her offered hand. "How do you do, your Ladyship?"

"Hughes?" Lady Devereux looked puzzled. "I don't recall that name. Are our families acquainted?"

"No, mother." Stuart maintained his politeness but had the air of one speaking patiently to a child. "Kate is an American. She's studying at St. Hilda's this term."

"American? How charming. I do have some friends in New York. The Brandons. Do you know them? No...I don't suppose you do... America is such a huge country...Stuart, do ring for Fanny. *Je suis très fatiguée.* I'll wait for her here."

"Yes, mother." He walked over to the telephone and, picking up the receiver, dialed 1. "Collins, send Fanny to attend her Ladyship in the game room." He hung up. "She's coming right up, mother. May I see Miss Hughes to her room?"

"Of course, darling." She tilted her cheek again for his peck. "Good night, Stuart, dear. Good night, miss."

Stuart and Kate murmured their good nights. Tucking Kate's hand into the crook of his arm and holding it tightly, Stuart walked her through a long Tudor gallery to the baroque wing that housed the guests' bedrooms.

He sighed. "Well, now you have it—the dirty little Devereux secret. Or not so secret. The Lady Devereux is a boozer. Her son, the Viscount of Essex, is ashamed of her, and thus would rather avoid introducing her to his friends. Unfortunately, or perhaps fortunately, she is oblivious. But usually she is too tanked to go anywhere, so it does not pose too great a difficulty for him."

"What about your father? Has he tried to get her help?"

Stuart laughed, but it sounded more like a harsh bark. "Do you want to know the whole dirty secret? Why she drinks?"

Kate wasn't certain that she really did want to know, but Stuart went on bitterly. "She is an unloved woman. My dear old dad married her for her money. It's an old story among the British aristocracy. She was the daughter of a baronet who had made his fortune in shipping. My father needed her funds to keep this house and the one in London running with two staffs, so he married her. She gained his title and hoped for love. As soon as she produced an heir—that would be me—he spurned her for other women. Lots of them. He lives his life totally separate from her. Their marriage is a travesty—so, she finds comfort in a bottle."

The thought occurred to Kate that Stuart himself had difficulty controlling his liquor, but she held her peace. As if reading her mind he went on, "I know you probably think I drink too much as well, but I only drink to celebrate—well, mostly—whereas she drinks if she's celebrating or if she's sad or if she has no cause at all. I feel quite sorry for her. What a miserable, lonely existence."

They were climbing a broad staircase now, and Kate thought, *So that's what it would be like to be the Lady Devereux. How sad. To have all this and yet not have love.*

"Stuart?" she asked. "I hope this doesn't sound like a cliché, but have you ever prayed about any of this? Have you ever asked God to help you and your mother?"

He barked out another non-laugh. "Maybe when I was a little boy. I think God is a little too concerned with running the universe to take any time with an alcoholic woman."

"But you're wrong!" Kate argued earnestly. "Haven't you heard the scriptures about how God cares for even the tiny sparrow? And in First Peter, it says that we should 'cast all our cares on Him, for He cares for us.' "

"Kate, I'm glad you find comfort in your religion. But I really don't believe that God cares two wits about the details of my life. And even if He did, I wouldn't want Him to tell me how to run mine. I don't need Him to."

Kate started to protest, but he held his finger up to her lips. They were standing outside her room now, and he leaned over her.

"Those lips of yours are too pretty for all this talk. They need to be kissed more often." And he kissed her—first softly and then with more passion. She gently pulled away from him.

He looked at her hungrily. "Please, let me come in for just a little while."

She shook her head and stepped inside her door.

"Please," he pleaded. He looked so vulnerable and dejected that she almost relented.

"No, I can't," she said with resolution. "I'll see you in the morning. Thanks for a wonderful evening."

Before she could shut the door, he kissed her again, long and hard. She broke off breathlessly, and quickly closed the door, murmuring, "Good night."

A glint of coldness flashed in Stuart's eyes over the dejected look that had tugged at her sympathies. But Kate had not seen it.

17

End of Term

The next morning dawned gray and rainy with sharp winds; however, by the time they had finished breakfast, the sun broke through and beckoned them outside. Lady Devereux left early for London without saying good-bye to their party. Lucy and Lydia, the two young women from Somerville College, elected to forgo horseback riding and instead wandered through the gardens and the house. That left Kate, Connie, Twila, and the five men to share the seven available mounts. Stuart offered to have Kate ride with him, and she was most happy to oblige. Although she adored horses, she was quite content to let him take the reins and keep her safe in his capable arms.

They rode across the estate's fields, many of them flattened from the recent harvest of hay and oats. Stuart explained that the farming turned some profit, but to ensure a reliable cash flow, he had finally convinced his father to open the house to the public for tours during the summer months. High taxes made much of the gentry land-rich but cash-poor, and necessity more and more forced them to place their homes on public display.

"Well, everyone benefits, don't you think?" Kate asked. "The estate owners get the funds to support these beautiful old houses and the common folks like me get to enjoy them vicariously."

Stuart squeezed her tightly. "You are not common, my dear," he whispered. "And you should never have to enjoy an estate vicariously. You belong on one."

Kate's heart caught in her throat as Stuart kicked his stallion into a gallop. He pulled up to a canter as they crossed over a stream on a stone bridge that that led to the carefully crafted 'wilderness' of the estate. The approach reminded Kate of the one at Blenheim, and Stuart confirmed that the same landscaper, 'Capability' Brown, had designed both in the eighteenth century.

That evening Stuart requested that they all dress in formal attire for a candlelight dinner and dancing. The young men donned their dinner jackets, and the ladies, their evening gowns. Kate wore the same one-shoulder strapless white sheath that had turned so many heads at the Blenheim Ball.

Several courses of appetizers—soup, salad, and stuffed pheasant, accompanied by appropriate wines—preceded the traditional English dinner of roast beef and Yorkshire pudding. For the pièce de résistance, Collins proudly bore in a massive Waterford crystal bowl filled with chocolate trifle topped by a mound of whipped cream.

The furniture of the formal drawing room had been cleared to the sides and the oriental carpets rolled up to allow ample room for dancing on the burnished hardwood floors. A stereo stocked with the latest LPs had been brought in, and champagne flowed freely. Kate felt slightly woozy and all but melted into Stuart's arms while they danced. As the evening wore on, the other couples, one by one, slowly wandered off.

Stuart held Kate tightly, swaying to the soft music and swirling her around until she felt giddy. She pressed her cheek against his satin lapel. He caressed her hair and kissed it lightly. It was an exquisitely romantic setting, and Kate's defenses gradually fell.

Stuart began to kiss her ardently, and she yielded to his caresses. With his arms around her, he nearly carried her to a settee in a far, dark corner of the room.

"Now, at last we are alone," he murmured. "I have wanted to make love to you since the first day I laid eyes on you." And he kissed her again.

"Stuart," Kate said breathlessly. "I can't. Please stop!"

"You can and you will." He kissed her neck and moved his hand to the strap on her shoulder.

Kate struggled to sit up. "No, Stuart, really. We should be getting back with the others. We shouldn't be here alone."

He laughed—that hard, short, barking laugh that signaled irritation, not amusement. "Of course, we should be alone. There is no one to interrupt us now. The others have gone their own ways. The servants are in bed. Mother has returned to London. And there isn't even that pesky Mr. MacKenzie to barge in on us. This is the perfect time and place." He leaned over her and kissed her again. "I want you, Katherine Hughes. I've waited too long for this."

The mention of David MacKenzie brought Kate up sharply. *What am I doing? Why did I let myself get into this? David tried to warn me...*

"Stuart, no. I can't do this. It isn't right."

He barked out another laugh. "Isn't right? Why shouldn't two people in love, make love? Nothing could be more right."

"But, Stuart." She sat up and pushed a strand of hair out of her face. "I believe in saving this for marriage."

He laughed again. "You're jesting, right? What does a little piece of paper mean? That's all a joke, anyway."

"Not to me. Not to God."

"Oh, all right," Stuart sighed, backing off slightly. "What if I promise you before God that after we make love, I will marry you? Will that do?"

"Stuart, don't tease me like that."

"Well, I'll promise whatever you want me to." He smiled, but his eyes had a dark, hard look.

He leaned toward her and began to kiss her again, insistently. She tried without success to push him away. She thought frantically, *He's stronger than I am. If he tries to force me, no one will even hear me scream. Oh, God, help me!*

Suddenly, her head cleared. She took a deep breath and forced herself to smile and speak lightly. "Stuart—wait. How about some more of that champagne?"

He grinned at her, leering. "Marvelous idea."

He got up and wandered over to the beverage cart. She followed him, making a pretense of looking at the portraits as she slowly walked towards the door. He poured two glasses of champagne and sauntered towards her, sipping his. He extended a glass to her. Smiling, she took it and stepped back. Suddenly, she threw the drink in his face and dropped the glass, shattering it. She raced out the door, through the foyer, up the stairs, and into her room, not stopping until she had shut and locked her door.

He did not pursue her.

Ninth Week

Kate slept poorly that night. The champagne had left her feeling slightly nauseated, and the evening's events ran over and over in her mind. She fluctuated from outrage to remorse.

How could he do this to me? Why did he tease me with a proposal? Was he at all serious, or was he saying what he thought I wanted to hear? Was I really threatened? Did I overreact? Why did I throw the drink at him? Wasn't that a little too dramatic? But how could he do this to me?

Her thoughts went round and round with no conclusion, except that she wanted to get away. She didn't want to see Stuart again until she had some distance and time to think through things clearly.

Kate knew that Nigel and Connie were heading back to Oxford in the early morning, and she decided to join them. Before anyone else was up, she packed her bags and took them quietly down to the entrance hall. Nigel and Connie were surprised to find her in the breakfast room drinking coffee and picking at her food, but they readily agreed to give her a ride back. Connie tried to search Kate's face for some explanation. Finding there distress and agitation, she wisely held her questions. After leaving with Collins their regards and thanks to Stuart, they took off in Colin Russell's Rover sedan. Connie and Nigel chatted easily on the drive home. Kate sat silently watching the rain run in rivulets down the window. It suited her mood exactly. The replay button was stuck in the tape recorder of her mind, and she couldn't shut off her dismal thoughts.

By the time they returned to Oxford, early church services were over. Kate briefly considered going to Evensong but quickly dismissed the idea with a simple: *I can't possibly go. I can't face anyone.* Most of the afternoon and evening she spent curled up in bed under her covers, sleeping or staring at the ceiling and listening to her thoughts replaying. Connie convinced her to come down to Hall for supper. Kate reluctantly dragged herself out of bed and joined the other young women. The notion flashed through her mind that Stuart would once again surprise her at dinner with a bouquet of roses and a contrite letter begging her forgiveness. But no note and no flowers arrived.

On Monday morning, Kate steeled herself for her last visit with Mr. Croft at Christ Church to collect her essays and grades. She dreaded an encounter with Stuart. Suddenly, she felt very eager to go home for the holidays, and she even flirted with the idea of not returning to Oxford for the winter Hilary Term.

She walked from St. Hilda's to Christ Church on the path along the meadow, deep in her thoughts and barely noticing the beauty of her surroundings. She was early for her tutorial and decided to sit on a bench in the Memorial Garden, dedicated to those lost in the Great Wars. She chose the spot where most tourists take pictures of themselves with the massive Hall of Christ Church and its cathedral bell tower looming behind the pretty hedges and flowers. This day, no tourists were vying for the spot. Clouds, threatening rain, scudded rapidly overhead—and Kate had the garden almost to herself and her gloomy thoughts.

Kate noticed an odd-looking woman dressed in an old raincoat and oversized green Wellington boots. She was thrusting her hand rapidly in and out of a paper sack as she threw breadcrumbs to the pigeons that had gathered around her. She clucked, cooed, and fussed at them as if they were her children. The woman's gray hair but smooth skin and childlike face left her age a matter for conjecture.

Kate could not recall having seen her before. She thought she surely would have remembered someone with such a singular appearance.

Before long, the woman sat beside Kate and offered her some bread crusts to feed the birds. As the pigeons landed about her feet and on the tips of her boots, the "Pigeon Lady," as Kate mentally dubbed her, identified each one by name.

"That shy one hanging back is Charles Dodgson, or Lewis Carroll as you would know him. The bossy one, squawking at everyone and trying to keep them in order, is John Wesley. And Ridley, Cranmer, and Latimer are that somber trio named for the martyred bishops. And those two, who look like they're conversing, are Jack and Tollers. They are very smart birds—you know, like the dons C.S. Lewis and J.R.R. Tolkien."

Her companion's observations delighted Kate. "I can't believe you've named them all!" she exclaimed.

"And, why not? God's eye is on the sparrow—and if He knows the number of hairs on your head, His servants can name a few pigeons."

"So, are you a believer?"

"Oh, yes!" The woman's bright blue eyes sparkled. "I have been for a long time. And what about you, dearie?"

"Yes, ma'am, I am too."

"Well, my dear. I couldn't help but notice that you look troubled about something. Would you like to tell an old lady about it? I've listened to many a student and professor over the years."

Kate did not doubt it. Something about the curious woman's face and manner elicited instant trust. In a torrent of words and tears, Kate began to pour out everything on her heart. She talked of her indecision about returning to Oxford for the next term, of the positive experiences she had had with the Inklings Society and St. Aldate's, and of David MacKenzie and his family. Then she talked of Stuart—and as she shared about that last night at Clifton Manor, her story was punctuated by sobs. The Pigeon Lady patted her gently on the back, murmuring, "There, there," but did not interrupt or comment. She listened until Kate's weeping and words ebbed, and then she spoke.

"Life is full of choices and trials, my dear. Sometimes, bad things happen to us from no fault of our own, but just because we exist in a fallen world. But sometimes we bring things on ourselves by poor choices we make. Yet 'God does work all things together for good for those who love Him and who are called according to His purpose.' When we fail, we need to ask His forgiveness and that of anyone we've offended and then move on. But we should learn from our mistakes and grow from them, not try to justify or defend them, or we'll end up repeating them." She handed some tissues to Kate, who was sniffing but listening closely.

"God does have a plan for your life, and as you delight to walk in His will, He will give you the desires of your heart." The lady's eyes twinkled with merriment. "Since we don't always know what is best for us, I like to think that, as we yield to Him, even our desires become His. Now, I suppose that you have a desire to be married someday?"

Kate nodded.

"And do you want God's best for you?"

Kate nodded again.

"Well, now. What do you think would be most important to God about the spouse He has chosen for you?"

Kate thought carefully. "I suppose that He would want me to marry someone who believed in Him too."

"Correct!" The Pigeon Lady praised her like a teacher. "Now, then," she said gently, "why did you spend so much of your time with Lord Devereux?"

"Maybe, because he *is* a lord," Kate answered truthfully. "And because he's handsome and rich and smart and charming—well *most of the time.* At first it was all so fun and exciting and romantic. He took me to lots of really wonderful places. And I didn't think there could be any harm in it. Neither of us was very serious about it."

"But why would you spend so much time with someone who doesn't share your beliefs?"

"Well, at first I wasn't sure what he believed, and then I sort of hoped that if he came to Christian meetings with me it might have a good influence on him."

"Missionary dating?" the lady asked with a wry smile.

"Yes, I guess so. And he did come to Evensong with me and to the Inklings Society a few times."

"But you also skipped meetings and services to be with him?"

"Well, yes, I did." Kate answered slowly. "But how would you know?"

"I've been around a long time, dearie. But tell me, besides being a believer and a growing one, what else do you think would be important for you to look for in a husband?"

"I think a couple should be friends. That they should have common interests and be able to share their hearts with one another. I would want to marry someone who would be my best friend my whole life, even after we had grown old together."

"An excellent answer. What else?"

"I guess I would want someone with character. Someone I could honor and respect, and someone who would honor and respect me and want the best for me. And someone who has a plan for his future, who works hard, and would be a good provider."

"Good. Anything else?"

"Well…" Kate hesitated. "I would want to be attracted to the person. I mean, he doesn't have to be drop-dead gorgeous, but it would be nice if I had feelings for him and it wasn't like marrying my brother or something."

The Pigeon Lady chuckled. "Don't worry. The Lord wants to give you the desires of your heart, remember? The Bible says that the way of a man with a maid is a mystery, and perhaps it is referring to 'chemistry,' as some people call it. Yet one must be careful. It is entirely possible to be attracted to the wrong person and think it's love when it's just a passing fancy."

"But how can one know for sure?"

"If you seek first the kingdom of God and His righteousness, then all these things will be added unto you. Make the Lord your first love, and He will bring the right person along at the right time. And then remember that love is a commitment. The feelings will come and go, but love never fails."

"You know, talking to you makes me feel like I've been to church...which is a good thing, I guess," Kate said with regret, "because I didn't go yesterday. Thank you for stopping and listening to me. I didn't really have anyone I felt I could share this with. You've been a big help." She stood up and shook hands with the woman. "Good-bye. I'd better get on to my tutorial. I hope to see you again sometime."

Kate hurried to the cathedral gate of Christ Church before realizing she had never learned her new friend's name. She turned to look back and wave, but the Pigeon Lady was gone.

Kate's final session with Mr. Croft went well. His role as an intimidating don fulfilled, he took on the relaxed air of an English country gentleman as he smoked his pipe and told her how pleased he had been with her progress. Kate was equally pleased to learn that he regarded her essays highly enough to give her a mark of Alpha Beta, which would translate to an A-minus in her American college.

Mr. Croft fairly insisted that she come to dine in hall since this was their last tutorial. With ambivalence, Kate agreed. She dreaded running into Stuart, yet almost hoped to as well. Her emotions were highly strung, ready to snap, even after the catharsis of weeping with the Pigeon Lady. Perhaps if she could just get over the tension of seeing Stuart again and have an opportunity to talk to him, all would be well.

Kate scanned the large dining hall as she took her seat, but she saw no sign of Stuart. Then just before the Latin blessing, he strode past her with his coterie of friends. He looked directly at her and through her, but gave no indication of recognition. After grace, Nigel came and sat across from her.

"Hello, luv." He smiled kindly as he filled his plate with food. "How are you doing?"

"Okay." Kate tried a feeble smile.

"You know, I don't know why you wanted to come back early with us, nor do I need to, unless you want to tell me. But Colin said that Stuart's behavior was beastly after we left."

"How so?"

"He started drinking at breakfast and went on until everyone left. And he flirted outrageously with the Somerville birds, which did not make Tom and Robert too happy with him." Nigel looked sheepish. "Nor you either, I suppose. Sorry. That was rather insensitive of me. Anyway, I think we left at a good time."

"Yes, it was a good time to leave," Kate agreed. And yet her abrupt departure from Clifton Manor had left her ill at ease and her relationship with Stuart, unresolved. "Do you think he'll talk to me now?"

"Why, certainly. I mean, why wouldn't he?" Nigel thought for a moment. "Did he see you when we came in?"

"I think so. But things ended unpleasantly for us at Clifton Manor. So he may not want to see me."

"Ah!" Nigel did not know how to reply. They finished their meal with superficial chitchat. Then giving her thanks to Mr. Croft, Kate excused herself and walked with trepidation over to Stuart's table. She could not endure this turmoil. Perhaps she would apologize for throwing the drink. Perhaps he would apologize for trying to take advantage of her. She did not know what to expect, but she knew she needed closure.

The students at Stuart's table were roaring with laughter at some anecdote he had just told with great aplomb. Stuart looked up, laughing, and saw Kate. His expression hardened and, ignoring her, he turned to one of his friends to begin a new story.

Kate stopped him before he spoke. "Hello, Stuart."

Everyone stared at her.

"Hello." His reply was politely noncommittal.

Her voice trembled, but she went on. "May I please talk to you?"

He waved his hand to include the entire table. "Certainly. Go right ahead."

Kate chewed her lip; her heart raced. *He's not going to make me cry in front of all these men. I won't give him that satisfaction.*

She took a deep breath and said, "Alone, please."

He paused, his eyes cold and fierce, as was his tone. "No. We have nothing to say to each other. Now, if you'll excuse me, Miss Hughes, I'm in the middle of my dinner." He dismissed her as if she were nothing more than his serving girl, and with loud laughter, resumed his conversation with his friends.

Kate stood for a few moments in indignation and disbelief. Then humiliation washed over her. She maintained a measured walk to the doors of the great Hall and then nearly ran down the wide marble steps. Reaching Tom Quad, she pulled her hood up in protection from the falling rain.

Good. I'm glad it's raining. No one will notice me crying.

She hurried past the Mercury fountain and through Old Tom portal, so intent on catching the bus back to her college that she did not even take a last glance around Christ Church. As she stepped from the curb to cross the street, a voice went off in her head.

Watch out, Kate! She turned her head to the left and then realized too late, she needed to look right. A car was heading straight towards her. She heard the squeal of brakes and thought, *Oh, God, help me! I'm going to be hit!*

Ninth Week, Monday Afternoon

As Stuart and his friends dashed through Tom Quad on their way back to their rooms they heard the distant wail of a siren.

"Sounds like an accident," someone observed.

"Probably an American tourist looking the wrong way," Stuart quipped, and they all laughed.

Nigel came running into the quad from the street, his shout breaking the stillness of the ancient sanctuary.

"There's been an accident!" Breathless, he ran up to Stuart.

"Buzz, Buzz!" Stuart answered his friend with a line from Hamlet.

But Nigel was too distressed to play their old game. "Stuart, it's Kate! She's been hit by a car!"

The smile and color drained from Stuart's face.

The Pigeon Lady knelt over Kate, holding her hand and praying. Kate briefly opened her eyes, and moaning, shut them again.

The St. Aldate's Coffee Shop had emptied of customers as soon as they had heard the squeal of brakes and the sickening thud of the impact.

The cashier grabbed the telephone and rang for an ambulance. Annie MacKenzie ordered Hannah to stay inside the shop while she went to see if she could be of some assistance.

She pushed her way through the crowd that had quickly gathered.

"Pardon me, I'm a nurse. Please let me through." People parted, and she came upon the victim.

"Oh, no—Kate! Dear Jesus, have mercy!" Annie knelt down beside an oddly dressed woman who was holding Kate's hand. She felt for a pulse. It was slow but strong. "I'm a nurse," she explained to the woman. "And I know her. Has she been conscious at all?"

"Yes. She opened her eyes and I believe she recognized me," the Pigeon Lady answered. "Annie." She put her hand on the younger woman's arm. "The ambulance will be here any minute. You need to call David right away."

Annie nodded and then looked more closely at the odd woman. She didn't recognizer her, but then their parish was large and many people knew the rector and his family.

The crowd parted for the rescue crew.

"Where are you taking her?" Annie asked one of the medics.

"Radcliffe Infirmary," he answered gruffly.

Annie watched as the men checked Kate, placed her gently on a stretcher, and carried her to the waiting ambulance. She looked about for the kind woman who had spoken to her, and saw her comforting the distraught young man who evidently had hit Kate with his car.

Annie headed back to the coffee shop. She asked one of the women from the church to watch Hannah, and then she phoned David.

After eating lunch in hall, David trudged wearily back to his flat. He had a stack of essays to mark in his rooms in the New Building, but he couldn't face them as yet. He wanted an hour of solitude. Maybe he would listen to some good music or read the dailies before he got back to the onerous chore of student essays. The pressure was now off the students and onto the professors to get in their grades. David dreaded assessing papers more than he had dreaded taking his own exams.

He walked down quiet and quaint Holywell Street in the falling rain, hoping Mrs. Bingley would be out. He gently unlocked the front door, but a chorus of barks greeted his unsuccessful attempt to enter unobtrusively. Shushing the dogs, he dodged for his door. He sighed as he heard the familiar ringing voice of his landlady.

"David? Is that you, my dear? Oh, my gracious sakes! I'm so glad you came 'ome."

The good-hearted woman gingerly walked down the steps. David opened his door to make room for her wide girth. She entered his apartment breathlessly speaking.

"Your mother 'as rung up at least three times. She tried to get you in college but you musta been on your way."

"What's the matter, Mrs. Bingley? Did she tell you?"

"There's been a terrible accident, David."

David felt gripped by fear. "My father?"

"No, no, dear boy. No one in your family."

Relief flooded him. "Then who, Mrs. Bingley? Did she say?"

"Yes, yes! Now let me see..." Mrs. Bingley sat down in his rocker and began rocking and fanning herself violently. "She said it was one of your students. She said 'er name is— 'er name is—Kate!" She pronounced the name with a flourish, proud of her memory.

David reeled back as if the wind had been knocked out of him. "Is she dead?" he barely whispered.

Mrs. Bingley stopped rocking. "Are you all right, my dear? Maybe you should sit down."

"Is she dead?" he repeated, his voice cracking.

Mrs. Bingley paused. "I don't know. She didn't say. All she said was to tell you there 'ad been an accident. That your student, Kate, 'ad been 'it by a car and taken to Radcliffe—"

David was gone before she finished her sentence.

He rushed into the crowded waiting room at the Radcliffe Infirmary. He vaguely recognized several students and saw Nigel with his arm around Connie, whose eyes were swollen and red from weeping. David spied his mother, who jumped up and embraced him tightly.

He choked out his question. "Is she dead?"

"No, honey. She was hit by a car right outside the coffee shop. She hit her head. They've done X-rays already and there's a slight skull fracture. She's lost consciousness, so it's still hard for them to judge the severity of the concussion. And they'll have to watch her for swelling or other symptoms that would indicate internal bleeding."

He looked up at the ceiling and exhaled slowly to maintain control. "Any other injuries?"

"Just cuts and scrapes. Miraculously, no broken bones or neck injury."

"Thank God." He looked around anxiously. "Is Dad here? Can we go in to see her?"

"I doubt they'll let you in, David. Your father went to Abingdon for the day."

David strode up to the staff desk and demanded to be allowed in to pray for Miss Hughes. The nurse eyed his blue jeans with suspicion. "Are you a clergyman?"

Annie spoke up. "This is David MacKenzie. His father, the Reverend Eric MacKenzie, is the rector of St. Aldate's, which is Miss Hughes' church. The Reverend MacKenzie is in Abingdon on diocesan business, and his son is here as his representative."

The nurse's manner softened. "All right, Mr. MacKenzie, come this way, please."

David shot his mother a look of gratitude as he followed the nurse through the swinging doors to the emergency care triage.

Kate, pale and still, lay on a gurney. Her face was bruised and scraped. An ice pack was draped across the top of her head. The nurse checked her pulse and blood pressure and recorded them on a chart.

"You may stay with her for a few minutes, Mr. MacKenzie. Let us know if she wakes up."

As soon as the nurse walked out, David sank to his knees by the gurney, burying his face in the bedding.

"Oh, God," he groaned. "Oh, Father. Please have mercy on her. Please, please heal her. Please let her wake up. Please, Lord, don't let her die. Don't take her yet." He looked at her serene face and listened to her slow breathing. He took her small hands in his and covered them with kisses. "Please, God. Have mercy on her. Have mercy on me. Oh, God, I love her so. Please..." He choked on a sob and silently but fervently continued praying.

Suddenly, the hand he was clutching squeezed his. He raised his head and looked at her anxiously. Kate's eyes were open. She smiled weakly at him and stroked his hair.

"David, what's wrong?"

Tears glistened in his eyes, but he brushed them away. He tried to keep his voice steady. He didn't want to alarm her and send her into shock.

"You've been in an accident. You're in the Radcliffe Infirmary. You have a concussion but will be just fine. Everything is going to be all right." He picked up her hand and kissed it again.

She tried to lift her head and groaned. "Oh, my head!" A wave of nausea hit her. "I think I'm going to..."

David grabbed a basin and held it under her chin, gently supporting her head as she vomited.

"Oh...I'm so sorry," she whispered, tears springing to her eyes.

"Hush. It's all right," he said, dabbing her mouth with a tissue. "Just lie back and rest. I need to call the nurse and let her know you're awake."

As soon as David buzzed the nurse's station, an orderly appeared, who took the basin from him. David stroked Kate's cheek and kissed her gently on the forehead.

"You're going to be all right," he assured her again. "The doctors will want to check on you some more, so I'd better go. But I'll be out in the waiting room if you need me."

He gave her hand one more squeeze before the medical staff surrounded her gurney.

20

Ninth Week, Tuesday Through Friday

Kate slept fitfully. Her head throbbed, and any movement made her dizzy. It seemed as if, each time she just managed to doze off, someone would come into her room to check her vital signs. The night dragged on interminably until daylight brought its welcome relief. The nursing staff changed shifts, and the morning nurse breezily brought in a breakfast tray.

"Good morning! How did you sleep?" she cheerfully asked.

"Not very well," Kate answered truthfully.

The nurse took her pulse. "From what I hear, you are a very lucky girl. You must have someone upstairs looking out for you. No broken bones—it's amazing. How do you feel?"

"Pretty lousy. My head..."

"Here, I've brought you some painkillers. Now that you are out of the woods, we'll try to keep you more comfortable." She handed Kate some pills and a cup of water and watched her swallow them. "You should try to eat something. Maybe just some tea and toast, but you'll feel better with something in your stomach. And there's a very handsome young man out in the waiting room, very anxious to see you. The last shift said he had been in to pray for you yesterday and then stayed in the waiting room all night long. He's just come back from breakfast. Shall I let him in?"

Kate felt like her brain was stuffed with cotton balls. She had no idea who this could be.

"Who? I don't remember anyone."

The nurse sympathetically patted her on the shoulder. "Don't worry, dear. It's common to have a loss of memory of what occurred just before or after a head injury. But usually it's only temporary. Are you up for a visitor? He's the son of your rector."

"David! Oh yes, please send him in."

David stood awkwardly in the doorway. The nurse had warned him that Kate had no recollection of his being there after the accident, and he was uncertain how to act. With her pasty skin and bruised face, she looked pitiful. Pitiful and—oh, so beautiful. His heart ached to see her lying there so fragile and vulnerable. Yet she was alive and alert and well. He offered up a prayer of gratitude in his heart.

He took a deep breath and walked into her line of vision. "Hello, there."

"Hello, David."

"How are you feeling?" he asked as he pulled a chair to the side of her bed.

"Terrible."

"You look good."

"Liar." She smiled weakly. "If I look the way I feel, I look awful. I don't even want to see a mirror."

"Kate." David leaned forward. "I want you to know how sorry I am that this happened to you. I wish I could have stepped in front of that car for you, and I know others would say the same. Last night the waiting room was full of your friends. And my mother and I rang your parents. Lots of people have been praying for you."

"Thank you. But don't worry about me. I'm going to be okay. The Lord must have been watching out for me. I guess I should be very thankful I don't have anything worse than a headache."

"Do you remember what happened?"

Kate tried to think. "I remember the Pigeon Lady. We had a nice long talk...and then my tutorial at Christ Church...and lunch...and

Stuart…and…" Her voice trailed off. "No, I don't remember the accident…"

The nurse brought in a large vase with a dozen long-stemmed white roses. "This was just delivered by the florist. He said they're from Lord Devereux, Viscount of Essex. You have lots of admirers, Miss Hughes." She arranged them on the windowsill. "Aren't they beautiful? Shall I read the card to you?"

Kate started to shake her head but the pain stopped her. "No, thank you. You can leave it on the bed table."

David stood up. "Well, I guess I'd better get going. I just wanted to see how you were getting on. You need to eat your breakfast and get some rest. Would it be all right if I stop by before the Inklings meeting tonight?"

Kate hated to see him go. He made her feel safe and protected. She would have been content to have him sit beside her all day.

"Yes, please come."

"Right. I'll come back this evening, then." He longed to touch her cheek or stroke her hair or kiss her on the forehead as he had the night before. Instead, he ran his hand through his own hair. "Uh, you take care of yourself, I'll see you later, all right?"

"Right." She smiled.

Kate assumed the unfamiliar handwriting on the card with Stuart's flowers belonged to the florist. The note simply read, *So sorry. Stuart.*

Was he sorry about her accident, his snub at Christ Church, or their parting at Clifton Manor? Perhaps the message was intentionally obscure; nevertheless, Kate's thinking was too clouded to dwell on it. She did enjoy the beauty and fragrance of the roses, and her room soon filled up with other flower arrangements from her parents and her new Oxford friends.

These friends also streamed by her room during visiting hours. David returned as promised before the Inklings Society met down the road at the Eagle and Child, but could only give a smile and hello in the crowded room. Each day he would come by to check on her; however, since others were always present, he didn't linger.

It touched Kate to see the concern of so many from St. Hilda's College, St. Aldate's Church, and the Inklings Society. She hadn't realized she had made so many friends in her short time at Oxford. But despite their good intentions, their stays exhausted her, and she met the end of visiting hours with some relief.

More welcome over the next few days were the visits from Reverend MacKenzie. Years of experience had taught him to keep his hospital visitations brief. Kate appreciated his sensitivity as well as the sincerity of his prayers. Each time he anointed her with oil and prayed, her own faith quickened and she sensed her strength returning.

On his first visit, Eric MacKenzie had said, "We're all so grateful you were spared serious injuries. A lot of people are very concerned and praying for you—and David most of all." He had hesitated and then added, "He cares a lot for you, lass."

The next day he had looked about with a bemused expression and said, "You know, this is the hospital where David and all our children were born. Some people think of hospitals as places of sickness and death, yet they can also be places of hope and new life."

The next few days passed in a fog of groggy dozing and streams of visitors. On Friday, Annie MacKenzie stopped by.

"How are you, my dear? Much better, I hope?" She tenderly kissed her cheek, much as Kate's own mother would have done. That simple, kind action brought tears to Kate's eyes.

"Yes, much better. My thinking is clearer and I'm not so dizzy, so I'm supposed to be released tomorrow."

"Yes. That's what the doctors told your parents. I've been in contact with them almost daily since the accident. If it's all right with you, they have agreed to have you come to stay with us while you continue your recovery and before you fly home next week. That way you can be looked out for until you feel up to being on your own."

The tears sprang to Kate's eyes again. "Oh, you're so kind. But, Mrs. MacKenzie, I know how busy you are with your children and the church and all, and I don't want to be a burden to you."

"Nonsense. I enjoy nursing and don't get to practice it much anymore except when the children are sick. Besides, it was David's idea. He absolutely insisted, and we're happy to be of help. I know if one of my children were across the ocean and in need of care, it would be such a comfort to me to know that a family was watching out for them. Your mother seemed very relieved at the offer. So, will you come?"

"Of course, thank you. You're very kind."

Annie stood up to leave. "Oh, I almost forgot—and Hannah would be most cross with me." She gave her a rumpled piece of paper with a crayon drawing of a long-haired stick figure, a giant bump growing out of its head. "That's supposed to be you." Annie smiled. "That's not a horn but a 'boo-boo.' Hannah sends her best wishes and is really looking forward to your coming home with us tomorrow."

"Tell her thank you. I'm looking forward to it too."

As Annie left, Kate looked again at the drawing and smiled.

Ninth Week, Saturday

David picked up Kate on Saturday morning as an orderly wheeled her out of the infirmary. Clutching a small overnight case, Kate wore her long winter coat over her pink flannel pajamas. David looked with amusement at her fuzzy pink slippers, then swept her up in his arms and carried her to his little car.

"We shan't risk getting your slippers dirty," he joked. Against her faint protests, he carried her again from his car into the rectory, up the first flight of stairs, and placed her gently on the guestroom bed.

Annie and Hannah put away Kate's belongings, then quietly shut the door and left her alone to rest. In the middle of the afternoon, a knock on the door awakened Kate from a nap.

"Come in," Kate called groggily.

It was Annie. "Sorry to disturb you. There's a young man downstairs who would like to see you. I told him you were resting, but he says he's leaving town for the holidays and he's dreadfully worried he won't see you before you go home to the States. He's Lord Stuart Devereux, Viscount of Essex. Shall I send him up, or would you prefer not to see him?"

Kate rubbed her head. "No, please send him up. But, Mrs. MacKenzie? Would you mind getting my brush and mirror? I must look awful."

Annie handed Kate her cosmetic bag and mirror. "I'll detain him for a few minutes."

Kate sat up, combed her hair, dabbed some makeup over her bruises, and brushed her cheeks with blush. She shoved her mirror under the covers as Annie showed Stuart in.

He looked haggard and ill at ease. For once, he seemed at a loss for words.

"Hello, Stuart." Kate spoke first. "It's good of you to come. Please sit down."

He slid into a chair next to the bed. "I had to see you before I left for London. I couldn't quite face the hospital, but Nigel said you were staying here now, so I came right over."

He put his head in his hands. "I've felt absolutely dreadful since I heard the news. You can't imagine the torment I've been through. I know it was my fault. If I hadn't been so beastly to you—I've been to Chapel every day trying to make some atonement."

The irony of his dwelling on his own feelings with no concern for hers did not escape Kate.

"Stuart," she chided. "You sound like Scarlett O'Hara crying after Frank Kennedy's funeral. She wasn't sorry for what she had done or that Frank had died, just that she might go to hell for it."

He thought about it and smiled contritely. "You're right, as always. I haven't even told you how glad I am that you're all right. That's one more reason I probably deserve hell as well."

"I thought you didn't believe in hell."

"I don't. But if there is a hell, I don't suppose my protestations to the contrary would do much good. Rather like Captain Hook yelling to the crocodile that it can't exist while it's champing off his arm, eh? But I didn't come here to talk religion with you. I suppose God has to forgive me because that's His business. But what about you?" He leaned forward and took her hand. "Will you forgive me for everything? I'm sorry I treated you so dreadfully."

"Yes, Stuart. I do forgive you." She withdrew her hand and then added, "And I'm sorry about throwing that drink on you."

He grimaced. "I was furious with you. But since the accident, I've thought that I probably left you little choice. No—I absolutely deserved it." He smiled expectantly. "So, is everything all right now?"

She nodded, and he sighed with relief. "Good! Well then, are you coming back for the Hilary term?"

She slowly shook her head. "I don't think so. My parents are really urging me to take some time off because of the accident. I think they want me close to home to be sure everything is all right."

"Trinity term then, in the spring?"

"I really don't know, Stuart. I need time to let my head clear. I can't make any plans right now."

"Well, all right, then. Whenever you come back, may we still see each other and forget all this dreadful business ever happened?"

Kate hesitated, then said, "I just don't know, Stuart. But I can't—" She took a deep breath. "I've done some thinking too. I'm not sure I want to date anyone anymore. I mean, it seems like it would be better just to do things as friends, until you find someone you want to marry. Otherwise, what's the point of dating? It just causes hurt feelings or puts you into bad situations." She sighed. "Oh, I don't know if I'm making any sense. When it's all said and done, our lives and beliefs are so different. So I'm not sure we should see each other—except maybe as…friends."

"Friends?" He raised his eyebrow. She nodded unhappily.

"I see. Friends." He drew himself up and cleared his throat. "All right, then. Friends write, don't they? You will write to me, at least?"

"Yes. Of course."

"Excellent." He stood up. "Perhaps, absence will make the heart grow fonder and you will reconsider this 'friends' business."

He leaned over and kissed her cheek. "Good-bye, my gorgeous *friend.* Please come back soon. I'll miss you."

"Good-bye, Stuart."

He strode out of the room, almost tripping over little Hannah who stood in the open doorway. On the stairs, he nearly collided with David.

"Mr. MacKenzie, please pardon me. I was just saying good-bye to Miss Hughes. Well, good day to you too and happy holidays." He gave a polite nod and swept down the stairs before David could reply.

Hannah appeared at the landing. "David, did you see that man? He's a lord!"

David gripped the banister to collect himself. The idea of Stuart Devereux visiting Kate in his family home infuriated him. He swallowed. "Yes, Hannah."

"I saw him kissing Kate," she sang.

His jaw tightened, but he spoke kindly. "Hannah, sweetheart, be a good girl and take this flower to Kate." He handed her a long-stemmed red rose. "Tell her it's from you, all right?"

Hannah sniffed the rose and nodded.

"And ask Mummy if she'll get a vase for it, please." He kissed her and added, "Remember to tell Kate it's from you. Now go on, darling. I'll see you tomorrow at church."

He watched Hannah go, shoved his hands in his pockets, and trudged back down the stairs.

Hannah stood shyly in the doorway of the guestroom, twirling the rose, and waiting for Kate to notice her. Finally, her mother came by, and petting her curls said, "Is that pretty flower for Kate, honey? Go on in and give it to her. Who's it from, sweetheart?"

Hannah tiptoed in and gently handed the rose to Kate. "Here. David said this is for you and it's from me. And to ask Mummy for a vase."

"Oh." Kate wasn't sure how to interpret this wealth of information. "Why, thank you, Hannah. It's very beautiful." She inhaled the rose's sweet scent.

"Why didn't David stay?" Annie asked Hannah, who shrugged in reply. "I thought he was coming to tea," she wondered aloud to herself.

"Must have too much work to do." She turned to Kate. "Do you feel up to having tea with us in the sitting room?"

"Oh, yes. I would *like* to get up. I'm getting rather sick and tired of feeling sick and tired."

Annie helped Kate stand up and walk to the sitting room, where she had a tea tray set out.

"It's a good sign that you're feeling restless. Normally, they advise concussion patients to rest in bed until they want to get up." She poured Kate a cupful of tea.

Kate looked about the pleasant room. "It seems so quiet around here. Where is everybody?"

"Mr. MacKenzie is in his study working on tomorrow's sermon. I already took his tea in to him. I asked the boys to go visit some friends so it wouldn't be so noisy. I figured with all the commotion around here on Sundays, you could use a little peace and quiet today." She sipped her tea thoughtfully. "I did expect David, though." She changed the subject. "So, did you have a nice visit with Lord Devereux?"

"I saw them kissing!" Hannah chimed in.

"Hannah!" chided her mother.

"It's okay," Kate said. "He was just kissing me good-bye, Hannah."

"Are you going to marry him?" Hannah eyed her inquisitively.

"No. We're just friends."

"I'm going to marry David," asserted Hannah.

Kate laughed. "Are you?"

"She's at that age where she thinks everyone should be married and she wants to marry every man she loves," Annie explained.

"Well, who can blame you, Hannah?" Kate smiled at the little girl. "I'm sure lots of girls would like to marry David."

"*I* am going to marry David," Hannah replied stubbornly.

"Now how does Charlotte deal with this competition?" Kate asked Annie under her breath.

An odd expression crossed Annie's face while she considered how to answer, but Hannah spoke first.

"Mummy, David isn't marrying Charlotte now, is he?"

"No, pumpkin. He's not."

"So see?" Hannah popped a scone into her mouth. "*I'm* going to marry David!"

"Hannah, don't talk with your mouth full," Annie admonished her. "And please go play now and let Miss Kate enjoy her tea."

As Hannah scampered off, Kate looked in astonishment at David's mother. "Isn't David engaged?"

"No, honey," Annie said gently. "Not now. They were engaged but broke it off about a year ago. The day of Jack Lewis's funeral, in fact."

"But I saw them," Kate protested. "In his rooms...they were...it was just a few weeks ago."

"Yes, well. Charlotte was up from Cambridge a few weeks ago and David said she was trying to get back together. But he wasn't interested."

Kate sat in dumbfounded silence.

"You see," Annie went on to explain, "Charlotte isn't a believer. David was so taken with her intelligence and attractiveness that he tried to overlook that. He thought if they loved each other enough they could overcome it, or he could win her to the Lord. But instead, she drew him away and he began to drift from God. His father and I were very concerned, as was Jack Lewis, who was at Cambridge with him and could see more of what was happening. But David couldn't hear it from us. It made him angry and defensive whenever we brought it up."

"Yes. I've been like that too," Kate said thoughtfully. "David tried to warn me about Stuart, actually, and it just made me mad."

"Sometimes when we know deep down that something is wrong, we lash out at the people who love us enough to tell us the truth. We think that if we can find fault with them, that will somehow justify what we're doing."

"Yeah," Kate agreed quietly. "But what happened with David and Charlotte?"

"Jack's funeral. You could say, it woke David up."

"Oh." Kate began to recall what David had told her that day in the cemetery at Headington Quarry. "He did tell me about the candle on the coffin that burned so brightly, and how he realized he wanted to be a light, like Mr. Lewis had been, here in Oxford—to really live his life for God and to bring others to know Him. And that's how the Inklings Society got started. So, did he realize then that things wouldn't work out with Charlotte?"

"No, I wish it had been that easy. She, in fact, was the one who made it clear she wanted no part of this new vision for his life. I don't know if David's incredibly hardheaded or just fiercely loyal, but it wasn't until this term he was emotionally able to let her go and begin to trust God for the right wife."

"Do you think he's found her yet?" Kate asked.

"I don't know, honey." Annie watched the younger woman carefully. "Now, I have a question for you—and you don't have to answer this if you don't want to—but what did you mean by saying that David tried to warn you about Stuart?"

Annie's compassion and acceptance filled Kate with absolute trust. She shared without reluctance what David's concerns had been and how, sadly, they had come to be justified.

"I'm sorry, Kate," Annie said sympathetically when she finished her story. "I'm sorry you had to go through any of this. I'm sure David knew from experience the pain you might be putting yourself through, and he wanted to spare you from it."

"Yes—and maybe if I had listened, I wouldn't have had to be knocked silly by a car," Kate answered.

"Well, thank God, you're on the mend and no lasting harm is done." Annie looked at the clock on the mantelpiece and jumped up. "Gracious! I have to get supper ready. Why don't you sit here and relax and then I'll bring a tray up for you."

Annie picked up the tea tray. "I've enjoyed talking with you, Kate. Thanks for sharing this with me." She hesitated and then continued.

"You might consider telling some of your story to David. I think he'd appreciate hearing it."

Kate did consider it. The idea of sharing with David MacKenzie her sorry saga with Stuart Devereux was mortifying to her. Yet as she ate her supper and prepared for bed in the home of David's family, she could think of no one but him. The revelation that David was not in fact engaged sent her thoughts whirling. In her mind, she relived their every conversation with this changed perspective. A new clarity swept away the cloudiness of her memory, and she began to recall in vivid detail the events before and after her accident. She could now clearly remember David kneeling by her bed, praying for her with tears in his eyes...and his joy and relief at her awakening, the tender way he had kissed her hands and face.

And she began to hope.

22

Tenth Week

Kate sat with the MacKenzie family during her last service at St. Aldate's. The festive decorations around the church and the special advent hymns left Kate longing for home and the Christmas holidays. Yet the poignancy of facing all the "lasts" at Oxford also tugged at her heart.

David treated her with kindness and even gallantry, but did not attempt to engage in any private conversation. Rather, he greeted all the students at the luncheon with equal warmth and solicitude. After lunch, the Reverend Eric MacKenzie gave a practical talk on handling holiday family dynamics. Kate noticed with disappointment that David slipped out early without saying good-bye.

David headed back to the family kitchen, where he found his mother working at the sink and wearing her familiar apron over her Sunday dress. He gave her a peck on the cheek.

"You're not leaving?" Annie asked.

"Yes—I'm sorry, Mum, but I'm swamped with work. I still have stacks of essays and marks to get in, plus all those beastly end-of-term faculty meetings and dinners. I'll be glad when it's all over."

"But you haven't even talked to Kate," Annie protested.

"No. I haven't." He sighed heavily. "But, Mum, I did want to thank you for taking care of her. You've been fabulous, an absolute brick."

"It's been my pleasure. You know I enjoy nursing, and she's a dear girl."

"Yes, she is," he quietly agreed.

"What's bothering you, David? Is it that she's leaving soon?"

"Yes…but also—did you know Devereux came here to see her? And worse, Hannah said she saw him kiss her." He began to pace around the room. "Honestly, Mum, I know it's positively uncharitable of me, but I would love to throttle the bloke—or better yet, decimate him on a rugby pitch."

"David, really."

He stopped pacing and gripped the back of a chair. "Yes, I know, I know. Love your enemies and all that. I do pray for the chap. But it's just that he's so wrong for her!"

"And you're so right?" Annie's eyes sparkled with amusement.

"Well"—David grinned—"of course. I'm perfect. After all, you raised me."

"And is she right for you?"

"I think she might be. I think so, but I wish I had the chance to find out."

Annie dried her hands and sat down. "Well, I had a nice long chat with Kate yesterday over tea—which by the way, you were supposed to come to. But perhaps it was for the best you weren't there. Anyway, there are some things you should know."

David sat down and offered his undivided attention.

"First of all. The kiss Hannah saw was a friendly good-bye kiss. I suspect what Kate saw of you and Charlotte was far more incriminating."

"Doubtless," David acknowledged with chagrin.

"Anyway, from what I could glean from Kate, she pretty much sent Lord Devereux packing without much hope of anything more than friendship." She paused then reached across the table and covered his hand with her own. "Maybe some day she'll share the whole story with you. Suffice it to say that your concerns about his character were warranted and Kate knows that now."

Clenching his jaw, David nodded.

"The other thing is that, all this time, Kate thought you were still engaged to Charlotte, and seeing you together only reaffirmed that misunderstanding."

"Oh, no," David groaned.

"But I straightened her out on that score. So it all boils down to this—you should talk to her now."

"I can't," David sighed. "At least, not until after the Inklings meeting Tuesday night."

"You know she flies out on Wednesday morning?"

"Yes—I know."

"And do you know she's not planning to come back for the Hilary term?"

David was stunned. "No!"

"Her parents want her to take some time off, to be really sure she's recovered from the accident. She's been leaning towards not coming back at all."

"But, but—she has to. How can she not come back? Connie's coming back, isn't she? Why wouldn't Kate?"

"Maybe she doesn't feel she has any reason to." Annie looked steadily at her son.

David returned the gaze. "Right." He stood up and gave his mother another peck on the cheek. "Thanks, Mum. For everything. I'll talk to her."

On Monday morning, Annie drove Kate back to St. Hilda's. The two women parted on warm terms, with Annie urging Kate to return soon to Oxford. Kate spent her last two days packing, saying goodbye to the girls on her hall as they departed for the holidays, and visiting her favorite haunts. Despite a chilly drizzle, she wandered around Addison's Walk hoping to bump into David, yet she encountered no one on her lonely walk. Then she meandered around the Botanic Gardens and along Christ Church meadow, but even the Pigeon Lady was nowhere to be seen. As she remembered that odd figure, a sonnet formed in her head, and she rushed back to her room to write it down before it slipped from her memory. She would share it that night at her last meeting with the Inklings Society.

Leaning her head back against the dark wainscoting of the Eagle and Child, Kate listened absently to Nigel Elliot read a selection from *The Four Loves* by C.S. Lewis. She couldn't believe the term was over, her stay in Oxford was over, and this chapter of her life was over. It seemed as if it had hardly begun. How had the time gone so quickly?

She recalled and mused over something Lewis had written in *Reflections on the Psalms,* about how little reconciled we are to the passage of time, which only proves that we are creatures destined for eternity: "*It's as strange as if a fish were repeatedly surprised at the wetness of water. And that would be strange indeed; unless the fish were destined to become, one day, a land animal.*"

Kate looked up at the yellow walls. In this back room of the pub where once the original Inklings had met each week, their pictures were now hanging. She recognized Lewis, of course, and also Tolkien, looking very much like the slender, quiet man who had read to them from his unpublished writings. She saw a small photo—unlike later ones—of a young and surprisingly pretty Joy Davidman Lewis.

Then she looked about at the faces of the small circle of people, who sat listening intently in the soft glow of the coal fire. At her first meeting, they had all—with the exception of Connie—been strangers to her. Now they really were a band of brothers: Nigel, Colin, Twila and the others, and of course Austen and David. She studied David's handsome face with longing. How could she bear to leave and not ever see him again?

As if sensing her stare, David looked at her. He held her gaze steadily while a sad smile played around the corners of his mouth. A blush crept over her face, and she glanced away in confusion.

When Nigel finished his reading and they had discussed the passage, David opened the floor to anyone wanting to share other works. Many students had already left for home, and Kate mustered up her confidence to trust this small circle of friends with her sonnet about the Pigeon Lady. She tentatively raised her hand and was recognized by David.

"The day I had my accident," she spoke slowly, "I was sitting in the Memorial Garden at Christ Church and I saw an eccentric-looking woman in large green Wellies, talking to and feeding the pigeons. She taught me to sit with my legs out and my feet crossed like this"—Kate demonstrated—"so that the pigeons would perch on my shoes and I could feed them too. Anyway, she talked to me about a lot of things and..." Kate paused, searching her memory. "I think she was there with me right after I was hit by the car. Well, today when I was walking in Christ Church meadow, a sonnet about her and the pigeons popped into my head, and I would like to share it with you. Oh, and the Bible verse that came to mind with it was from Matthew six: 'Do not be anxious about your life...Look at the birds of the air: they neither sow nor reap nor gather into barns...Are you not of more value than they?'"

Kate stood and read from a paper she clutched in her hand.

The pigeon lady sat with crosséd boots,
A soft gray beggar resting on her toe.
The crisp December sky exposed bare roots
Of trees that held the magpie and the crow.
"Come, come, my precious, pretty, little girl,
Take, eat, for you to others must provide."

The harsh, cold wind op'ed wings of muted pearl
That kept her perch. And so the bread she eyed
Through crimson spectacles; her world entire
The portion of a portion of a crust.
She poked, her gulp then dowsed the flaming fire
Of hunger, that now-satiated lust.
"Shoo, shoo, go fly and spread the message round
Where trust and satisfaction can be found."

When she concluded, she sat back down.

"Well done!" David exclaimed. "Really excellent. Thank you for sharing. I'd really like to see that written out. Brilliant, Kate."

Kate blushed happily.

"Anyone else?" When no one volunteered, David drew the meeting to a close and reminded everyone that they would reconvene when the Hilary term began in January.

As the group made their farewells, David approached Kate and quietly asked if he might see her home. She was pleased to accept and remained seated at her table while calling out her good-byes and best wishes for the holidays. When everyone had departed, David slipped into the chair across from hers.

"How are you feeling?" he asked.

"Good, thank you. The dizziness and headaches are all gone. I'm still sore all over and I get tired easily, but that's to be expected."

"We're all so glad you've recovered so quickly. But here," he said, smiling. "I have some things for you." He drew from his satchel a sheath of papers. Kate recognized her own handwriting.

"We never had our last tutorial for you to collect your papers because of the accident. So here they are." He handed them to her. "And, I must say, they are really well done. Your ideas and insights are most perceptive. I showed you a few instances where you could improve your writing technique, but over all I found your essays to be quite excellent."

Kate's initial disappointment, that David had wanted merely to return her papers, turned to pleasure when she saw the high marks of Alpha Beta and Alpha on her essays.

"Do you have any questions?" he asked.

Kate looked the papers over and shook her head.

"All right, then." He took a deep breath. "I would like for you to consider that our tutorials are now officially over and that I am no longer your tutor."

Kate looked at him quizzically.

"That is to say..." he fumbled on, "from now on, I hope you will consider me not just as your tutor, but as your friend."

"I've always considered you my friend," Kate said slowly, not certain what he was really trying to express.

"Yes, quite right. I am. But I'm no longer your teacher. And so I hope that means we can be better friends." Rubbing his forehead, he scowled and muttered, "That's not really what I mean either." He tried again. "Look, Kate, I have something else for you and I would like you to have it, not as my student, but as my—very special friend."

He opened his satchel again and pulled out a slim brown leather book decorated with gold tooling in an intricate design. The gold letters read, *The Sonnets of William Shakespeare.*

Delighted, Kate turned over the exquisite volume in her hands. "Oh, David, it's beautiful! Where did you find it?"

"The old used bookshop near the Covered Market. It's Victorian. The border design is by William Morris, the same poet and artist who designed some of those Pre-Raphaelite stained glass windows at Christ Church Cathedral. It's a lovely little volume, isn't it? It's one of my favorite books, and I'd like you to have it, as a sort of keepsake."

Kate traced the gold tooling with her finger and murmured, "How can I ever thank you? I'll always treasure it." She began to turn the pages—and found a slight bump in the middle of the book. Opening it to that spot, she discovered a pressed red rose like the one she had received from Hannah on David's behalf.

"Ah—that marks a particular sonnet I would like to recite to you, if I may. It speaks so much better than I can of some things I would like to say. I know it seems rather odd that David MacKenzie would ever be at a loss for words, but these are uncharted waters for me." He took a deep breath and exhaled quickly. "Right. So here goes. Sonnet 91."

Some glory in their birth, some in their skill,
Some in their wealth, some in their body's force;
Some in their garments, though newfangled ill;
Some in their hawks and hounds, some in their horse;
And every humour hath his adjunct pleasure,
Wherein it finds a joy above the rest.
But these particulars are not my measure;
All these I better in one general best.
Thy love is better than high birth to me,
Richer than wealth, prouder than garments' cost,
Of more delight than hawks or horses be;
And having thee, of all men's pride I boast;
Wretched in this alone, that thou mayst take
All this away, and me most wretched make.

He did not quote the lines as if reciting a poem. He quoted them naturally as if he were speaking to her from his heart, all the while holding her gaze.

Kate scarcely breathed as she listened. In the silence that followed, she thought he would surely hear her heart thumping. For a few moments, neither of them spoke.

Then David said, "Kate, my mother tells me that you are thinking of not returning after the holidays."

Kate looked away briefly, then returned David's gaze.

"Yes, well, you see my parents thought it best for me to skip the Hilary term and stay home so that they could be sure I had fully recovered from the accident. And then I started thinking that maybe I should just stay home for the whole semester. Maybe God has taught me all He wants me to learn here in Oxford."

"Do you really think you've finished all God has for you here?"

"What do you mean?"

"Perhaps you feel like you've gotten out of Oxford all you're supposed to. But what about what you can *give?* Perhaps God had more for you to do here."

Kate considered this. "I'm not sure what I can do, what I would have to offer to Oxford."

"Kate, we need you here."

"Who?"

"We do. The Inklings Society and St. Aldate's."

Kate wasn't convinced. "We?"

"No, you're right." David took her small hands in his. "*I* do. I need you here, Kate. Please reconsider. As the sonnet says, I would be most wretched if you were not to come back."

He gently traced the outline of her cheek with his hand. "When I first heard about your accident, I didn't know if you were alive or dead. But I didn't think I could bear the pain of losing you. I knew then for certain how much you mean to me. I would gladly have been hit by that car for you. But now, when you talk of not coming back, of my possibly never seeing you again...I..." His voice nearly broke. "I don't think I could bear that either."

Kate cradled her cheek against his hand. "Nor could I," she whispered, her eyes glistening with tears.

They both smiled.

"Kate," David went on, "I don't know for certain what God has in mind for us. I've been presumptuous in the past and made some dreadful mistakes, letting my passions run ahead of His will."

Her smile faded.

"Yes, I'm speaking of Charlotte," he said. "But I have determined since then, with God's help, that I will love in purity. Then when I'm certain of His will, I will have no cause for regret, and neither will the young lady in question. Do you understand what I'm saying?"

"Yes," she answered quietly. "I understand exactly and totally agree. I have my own cause for regret."

"Devereux."

Kate quickly covered his hand with her own. "Yes, but nothing terrible happened. It's just that it *could* have, and I never should have opened myself to that possibility."

He nodded. "So then, Kate. Please—say you will come back."

She smiled.

"Yes. I will."

David sighed happily with relief and contentment. Pushing back from the table, he stood to help Kate on with her coat. Her thick dark hair got caught in her collar, and he gently pulled it free. This time, he held her long tresses to his lips and kissed them before letting them fall down her back. She turned into his arms, and he held her tightly, slowly kissing her hair, her forehead, and the tip of her nose. He cupped her cheek in his hand and traced her lips with his thumb.

"I'll wait for that first kiss," he said hoarsely. "Now let me take you home."

Part 2: Intentions

To my husband, Bill

"This is my beloved and this is my friend."
—Song of Solomon 5:16

Let no one despise your youth, but set the believers an example in speech and conduct, in love, in faith, in purity… Treat younger men like brothers, older women like mothers, younger women like sisters, in all purity.

—1 Timothy 4:12 and 5:2

When I have learnt to love God better than my earthly dearest, I shall love my earthly dearest better than I do now. In so far as I learn to love my earthly dearest at the expenses of God and instead *of God, I shall be moving towards the state in which I shall not love my earthly dearest at all. When first things are put first, second things are not suppressed but increased.*

—C.S. Lewis,
from *Letters of C.S. Lewis*, November 8, 1952

Good and evil both increase at compound interest. That is why the little decisions you and I make every day are of such infinite importance.

—C.S. Lewis,
from *Mere Christianity*, book III, chapter 9

Oxford, England
April 1965
Trinity Term, First Week, Sunday Afternoon

The train was running late.

David MacKenzie paced up and down the platform, stopping only to check his watch, as if by this gesture of frustration he could will the train to arrive.

"Blast!" He muttered the impatient imprecation to no one in particular and resumed his pacing.

He had endured the long dreary months of the winter Hilary Term—"the winter of my discontent," he had called it, in a typical allusion to Shakespeare—by immersing himself in his usual round of lectures, tutorials, and studies as an Oxford don. All winter he had purposely stayed busy.

But alone at night in his little flat, he would allow himself to think of *her*. And his heart ached. He would stare at the fire, remembering how its glow had danced in the auburn highlights of the thick dark brown hair falling luxuriously down her back. The verse from the Song of Solomon often came to mind: "The king is held captive in her tresses." And though not a king, David found that certainly he had been captivated.

Yet try as he might, David could not recall Kate's face. He could remember the details—the large dark eyes, the high cheekbones, the sensuous lips—but they melted more into a blur the harder he tried to focus on them. He had no photograph of her and often wished he had the memory of a painter, rather than a poet.

"Blast the trains! Typical!" he muttered, denouncing under his breath the British nonchalance about travel schedules.

He had borne the long winter months of separation by pouring out his passion in lengthy letters and poetry. The poetry lay secreted in his desk drawers. The letters, carefully edited of his passion, had taken the long journey across the Atlantic to Kate's home in Virginia.

Kate had eagerly searched each line for a deeper display of emotion, then disappointed, replied in an equally measured tone. Their letters had shared much of their feelings about faith or family or familiar things, but little about their feelings for one another. The slow correspondence was augmented by Kate's essays on Shakespeare, as she continued her studies, and by David's critical evaluations of them, as he resumed his official role as her tutor.

Thus he had patiently awaited her return, but as the time grew closer his patience had run thin. *Only one more week and she will be here...only three more days and she will be here...only one more hour*...and the train was late.

"Blast!" he repeated, glaring again at his watch and glaring at the empty track.

Finally, the train roared into the station. The doors slid open, and passengers spilled out onto the platform. David anxiously searched their faces. Then he spied her, anxiously searching for him.

"Kate!" he called as he plunged through the crowd. At the sound of his voice, her face lit up in relieved recognition.

Suddenly she was in his arms.

I'd forgotten how petite she is, was his first thought. As his lips brushed the top of her head, he caught the herbal scent of her hair and he suddenly felt intoxicated.

"Kate—oh my word, I can't believe it. You're back! You did come back."

Laughing and crying at the same time, she gazed up at him. "I promised I would, didn't I?"

"Let me look at you." He held her at arms' length, admiringly. Now he wondered how he ever could have forgotten her beautiful face.

"It's so good to see you!" They spoke simultaneously, and laughing, embraced again.

"How touching." A smoky voice sliced through their joy. "The tutor is reunited with his student. Sweet—but rather unprofessional, wouldn't you say?"

Kate turned in confusion towards the sardonic stare of an attractive redhead in a tight leather miniskirt.

David reluctantly released Kate, his jaw tightening. "Charlotte. What brings you to Oxford?"

"Well," she replied lightly, "obviously not my former fiancé, although I was hoping to run into you. No, luckily—or unluckily—" Charlotte glanced meaningfully at Kate, "I'm here for the Trinity term, guest lecturing and sharing my research at Somerville College." She put down her luggage, searched through her handbag, and pulled out a business card. "Here's my number, darling." Leaning close to David, she pressed the card into his hand and whispered, "Ring me up when you tire of fraternizing with the students." Before David could reply, she turned and sauntered off in her thigh-high boots.

Kate noted David's befuddled expression with a rush of jealousy. "Have you been seeing her much?" she asked peevishly.

Her tone caught David off guard. "Sorry?"

"Have you been seeing much of Charlotte?"

"No!" he hastened to mollify her. "Not at all. I had no idea she was coming to Oxford for the term. Anyway," he tilted her chin and searched her face with his deep blue eyes. "I told you it was all over between Charlotte and me."

Kate caught her breath as she returned his gaze. *How handsome you are and how terribly I missed you!* She swallowed hard. "…I'm sorry," she stammered.

David smiled, and then bending to pick up her suitcases, playfully pretended he couldn't lift them. "What did you pack in here?" he teased. "You may have to sit on them. I'm not sure my MG has room in the boot for all this."

Kate blushed.

"Don't worry," he reassured her. "If all else fails, I have a boot rack. Thank God, it's not raining." He carried the luggage into the waiting room of the station, which was thronged with returning students. Kate gingerly held on to the edge of his jacket so as not to be separated.

"Katherine Hughes!" A voice boomed over the heads of the crowd, and suddenly a tall handsome youth swooped her up and twirled her around.

"Stuart!" she laughed breathlessly as he put her down.

"My, but you look absolutely marvelous! I was hoping to see you. You can't imagine what a beastly bore Hilary term was without you. Only your letters kept me from going mad. Do you need a lift?" he continued. "I'm here to pick up a friend so I have my car. You're back at St. Hilda's, I presume. Where are your bags?"

"Here." David stood by, holding the suitcases while struggling to keep his jealous anger in check.

"Ah. Mr. MacKenzie!" Stuart greeted him cheerfully.

"Lord Devereux." David nodded curtly.

"Well, now. How kind of you to help Miss Hughes. I'm looking forward to attending your Shakespeare lectures again this term." He leaned over Kate and murmured, "I hope to see you before then, Gorgeous." Then he slipped off into the crowd.

Incredulous, David shook his head. "You wrote to him?" he asked.

"Why, yes," she answered faintly, "just a few times."

"Right." He strode towards the station doors with her luggage. Suddenly he stopped and dropped the bags. "Kate, that man attempted to take advantage of you more than once. Why in heaven's name would you keep up a correspondence with him?"

"Well...because I promised him I would...just as friends."

"Friends," David repeated, shaking his head. "Right. Yes, he was rather friendly."

"David, he really felt badly about how he had treated me and asked me to forgive him. I *did* forgive him, and promised I would answer if he wrote me. But I also told him that we could never be anything other than friends, and I still believe that."

To control his agitation, David took a deep breath and exhaled slowly. "All right. Let's get out of here before we run into someone else."

This was going to be much more difficult than he had anticipated.

First Week, Sunday Evening

"It's so good to have you back!" Kate's suite-mate, Connie, sat on the bed watching Kate unpack in their shared set of rooms.

"It's good to be back," Kate replied. "But in some ways I feel like I've hardly been gone at all...and yet when I was back home in the States, it seemed like I was away forever." Kate paused thoughtfully as she hung up a blouse in her wardrobe. "It's kind of like Lucy stepping out of the Wardrobe. She had been in Narnia for ages, but no time had passed at all in England while she was gone. I feel as though I've been in a time warp and now I'm back to 'real' life." Kate sighed as she sank tiredly onto the bed. "I'm still on American time. I'm probably not making any sense. Now, tell me, what have I missed while I've been gone? Are you and Nigel still an item?"

Connie's rather ordinary face was transformed with the light of an inner beauty. "Yes, I guess you could say we are. But the thing I've wanted most to tell you is that while you were gone, Nigel and I both decided to become Christians."

"*Really?*" Kate's surprise was apparent. And after a moment of amazed silence, she threw her arms around her friend's neck and hugged her warmly. "Oh, Connie, I'm so glad! What happened? When? How?"

"Do you remember that night we all attended the Jacqueline du Pré concert at the Sheldonian, and afterwards we went to the Bird and

Baby and Mr. MacKenzie and Mr. Holmes shared with us about their beliefs?"

Kate nodded.

"Mr. MacKenzie talked a lot about C.S. Lewis's writings and how much they had influenced him. He gave Nigel two of Lewis's books to read—*Mere Christianity* and *Surprised by Joy,* and after he read them, Nigel loaned them to me. Then Mr. MacKenzie was Nigel's tutor for the winter term, and they had lots of time to talk about things, and we both have been regularly attending the services at St. Aldate's. So I guess it's been a cumulative thing, first Nigel and then me. We began to believe that Christianity was true and not just another myth, and both of us made a decision to follow Christ." Tears of joy glistened in Connie's eyes.

Kate's eyes mirrored those tears, and she hugged her friend again. "I can't tell you how happy this makes me! I've been praying for you since we first met, and now I know we'll not just be friends, but sisters as well."

Connie nodded and smiled. "So, sis, how are things with Mr. MacKenzie? Are you still an item?"

"Connie, please don't call him Mr. MacKenzie! It makes him sound so ancient."

"And you were the one telling me last fall that because Mr. MacKenzie...I mean, David...was a tutor, he was so much older than us. How old is he anyway?"

"I think he's around twenty-four or five and I'll be twenty-one in June, so we're only about four years apart."

"Right." Connie intentionally used the British pronunciation, and they both giggled. "Age is a funny thing. Your tutor can be four years older and it seems like he's another generation...but if you happen to fall for him, it's 'only' four years. But then, weren't we just talking of the passage of time and what an illusion it is?"

"Hmm," answered Kate dreamily as she exchanged logic for thoughts of David.

"So, did you write each other a lot?" Connie prodded. "Did he write any mushy poetry?"

"Yes. We wrote a lot. But there was no mush and no poetry, except for Shakespeare..." Kate's voice trailed off. "I must confess I was hoping for some. We wrote about what we were doing, or our families, or some fresh new insight into our Bible readings—and I also continued my studies with him via correspondence."

"*Studies?* How unromantic," Connie sighed. "But what about Stuart Devereux? Did you write him?"

"A few times. But strictly as friends."

"Well, keep it that way," Connie warned. "He really went wild this term. Parties. Bingeing on liquor. And messing around with those two girls from Somerville that went to his house party with us. Plus he's been pretty belligerent to his friends who've tried to warn him. Nigel was worried that Stuart would flunk out—be 'sent down' as they say. But somehow he managed to turn in his two essays each week and wasn't expelled. He claims he's going to buckle down this term."

Kate tried to take in all of this. "You know, I saw Stuart at the train station. He told me how 'beastly boring' the term was without me. He was perfectly charming as usual."

Connie eyed her friend skeptically. "Oh. I'm sure he was. Did Mr. MacKenzie find him charming too?"

"Not at all." Kate smiled sadly and yawned. "He was upset with me for having written him..." She stopped, remembering the scene at the train station. "But, Connie, do you know who else was there?" Not waiting for a reply, she rushed on. "David's fiancée. Well, former fiancée, I should say. She's here for the term too, as a lecturer. You know, Connie—this is probably wrong of me, but I don't like that woman."

"Well, why should you? You're sort of rivals, aren't you?"

"That's it exactly," Kate agreed. "She acts like he's still hers. And I think she wants him back."

David polished off his fish and chips and leaned back in his chair at the King's Arms pub, listening contentedly as his colleagues discussed the upcoming term while they ate. He didn't share the European penchant for savoring a meal with conversation. His family teased him that he inhaled his food— the only explanation they could find for how quickly it disappeared.

His friend Austen chatted comfortably with their new colleague, Yvette Goodman. Yvette had recently been elected a Junior Fellow at St. Hilda's College; but she was still something of an anomaly at Oxford, and not because of her gender. Although the individual colleges were still decidedly segregated by sex, the University had been coeducational for many years. In fact, as far back as the 1920s, C.S. Lewis himself had been tutored by a woman.

Nor was Yvette's distinction that she was a Christian. Believers were few in number and arguably somewhat disdained, but she and others like David and Austen had banded together for support and fellowship.

Rather, what made Yvette Goodman an anomaly at Oxford University was her color. In that bastion of English education and society, people of color were rare, especially as instructors. Yvette's English mother was white and her West Indian father, brown. She had grown up in a crowded Georgian row house near Paddington Station in London, where her father drove a large black taxi. Yvette had not only overcome the color barrier, but the class barrier as well—and against all conventional odds, had worked her way through the University of London—now finding herself on the English faculty of one of the most prestigious universities in the world.

It cheered David to see Austen talking animatedly. Always reserved, Austen had grown somewhat melancholic since the death of his wife. Yet with their new friend, he seemed at ease and even happy. Yvette wasn't particularly pretty, but inner joy radiated from her broad features. After discovering the source of her joy, David and Austen had welcomed her into their tiny fellowship, and together they had become something of a triumvirate. The two young men now often thought of her in the way they would a sister, and her coffee-and-cream skin had become to them as familiar as the charming gap between her two front teeth.

"So, David." Yvette turned her dark brown eyes on him. "You've been very quiet. What grand plans are you hatching for this term?"

David tilted his chair back and put his hands behind his head. "Two things," he said, smiling. "Next week I'm going up to Cambridge. Some friends of mine want to get an Inklings Society going there and have asked me up to give the opening talk."

"That's splendid!" Austen was genuinely pleased.

But Yvette was puzzled. "Does Cambridge have any connection to the Inklings, or do your friends just admire their writing?"

"Both," David replied. "Tolkien and Lewis have their share of admirers worldwide. But the only Inkling to have a real connection to Cambridge was Jack. He held the Chair there in Medieval and Renaissance Literature after Oxford kept passing him over for a professorship. I took my undergraduate studies with him there."

"Well, this must be very exciting for you," Yvette remarked.

"Indeed, 'tis." David righted his chair and leaned forward. "To think that just a bit over a year ago we had the idea of continuing the Inklings' legacy here in Oxford…and now it's spreading to Cambridge."

"So, what's number two?" Yvette asked.

"Sorry?"

"You said you had two grand plans for the term. What's the second one?"

David grinned mischievously. "I'm thinking about getting married."

Austen and Yvette were so surprised at David's news that they both burst out laughing.

That wasn't the reaction David had expected. "What? What's so funny?"

"Just like that?" Austen asked. "You pick Kate up at the train station this afternoon and already you're thinking of getting married?"

"Well, obviously, I've been thinking about it longer than that," David replied defensively. "I thought about it before she left and all winter while she was gone."

"Wait," interjected Yvette. "Is this the girl you tutor in Shakespeare and whom I have this term for Romantic Poetry?"

"Yes, the same. Katherine Hughes. She's American."

"Oh, so sorry," Yvette teased.

"Watch it, my mum is American."

"Pity." Yvette wouldn't let it go.

"Which makes me half-American, woman," David said, laughing. "So enough! Besides, Americans have certain redeeming qualities—like they're friendly and resourceful, and—"

"Rich..." Yvette continued, "and rude and loud and—"

"But, David," interrupted Austen, returning to the real subject. "Don't you think this is all very sudden?"

"Keep your shirt on, old boy. I just said I was thinking about it. I didn't say I had reached a decision. But the way I figure it, Kate is here just for the term, maybe a bit longer if she does some touring afterwards. But then she will go back to the States for good—unless, of course, she marries a Brit. So I have eight weeks—or really, less—to make a decision."

"*Wisely and slow,* old chap, *they stumble that run fast,*" cautioned Austen.

"Yes, yes, Friar Lawrence. I shan't be as precipitous as Romeo." David's face darkened. "Besides, I've been wrong before...You know, I saw Charlotte today at the train station."

"What's Charlotte doing in Oxford?"

"She's here for the term, guest lecturing for Somerville. I hope I can stay clear of her." David glanced at their friend, who clearly hadn't followed the digression. "Sorry, Yvette. I should explain. Charlotte was my fiancée. We met as undergraduates at Cambridge and she stayed on there in biochemical research. She's an agnostic, and when I recommitted my life to Christ around the time of Jack Lewis's funeral, she broke our engagement."

"Oh, my." Yvette took this information in. "So, do you still have feelings for her then?"

"No," David answered decisively. Then he hesitated and muttered. "Well, not the kind you mean, anyway." Uncharacteristically, David's face reddened.

"David no longer loves Charlotte in a romantic way," Austen tried to explain. "But Charlotte is rather...well...she's a seductress, to put it bluntly."

"Aye, she is that," David unhappily concurred.

"Ah. I see." Yvette completely comprehended the situation. "Well, then you *had* better steer clear of her."

3

First Week, Monday

David jogged back from University Parks, where he had helped train the University of Oxford Men's Football Team. He felt the exhilaration of the well-conditioned athlete after a successful workout as he bounded up the stairs of the palatial Georgian era "New Building" of Magdalen. Although his flat was nearby, he had decided to shower and change in his college rooms before dinner. He also needed to go over his lecture notes for Wednesday—and did not want to get entangled in a discussion with his well-meaning but nosy landlady.

His rooms—like those of C.S. Lewis, who had been one staircase over in the magnificent Palladian building—were spacious but Spartan. He had bath and bedroom, in which he kept a rarely used cot and extra clothing. The sitting room, with desk, bookcases, and functional but nondescript sofa and chairs in front of the fireplace, overlooked the acres of meadow called the Deer Park on one side and the turrets and yellow stone walls of Magdalen College on the other. But today, he had little regard for the views, as splendid as they were.

Shuffling through the papers on his desk, he unearthed his lecture notes. David, like his mentor Lewis, was a popular lecturer at the University, drawing large audiences of students. This was gratifying to the young tutor but added pressure to live up to his reputation. He expected excellence from himself and couldn't let down his students with a mediocre delivery.

Never able to sit still for long, he grabbed a book and began pacing about the room as he rehearsed his speech. Suddenly he felt the presence of someone else in the room, and he turned with embarrassment towards the door.

It was Charlotte.

"You look like Hamlet, walking about with that book in your hand," Charlotte said, laughing. "What are you reading with such expression?"

"*Words, words, words,*" he quoted warily, putting down the book.

His former fiancée stepped into the room. She was wearing a short, bold, geometrically designed dress and fishnet stockings that had turned many a head as she walked by. "Oh my, I haven't seen you in your football kit in ages. I had forgotten how marvelous you look in those shorts."

David cleared his throat uncomfortably. "Charlotte, I don't have much time. I still have to change before dinner."

"Don't worry, darling," she cooed as she sat on the sofa, making a great show of crossing her long legs. "I shan't keep you. I have to get to dinner as well. I came because I have a proposal for you."

David turned away from her and gripped the mantel of the fireplace. "Look, Charlotte, it was your decision to break up with me," he said, struggling to keep his voice even. "But it was the right one. We could never be happily married."

"Dear boy." Her laugh had the brittle edge of crashing icicles. "Who said anything about marriage? You're right, it wouldn't have worked."

He turned to face her. "Then what proposal?"

She ran her tongue over her lips. "Since we're both in a hurry, I'll get to the point. As you know, I'm here in Oxford for eight weeks—eight lonely weeks. I certainly don't know any other desirable men here. What I propose is this: For these eight weeks, we resume our relationship—as lovers—but with no strings attached. We will be entirely discreet. No one need ever know—particularly that American girl you're so fond of. We enjoy ourselves for the term and when it's over, I go back to Cambridge, you go back to the girl, and no one will be the wiser." She made a show of tugging at her skirt, which had crept up her legs. "So, what do you say, darling?"

At first David could not think at all. He was utterly stunned. Then he slowly answered, "Sounds more like a proposition than a proposal."

"Oh." She laughed again. "You always were a stickler for words."

"But why me?" David was flustered. "Any man would want you—I mean..."

"Except you?" Charlotte smiled sadly. "Darling, when we broke up that's what I thought. The trouble is, I don't want them. The fact is, I've missed you, David. I haven't found anyone like you." She looked at him pointedly. "It's you I want."

"But things are different now. Things have changed." In agitation, David started pacing again.

"The American? I told you, she will never know about us. And after the term, you can go back to pursuing her—if that's what you still want."

"But, Charlotte"—he stood still and looked straight into her eyes—"it's wrong. I couldn't break God's commandments like that."

"What difference does it make?" She was getting annoyed. "Why do you have to bring God into everything? Like I said, no one need ever know. You can protect your precious honor and reputation here at Oxford."

"But God would know and so would I."

"That didn't seem to bother you before," she answered huffily. "Besides, I can't see why God would care if two people are happy and having a bit of fun. And according to your beliefs, God forgives sin, doesn't He? If He is such a killjoy, then you can beg His forgiveness later."

She stood up to leave. Leaning very close, she brushed some loose strands of his dark hair off his forehead. "Remember the good times we had at Cambridge?" she asked huskily. "I'll give you whatever you want, David—and expect nothing. No emotional strings. What more could a man want?" Her hand caressed his neck, his shoulder, and the length of his arm. She squeezed his hand. "Think about it and ring me."

Indeed, thought David as he watched her leave, *what more could a man want? Only an imbecile would pass this up!* All the memories of her, which had been banished from his thoughts, came rushing back to him with desire. He groaned and sank down into his chair. *No one need ever know. What harm could there be? And she's right. God would have to forgive me because He promised He would.* He stared at his hands and noticed they were shaking. *But I would have to ask His forgiveness because it would be wrong. And Kate...what about Kate?* Charlotte's voice taunted him. "*What difference does it make? No one need ever know...*"

4

First Week, Monday Evening

Plunging himself into a hot bath, David cleansed his body while struggling to purge his mind of the thoughts that were plaguing him. Finally, as he toweled off and dressed, he began to pray. *Lord, Your word promises that we will not be tempted beyond our strength but that You will provide the way of escape. I confess I am sorely tempted by this woman. I confess that, left to myself, I don't really want an escape. But help me. Keep me from temptation and deliver me from the evil one—*

The persistent ring of the telephone interrupted his prayer, and he strode out to the sitting room to answer it.

"MacKenzie here."

"Hi, David. It's Mum. Is everything all right?"

"Yes, everything's fine. Why?"

"You've really been on my heart today and I've been especially praying for you."

"Well, thanks, Mum. I need it."

"Anything you want to tell me?"

"No, I'm fine. But I appreciate you ringing."

"Well, what are you doing after supper? I was wondering if you could bring Kate over. Hannah and I would like very much to see her and don't want to wait until Sunday, when there's so much going on here."

"That's a brilliant idea, Mum. I'll phone her and see if she's free...and, Mum," he added quietly, "thanks for ringing me. It means more than you know. Cheers."

David was thoughtful as he placed the telephone back in its cradle. He took a deep breath and exhaled slowly. *And thank* You, *Lord.*

That evening David and Kate found themselves wrapped in the warm embrace of the MacKenzie household. Again, Kate had the sensation that she had been in a time warp and had never been away from Oxford or the St. Aldate's rectory. David's mother and baby sister Hannah were genuinely happy to welcome her back. His teenage brothers greeted her in their shy, awkward way and quickly returned to their studies. While three-year-old Hannah played with Kate's long dark hair, Annie and Kate chatted away like old friends about her winter at home and her recovery from her accident. Two things always surprised Kate about Annie MacKenzie: how the mother of an Oxford tutor and six other children could look so pretty and youthful—and how at ease she felt with her. With her petite figure and golden-brown hair pulled back into a ponytail, Annie could have passed as Kate's sister. They were kindred spirits, and Kate felt she could share with her much more easily than she could with her own mother. David's deference towards and affection for his mother also increased Kate's respect for him.

"David?" asked a slender teenaged boy whom Kate remembered as the brother named Richard. "Could you please help me with my Ovid? I can't figure out this one passage."

"Oh, no, not good old Ovid!" David moaned, laughing. "Listen, my Latin is rather rusty. Where's Dad? He's better at this than I am."

"He's counseling," Annie answered. "But I'm sure you're scholar enough to help your brother translate."

"Oh, all right, I'll give it a go." David reluctantly excused himself from the women and sat down with his brother across the spacious sitting room. A few minutes later, the older, stockier brother, William, came in laden with a French book. David greeted him with a mock groan.

"Hey, lads, I'm here for a friendly visit," he protested, "not to have to do homework!"

"Come on, David. It's poetry," William coaxed. "Baudelaire."

"Ah, Baudelaire! *C'est différent*, David declared, taking the book. *"Il est magnifique, n'est ce pas? Écoute."*

David began to read the poem, the French rolling naturally off his tongue. Kate stopped speaking in mid-sentence as she listened. He read French poetry as beautifully as he did Shakespeare. She had excelled in French, at one point considering it as her major, but had realized she preferred English literature to the arduous work of translation. Now she sat stunned as she listened to David read and then energetically discuss the poem with his brother in perfectly fluent French.

Annie noticed her astonishment and explained. "We were blessed with a year's sabbatical in Paris when David was in prep school, so the boys are all fairly fluent. Do you speak French?"

"Un petit peu," answered Kate truthfully. "But I'm nowhere near as fluent. How can he know so much? You know, sometimes he makes me feel really stupid."

"Perhaps ignorant would be a better word," Annie suggested gently. "I remember being overwhelmed with Reverand MacKenzie's vast store of knowledge. But keep in mind that David was classically trained by his father and by Mr. Lewis. The requirements at Oxford aren't nearly so stringent now as they were even five years ago. Latin and Greek are no longer mandatory."

When David finished assisting his brothers, he opened a volume from the Chronicles of Narnia—*The Horse and His Boy*—sat down with Hannah on his lap, and began reading to her, using different voices and accents for each character. The boys feigned indifference, but slowly migrated closer to the sofa. Soon the whole family had become enthralled by the story. As Kate observed the scene, a sense of yearning tugged at her heart. *This is what I want. This is the way I want my family to be.*

Then with a shout of joy, Hannah suddenly scrambled down.

"Daddy's home!" she cried.

Scooping up the little girl in his arms, Eric MacKenzie greeted his family, kissed his wife, and then turned to Kate.

"Welcome back, Kate. It does me good to see ye again," he said with his slight Scottish burr, as he warmly shook her hand. "Ye've been missed around here, lass." He nodded his head toward David and gave her a knowing wink.

"How was the counseling, Dad?" David interjected. "Successful?"

Eric MacKenzie sighed. "I gave it my best shot, but it really depends on the couple. If they decide to obey God's word and keep their vows, their marriage can be saved. But sometimes people really don't want to change and there isna' much I can do about it."

He sank wearily into his chair and snuggled with Hannah. "Of course, they'll blame me when it doesna' work out," he added, smiling sadly, "and then tell all their friends that they tried everything, even counseling." Stretching out his long legs under the coffee table, he directed his attention back to Kate. "But how are ye, lass? Please tell me all ye've been doin'."

Annie excused herself to prepare tea, and David followed her, ostensibly to help. When he entered the rectory kitchen, Annie had struck a match and was adjusting the blue halo of gas under her teakettle. She blew out the match and turned to him with an affectionate smile.

"And to what do I owe this honor?"

He bowed. "I came to offer my services, Madame."

"Well. I'm grateful for the gallantry, but I suspect you wouldn't be tearing yourself away from Kate unless there was something you wanted to talk about."

David grinned as he sat down at the table. "Perceptive as always, Mrs. MacKenzie. All right, here it is. Uh...um..." He cleared his throat. "How did you know Dad was the right one for you?"

Annie looked amused as she began to arrange the tea tray. "Well, now that's a long story—much of which you've heard before. And I think you are really asking a more general question, aren't you?"

"Right again. Well, then. How does one know for certain that someone is the right one for them?"

"Your father is the one to go to for premarital counseling, you know."

David pushed his hair back from his forehead. "Yes, but I'm asking for pre-premarital advice."

"I think you know the general guidelines, honey," she answered, stacking the cups and saucers. "Your intended should be a committed and growing believer; you should have the agreement of both sets of parents and the blessings of your pastor." Annie began ticking her list off on her fingers. "You should be compatible with similar interests, goals, and vision regarding your future life together; you should be the best of friends; and you should stay sexually pure so that your judgment and emotions are not skewed."

"Meaning?"

"I mean, how can you hear what God is saying if you are living in sin?"

"Right. But what if..." David found it hard to look at his mother and began to fiddle with the saltshaker. "What if everything seems to be lining up but you still notice other people? I mean, how can someone be the love of your life if you're still attracted to other women?"

The kettle whistled, and Annie switched off the burner. Pouring the water into her china teapot, she pondered her response. Then she slid into the chair next to him.

"You know, honey, you'll always notice other women. Just as she will notice other men. In fact, women notice other attractive women too. I think all of us admire beauty in others, and there's nothing wrong with that. Beauty is one of God's gifts. But the key is to leave it at admiration and not act on it."

"But how?"

"'Forsaking all others, I take you.' When you marry, you take those vows before God and man. You make a lifelong commitment. And you never put yourself in a situation that would tempt you to do otherwise."

"Right," he sighed. "I suppose it's rather like making a commitment to Christ. Isn't it?"

"Very much so," Annie agreed. "Your father is fond of saying that love is a decision, just like faith is. We may not always have warm fuzzy feelings for one another, but the decision to love carries us through tough times—and then often, the feelings follow."

She stood up and patted him on the back.

"Now then, help me carry up this tray before they wonder what happened to us."

David pulled up to the front gate of St. Hilda's College. Switching off the motor of his MG, he turned to look at Kate.

"You've been rather pensive tonight. What have you been thinking about?"

"You've been quiet too," Kate countered.

"Yes, but I asked first."

Kate sighed. "Okay. But I know this is going to sound dumb."

"Try me."

"Well, it's that you know so much. I knew you were an expert on Shakespeare, but then tonight I find out that you know Latin and can speak French fluently. And your mother said you've studied Greek too."

"Don't forget Anglo–Saxon, Middle English, German, and uh...Italian," David added helpfully.

"You see! That's what I mean. You're just so smart and—I don't know— you make me feel stupid or something..."

"Kate, I don't follow this. You're bothered because I know more languages than you do? How does that make you stupid?"

"Well, you know so much more than I do, about almost everything."

David tried not to smile. "First of all, you're a student from William and Mary, one of the finest colleges in the South, and now here you are at Oxford. That hardly qualifies you as stupid. And second, may I remind you that you *are* a student and I am your tutor. If I didn't know a little more than you, I would be out of a job." David couldn't resist a grin. "And I would hate not being your tutor anymore."

"Oh," Kate said in embarrassed frustration. "I knew this would sound dumb."

"No, not dumb, but perhaps rather silly." He lifted her chin. "What's this *really* all about?"

Kate sighed again. She could not meet his eyes. "Maybe...maybe, I'm afraid that you'll get bored with me or something."

"I can assure you, Katherine Lee Hughes, that I find you endlessly fascinating."

She looked up at him and smiled shyly. "Really?"

"Uh-huh."

Her face suddenly clouded. "But I know that other women truly are smarter than I am and I just can't compete with them."

"To whom are you referring?"

She almost choked on the name. "Charlotte."

"Ah." David grew thoughtful. "You know, Charlotte *is* quite intelligent. But her interest lies in science." He gave a low whistle. "Now that stuff is totally beyond me…molecular structures and genes—it's all Greek to me. Well—" He grinned. "I guess more like Chinese.

"Really, Kate," he said gently, reaching over to touch her hair. "I'd much rather talk to you—" He checked himself, cleared his throat, and quickly resumed his teasing tone. "Now if you suddenly discover you have a passion for mathematics and a disdain for literature, we will reopen this discussion. But until then—no more of this."

Hopping out of the car, he opened her door and helped her out. She hesitated before unlocking the entrance gate.

"David? There is another thing. And maybe I can't articulate this any better. But, you know, I really do love your family."

He smiled. "I'm glad. I do too."

"But what I mean to say is that—well, you know, I've always thought I wanted some kind of career. That after all this education, I couldn't see just having a family and staying home with them. It would seem like such a waste of my abilities."

Having heard this before from Charlotte, David's stomach tightened with dread as he waited for what he thought Kate would say next.

"But seeing your mom with you and your brothers and Hannah…and your Dad too…" she continued, "and seeing you sitting there reading with Hannah on your lap…I can't express it very well, but it put such a longing in my heart. I can see that being a homemaker and raising a family is perhaps the most important career a woman could have. And I realized that…well…that a family *is* what I really want most of all."

With relief, he drew her to him and rested his cheek against the top of her head. "Oh, Kate, darling. It's what I really want too."

First Week, Wednesday

Gratified by the reception of his lecture, David bowed his head in acknowledgement of the enthusiastic applause that followed it. He felt exhilarated by this connection with the University students and by his contribution to inspiring them in their studies.

The term had begun auspiciously. The previous evening's meeting of the Inklings Society had been so well attended that they had moved it from the Eagle and Child to the Friend's Meeting House next door. True, the acclaimed J.R.R. Tolkien himself had been there to discuss Elven-lore and the Elvish language in his trilogy, The Lord of the Rings. Although they couldn't expect that kind of turnout again as the term progressed and examinations loomed closer, it was encouraging nonetheless. Yes, David felt that they were making a difference at Oxford.

He waited at the lectern for the inevitable crush of students who would want to speak to him afterwards. A bevy of young women quickly surrounded him. Austen teased him unmercifully by calling him the "new Charles Williams," referring to the fellow Inkling and friend of C.S. Lewis who in his day had attracted a large following of females. As David talked cordially with the students, his eyes scanned over the departing crowd, searching for Kate.

He finally spied her standing in the back with her friends Connie and Nigel and—*Oh, no, not Stuart Devereux again.* David waved to catch Kate's attention. She waved back, smiling broadly, and then her face fell. He followed the line of her gaze to the front row, where an attractive redhead sat: *Charlotte. What is she doing here?* David glanced back again to Kate, but she was gone.

Charlotte waited for the last of the students to depart. Her long, slender fingers trembled slightly as she lit a cigarette, inhaled deeply, and slowly blew out the smoke.

"You're surprised to see me?" she asked. Then without waiting for his response, she continued. "You've earned quite a reputation here in Oxford, so I hear, and I'm glad to see for myself that you deserve it. Really, David, it was an excellent lecture. You know Shakespeare isn't my cup of tea, but you caught even my interest."

"Thank you."

"Well, then." She crossed her long legs. "Have you thought about my proposal?"

"Yes."

She smiled. "Yes?"

"No!" Flustered, David quickly corrected himself. "I mean 'yes,' I've thought about it, but the answer is 'no.'"

"Oh." Her smile faded. "May I ask why?"

He sighed and rubbed his forehead, avoiding her eyes. "I told you why before."

"Humor me. Explain again. I thought it was an offer no man could refuse."

"This man can. I'm a Christian, and it's time I start behaving as one."

Charlotte took an angry drag on her cigarette. "This is what I detest about religion. All the ridiculous rules and laws."

"It's not about rules, Charlotte. It's about love. Love for God and for the one person God intends for me."

"You used to think I was that person, didn't you?"

David finally looked at her. "I did love you, Charlotte, and I intended to marry you. And I convinced myself that, since we were going to be married, it wouldn't be wrong. That it would all work out. But *I* was wrong. We don't know what the future holds and we can't presume to. I've asked your forgiveness before, but I want to say again that I'm truly sorry."

"Well, I'm not!" she snapped back. "They were some of the most wonderful days of my life." She took another drag on her cigarette. "Are you telling me that you're going to be celibate until you're married? That even if you find Miss Wonderful, you aren't going to share your bed with her?"

"That's right."

"I don't believe you."

David shrugged. "With God helping me."

"So, God disapproves of sex, I take it?"

"No, of course not. God created sex, both for man's procreation and for his pleasure. It's a wonderful gift, but it's meant to be enjoyed only in the sanctity of marriage." David began pacing thoughtfully.

"Here," he said turning back to her. "Let me give you an analogy."

"Oh, spare me."

"It's short. I read it somewhere and it's a good illustration of what I'm trying to say. You've heard fire used as a metaphor for love?"

"Yes," Charlotte replied impatiently.

"And fire for passion as well—fire brings warmth and light and a certain romance and excitement."

"Yes, so where's the analogy?"

"Well, fire is wonderful, but only so long as it's kept under control where it belongs: in the hearth. But if you extend it beyond its proper boundaries—say onto the rug—it can burn the house down and cause all manner of loss and destruction in people's lives. Do you see what I mean? God has ordained sexual intimacy for marriage where it brings warmth and life—but outside of marriage it produces a lot of pain and heartache."

Charlotte sighed. "I get the point, but I still don't agree with it."

"Aye, and there's the rub," David said sadly.

Charlotte crushed out her cigarette in an ashtray near the lectern. "You're really serious about this Christianity bit now, aren't you?"

"Yes, Charlotte."

"A pity it has to divide us. I wish I could believe like you do."

"I do too, Charlotte. I pray for it often."

Her eyes glistened with tears. Catching herself, she lifted her chin to keep from losing control. Putting her palm against his chest, she reached up and kissed him gently on the cheek.

"I'll see you around, David."

David nodded but didn't answer as Charlotte closed the door behind her.

6

First Week, Thursday Afternoon

Kate sat on the small sofa in her tutor's Magdalen rooms, reading aloud her essay on *Love's Labor's Lost.* Across from her, David sat hunched over, chin in hand, listening.

"Stop!" he suddenly exclaimed and jumped up from his chair. "This won't do!"

Kate froze, then looked up anxiously. "What's wrong? What'd I do?"

David shook his head and started pacing. "This is ridiculous."

Kate's face grew hot. "I'm sorry," she faltered. "I really did work hard on it. Is it the thesis you don't like, or the writing?"

David stood still and looked at her uncomprehendingly. "Sorry?"

"Is it what I said or how I said it?"

His manner softened. "Oh, good grief! It's not your paper, Kate. It's me. I must confess I don't have the slightest notion what you wrote. You lost me after the first paragraph."

"Is it that...boring?"

"No, no, no! I just wasn't paying attention." He sighed. "I'm sorry. You know, Jack once told me he had to give up tutoring female students altogether. He said their beauty so distracted him, he couldn't think of a thing to say. I thought it rather peculiar at the time, but well...now, here I am." He rubbed his forehead, then said quietly, "Perhaps it would be better for you to have another tutor."

"But why? I thought you liked teaching me!"

"I do." He looked at her with longing. "I do ever so much. But perhaps that's why I shouldn't. I can see now why Jack gave it up."

"But I don't want another tutor!" Kate's eyes brimmed with tears. "I returned to Oxford to study with you. Not anyone else."

"Oh, please don't cry, Kate," he implored her, nudging a box of tissues across the coffee table. "Don't. You'll make me want to hold you and I mustn't. Not here." He turned his back on her and leaned his forehead against the cool marble of the fireplace mantel. "I'll think about what to do. Just leave your essay for me to assess."

"But what should I write about next time?" She dabbed her nose with a tissue and sniffed. "If there is a next time, that is."

"I don't know. I've forgotten." He turned around to face her. "I'm dreadfully sorry. I'll ring you up or...um...put the assignment in your pigeonhole."

David stared at Kate and then abruptly blurted out, "Just why are you wearing such a short skirt, anyway?"

"What?"

"Your skirt. Why is it so short?"

Kate tried unsuccessfully to pull it down. She squirmed uncomfortably. "Well, it's the style, and I thought you would like it."

"Of course I like it. That's the problem!" David started pacing again. "And what about the other chaps? Do you think they'll like it too?"

"Well, I don't know." She added defensively, "What if they do?"

"What do you suppose men are thinking when they notice you in a skirt like that?"

"Well...I suppose they think I look nice or pretty."

David stopped in front of her and sadly shook his head. "Yes, they are thinking that. But, my dear girl, they are also thinking all sorts of things—terrible things that you would really rather they didn't."

As his meaning dawned on her, Kate answered faintly. "I had no idea."

"Well, now you do. So perhaps you'll consider not stumbling the young men around here, including your helplessly sinful tutor." He added gently, "Would you please wear longer skirts or your student's robe to future tutorials?"

Kate nodded and covered her knees with her notebook. Then she scowled. "You don't seem to mind Charlotte's miniskirts."

"Charlotte? What does she have to do with this?"

"Every time I've seen her she's been wearing a miniskirt. You seem to like hers."

"I told you, it has nothing to do with liking the look—well, maybe it does. Just why are you bringing her up?" he cried in exasperation.

"Because you probably never told *her* not to wear miniskirts. Isn't there a double standard here?"

David shoved his hair back from his forehead in frustration. "Yes, absolutely! First of all, she's not a Christian, so I don't expect the same conduct from her that I would from a believer. There's your double standard. I hold *you* to a higher one. Second, she's not my student. If she were, I would *ask* her—I haven't *told* you to do anything— I would *ask* her the same thing. And third, she has nothing to do with me!"

"Then why was she sitting there waiting for you after the lecture yesterday?"

"She came to hear the lecture, same as you and all the others."

"But she waited," Kate countered stubbornly.

"She's never heard me before. She waited to give me her compliments."

"Is that all?"

"Truthfully?" He sighed. "No." David gave her a pointed look. "And let's leave it at that."

Kate opened her mouth to protest, but thought better of it. "Okay, I will," she huffed as she tossed her essay down on the coffee table. Then, fighting back tears, she walked out.

David watched her leave, immobilized by inner turmoil. Suddenly he shook his head, as if to literally shake himself free from his inertia, and, grabbing his jacket, raced down the stairwell in pursuit.

"Kate, wait!" His deep voice rang out, echoing against the stone buildings and startling a passerby. But David had arrested her. She waited without turning around or looking at him.

"Kate, I'm so sorry." He caught his breath as he pulled on his jacket. "May I walk with you?" He glanced about to see if they were still an object of notice. Satisfied that they were not, he reached for her books. "Here, let me carry these."

For a moment, Kate clutched them tightly.

"Kate?"

She finally looked up at him, his face earnest and anxious. Her pique dissolved—she released the books and took his proffered arm.

He sighed heavily with relief. "You know, I prefer to keep things on an academic and professional level when I'm in my rooms. Out here, I feel I can talk more personally. May we go to Addison's Walk? It's such a lovely day and there is something special I want to show you."

Kate nodded. "I'm sorry I got angry," she said quietly as they walked towards the meadow. "And I'm sorry I wore an immodest skirt—and that I distracted you."

He chuckled. "You can't help the last bit. That's what *I* need to sort out. I'm rather like the King of Navarre in *Love's Labor's Lost,* aren't I? Banishing women from my presence so I can concentrate on my studies. Well, this is the paradox of my life right now. You have no idea how I long to be with you, but then when you're around, I long for you so much more that I think it would be better *not* to be with you at all...But I'm sure you don't understand what I'm saying."

She leaned her head on his arm and sighed. "Oh, yes—I do." Suddenly, she gasped in delight. Before them a sea of tiny purple wildflowers bowed before the breeze, undulating like waves across the meadow. Above them the bright blue vault of heaven stretched over the bordering trees.

"They're snake's-head fritillaries," David answered her unasked question. "One of the wonders of Oxford in April."

"Oh, to be in England, now that April's there!" Kate quoted happily. "From the time I was a little girl, I would look at pictures in travel brochures and dream of coming here in the spring. It's almost like God Himself put this yearning in my heart. And here I am, in England in April!"

David smiled. "The reality is a lot of rain."

Undeterred in her enthusiasm, Kate continued, "And do you know, when I was in junior high school and it would be raining and I felt depressed, I would pretend I was in England and then I would feel better?"

"You were an odd little girl. So, now when you are here and it's raining, do you think to yourself, *Well, this is English rain. So I shan't be depressed?*"

"No," she admitted honestly. "Here the rain is depressingly dreary."

They both laughed.

"David, these flowers look like a carpet of tiny bells. I want to run through them and roll around."

"Not in that skirt or those boots, you don't," he teased. "Come back in jeans and tennis shoes." He took her elbow and led her along the bowered path around the meadow. "Do you recall that after your first tutorial we walked here, and I told you that this is where Tolkien and Lewis had their fateful talk about Christianity being the true mythology?"

"Yes, and you said that it's one of your favorite places in Oxford—and where you come to think and pray."

"Very good," David was obviously pleased at her recollection. "Did I tell you that I had my own walk here with Jack when I was in senior school, and he gave me a similar talk to the one he had had with Professor Tolkien?"

"Really?"

"Yes, I committed my life to Christ, right here by this meadow. I guess that's why this place means so much to me."

Kate squeezed his arm. "Thanks for sharing it with me."

"Oh, Kate, there's so much I want to share with you." He looked at her eagerly. "Will you come up to Cambridge with me on Sunday after church? I'd love to show you Cambridge."

"I'd love to see Cambridge!"

"Good. Some friends of mine are starting an Inklings Society there, and they've asked me up to speak and sort of kick things off. You can stay at Lucy Cavendish Women's College, and I'll be at my alma mater, Magdalene. We'll be back in time for the Inklings meeting here on Tuesday."

A recollection crushed Kate's excitement. "Oh, no. I can't!"

"Why not?"

"I have my tutorial with Miss Goodman on Tuesday morning."

"Could you possibly get your paper done early?"

"Maybe, if I have no social life this weekend."

"Hmm...Saturday is May Day. Did you have plans to go to any of the dances?"

Kate shook her head.

"Good. But you can't miss May Morning. How about if I pick you up bright and early for the festivities and take you to breakfast. Then you'll have the rest of Saturday to work on your essay. We'll make up for your social life in Cambridge. Does that sound amenable to you?" When she nodded, David continued, "I'll talk to Yvette for you about missing your tutorial, but I know she won't mind. Say, how do you like having her as a tutor?"

"She's fine."

"Just 'fine'? She's wonderful in her field. I'm surprised you don't adore her."

"Well, I've only just met her."

"I think you'll really like her once you get to know her better. Since last term, she and Austen and I have formed a sort of three musketeers—'one for all and all for one'—against the heathen hierarchy around here. She's a splendid person and has become a good friend. I know you'll love her."

"Well, if you say so." Kate smiled at his confident assertion.

"I do, and I'm glad you've come to recognize that I'm always right," he added facetiously. "But you sound like you think I'm the only don in Oxford who can tutor you."

"I told you that's the reason I came back."

"The only reason?" he teased.

"Well, maybe there's another." She peered coquettishly at him through her thick eyelashes.

"Stop your flirting, Katie Scarlett O'Hara, or I shan't be able to court you."

"Court me?" Kate nearly snickered at the archaic term.

"Well, what would you call it?"

"You're *seeing* me?" Kate suggested. "Or we're *dating?*"

"No, it doesn't sound proper to say a Magdalen Fellow is *dating* one of his students. Besides..." He lifted her chin and looked into her eyes. "I'm much more serious than that."

Kate could scarcely breathe. She took a gulp of air and swallowed. "You are?"

He traced the outline of her chin with the back of his hand, "Yes, my dearest Katherine. I am, indeed. Now my conundrum is to find a way to tutor you and court you—if you will—with honor."

7

First Week, Thursday

David's walk with Kate around the meadow and his change in demeanor had considerably altered her mood. She almost sang with joy as she strolled from Magdalen College to St. Hilda's over the stone bridge that spanned the Cherwell River. She tried to ignore a wolf whistle and beeping horn, but stopped when a familiar voice with an aristocratic accent called out.

"Hello there, Kate! Hop in! I'll give you a lift back." Stuart Devereux pulled alongside her in his sleek black Jaguar. She began to refuse, but he had already unlatched the door and pushed it open.

As she slipped into the leather seat, Stuart glanced at her appreciatively. "Nice skirt, Kate. Your legs look fabulous."

"Thanks," she answered tersely as she tried to hold her skirt down.

"Are you coming from Magdalen, then? Are you reading with MacKenzie again this term?"

"Yes."

"Lucky bloke." He looked over at her again and winked. "But I say, Kate, I'm the lucky one to run into you like this. In fact, I've been wanting to talk to you." He pulled into the circular driveway of St. Hilda's College and parked in front of the old brick Georgian Hall. He leaned back against his door and smiled. "There's a May Day dance Saturday night at the Oxford Union, and I would like it very much if you would go with me."

Kate found it difficult to meet his eyes. "Gee, Stuart, I... appreciate the invitation but I already have plans for Saturday."

"Oh, blast! I knew I should have rung you up earlier. Who's the chap?"

"Wordsworth. I have to get my essay done early because I'll be gone for a few days next week."

"Gone? When you've just arrived? Where are you off to? Sightseeing, are you?"

Kate wished that he wouldn't ask so many questions, or that she had more skill at evasion. "Sort of, yes. I'm going to Cambridge."

"Cambridge? Lovely town. Not far from my country house in Essex, if you remember."

How could I forget that? Or how horribly you behaved? "Yes," she answered. "I do remember. But I haven't been to Cambridge yet."

"I'm sorry I hadn't thought to take you myself. We could have stayed at Clifton Manor. Made a weekend of it." He looked at her quizzically with his green eyes. "With whom are you going, anyway?"

Kate tried unsuccessfully to sound nonchalant. "David...MacKenzie. He's going up to get a new Inklings Society started there."

Stuart stared at her in silent astonishment. Finally he muttered, "MacKenzie? I'll be buggered! You and Mr. MacKenzie..." Then he threw his head back and laughed loudly, the short barking laugh that signaled trouble to Kate. She felt uncomfortably trapped and desperate to escape.

"I don't believe it!" He laughed sardonically. "What an idiot I've been! I should have known. He's always hanging about and fancying himself your Lord Protector. I didn't put it together at all. No wonder he's always acted so stiff with me. This is unbelievable—right under my nose you've been having an affair with MacKenzie!"

Kate's face turned red. "I'm not having an affair! It's not that way at all!"

"Oh, right. You run off to Cambridge with your professor for a little holiday. You'd better watch it, missy. That MacKenzie has always been a snake in the grass."

"Stuart, that's not fair. He's been most...honorable."

Stuart threw his head back again in laughter. "I'm sure he is...'honorable,' as you say, with that stunning fiancée of his." He gave a low whistle. "I saw her at his lecture yesterday. She's quite a looker—well, I have to give it to him. He has good taste in his women."

Kate was indignant. "For your information, they are no longer engaged."

Stuart chuckled. "Ooh, I've hit a hot button there, I can see."

"I've got to go—thanks for the ride." Kate angrily pulled on the handle of her door and started to slide out. Stuart gripped her arm tightly; his face darkened.

"I'm sorry to offend you, Kate. But I do want to warn you. Most men are interested in only one thing." He looked significantly at her skirt and then full in her face until she blushed. His message had hit home. "Don't be naïve and think your Mr. MacKenzie is any different."

~

Connie was sprawled over the sofa in their common living area, stacks of books on either side of her, when Kate came storming through the door.

"Hey, how'd it go?" Connie peered over her wire-rimmed glasses at her obviously flustered friend.

"Terrible." Kate practically threw her books down. "That Stuart Devereux is so infuriating!"

"Stuart? What was he doing there?"

"Oh, he picked me up on the bridge and drove me back. Wanted to ask me to the May Day dance Saturday night." Kate yanked at the zipper on the side of her skirt.

"You're not going with him, are you?"

"No, but now he knows about David, and he said some very nasty things about him."

"Oh, well. I guess you can't blame him for being jealous." She watched Kate slip out of her skirt. "That's a cute skirt," she offered, hoping the compliment would cheer her up.

"You can have it," Kate said, tossing it on the couch. "It's caused me too much trouble. I'm not ever wearing it again."

Connie held it up doubtfully. "I don't think I could fit even one leg in this. But it looks great on you."

"Yeah. That's what Stuart said."

"So, David didn't like it?"

"No. Well, I guess he really did, but he forbade me to wear it again to a tutorial and gave me a lecture about modesty and then we got into a fight over it and then over Charlotte. And I asked him what in the world she was doing at his lecture anyway and he never would answer the question. Refused to answer, really." Kate thrust her legs into a pair of slacks, which she zipped up violently.

"Hmmm." Connie thoughtfully chewed on her pen. "I don't know if that's good or bad."

"Neither did I, so I just walked out."

"Wow. That wasn't much of a 'tut,' was it?"

"Oh, and he also said he wasn't sure if he should even continue to tutor me."

"Why?"

"He said I distracted him too much." Kate could not help smiling.

"The skirt?"

"Well, that was part of it." Kate sank into a chair as a dreamy expression erased her scowl. "But then he chased me out into the quad and asked me to walk with him. He took me down to Addison's Walk, down by the meadow. Have you seen the flowers there, Connie? They're just exquisite. Thousands of tiny purple flowers nodding like bells…or like Wordsworth's daffodils, 'fluttering and dancing in the breeze'…"

Kate sat up excitedly. "Connie, he asked if he could take me to May Morning, but more than that he asked me to go to Cambridge with him on Sunday! He's speaking Monday night to a new Inklings Society that's just getting started, and he asked me to come with him. Naturally, we'll stay in separate colleges, but I get to spend two whole days with David MacKenzie! Of course, that means I have to work like a Turk to get my paper for Miss Goodman done early. That is, if she'll let me. And I haven't even started—"

Her speech was cut short by a knock at the door.

"Come in!" the girls called simultaneously.

The door opened, and in stepped their scout, a broad-faced matronly woman who served as their housekeeper, courier, and even a sort of "den mother." She stood on the threshold, her cheeks flushed with excitement, clutching a bouquet of purple fritillaries.

"This 'ere pretty nosegay is for Miss Kate. A very 'andsome young gent just brought them by with this 'ere note."

Kate jumped up with a cry of delight. "Oh, look, Connie! These are the flowers I told you about. They must be from David." She took the flowers and note. "Thank you, Emma. Aren't they beautiful?"

"They are indeed, Miss. Picked by the gent 'imself, right from the meadow, I warrant. You've got yourself a 'andsome admirer, Miss, to be sure."

"Oh, yes. Thank you, Emma." Kate repeated, as the stout woman closed the door.

Kate ripped open the envelope.

My Dear Kate,

Please accept this token of remembrance from me. My hope is that it will give you inspiration for your Wordsworth essay. I spoke with Yvette and she has agreed to let you miss the tutorial on Tuesday. Please ring her up to schedule an alternate time. My guess is that she will let you turn the paper in when you next meet. I also discussed with her my dilemma about teaching you, and she wisely suggested that you join me with another student for your tutorials. Why don't you come with Nigel Elliot? I meet with him the hour before yours. We are reading Henry V for next week. I hope this will work for you both.

I am very much looking forward to seeing you this weekend for May Morning and especially for our excursion to Cambridge. I will call for you very early Saturday morning—sorry, but it will have to be around 5:00 to beat the crowds at the bridge. Then on Sunday, I'll pick you up before church, and we'll leave directly after the student luncheon. Please pack lightly—remember the boot of my car is small—and bring your mackintosh and umbrella. It always rains in Cambridge.

May the Lord bless you richly, and may He enable you to finish your tasks.

Yours,
David

Kate refrained from kissing the note as she passed it over to Connie, who was eagerly awaiting her turn to read it.

Connie looked up after finishing. "He signed it 'Yours.' Did you notice?"

"Yes, I did." Kate smiled happily as she gazed at the bouquet. "I guess I'd better get started on my Wordsworth."

Second Week, Sunday

Very early on the first day of May, David escorted Kate to Magdalen Bridge. The span stood silently wrapped in a blanket of gray mist laced by dancing torch lights from the bobbing punts on the river. They stood shivering with countless others in the cold morning air, impatiently awaiting the arrival of dawn but warmed by communal cheer and muted laughter. A hush fell on the festive gathering as the first fingers of sunlight touched the slender spires of Magdalen's elegant stone tower. On cue, the choristers, standing high above them on the tower roof, burst into "Te Deum Patrem Colinus," the hymn sung every May morning since Elizabethan times. Then a clamor arose from the riverbanks as town boys blew on tin horns and students bellowed their approval. The choristers raced down the steps of the tower and began to vigorously pull on the bell ropes. Soon bells throughout the city answered with peal after peal. Fountains of champagne spouted from uncorked bottles, and young men—still dressed in their dinner jackets from the previous evening's dances—leaped with abandon into the river. May Day had officially arrived in Oxford.

David treated Kate to breakfast in the nearby Turf Tavern, down a cobblestone alley off Holywell Street, where he kept his own flat. In this warren of wood-beamed and stone rooms snuggled against the ancient city wall, they tried in vain to talk amidst the scores of students still boisterously celebrating. Later, with reluctance, he left her at St. Hilda's so she could read *Henry V* and complete her Wordsworth essay.

On Sunday morning, as promised, David called for Kate before church. He stowed her powder-blue Samsonite overnight bag and matching train case in the trunk of his MG and carelessly tossed his own duffel bag behind the bucket seats.

After the student lunch at St. Aldate's, Kate stepped into the rectory powder room and combed her long dark hair into a ponytail. She knew that as long as the weather held, David would want to keep the top down on his convertible. The prospect of a nearly three-hour drive alone with him had her stomach churning with anticipation and anxiety. She wondered if she would be able to keep up an interesting and entertaining conversation.

She need not have worried. As soon as they passed the outskirts of Oxford, David began to talk. Like a butterfly emerging from his chrysalis, he shed the professional constraints that bound him as a Fellow of Oxford University and became a young man earnestly telling a young woman all about himself. It was as if he wanted to impart his entire life story in the brief time they had alone together. The sluice gates of his soul opened, and out poured a torrent of words, ideas, and memories.

Kate barely spoke, but she didn't mind. She had the advantage of being able to study him unimpeded. In other contexts, she had felt it would be rude to stare at him so, but she loved watching him now: his handsome profile animated with an array of expressions; the glances and smiles he cast her way. And she loved listening to him. She longed to hear his stories as eagerly as he longed to tell them. She yearned to know everything about him; she yearned to embrace his very essence.

The trip passed all too quickly for both of them. As soon as they left behind the rolling hills of the Cotswolds, dotted with sheep and stones, David had to put up the car top. The descent to the flat plain of the fens greeted them with chilly showers. David explained how much of the land of East Anglia had been under water, and that by the engineering genius of the Dutch with their dikes and windmills, the English had reclaimed the marshes as rich, fertile farmland. The flat landscape of wheat fields stretching all the way to the horizon suggested to Kate the prairie lands of America. David theorized to her that the winds of the North Sea could sweep unimpeded across the largely treeless fens, bringing a constant barrage of the chilly, wet weather for which England was renowned. Kate had heard some of this the previous autumn when she had visited nearby Clifton Manor, the country estate of Stuart Devereux, but she prudently didn't mention it.

Then suddenly, rising like a colossus out of the flat countryside, a massive cathedral loomed ahead of them.

"What is it?" Kate exclaimed.

"Ely Cathedral, known as 'the ship of the fens.' I've taken a bit of a detour for you. I think we'll be just in time for Evensong, and I wanted you to see it while it's still daylight because it's quite spectacular."

"Is Ely the name of the village, too?"

"Yes, but first the church was built—on an island in the middle of the marshes. Remember the fens weren't drained in medieval times and all the materials were brought over by boat. Bede's *Chronicles* attributes the name to the huge quantity of eels in the marshes, and the name probably means 'isle of eels.' But there are those who credit the name to St. Dunstan, who—according to the legend—transformed the local monks into eels because of their lack of piety."

As they entered the church, Kate looked up and gasped with delight. The entire ceiling of the long vaulted nave, which stretched endlessly to the transept, was painted predominantly with greens and gold.

Catching her gaze, David answered her unvoiced question. "Victorian."

Kate was amazed. Often Victorian decoration seemed ostentatious and overpowering to her, but the effect of this beautiful ceiling was delicate and light. Just on the edge of her memory hovered some lines from *Hamlet* that would perfectly describe the sight.

"This brave o'erhanging firmament, this majestical roof fretted with golden fire..." David whispered.

Kate smiled at him in puzzlement. *How did you know what I was thinking?*

Placing her hand in the crook of his arm, he led her down the long nave towards the altar, where the light grew steadily brighter. They stood in the transept as light flooded from the brilliant stained-glass windows of an immense octagonal lantern tower rising over them, a seemingly weightless miracle of glass, lead, and stone supported by eight massive pillars. It was breathtakingly beautiful. Awestruck, Kate sighed. One's heart could not help but soar heavenward in such a place.

The couple found seats in the transept across from the boys' choir, whose singing resonated throughout the cathedral—Kate always enjoyed the ethereal purity of boys' soprano voices. As the congregation joined in the opening hymn, David held the hymnbook with her, their fingers lightly touching. She felt a thrill of joy as David's strong baritone mingled with her clear soprano and their voices rose with the others, filling the vaulted roof with praises to God.

The priest began reading the Scriptures and liturgy, and Kate followed the service carefully in The Book of Common Prayer, repeating the appropriate responses with the congregation. David, who had grown up reciting the liturgy as soon as he could speak, had the luxury of rattling off the responses without thought while his mind was far away. Not that his thoughts were far from God. On the contrary, while his lips mouthed the liturgy, he was having his own interior conversation with his Lord.

Father, You know my frame and my failings. And You know my feelings for this precious girl beside me. Oh, God, I am consumed by her! It's overwhelming me. The weight of my love and longing is crushing me...I do believe You have drawn us together. Please make Your will clear to us both. Confirm it in our hearts. And if this is Your will, continue to bind us together with cords of love. And if this is not of You, please show that to us clearly now before our feelings run astray. Not my will, but Thine be done. And keep us from temptation and deliver us from the evil one. Have mercy on me, and give me grace and strength to love her in all purity as Christ loves the church, and to present her as a spotless bride, holy and acceptable unto You...

The organ sounded the chords of the final hymn. David rose from the kneeler and gently took Kate's elbow to help her up. They both smiled.

They reached Cambridge at dusk and dined at Midsummer House, romantically situated in a riverside house and conservatory. This was David's opportunity to treat Kate to their first dinner out together—and he chose what he considered the best restaurant in Cambridge, asking for a table upstairs by a window directly overlooking the River Cam. The setting was undeniably idyllic, and the French cuisine, superb. Kate knew the financial sacrifice David was making to please her, and her heart swelled with gratitude.

They lingered long over their meal and coffee, talking late into the evening. Kate, who usually felt reticent about sharing her inner life, was now the one to pour out her thoughts and memories. She found that David was a good listener as well as communicator, and he seemed genuinely interested in everything she wanted to tell him about herself. Occasionally as she talked, he would reach across the table to play with her bracelet or gently brush a strand of loose hair from her face. Those brief touches, which spoke clearly of his desire to connect, sent butterflies flurrying through her.

Reluctantly, they finally parted. David left her in the care of some girls at Lucy Cavendish College, with a promise to return for her the following morning after breakfast for a day of exploring Cambridge together.

Second Week, Monday

After attending matins in the Magdalene chapel and breakfasting in hall, David appeared at Lucy Cavendish College with two borrowed blue bicycles. Because the road that wound through the university center of Cambridge was closed to traffic during the day, Kate found Cambridge more of a bustling rural village than Oxford's urban metropolis. She felt quite safe on her bike, navigating the winding streets in David's wake.

He took her first to King's College, its wide stone quadrangle dominated by the cathedral-sized chapel. Blackened by years of coal soot, the chapel's stone façade belied the light-filled interior. Kate felt overwhelmed as she stepped inside the sanctuary and looked upwards at the delicate fan vaulting, stretching nearly the length of a football field. She had seen this architectural marvel before at Oxford—in the magnificent stairway of Christ Church's dining hall as well as in the Divinity School Library—but this, she knew, was the largest expanse of fan vaulting in the world. While she gazed up, her studies of Wordsworth's *Prelude* tugged at her memory.

"David," she whispered, as they walked through an intricately carved dark oak choir screen to view Ruben's painting *The Adoration of the Magi*, "didn't Wordsworth write about King's Chapel in *The Prelude*?"

"Yes, he did." David looked pleased with her. "In Book Three, he writes about his undergraduate days at Cambridge and perfectly describes seeing the chapel in the dismal weather here. Let's see, it goes... *'It was a dreary morning when the wheels rolled over a wide plain o'erhung with clouds, and nothing cheered our way 'til first we saw the long-roofed chapel of King's College lift turrets and pinnacles in answering files, extended high above a dusty grove.'* " He looked up at the ceiling appreciatively. "It does cheer the spirits, doesn't it?"

The couple rode their bikes back down King's Parade and stopped to look in the Great Court of Trinity College, where Sir Isaac Newton had conducted his experiments on the speed of sound. Then they carefully threaded their way over the heavily trafficked Magdalene Bridge and parked their bikes in the racks by the Porters' Lodge.

David led Kate into Magdalene's First Court, tiny in comparison to Trinity's. But its fifteenth-century-brick simplicity charmed her. He showed her the lovely but unpretentious chapel and pointed out the rooms above the stairwell that had been C.S. Lewis's for the eight years he served as professor of Medieval and Renaissance Literature at Cambridge.

"I spent a lot of time in those rooms," David mused. "Jack always made time for me and would keep the conversation going through several pots of tea. He loved tea. In fact, the signal that the matins service should be over was Jack's teapot whistling madly away. Every morning, he would give a hurried apology and race upstairs to turn it off. We were always grateful for the signal that the priest should end the service and suspected that Jack did it on purpose to get us to breakfast on time."

They stepped into the narrow passageway connecting the kitchen to the dining hall. Modest in size like the front court, this dining hall was tastefully painted in hunter green with gold trim and hung with the requisite portraits.

"This is where we'll have our meeting tonight after dinner—by candlelight, I might add. We've clung to tradition here, and there's no electric lighting in the hall."

David poked his head into the kitchen, where he bantered with a blushing kitchen maid from whom he cajoled a picnic lunch. Sandwiches and drinks in hand, he motioned Kate to proceed with him to the next court, where they faced a lovely eighteenth century stone building graced by large hanging pots of flowers.

"Have you read any of Samuel Pepys' diaries for Restoration lit or history?" he asked.

Kate nodded.

"Well, Pepys was a student here, and the originals are on display in this building. We'll take a look at them after we eat."

David opened a wooden door in the wall adjoining the Pepys' building, and they stepped into the Fellows' garden. Following the footpath, they settled on a bench overlooking the Cam and unwrapped their sandwiches. David offered a blessing and then began to share more about his days at Cambridge and his unusual friendship with C.S. Lewis.

Just as they finished eating, a sharp wind threatened to end their tranquility with a sudden shower. They dashed up the stairs of the Pepys Library and perused the extensive collection of Samuel Pepys' renowned diaries of seventeenth-century life. Before long, David looked through the windows and caught a glimpse of sunshine breaking through the clouds. He signaled to Kate to follow him outside.

"We need to make hay while the sun shines and go punting," he explained as he stepped into the Porters' Lodge and emerged with keys to the boat sheds.

He held Kate's elbow tightly and reassuringly as they stood on the narrow curb outside the college's main gate, waiting for a break in the traffic. He sensed intuitively that Kate hadn't recovered sufficiently from the trauma of her accident not to be intimidated by the rush of cars and trucks. This strip of road, dividing Magdalene's Hall and Chapel from the courts that accommodated the students' housing, was exceedingly narrow—and even more dangerous than the crossing between Christ Church and St. Aldate's in Oxford, where Kate had been struck down. Trucks and buses roared across Magdalene Bridge with reckless disregard for the pedestrians and cyclists, who pressed against the walls of the college to avoid being run over.

David waited patiently and protectively until he felt assured Kate would feel safe crossing. They passed under an arch into a small, quiet quadrangle of old stone buildings surrounding a perfect green carpet of thick grass. Climbing rose bushes grew along the borders and clung to the walls. Always delighted with the English penchant for filling every available space with flowers, Kate stopped and literally took time to smell the roses.

David pointed out the new brick buildings off to the right of the quad. "Those ugly things in the next quad are the residence halls I lived in. But what they lack in beauty, they make up for in comfort. I had my own bedroom and large sitting room and shared a bathroom and kitchenette with my mate, Kevin. He's stayed on for his graduate studies and is the chap who's launching the Inklings Society here. You'll meet him tonight at dinner."

Carefully staying on the walkways and keeping off the grass, David led Kate across the quad to the bank of the river. Magdalene had its own supply of punts tied to a tiny landing, and he quickly unlocked and readied his craft with the ease of experience.

He confidently poled out into the River Cam while Kate relaxed and leaned back against the cushions of the bow. When he had taken her punting in Oxford, David had told Kate that as a student he had earned extra money by navigating for the tourists through the universities' waterways. She was grateful for his expertise now, as it seemed that as soon as the sun appeared, everyone else in Cambridge had shared David's idea. A small flotilla jammed the narrow canal. Kate couldn't refrain from laughing at the hapless tourists who spun helplessly in circles or rammed each other as they struggled to control the awkward flat-bottomed crafts. David deftly avoided these obstacles and soon had their punt smoothly gliding along as he pointed out the colleges and their 'backs,' the expanses of meadows and gardens bordering the riverbank.

David ducked as they passed under a bridge, and Kate realized it was a tiny replica of the Bridge of Sighs in Venice. Oxford had its own version at Hertford College—but it crossed a cobblestone lane, not a river. Standing in the stern of the punt with the long pole in his hand against the backdrop of the crenellated covered bridge, David reminded her of a Venetian gondolier. Smiling, she told him so.

"Have you been to Venice?" he asked.

"Not yet, but I hope to. Have you?"

"Ah, yes. Wonderfully romantic city." He grinned. "A pity I was there with Austen, which rather spoiled the romance. We did the Grand Tour together during the Long Vacation. Well, not really a *grand* tour. We did the whole bit with backpacks, staying in youth hostels. But it was a splendid holiday. Do you see King's Chapel there over your right shoulder?"

Kate turned to look. "Wow," she said.

"Impressive from the river too, isn't it?" He poled them towards a lovely stone bridge and the bank on the opposite side from King's. Then trying to keep his tone light, he asked, "So, what are your plans after the term? Are you thinking of making the Grand Tour?"

"Well, yes, I'd like to, but I haven't figured it out yet. Connie and I have talked of doing something like you and Austen did, but my parents aren't very keen on two girls traipsing about Europe by themselves." Kate trailed her hand thoughtfully through the water. "My dad wants me to take one of those bus tours, so maybe we'll do that. I don't know what to do, but I guess we'll have to get serious about our plans soon. Do you have any recommendations?" She glanced up at him. His eyes, reflecting the bright spring sky, seemed impossibly blue.

David looked at her with longing. *Come with me!* he yearned to say.

"Uh...no," he answered instead. "There are pros and cons to going with a tour group. Certainly you would be safer with a group but..."

he hesitated and then suddenly blurted, "Oh, Kate, I would love to show you Venice. And Paris. It's an incredible city. Did you know I lived there? My father took a sabbatical for a term when I was in senior school. We lived right in the city—Passy, sixteenth arrondissement. We could see the top of the Eiffel Tower from our kitchen window."

"Really?"

"Yes, it was marvelous." He moored the punt to the bridge and slid the pole along the bottom of the craft. Sitting down, he earnestly fixed his gaze on her. "I would very much like to show you Paris sometime, Kate."

She smiled, pleased at his evident enthusiasm for her company. "First you want to show me Cambridge, now it's Venice and Paris," she teased gently. "Would you like to be my personal tour guide?"

He grinned. "I'd love to."

"No, seriously. Why do you want me to see all these places? Are you thinking about my education, or what?"

"Partly. But, honestly..." He paused, considering. "Honestly, I selfishly want you to be educated about *me.* Cambridge and Paris are a part of me, of who I am. And I don't know—I would just like you to experience them with me, and then you would know and understand me better. It's as if my life is a large house and these places are rooms I want to open the doors to and share with you."

"But I don't think you would want to see Richmond, Virginia, to know me better."

"You're wrong. I would love to see you in your native habitat, as it were. But I do have an advantage over you. Remember that my grandparents live in Virginia. And I have seen William and Mary and have, at least, visited the Capitol Building in Richmond and driven down Monument Avenue. So I can create some pictures in my mind."

He stood up and stepped onto the grassy bank. "Still, I should like to see you in your home, with your parents and sister and brothers. Now, you've had that advantage. You've met my family, even staying at the rectory for a few days." He stretched out his hand to her, and she grasped it, gingerly creeping forward, anxious not to tip over the boat.

"I don't know what it is about traveling, though," he continued. "There's this shared experience that creates a unique bond with fellow travelers because you are seeing and doing all these new things together. Maybe you have experienced that with Connie over here. All I know is that Austen and I were good friends when we set out on our journey, and we came back as brothers. And I suppose that's why I've gone on about hoping to share these places with you."

He held her hand tightly as she stepped out of the punt. Kate felt like a princess disembarking from her barge. She laughed almost giddily. "So, do you really want to share Paris with me?"

David turned her hand over and pressed his lips against her palm. He looked at her steadily. "I want to share everything with you."

Kate's giddiness ceased. She did not know how to answer. She felt her knees go weak, and she faltered. He caught her in his arms. A moment passed. Then another. Kate dared not breathe. His longing was undisguised. Surely now he would kiss her. *Oh, please, David, kiss me!*

He bent down and gently kissed her forehead. Then with a deep sigh, he released her. But he did not let go of her hand.

10

Second Week, Monday Afternoon

David led Kate by the hand up the bank to a vast garden. "This is the Garden of Clare College, one of the prettiest in Cambridge," he explained. "I know how you love flowers, so I wanted you to see it."

Hand in hand, the couple meandered through the hedges and around vast flowerbeds, whose profusion of blossoms and plants spilled over with a variety of colors and textures. Running alongside it all was the river and the backdrop of the spires of the Cambridge colleges. The beauty and serenity of the place evoked a poignant yearning in her heart.

"This may sound crazy," Kate said, "But sometimes when I see the overpowering beauty of God's creation, it pierces my heart. When the sky is so blue and the flowers so bright, the world is so beautiful it almost hurts. Yet even with such beauty before me, I have this intense desire for something even more—but I'm not sure what it is." She glanced at David. "Do you have any idea what I'm trying to say? I mean, do you ever have these feelings?"

"Let's see...when I contemplate exquisite beauty, am I ever pierced to the heart and do I have an intense desire or longing for something more?" His eyes sparkled with mischief. "Yes, I definitely would say so—every time I look at you, in fact."

"David!" she protested. "Be serious."

"I'm being perfectly serious." He smiled. "But, yes—when I'm looking at God's creation as well. The Romantic poets you're studying wrote of it. They would call it 'the sublime.' Lewis also described it. He called it 'joy.' And it was his yearning for joy that drew him to heavenly things. He writes quite a bit about it in *Surprised by Joy.* He would say that the longing we feel is really our longing for heaven and eternity. That we are not mere mortals—we are immortals. And our desire—for the immortal or for something beyond this—is evidence that we are creatures designed for eternity."

"Then I'm not crazy or just being an emotional female."

"Well, I wouldn't go that far." He grinned. "No, seriously, your thoughts put you in good company with poets and philosophers. But here, sit down on this bench for a minute. You can contemplate the beauty of creation while I read you a sonnet."

Pulling a slim volume from the pocket of his brown leather flight jacket, David stretched out on the grass at her feet. He cleared his throat as his entrée and began to read in his deep melodious baritone.

Shall I compare thee to a summer's day?
Thou art more lovely and more temperate:
Rough winds do shake the darling buds of May,
And summer's lease hath all too short a date:
Sometimes too hot the eye of heaven shines,
And often is his gold complexion dimm'd;
And every fair from fair sometime declines,
By chance, or nature's changing course untrimm'd;
But thy eternal summer shall not fade,
Nor lose possession of that fair thou ow'st,
Nor shall death brag thou wander'st in his shade,
When in eternal lines to time thou grow'st;
So long as men can breathe, or eyes can see,
So long lives this, and this gives life to thee.

Kate sighed. "That was lovely. But, what about you? Have you been immortalizing anyone in verse lately?"

"Hmm," David rubbed his jaw. "That's a leading question. The answer is…no…and yes. I have written some poetry, but I doubt it will ever see the light of day to immortalize anyone."

Her eyes lit up eagerly. "You have written about someone?" She almost laughed. "Did you write any poems about me?"

"Do you think I'd tell you?"

"Well, why not? Did you?"

He nodded his head, smiling sheepishly. "Yes," he admitted.

"Will you show them to me?"

"No, definitely not."

"Why not?"

"Because I suspect they're rubbish and it would be dreadfully embarrassing."

"Please, David," she begged. "Your Celtic saga was wonderful. Won't you let me see them?"

"No!" He declared firmly. "At least, not any time soon. The Celtic poems were meant for public consumption. These others are personal. So let's forget it." He grinned at her and changed the subject. "Now how many men do you know who would take a young lady to a garden and read Shakespeare to her?"

"Not many," Kate admitted. "But Colonel Brandon read sonnets to Marianne in *Sense and Sensibility*."

"That's in a book," he countered.

"I'll bet you Mr. Lewis read poetry to his wife."

"Doubtless he did. Well, he probably quoted it from memory." David rolled over on his back and laced his fingers under his head. "You know, my dad read to my mum. Still does. She thinks it's wonderfully romantic."

"Will you still read poetry to your wife after you've been married for years?" Kate asked. "Or just to impress her while you are 'courting,' as you say?"

He smiled. "Hmm...I sense some cynicism. No, Austen tells me I'm an incurable romantic, and I hope I won't change in that regard. Besides," he rolled back over on his side to face her. "Reading poetry is my profession. And the Bible says that he who doesn't care for his wife and family is worse than an infidel. So I may as well fill her soul with poetry as fill her belly with the profits, don't you think?" He plucked a long stalk of grass and chewed on it thoughtfully. "Honestly, I would want to keep my wife happy, and I hope I'll continue to 'court' her as long as I live." Then throwing the stalk down, he said, "But speaking of courtship, there is something I'd like to discuss with you."

Kate held her breath expectantly.

"Back there by the bank when you got out of the punt, I wanted to kiss you so much." He fiddled with the shoelace on her sneaker, not able to meet her eyes. "I don't mean just kiss you on your forehead. But *really* kiss you."

Kate slid off the bench next to him on the grass. She put her hand over his, and he let go of the shoelace. "I wanted that too," she whispered.

"Kate." He rubbed his thumb across her fingers. "What do you think of not kissing until your wedding day?"

Kate felt like the breath had been knocked out of her. "My wedding day! But, why wait till then?"

"You know, the Bible talks about how husbands should love their wives as Christ loves the church. Christ was willing to die for the church to present her as a pure and spotless bride. I've been really convinced that God wants me to come to my wedding day presenting a spotless bride."

Kate didn't like where this was leading. "But doesn't that mean you shouldn't make love to her? Not that you can't kiss her!"

"I've been thinking a lot about the scripture in First Timothy that speaks of treating the younger women as sisters in all purity. Ever since my own sisters went off to college, I've thought about how I want them to be treated and how I'd want to kill any bloke that lays a hand on them."

"But surely they could be kissed, couldn't they?"

"Look at it this way," David said. "If they treat young men as brothers and I treat women as sisters, we wouldn't be kissing them. Not more than a friendly peck, anyway. I try to use that as my standard. I'm affectionate with my sisters, but I certainly would never make out with them."

"But everyone kisses, David. Even Christians make out. It's expected between two people who are dating. As long as they don't go all the way..." She floundered in confusion. "I mean, it's customary to give your date a goodnight kiss."

"Oh, Kate. '*Nice customs curtsy to great kings.*' Why can't we as Christians set a higher standard? Show the world the way courtship should be conducted? Remember Henry V's other line to Princess Katherine, his intended queen? '*Dear Kate, you and I cannot be confined within the weak list of a country's fashion: we are the makers of manners, Kate.*'" David added appreciatively, "Marvelous lines."

"Wait a minute," Kate challenged. "Wasn't Henry trying to convince Katherine that she *should* kiss him before they were married, not the other way around?"

He laughed. "Quite right. I was hoping you wouldn't notice. Still, the words can be used just as well for the reverse argument."

"But I *like* kissing!" Kate admitted.

David sighed and pressed her hand to his lips. "So do I. And I'm afraid that once I kissed you, my dearest Katherine, I couldn't stop at that. And anyway, don't you think it would set a splendid example for a couple to wait for their wedding day for their first kiss?"

Kate considered this for a moment, then said, "Theoretically, yes. But I don't know anyone who has done that."

"I know some who have. In fact, Austen and his wife Marianne did. It was a wonderful witness."

"But if a girl has been kissed before, then what difference would it make if she kisses her fiancé? Why should she save that for her wedding day?"

"Kate, that's the argument non-virgins use for jumping in bed with anyone that comes along. You know that when we ask forgiveness for what we've done wrong, God cleanses us. We can start over with a clean slate."

Kate was upset. She knew in her heart that what he was saying made sense, but her own desires fought the idea. "So, are you saying that you have a clean slate now, since Charlotte?"

"Well, yes," he answered cautiously. "I do."

"Did you hold these same standards with her?" Kate angrily pulled her hand away. "I know you didn't, David. I saw you kissing her that night in your rooms. What else did you do besides kiss?"

David's jaw clenched. "Kate, this is not the time to discuss this."

"Why not? Don't I have a right to know? If you expect me to be so holy, why don't you tell me how well you and Charlotte did? Can't you be honest with me—or are you a hypocrite?"

The shadow of shame clouded David's face. "I can be honest with you, Kate, but I don't want to hurt you."

"So, you did do more than kiss her!" Kate knew she was carrying this too far, but she recklessly forged ahead anyway. "Did you...go all the way with her?"

"I don't want to discuss it now. I don't see where it could lead—except to hurt. All I'll say is that I have regrets. And I don't want us to have any."

"I knew it! You made love to her and you won't even kiss me!" Kate burst into tears. "It's not fair!"

David always felt helpless when women wept, but he knew from his experience with his sisters it was best to let the tears run their course. He pulled Kate to him and held her head against his chest. "Oh, Kate, please don't cry. I'm so sorry. I never wanted to hurt you." He stroked her hair gently, feeling abjectly miserable. "That's why I want to do things *differently* this time."

His gentleness only made her feel even sorrier for herself, and she began sobbing softly. *We've been having the most perfect day and I ruined it. Or he ruined it. Why can't there ever be an entire day that is perfect? Why do I ask stupid questions I don't really want the answers to? To think of him with her! That he didn't save himself, but he expects me to. It's so unfair!*

"Take me home," she finally sniffed.

"To Oxford?"

"No. I know you have the meeting tonight. Just take me back to my room, please. I need to be alone to think."

Second Week, Monday Evening

By mutual consent, David and Kate dined separately in their respective colleges. David spent the rest of the afternoon preparing for his talk to the newly formed Inklings Society of Cambridge. Kate tried to nap on the sofa in the set of rooms she was sharing in Lucy Cavendish College, but ended up staring at the wall while her emotions roiled within her.

After dinner, her hostesses walked her over to Magdalene's Hall for the meeting. She was surprised and heartened by the large turnout. She counted perhaps forty people already seated and more arriving. David had expressed his hope that many students who had actually known Professor Lewis would be interested in coming, and that perhaps they could be persuaded to join the fledgling group.

She could see David making his way through the crowd, heartily greeting people he knew and graciously welcoming those he did not. *He could be a pastor...or a politician...*she thought. His ease at "working the crowd" reminded her of her own father at campaign functions when he had run for Virginia State Delegate. She felt a surge of pride in him.

Suddenly David was squatting beside her chair. "Kate, please wait for me after the meeting. I'd like to see you back."

"Oh, it's okay. I can go back with the girls."

"But I want to talk to you."

Tears filled her eyes. "I'd rather not."

He looked pained and covered her hand with his own. "Kate. We need to talk. *Please.*"

She glanced away without speaking. She did not want to burst into tears again in front of all these people.

"I'm taking you back," David said with a finality that closed off any more discussion. He stood up and strode to the front of the hall, where his friend Kevin was bringing the meeting to order.

At the beginning of his speech, David drew an appreciative laugh from the gathering for commending Cambridge on its great wisdom and foresight in offering C.S. Lewis the chair of Professor of Medieval and Renaissance Literature—as opposed to the bumbling inanity of "the other place," which had passed him over for thirty years. After regaling them with some of his reminiscences of C.S. Lewis as teacher and mentor at Magdalene, David read portions of "De Descriptione Temporum," Lewis's inaugural address to what had been a packed lecture hall of Cambridge students on his 56th birthday. Kate knew that David's melodic baritone did not exactly match Lewis's reputed *basso profundo.* Nevertheless, his delivery was excellent—and if they closed their eyes, those assembled could pretend that Lewis himself was speaking to them.

Enthusiastic applause followed David's rendition, and Kate again felt a tremendous surge of pride in him, conquering her resentment. When the meeting concluded, Kate tried to make her way through the throng of admirers that surrounded him. He spotted her, drew her to his side, and introduced her to Kevin Ryan.

Kevin's laughing blue eyes, strawberry-blond hair, and fair round face sprinkled with freckles reflected the Irish origin of his name. The lilt as he spoke only confirmed it.

"Hello, Katie darlin'. 'Tis a pleasure to meet you at last. MacKenzie has not stopped jabberin' about ye since he arrived and I can see why. Now I can't understand yer botherin' with the likes of him, and if ye change yer mind remember his good mate Kevin Ryan will be waiting for ye." He kissed her hand, flashed a charming crooked smile, and winked.

Amid cheerful banter, the meeting dispersed, and David and Kate started back to Cavendish College. Although chilly, the night was clear, and David made a quick calculation to himself that they would have more time to talk privately if they walked rather than drove. Walking side by side in the darkness would also preclude the necessity of scrutinizing each other's facial expressions. He knew it was sometimes easier to say things frankly without making eye contact. Moreover, this way he could draw her hand through his arm and walk closely beside her.

After eliciting her reactions to the meeting and his address, David took a deep breath and plunged into the issue at hand.

"Kate, I was hoping we could avoid this subject until we knew each other better. I guess I held out some vain hope that we could avoid it altogether. I know it causes you pain—and believe me, to even speak of it causes me great pain and shame as well. But since we have opened Pandora's box, as it were, I think it's best to bring it out in the open."

Kate's response was silence. She still didn't trust herself to speak. David correctly interpreted her silence as an assent to continue.

"I met Charlotte my third and final year here at Cambridge. I was dreadfully infatuated with her. I can see now that my attraction was completely 'eros,' or physical. We weren't ever soul mates or kindred spirits, and we certainly never shared anything spiritually. I rather stupidly thought that God had brought her into my life so that I would be the means of saving her, and I began the relationship with a naïve zeal to win her to faith.

"But it wasn't long before the opposite occurred. She began to draw me away from my friends and any Christian fellowship. She enjoyed going to parties or meeting with her friends at pubs, and I wanted to keep her happy. And I thought I *was* happy. Jack and my parents became very concerned and tried to warn me, but I had gotten too involved to listen. I convinced myself that they were being narrow-minded or too judgmental and that I shouldn't pay attention to them."

He paused, remembering how Kate had argued with him in a like manner when she had been dating Stuart Devereux. "If I recall correctly, you said some similar things to me before you went off to that house party in Essex last autumn."

"You're right, I did," Kate replied.

"Anyway, after I took my undergraduate degree here, I went back to Oxford for my graduate studies. Charlotte had no intention of leaving Cambridge, and we carried on a long-distance relationship for that first year. During the second year, I began to suspect she was seeing other men back here—and she as much as threatened to break things off with me if we weren't engaged. Stupidly, in desperation I proposed to her over the objections of my parents, Jack, and even my close friends like Austen and Kevin."

He paused, considering how much to reveal. Sighing heavily, he continued. "So, we maintained the long-distance relationship, visiting each other on weekends whenever we could. And since we were engaged, we became more physically involved. It was something she wanted, but I take full responsibility for letting it happen. I rationalized to myself that since we were going to be married, in the end it wouldn't matter. It was the same sort of foolish thinking that had me convinced that, at some point, she would come to share my faith—although sadly my witness had long been negated by my immature and selfish behavior. And things remained in this murky quagmire of immorality until Jack died and I came face-to-face with my own mortality and disobedience. I did share with you about Jack's funeral and the impression that the candle, burning so stalwartly in the cold, made on me?"

Kate nodded.

"So, as you know, that very day I made a commitment—a recommitment really—to dedicate my life to God. And that was the beginning of the Inklings Society—and the end of my engagement to Charlotte."

They were crossing a bridge now, and David stopped to lean on the railing and watch the river flow by. He spoke very quietly. "I can never express to you the depths of my regret. I am so very, very sorry. Would you—could you—find it in your heart to forgive me, Kate?"

Kate silently stared at the water. She did not want to forgive him. She wanted to cling to the hurt and make him suffer even more.

"Kate. *Please* forgive me." He put his hand under her chin and lifted up her face. Tears were coursing down her cheeks.

"Okay," she whispered. "I will."

He wrapped his arm around her, and she cried softly in his embrace. After a few minutes she sniffed. "Do you have a handkerchief?" She laughed as she brushed away her tears. "I'm afraid I'm ruining your father's RAF jacket."

David promptly produced one, and Kate blew her nose.

"Kate, I know this has hurt you terribly, and although you and God have forgiven me, I also know this will always haunt me. And it's because I never want to cause such pain to anyone else that I have made a solemn commitment to God to conduct my relationships in absolute purity from now on. Even if we think we may marry a certain person, I know now that we don't have any guarantees until we're actually standing at that altar. It may not work out, or it may not be God's will."

"But," Kate objected, "does that mean you can't even kiss until you get married? Isn't that being legalistic? I mean, do you think kissing is sinful?"

"No, not in and of itself," David replied. "Of course, the Bible says to 'greet one another with a holy kiss,' and I think every couple has to work out just how much kissing—if any—keeps them in a pure relationship. I'm not legalistically saying, 'No one should ever kiss before they are married.' But I do know that God does have a stricter judgment for teachers, and I am a teacher of Christianity, not just literature. I know people watch me—either hoping I'll mess up and discredit my faith, or hoping to see that it *is* possible to live one's life by biblical principles. I just think that being able to say, 'They saved their first kiss until their wedding day,' would attest so strongly to the fact that, even in this era of free love, it is still possible, by the grace of God, to keep oneself pure."

But Kate had another argument. "I have friends who say that sex is like a long corridor—and that kissing and making out are like opening doors down that corridor. And that it would be too much for a couple to go through all the doors at once on their wedding night. That they should experiment and open some of the doors first."

David shook his head. "Right. That sounds like a line some bloke came up with to convince his girlfriend that they should mess around. I've known plenty of people who have rushed through all the doors on the first date without any trouble. I've also known plenty of girls who have given themselves away too easily and were bitterly disappointed. With all the counseling my father has done, I can assure you that experimentation *before* marriage has little to do with sexual satisfaction *in* marriage. On the contrary, the wonderful thing about marriage is that you have a lifetime to work on your love life. My dad also asserts that a man's faithfulness to premarital purity will be a good indication of his remaining faithful when married."

Kate nodded and sighed resignedly. "Okay, you win."

David gently twisted a strand of her hair between his fingers. "It's not a question of *me* winning. It's *us* winning. I can't do this without you, Kate. The Lord knows what a weak and sinful man I am. I need your help. If you can't agree to this, then I am undone."

"All right, David." She looked up at him and smiled. "I agree."

"Really?" Relief and joy spread across his face. "You're wonderful. Oh, Kate, I could kiss you for that!"

The irony of his declaration hit them both, and they burst into laughter.

12

Second Week, Tuesday

The next morning dawned wet and gray in customary fashion but failed to daunt David and Kate as they pedaled their bicycles through Cambridge's twisting streets. They admired the half-timbered President's Lodge in the original Tudor courtyard of Queens' College, and walked over the famous Mathematical Bridge that once had been constructed without any screws or fastenings, but held together merely by mathematical principles. They lingered longer over the art treasures in the Fitzwilliam Museum. Kate was particularly delighted to see original drawings and manuscripts by William Blake, whose work she was reading in her study of the Romantic Poets.

The weather eventually cleared, and they happily biked along the River Cam to the small village of Grantchester, where they lunched in the Orchard, the picturesque pub frequented by poet Rupert Brooke. The conversation and laughter flowed easily, and their time together seemed all too brief for all they wanted to share. As they drove back to Oxford, and the flat fens rose into the rolling hills of Oxfordshire, a sobering awareness settled on them that they must soon resume their roles and responsibilities as student and tutor.

David was pleased, however, with what had been accomplished both professionally and personally on their excursion. Besides helping to launch the Cambridge Inklings Society, he had reached some important conclusions about Kate. She had acquiesced to his commitment to conducting their courtship in a chaste manner, and he was more convinced than ever that she was indeed the life partner he had longed for. She silently shared this unspoken conviction. They both returned to Oxford with hearts full and hopes high.

Before dropping her off at St. Hilda's, David elicited two promises from Kate: that she would come to cheer him on at his next football match, and that she would accompany him to the Magdalen Fellows' Dinner Dance during Eights Week.

David planned to keep his routine meeting with Austen and Yvette for dinner at the Eagle and Child before their weekly Inklings gathering. But first, he stopped by his Magdalen rooms to review his lecture notes. Humming happily to himself, he glanced through the papers stacked on his desk and was surprised when his scout Watson poked his head through the door.

"Excuse me, sir," The bald middle-aged man always addressed his much younger don with the utmost deference. "Welcome back, Mr. MacKenzie. Did you have a good trip to the other place, sir?"

"Yes, thank you, Watson. I did," David answered smiling. "A splendid trip."

"Very good, sir. Before I leave, I wanted to be sure to give you this message President Palmer sent over this afternoon." He handed David an envelope.

Puzzled, David asked, "Do you know what this is about, Watson?"

"No, sir. Haven't the foggiest. Will that be all, Mr. MacKenzie?"

"Ah, yes, Watson," David replied in a distracted manner. "Thank you. I'll see you in the morning." He tore open the envelope and quickly read a summons to an interview with the college president at nine o'clock the next morning.

"What the deuce?" he asked aloud. He could not fathom why he had been called up. It seemed too early in the term to discuss student progress or his lecture topics. Had he inadvertently done something wrong? Or was he to be commended for something? David wished he could talk to Dr. Palmer right away; but even if he had planned to dine in hall, the president only rarely came to dinner. There was nothing to be done before morning. As much as David hated putting things off, he would just have to stay in suspense. *Possess my soul in patience,* he told himself as he slipped the message into his jacket pocket and headed to the Eagle and Child.

~

" 'Ello, mates." David cheerily affected a cockney accent as he put his plate down on the table and slid into the seat next to Austen. "How is everyone this evening?"

Yvette looked up from her dinner and returned the greeting with a smile. " 'Ello, mate. How was your trip to the other place?"

"Splendid! The Cambridge Inklings Society has officially begun—and with quite a bit of interest." He went on to share the details as he rapidly vanquished his roast beef and Yorkshire pudding.

Yvette hesitated and then asked, "And how did it go with your American friend?"

"Equally splendid!" David beamed. "We were able to spend quite a bit of time together and really got to know one another. Only one dispute, and we resolved that fairly quickly, I think. Anyway, I'm more convinced than ever that she is *the one*."

Yvette and Austen exchanged glances.

"David," Yvette said slowly. "Would you please get me some coffee?"

"Certainly. Austen?"

Austen shook his head. "I'm fine."

David went to the back of the pub and ordered two coffees with cream at the bar. Reaching into his jacket pocket for his wallet, he felt the letter from President Palmer. He pulled it out, puzzled over it again, and carried it back to their table along with the steaming mugs of coffee. Austen and Yvette were leaning over the table whispering furiously, but broke apart as soon as he returned.

"You know, this is really rather odd," David said as he tossed the envelope on the table, "but Watson brought me this message from President Palmer this afternoon. He wants to see me straight after breakfast tomorrow morning. I don't recall ever being called up before." David shoveled raw sugar into his coffee. "Can't for the life of me think why he wants an interview. I still feel like enough of a kid to wonder if I've done something wrong and am being called on the carpet. I just wish I knew what it was."

Austen glanced over the missive and then pensively tapped it on the tabletop. He and Yvette exchanged glances again. David took notice.

"What is it? Do you know something?"

Yvette looked down and stirred her coffee. She would let Austen do the talking; he was the older friend.

Austen ran his finger over the edge of the envelope. "Yes. But it may or may not have anything to do with your summons."

"Well, what it is it? Out with it, man!"

Austen looked at his friend steadily but sadly. "Since you left for Cambridge, old boy, there's been talk. The buzz must have started in the Senior Common Room at Magdalen and found its way over to Merton and apparently to St. Hilda's as well. Both Yvette and I have tried to quell it, but you know how rumors take on a life of their own and..." He hesitated and looked down.

"Go on."

Austen took a deep breath. "People have been saying that you...had an assignation in Cambridge with one of your students."

David silently stared at him.

"That you're having an affair with one of your students." Austen rephrased it.

"People are saying," David clarified in disbelief, "that Kate and I are...?"

"Yes...more or less," Austen uneasily concurred.

David put his head in his hands. "Unbelievable!" After a moment he looked up. "Do you know, the one argument we had was about staying completely chaste in our relationship? She wanted to kiss. I *want* to kiss her, but we agreed to deny ourselves even that liberty in order to be absolutely above reproach. And here we're being accused of this!" He shook his head. "The irony of it all. *Incroyable!*"

"You mean to tell me you haven't kissed her?" Yvette questioned him incredulously.

"No! I haven't!" David closed his eyes and slid dejectedly down in his seat. "I told her I want to save the kiss for my wedding day."

"You mean your very first kiss won't be until you're married?" Yvette asked.

David nodded.

"Are you batty? I've never heard of anyone doing that!"

David and Austen's eyes locked in silent understanding. "I have," David said. An appreciative smile played around Austen's mouth. He gave David an encouraging nod.

"I don't get it," Yvette continued undeterred. "What's so romantic about having your first kiss in front of all those people?"

David couldn't help smiling. "It's not about what's romantic, Yvette. It's about what's right—what's right for me in terms of setting an example for others to follow—but now..." His jaw tightened. "I'm not much of an example if people believe this rot." He felt a surge of indignation. "Who started these beastly rumors anyway?"

Austen shook his head. "Don't know. The buzz from the S.C.R. was that someone went straight to the President."

"Someone who wants me to lose my job, perhaps? Why would anyone do such a thing?"

"'*Blessed are you when men revile you and persecute you and utter all kinds of evil against you falsely on my account,*'" Yvette quoted in an attempt at consolation.

"Losing my job won't be much of a blessing," David replied grimly. He looked at his friends imploringly. "You will vouch for me?"

"Of course," they both assented.

"You say this has spread to St. Hilda's, Yvette? Are the students talking too?"

She nodded.

"Oh, Lord, help us." David agitatedly pressed both his hands to his forehead. "And here I've been so self-pitying and worried for my own reputation that I haven't thought about Kate. If she's caught wind of any of this, she won't want to show her face at tonight's meeting. But that would only seem like an admission of guilt. She's got to come!" He pushed his chair back. "Austen, you cover for me. I'm going to go get her."

Yvette reached across the table to stop him. "David, just wait a minute. If you go charging over to St. Hilda's now, you'll just cause a big scene. What are you going to do? Bang on the doors for her to come out?"

David sank back down dejectedly. "What shall I do?"

"You and Austen start the meeting same as always. I'll bring Kate."

They had correctly surmised what Kate's reaction would be to any disapprobation from her fellow students. Yvette found her ensconced in her room weeping. She gently prodded Kate to make herself presentable and come with her to the meeting.

David had been anxiously watching the students file into the Eagle and Child for the Inklings Society meeting. As Connie came in, he searched her face for some clue as to Kate's welfare. Connie caught his eye and shook her head as she sat down beside Nigel.

Austen opened the meeting with some comments about Charles Williams and a reading from *Taliesin to Logres.* David remained uncharacteristically quiet during the ensuing discussion of the complicated poem. Then Austen invited David to share about the inception of the Cambridge Inklings Society. David wondered if he was being hypersensitive, but there seemed to be some constraint in the students' reception of his talk. Was it his imagination, or were some of the young men elbowing each other and snickering?

His suspicions were confirmed when Yvette and Kate slipped into the back of the room. Their arrival set off a hubbub that interrupted his remarks. Kate looked crushed. His heart was torn in compassion and was then filled with indignation. He could understand someone disliking him and trying to wreck his reputation, but why would anyone want to hurt Kate? He had silently debated all evening whether or not to address the issue. Austen was inclined to leave it alone because of the potential of highlighting the allegations and causing further embarrassment to Kate. But David was not one to leave things alone.

"Welcome, ladies," he addressed Yvette and Kate directly. "Thank you for coming." He tried to give Kate a reassuring smile, then turned back to address the gathering. "I was just telling the group about our sister society in the other place. And since I'm on that topic, I feel it is imperative that I address an issue that has come to my attention tonight." He took a deep breath and plunged in.

"I don't wish to embarrass Kate Hughes by mentioning this, but it is incumbent upon me to speak. Some of you know that I invited her to accompany me to Cambridge. Some of you might also be aware that a vicious rumor has been circulating that Kate and I stayed together in Cambridge and that we are involved in an illicit relationship. I want to state publicly and emphatically that this is a pernicious lie with absolutely no basis in truth." David's eyes flashed, defying anyone to say otherwise. Except for the clink of glasses and murmur of conversation from the bar, the back room of the pub was silent.

"Permit me to state the facts clearly. Kate did go with me to Cambridge, but we did not stay together. She stayed at Lucy Cavendish

College and I stayed at Magdalene...and we both kept the college curfews. We were not alone except in a public setting. Now since most of you are friends or students of mine, I will make a confession that will not come as a surprise to very many of you. "

Kate glanced up at this and caught David's gaze.

"I confess I do care very deeply for Kate," he continued, looking at her. "And because I do, I have determined to treat her with the utmost respect and honor. Part of that means staying above reproach in my conduct. And that includes standing here before you and defending her reputation." David squared his shoulders and boldly eyed the quiet gathering. "Now most of you know that the Inklings were Christians, as are Kate and I and many of you. And because we are representatives of Christ, our reputations are very important to us. So I would humbly implore you, if you do hear any such rumors, to silence them with the truth. And if the perpetrators persist, tell them I will have words with them, face-to-face."

David surveyed the room of students and felt reassured by their heads nodding in visible support. "Thank you. I think that's all I have to say." Relieved, he sat down and turned to Austen to close the meeting.

"Mr. MacKenzie?" Nigel flashed his toothy grin. "If we do discover the perpetrators of this rumor, may a few of us mates rough them up a bit?"

"No, thank you, Nigel. That wouldn't be a very Christlike response, now would it? But"—David smiled grimly—"I would be happy to challenge them to a rugby match."

Knowing grins and guffaws broke the tension in the meeting.

Well, I've got the students on our side, David thought. *Now all I have to do is convince President Palmer.*

Second Week, Wednesday

David decided to dress conservatively for his morning interview with Dr. Palmer. Although his dark, wavy hair still curled unconventionally over his shirt collar, he had put aside his comfortable Levi's and penny loafers and chose instead the frumpy flannel trousers and British brogues of the traditional Oxford don. Straightening his Magdalen College tie and pulling on his Harris Tweed jacket, he strode through the cloisters from the Hall and across the lawn to the nineteenth-century stone building appropriately dubbed "The President's Lodgings."

In the ground-floor office, a gray-haired, bespectacled secretary greeted him with a coquettish smile. David was charmingly oblivious to his good looks, which made him a great favorite with women of all ages.

"Hello, Mr. MacKenzie. You're right on time."

"Hello, Mrs. Dalrymple. Top of the mornin' to you. You look very chipper today."

The middle-aged secretary blushed. "Thank you, Mr. MacKenzie. President Palmer is expecting you. You may go right in."

David knocked on the oak door and waited to hear Dr. Palmer's greeting.

"Come in, my boy. Please be seated. Tea or sherry?"

"Tea would be fine, thank you, sir." David traded pleasantries with the college president as he took the cup of tea. Anxious as he was to have the interview over, he knew that the social protocols had to be patiently observed.

President Palmer was a tall gentleman with silver hair and the large nose and ears that characterized many of his countrymen. His stature and demeanor were as intimidating as his position. But he was a just and kind man, and David felt confident that his case would be fairly heard.

After inquiring about David's latest football match, Dr. Palmer was finally ready to address the purpose for the interview. "Well now, David, I suppose you are wondering why I called you up today."

David put his teacup down. "Yes, sir. I must confess I've wondered whether I was to receive a commendation or a condemnation."

"*Probitas laudatur et alget*," the college president intoned.

David quickly translated. "'Goodness is praised.' Well, then I shall hope for a commendation, as I am not aware of any wrongdoing."

"Well—" Dr. Palmer coughed, picking a piece of lint off his trousers. "I am sorry to tell you that you have become the subject of some unsavory gossip that has been circulating among the Common Rooms."

Oh, boy. Here we go.

David waited.

"But knowing your stellar reputation, I thought it incumbent upon me not to give credence to this gossip without first ascertaining the facts from you."

"I appreciate that, sir. What would you like to know?"

Dr. Palmer cleared his throat. "Did you go up to Cambridge this week?"

"Yes, sir."

"To what purpose?"

"You may be aware, sir, that I—along with Austen Holmes, Merton Fellow in Anglo-Saxon—sponsor a club called the Inklings Society. We meet weekly to read and discuss the works of the original Inklings, the informal literary club that C.S. Lewis began here at Magdalen before the war. Anyway, since Lewis did become a professor at the other place, there has been a tremendous interest for a similar club there. You may recall that I took my undergraduate degree from Magdalene, Cambridge, and studied there with Professor Lewis. I went up there because I was invited to give the inaugural address at the Cambridge Inklings Society on Monday evening."

Dr. Palmer nodded. "Did one of your female students accompany you?"

"Yes, sir. But…excuse me, sir. Let me be frank with you, because I can guess where this is going. Last night Mr. Holmes apprised me of rumors he had heard, and I can assure you there is no truth to them whatsoever. I did invite Katherine Hughes from St. Hilda's to go with me. She is one of my students, and she is a member of the Inklings Society. She stayed at Lucy Cavendish College, and I stayed in the Fellows' Guest quarters at Magdalene. We kept the curfews, and I can have the porters attest to that, if you like. I can also have Mr. Holmes and Miss Goodman from St. Hilda's, as well as Kevin Ryan, a Fellow at Magdalene, vouch for the purpose of the trip and my conduct."

Dr. Palmer waved his hand dismissively. "That won't be necessary. But was taking this student purely academic or was there a personal element involved?"

"Frankly, there was a personal element as well. However, we were not alone together, except in public places."

"And in your car?"

"Yes, sir. We were alone in my car. But sir, I drive an MG Midget."

Dr. Palmer could not repress a smile. "So, you are telling me that you would not have had the opportunity of doing what you are accused of?"

"Yes, sir. And that is by deliberate design. Just as I don't tutor female students alone with the door to my rooms closed. I purposely avoid even the appearance of impropriety. Believe me, sir—I have been overzealous in this regard, and this is why I have taken such umbrage at these accusations."

"Nevertheless, you did invite this girl to go with you to Cambridge, and perhaps you had been wiser not to."

David could not reply. He did not regret the invitation.

"Permit me to ask you another question."

David nodded his acquiescence.

"Are you in love with this girl?"

David looked at him steadily. "Yes, sir, I am. I intend to marry her."

The older man raised his eyebrow. "Really?"

"Yes. And because I love her, I have not dishonored her and will not. You have my word on that."

Dr. Palmer thoughtfully poured himself another cup of tea. After silently stirring in his milk and sugar and taking a sip, he spoke. "I believe you, David, and I suspect that the source of these rumors is some jealous student. I certainly hope they didn't originate with the faculty. But you must be even more circumspect to avoid aggravating this. Perhaps we should find another tutor for the girl."

David's stomach tightened. "I've considered that and even suggested it to Miss Hughes. But she specifically returned from America this term to read Shakespeare with me, and so I have arranged for her to join a tutorial group. We will not be alone, even for tutorials."

Dr. Palmer nodded. "You have acquitted yourself well, David. I shall let you go, but with a warning to watch yourself."

David rose and shook his hand. "Thank you, sir, I shall."

"And, David," Mr. Palmer's voice arrested him at the door. "When shall I meet this young lady of yours?"

David smiled. "At the Fellows' Dinner Dance, sir."

"Very well. Now off to your lecture." Dr. Palmer said kindly, waving his hand. "I've heard excellent reports about them. And we don't want you starting more rumors by showing up late."

"No, sir. Thank you and good day, sir." David stepped out the door, pausing long enough to let out a sigh of relief.

"Everything all right, Mr. MacKenzie?" the president's secretary asked coyly.

"Couldn't be better, Mrs. Dalrymple. Couldn't be better." David flashed a broad smile that made the matron's day.

~

David dashed back to his rooms in the New Building to grab his lecture notes and slip on his black nylon tutor's robe over his sports coat. He raced down the stairs and across the quad. Then, unlocking his bicycle from the rack near the Porters' Lodge, he edged out onto the street. Pedaling furiously, he joined the throng of students whizzing by on their bikes. With their black robes flapping behind them, they looked like a flock of ravens flying down the High Street.

After delivering his lecture to an enthusiastic audience at the Examination Schools, David joined a group of students for coffee. Nigel and Connie were part of the group, as was Kate. In the hubbub of the crowd, David and Kate were able to talk quietly together without drawing attention to themselves. It comforted David to see that the sparkle had returned to her eyes. She relayed how Yvette had gone to the Principal at St. Hilda's and the rumors there had been subsequently squelched. David, in turn, shared about his interview with Dr. Palmer and his expectation that the truth would quickly filter down through the Common Rooms. They both expressed relief that this storm seemed to have blown over without too much apparent damage.

David then wondered aloud about the source of such malicious gossip. Kate had thought much on this. She had recalled her uncomfortable exchange with Stuart Devereux when he had given her a ride home from Magdalen Bridge. But she did not think it would be prudent to raise David's ire with this suspicion, so she held her peace.

The group broke up quickly as each had to return to studies or tutorials before lunch. David surreptitiously gave Kate's hand a parting squeeze under the table. Then he hopped on his bike and rode to

Blackwell's Bookshop on Broad Street to pick up a reference book he had ordered.

On his way out, he stopped at the sale table to look over the bargains. He caught a whiff of Chanel No. 5 and glanced over to see an attractive woman with shoulder-length red hair bending over the table.

He swallowed hard. "Charlotte."

She looked up with pleased recognition. "David, darling! You naughty boy. I'm quite surprised to see you showing your face in public after the terrible things I've heard about you lately. And to think you turned me down so coldly and then ran off with your little American without so much as a by-your-leave," she scolded. "I must confess I was rather shocked and hurt when I heard. I mean how could you be so hypocritical?"

David's reply had an edge to it. "I thought you knew me better than to believe such rubbish. From whom did you hear this, anyway?"

"Oh, no one in particular. Just the usual dining-hall gossip. So it isn't true?"

"Absolutely not."

"But you did go up to Cambridge? And with her?"

David sighed and then recited again his litany of explanation.

"Well, I feel much better not to have been totally ditched and lied to. But tell me"—she tossed her hair over her shoulders—"have you been called up by any of the faculty for this?"

"I talked with President Palmer this morning and was able to clear things up."

"And he believed you?"

"Why shouldn't he?"

"Oh, I guess I was secretly hoping he would send you packing and you would be back to Cambridge looking for a job."

A faint suspicion flitted across David's mind. "I'm flattered. But things are going excellently here. Well," he said, picking up his parcel from the book table, "I don't want to miss lunch so I'd best get going."

"Certainly. I'm glad to hear of your innocence and vindication. I'll..." Charlotte's voice trailed off as she grimaced and put her hand to her forehead.

David looked at her with concern. "Are you all right, Charlotte?"

"I'm fine," she answered faintly. "It's nothing. I...just feel...so... queer..." She closed her eyes and swayed unsteadily.

In a flash, David was beside her. With a moan, she crumpled into his arms.

"Oh, my word! Charlotte, what's wrong? Here, you should sit down." He practically carried her to a chair and called for the clerk to fetch some water. "Lean over," he said soothingly, "and put your head down to your knees."

She meekly obeyed, slumping over for a few minutes. Then after accepting a sip of water, she murmured, "This is so embarrassing. Please don't make a fuss over me, David. I'll be fine, really."

"What's wrong? Do you know?"

Charlotte leaned over, her head in her hands. "No, my head has been hurting a lot lately, and then suddenly, I felt very faint. It happened a few days ago as well. But then I felt fine. I thought I was over it."

"You should see a doctor. Do you want me to fetch my car and take you to the infirmary?"

"Oh, don't be silly. I'll be fine in a few minutes. Besides, I have to get back for lunch as well."

"But you're in no shape to get yourself back to college."

"Don't be so dramatic. It's nothing, really," she chided. "You go along to lunch. I'm a big girl and can get back just fine."

"At least let me hail a taxi for you."

"All right," she relented.

David flagged down a taxi and gently helped Charlotte out to the curb and into the backseat of the waiting vehicle. Handing the cab driver some pound notes, David directed, "This young lady is ill. Take her to the Porters' Lodge at Somerville and see that she gets proper attention, won't you?"

The driver tipped his cap. "Right, mate."

"David." Charlotte leaned her head back on the seat and smiled faintly. "You've been such a dear. I'll be fine. Don't you worry."

But he did.

Fifth Week, Trinity Term
Friday, May 28, 1965

During the next three weeks leading up to Eights—the annual spring intercollegiate boat races and festivities—David and Kate fell into a routine of activities that they followed more or less until the end of term. As a student, she attended lectures and spent long hours reading, researching, and writing papers. As a Fellow, his routine held little difference, except that he was the one giving the lectures and tutorials and marking the papers. But he too had to spend hours reading and researching in preparation. They managed, however, to devise activities that would allow them to see each other every day and to spend time together—but not alone.

On Monday evenings, they would meet as if by accident in the Radcliffe Camera, the octagonal domed reading library. They sat studying across from one another at a large reading table—Kate diligently working on her paper for the Romantics, David interrupting her studies by teasingly passing her notes or playing footsie under the table. Then they would stroll across Radcliffe Square and stop in the King's Arms or the Turf Tavern for a late-night snack and quiet talk before he walked her home across Magdalen Bridge.

On Tuesdays after her Romantics tutorial with Yvette Goodman, Kate always looked forward to the Inklings Society meetings at the Eagle and Child. She devoted Wednesday afternoons to preparing her

Shakespeare essay, while David helped to coach the Oxford University football matches. If the game were played at home, David would join Kate, Connie, and Nigel afterwards for St. Aldate's midweek fellowship dinner and Bible study.

Thursday was the day for their Shakespeare tutorial. Kate wondered how she would view sharing that time with another student, but her apprehensions were unfounded. Nigel contributed his unique insight and sense of humor, and their discussions were lively and stimulating. Sharing another person's perspectives and criticisms challenged her to grow as a writer and a scholar. Occasionally, Connie would join them, and their conversation would flow into the dinner hour, buoyed up by goodwill and pots of tea.

On Friday afternoons, Kate would gather a group of students to cheer David on at his football matches for the University Staff team at Mansfield Road. She began to share the English enthusiasm for soccer, especially since her man made the game so exciting with his playmaking prowess and propensity for goal scoring.

Saturday was field trip day. David would organize an outing, and Kate would invite her friends to join them. With Yvette and sometimes Austen as added chaperones, they visited Winchester, Salisbury, and Wells cathedrals, Warwick and Sudley Castles, Stonehenge and Amesbury, and attended plays in London.

But Sunday was their favorite day of all. They would attend the morning service at St. Aldate's, stay for the student luncheon, and then relax at the rectory in the afternoon with the MacKenzie family. Often Annie asked them to stay for supper, and once or twice, Kate had the courage to do the cooking. Afterwards they would attend Evensong at St. Aldate's, if David wasn't needed to read at Magdalen's service. Kate always felt at home at the MacKenzies and enjoyed watching David with his family. And Annie and Eric MacKenzie had the wisdom to give the young couple some time alone.

So David and Kate developed a routine as they deepened their relationship—seeing each other in different contexts and learning more about each other through their conversations and their interactions with others. But always they were circumspect, to avoid even the appearance of evil. And always they were mindful to keep their distance to avoid the temptation of yielding to their desires.

They both highly anticipated the Magdalen Fellows' Dinner Dance held on the Friday evening of the Eights boat races. Magdalen's Senior Common Room was renowned for its well-stocked wine cellar and the excellence of its cuisine on such formal occasions. It was an event the entire college staff looked forward to, and Kate knew its importance to David in presenting her to his colleagues.

The dinner was a black-tie affair, and Kate chose her evening gown carefully. She wore a long, emerald-green satin sheath with a matching wrap. She had debated about wearing her hair up in a French twist, and then remembering how much David loved her long hair, she decided to wear it down, tucking tiny pearl pins in the tresses and matching them with her pearl necklace and earrings.

David expressed his approval. "Whoa! You look...absolutely *stunning*." He took a deep breath and exhaled slowly. "I can't believe that someone so beautiful would want to be with me."

"Oh, come now," Kate was embarrassed but pleased. "In that tux, you're not so bad yourself."

"Well, having you with me will certainly improve the old guard's impression of me." He tucked her hand in his arm. "Thank you for coming with me tonight, Kate. I'm sure going to a stuffy dinner party with a bunch of crusty old men is not your idea of fun. But this means a lot to me."

She smiled up at him. "It means a lot to me, too. Thank you for inviting me."

They had entered the cloister and could see the dons and their elegantly dressed wives and dates gathering in the center lawn—a perfectly rolled, thick carpet of grass. The evening sky had turned a bright midnight blue above the crenellated molding of the Hall roof. The soft strains of Handel from a string quartet floated across the quad and intermingled with the hushed conversations. Waiters in white dinner jackets carried silver trays loaded with hors d'oeuvres and crystal goblets of wine.

Kate squeezed David's arm and sighed, "Isn't Oxford wonderful?"

He smiled. "'Tis indeed. But we can't just stand here soaking up the ambience. We do have to be sociable as well. Are you ready?"

She tilted her head with a look that said, "Of course," and he escorted her to the receiving line for the Board of Regents. Kate duly bestowed her most charming smile on those she met as she proceeded down the line, shaking hands and turning heads.

"President and Mrs. Palmer," David was saying, "may I present Katherine Hughes?"

With a twinkle in his eye, Dr. Palmer kissed her hand. His wife, a handsome woman with ash-blonde hair who looked a decade younger than her husband, patted Kate's hand enthusiastically.

"You know, my dear," she whispered leaning her head close to Kate's. "My husband, Charles, doesn't like this bandied about, but he was *my* tutor before the war. So don't let all these old fogies scare you off." To David she spoke more loudly. "She's absolutely lovely, David. Don't you dare let her slip away."

David beamed. "I don't intend to, Mrs. Palmer."

They drifted out onto the lawn, taking the proffered refreshments and making introductions. After a time of small talk, David turned to Kate. "They'll be at this for some time before going in to dinner. Would you walk with me for a few minutes?"

Kate nodded and then glanced down at her high heels.

"Don't worry. We shan't go far." He offered his arm, and they slipped into the cloister and out to the grassy open quad before the New Building. With the melodies of Mozart floating after them, David slowly led her through the wrought-iron gate and across the stone bridge to Addison's Walk.

They came to a bench just over the little bridge and sat, looking out over the meadow. The fritillaries had faded, but buttercups and violets abounded. Dusk had not yet fallen, and the sun had just dipped behind the trees, shooting its golden rays into the deepening blue of the sky. Kate couldn't imagine a more serene place, and for a few minutes the couple sat in awed silence.

Finally David spoke. "I've shared with you before how this is a favorite spot of mine, and it was here I made the most important commitment of my life when I prayed with Jack to give my life to Christ."

Kate nodded.

"And I've often thought," he continued, "that it would be very special to make the second most important commitment of my life here, as well."

David took Kate's hand in his.

"I want to tell you that I love you, Kate. I love you so very much, so much more than I can ever express with my inadequate words. I love you so much that I would like to spend my life with you, to show you every single day how much I love you. I...would like you to stay here in Oxford with me...and be my wife."

Kate's welled with tears. "Oh, David, I love you so much too." She stifled a sob into a smile. "But aren't you supposed to ask me something?"

David looked puzzled and then chuckled in chagrin. "Quite right." Still holding her hand, he knelt down on one knee before her.

"Katherine Lee Hughes, will you marry me?"

"Oh, yes, I will." She answered breathlessly. "With all my heart."

David turned her hand over and gently pressed his lips to her palm. Then he slipped a ring over her finger. "'And I will betroth you to me for ever,'" he quoted from the Book of Hosea. "'I will betroth you to me in righteousness and in justice, in steadfast love, and in mercy. I will betroth you to me in faithfulness;' and we shall know the Lord."

Kate looked down in surprise at a large sparkling diamond encircled by tiny emeralds. "Oh, David," she gasped. "It's absolutely beautiful!"

He rose to sit beside her and slipped his arm around her waist. "It was my grandmother Margaret MacKenzie's and my great-grandmother's before that. When I talked with my parents about proposing to you and asked their blessing, my dad gave this to me. He said that they couldn't be more pleased with my choice for a bride and that, should you accept my proposal, they wanted you to have this to welcome you into the MacKenzie clan."

Kate interpreted correctly that Charlotte had not been offered this priceless heirloom. Her face clouded with emotion as tears sprang to her eyes. "Thank you," she whispered.

David put his arms around her and drew her as close as he dared. He nestled his face in her hair, kissing it gently.

Kate looked up, and with a laughing sob said, "I'm so happy and yet I can't help crying."

"Shh, I know." He stroked her hair, and they clung to each other, prolonging the moment in quiet joy.

"My parents!" Kate suddenly lifted her head. "I'll need to talk to my parents."

"I posted a letter to your father asking for your hand in marriage. He should be getting it at the beginning of the week. But if you want to follow it up with a letter of your own, or ring him and tell him you *do* want to marry me, why that'd be grand."

"Yes. I will, of course. Oh..." she began to fret, "but then they'll want me to return home right after the term and start planning the wedding, and my mother will want to have a big to-do at the Country Club of Virginia with all their high-society set, and she'll need months to plan it, and...how can I ever leave you again for so long?"

"Well, here's what I propose, if you agree. Let your mother make her plans for her big to-do and we'll have it in September in Richmond, if she likes. I have the Long Vacation and don't have to be back for Michaelmas term until October."

"But—" Kate started to protest and David laid his finger across her lips.

"But," he continued, "I don't want to wait that long to be married. My dad says long engagements make for more temptations. I would like to have a small wedding with just family and our closest friends at St. Aldate's—say, the week after the term ends. That's a month away. Then..." he smiled. "You and I take the entire summer for our honeymoon and we'll do the Grand Tour together. I'll show you Paris, Venice, Florence, Switzerland, and all the places we've talked about. We'll save your dad the cost of a guided tour. Then in September, we'll go to the States and have the big celebration with your family and friends, and my American grandparents and aunts and cousins can come too. Well," he paused expectantly, "what do you think?"

"I think it's wonderful!" She hugged him excitedly. "But, oh my...I will still need to get a dress, and shoes, and flowers, and..."

"Whoa!" David laughed. "Please, Kate. Let's not think about all that right now. Let's just enjoy the 'now' of this—just being engaged. All right?"

She smiled and nodded. "Okay."

David kissed her forehead. "They'll be going in to the Hall for dinner, so we'd better get back. And now," he said, grinning proudly, "I can introduce you to everyone as my fiancée."

15

Fifth Week, Saturday
The Eights Boat Race

Yvette and Austen were quietly debating changes to the English Language curriculum, with David occasionally adding his comments. Kate sat beside him; the substance of their conversation beyond her realm of thought or concern. She happily leaned her head against David's shoulder and reflected on the events of the previous night, when David had asked her to be his wife. She remembered how the ancient Hall—lit by flickering candles, its long boards laden with delicacies and liquors—evoked an era and a world completely beyond her sphere. She recalled how David's introduction of her as his fiancée had stifled the snickering of some Junior Fellows as they eyed her, and how she was able to smile and converse pleasantly, although intimidated by the intellect of the people who surrounded her. David restored her confidence when, placing his hand firmly against her back, he swept her across the floor in their first betrothal dance. She was wrapped in a cocoon of sweet joy while the world of Oxford carried on, oblivious to her happiness.

They were sitting in the Head of the River, an old brick pub leaning over the Isis, a tributary of the Thames River by Folly Bridge, waiting for the final boat race in the annual competition of Eights. Originally, they had stood with the throngs of students lining the banks, but the chilly air and threat of rain sent them scurrying to the pub for a warm refuge. They were seated at a mullioned bay window thrust out over the river.

Kate looked down with pure pleasure at the ring on her finger as it sparkled in the light from the window.

Yvette took notice. "That's a beautiful ring, Kate. Is it a family heirloom?"

"Yes," Kate answered with a deep blush. "But it's from the MacKenzie family."

Yvette's jaw dropped in surprise. "Does that mean what I think it does?"

David and Kate smiled and nodded happily.

Austen let out a loud guffaw as he clasped David's arm in congratulations.

"Good show, old chap! When's the big day?"

"As soon as possible after term. I want to take Kate on the Grand Tour over the Long Vacation."

Austen grinned. "With me as chaperone?"

"Right." David smiled broadly. "No, Austen, old boy, your services as chaperone will no longer be needed."

"How about me?" Yvette teased. "I've always wanted to take a trip to Switzerland." With another admiring glance at the ring, she added, "Seriously, you two, this is wonderful! But you know," she cautioned Kate, "there'll be a lot of women in Oxford who will not be happy with you for taking David out of circulation."

"Yeah, right, Yvette." David said, laughing. "They'll be jumping off Carfax Tower in despair."

Shouts from the bend in the river commanded their attention.

"Sounds like they're coming," Austen said. "Let's go back to the footpath for a better look."

As Fellows, they could claim some privileges and were able to jostle past the gathering crowd to an open spot along the river. Despite the casual summertime frivolity, Eights was still a traditional event that required traditional garb. The men wore white slacks, navy blue sports coats, their respective college ties, and straw hats with wide, stiff brims called boaters. The women wore summer suits or dresses complete with hats and gloves. Kate wore her long dark hair pulled up in a loose chignon.

David stood with Kate in front of him and, resting his hands on her slender shoulders, pulled her close to him. Kate felt butterflies flutter about in her stomach.

"Mmm...you smell absolutely divine," he murmured. "What are you wearing?"

"Oh, it's just regular old 'White Shoulders,'" she answered, leaning back against him. At that moment she couldn't imagine ever being happier in her life.

A starting gun fired, the shouting swelled, and leaning over the river, they could see the boats whizzing around the bend. Kate recognized the black blades with white fleur-de-lis of Magdalen straining to catch up to or "bump" the boat of eight men ahead, whose royal blue blades rapidly flashed toward the finish line.

"Who's ahead?" she shouted to David above the fray.

"Christ Church! I don't think we can catch them! Come on Magdalen!" David's deep voice rang out with the chorus of shouts along the length of the bank as students yelled with excitement.

But when the race had ended, Christ Church had won the day.

Kate could make out the tall, lean figure of Stuart Devereux jumping from the boat and embracing his crewmates. Uncorked champagne bottles spouted their bubbly foam like fountains over the laughing victors. David took Kate's hand as they joined the festive crowd heading back to the pub.

She looked up at him. "Did you ever race?"

"Naturally. But at Cambridge, we called the race 'Bumps.' I rowed for Magdalene, but we were such a small college that we were always abysmally dreadful and could not struggle beyond the lowest divisions. Here Magdalen is always in the First Division but hasn't been able to win it all for many years."

"How many divisions are there?"

David shrugged. "Austen, do you know how many divisions there are here?"

Austen shoved back his boater. "Hmmm. Ten or so, I'd imagine. There must be a list inside."

"Ten?" Kate repeated incredulously. "But there aren't enough colleges to fill ten divisions."

"Oh, my dear," chided Austen, "each college enters several boats in various divisions and over one hundred boats participate. The placement all depends on how the crew places the year before. You can only move up a place in your division by bumping or catching up to the boat ahead and by not being bumped by the boat behind. It's very difficult to be Head of the River, and it's based on years of effort. The colleges take it all quite seriously. Except Merton perhaps…we haven't done so well lately."

Kate suppressed a smile, understanding that "lately" could refer to a decade. Another roar of victory arose from the banks of the river. "Sounds like they're taking their celebratory drinking seriously too," she observed wryly.

"Yes," David concurred, as they stepped back into the pub. "We should reclaim our table and finish our fish and chips before the hordes descend on us."

"I think I'll be excused first," Kate whispered. "Do you know where the bathroom is?"

David couldn't resist a grin. "Sorry, my love, but the pub doesn't offer baths to its patrons."

Kate rolled her eyes. "Okay, where's the *toilet?* You Brits prefer preciseness to politeness. Honestly, the word is crass. I think bathroom or restroom sounds much nicer."

"Well, you could say lavatory. But did I ever tell you about the little joke Jack played on his American secretary, Walter Hooper, when they first met?" David asked, his blue eyes twinkling merrily. "Well, he and Jack sat for hours out at the Kilns talking and drinking pots of tea.

Finally Walter couldn't stand it anymore and he asked Jack if he could use the bathroom. Without batting an eye, Jack showed him to the room with the tub, handed him a towel and some soap, and asked his guest if he needed anything else. When Walter was alone he looked around and noticed that the room held a tub but no toilet—fairly common in old houses—so very sheepishly he returned to Jack and confessed that what he really needed was the toilet. Jack threw back his head with that roaring laugh of his and declared, "That'll cure you Americans of your euphemisms!"

Austen and Yvette chuckled appreciatively.

Kate smirked. "Ha, ha. Very clever. Now would you please tell me where the toilet is?"

"Straight back to the left." David grinned at her.

"I'll go with you," Yvette said as the two women squeezed through the crowded hallway.

The two young men returned to their table. Austen looked at David with a quizzical expression. "Why do women always go to the loo in groups?"

"Don't know." David answered. "My sisters are like that too. One announces she has to go and the whole lot gets up. Maybe they feel safer together. Or maybe they do it to socialize."

"They socialize in the loo?"

The men laughingly shook their heads and then resumed their talk of the race. After a few minutes, Yvette returned alone.

"Where's Kate?" David asked.

Yvette looked worried. "She's surrounded out there by a bunch of drunken lads from The House. You'd better see to her."

David bolted to the pub's entryway, which was mobbed with young people. He spotted the blue-and-white jerseys of Christ Church and pushed his way through the crowd. He could barely see Kate, her petite frame shrinking back against the wall with a tall, and quite obviously inebriated youth leaning lasciviously over her.

David immediately recognized Stuart Devereux.

16

Fifth Week Saturday Afternoon
Eights

David anxiously shoved his way up to the celebrating crew from Christ Church.

"Pardon me, Lord Devereux." He spoke in a polite but authoritative tone. "I believe the young lady would like to return to her table now."

Kate looked over at David with relief. Stuart leaned with his hand flat against the wall over her head. He turned to the voice that had addressed him with the vacant, uncomprehending stare of someone who was decidedly drunk. Then he recognized David and smiled stupidly.

"MacKenzie! The Lord Protector. Your bulldog is here, Kate. I don't think she wants to go anywhere, MacKenzie. I think she prefers my company to yours—don't you, Kate?" He lifted up her chin. "Come on and give me a victory kiss, Kate."

"Stuart, please," Kate protested.

"Keep off her, Devereux!" David barked, pushing through the ring of men who surrounded them.

"Don't get your knickers in a twist, MacKenzie. I just want a little kiss. After all," Stuart leered, "she's done much more with you."

David shoved him back from Kate. "Keep away from her, Devereux. Kate," he spoke over his shoulder, "go back to the table."

With the possibility of a brawl brewing, the crowd around them had grown thicker, and Kate hesitated to push her way back through.

Stuart swayed unsteadily. "What gives you the right to give her orders? She was my girlfriend first."

"She's my fiancée now."

Stuart threw back his head and laughed. "So you're making an honest woman of her after all? Just like with that Cambridge bird?"

David's face turned red. It took every ounce of his self-control not to punch Stuart right then in his patrician jaw. "That's a bloody lie, Devereux. Apologize now to Kate or we'll take care of this outside."

Stuart noted the fierceness in David's eyes. He was not too drunk to reckon the strength and athletic prowess of his foe. His calculations sobered him up quickly, and he shrank from the challenge, holding his hands up in surrender. "Sorry, Kate. Sorry, Mr. MacKenzie. I misspoke. I'm dreadfully drunk." He smiled broadly at his crewmates and then shouted, "I'm dreadfully drunk, aren't I, lads? And we'll get plenty more drunk, won't we? Because we're 'Head of the River'! Let's hear it for The House!"

The hallway erupted in a chorus of "Hip, hip, hurrah!"

David pushed his way through the crowd to Kate. "Let's get out of here." He encircled her protectively with his left arm and used his right arm like a linesman clearing an opening.

Revelers jammed the sidewalks along Abingdon Road and Folly Bridge, but David and Kate at last broke out of the pack. Kate gulped the fresh air. The density of bodies packed together with the aroma of beer had made her feel slightly claustrophobic, and she had been close to panicking as Stuart made his unsolicited overtures.

David put his hands on her shoulders. "Are you all right?"

Trying not to cry, Kate nodded.

"I'm so sorry for taking you in there. I must have been daft not to think they'd all end up there after the race, and stone-drunk to boot. Really, I'm sorry. It's no place for a young lady."

"What about Austen and Yvette? They won't know where we've gone."

"I'm sure they'll figure it out and won't stay long themselves. Really, Kate, I'm so sorry at least not to have gotten you out of there sooner." He looked around at the crowd of carousing students spilling into the streets. "Here is the intellectual cream of the crop and all they can think of is drinking and wenching. It's a sad commentary on our society, isn't it? Reminds me of Hamlet's lament about the Danes and their drunkenness: *'It takes from our achievements, though performed at height, the pith and marrow of our attribute.'"*

"Why, David MacKenzie, only you could be quoting Shakespeare in the middle of Eights." At the sound of his voice an attractive redhead had turned around. "I'm surprised to see you down here in this den of debauchery, and with your little friend too."

"We were just leaving," David grimly replied.

"So soon? The fun's just beginning."

"You may not want to go in there, Charlotte," David warned. "It's a madhouse. How are you feeling, by the way?"

"Just fine." Then she added, "Oh, yes—the frightful incident at Blackwell's. Oh, you were such a dear to look after me. I have had one or two other minor spells, but nothing to worry about."

"Have you seen a doctor?"

"No, no, no," Charlotte clucked. "It's nothing, and besides the term's almost over. I can always check with a doctor when I get back to Cambridge." She looked at Kate. "I'm Charlotte Mansfield, by the way, David's ex."

"Yes, I know," Kate replied, raising her chin. "We've met before. I'm Kate Hughes, David's fiancée."

Charlotte blanched as the message registered. "Really? I'm, I'm...quite speechless! Well!" She scrambled to regain her poise. "When's the big day?"

"We hope the Saturday after the end of term," David answered.

Charlotte visibly wilted, and murmured, "So soon?" Then she perked up, "Well, I simply must get an invitation. Intimate friend of the groom and all that. After all, you have me to thank for getting you two together. I mean, really..." She took on the demeanor of a confidante as she addressed her remarks to Kate. "When I think of how I encouraged him to follow this career, I'm just thrilled at how well he's done. And if I hadn't broken things off with him, then you wouldn't be together now. I'm sure you two are just perfect for each other. He always wanted a little woman who would look up to him and be happy to stay home with a pack of kids. No, we weren't at all right for each other, my dear; you have nothing to fear there...But that's not to say that the sex wasn't fabulous. David is such an incredible lover, but then...oh..." She covered her mouth with her hand. "I'm sorry, I forgot you wouldn't know about that now, would you?" Her blue eyes, catlike, narrowed into slits.

Kate had never been quick with a clever repartée. She stood in shocked silence.

"Well, I suppose congratulations are in order." Charlotte placed her hand on Kate's arm. "Don't forget to invite me, dear. Cheers!"

She disappeared into the crowd, leaving Kate dumbfounded. David took Kate's elbow.

"Let's go."

"The nerve of that woman!" Kate fumed. "Did you hear her? I can't believe she had the gall to say that stuff. She claimed to be responsible for your success here. What did she ever do to encourage you? Can you believe her? Does she really think for one minute that I would invite her to our wedding?"

Kate mimicked Charlotte's clipped northern accent. " 'But that's not to say that the sex wasn't *fabulous.* David is such an incredible lover...oh, but you wouldn't know, would you?' "

"Sshh—come on, Kate. Let's go." They started walking towards town.

"That's so unfair! She rubs your relationship in my face and everybody else thinks we've done the dirty deed. How does she know we haven't, anyway? And when was this scenario where you helped her out at Blackwell's? You never told me about that."

"It didn't seem worth telling. About a fortnight ago I ran into her and she was taken ill, so I hailed a taxi for her, that's all. It was the same day I talked with Dr. Palmer after we got back from Cambridge and all the rumors were flying around. So I explained to her they weren't true. That's why she made the comment, Kate. She's just trying to rile you. Forget it."

"Forget it? Why do you think she's trying to rile me, David? She still loves you, that's why. She'd like nothing better than to get you back."

"She never loved me."

"Well, you could have fooled me! I still can't believe her audacity. You know, David, she is *not* a nice person. What did you ever see in her anyway? Oh, that's right—I forgot...the *fabulous* sex. The nerve! I mean she just goes right for the jugular, doesn't she? Nothing like ripping open a wound that hasn't healed yet. She thinks you're such an incredible lover, and she's right—I wouldn't know. That's what really hurts. She's got the gall to brag about your sex life together and I haven't even had a kiss. David..." Kate stopped walking. "Now that we're engaged, can't we at least kiss?"

David sighed. "Kate, we've been over all this before."

"But don't you want to? I mean, you do want me that way, don't you?"

"Of course I do, darling. That's why I don't want to put off getting married. I find you very desirable, just as any man would."

"Then why not kiss me? Everybody thinks we have, so what difference would it make?"

David turned away from her and resumed walking. "Please don't tempt me again. I fear I'm like Stuart Devereux; I wouldn't want to stop with a kiss."

"You're *not* like Stuart, at all. And besides, he's only like that when he's drunk."

"And how often is that? Kate, how many times do I have to explain to you that most men are obsessed with sex? It's just that alcohol lowers our inhibitions and makes it easier for us to show our true colors. The Bible says to 'flee youthful lusts' and to 'avoid even the appearance of evil,' and that's what I'm trying to do."

"Well, apparently we didn't avoid the appearance of evil when we went to Cambridge—and since everyone already thinks badly of us maybe we should just enjoy ourselves. It's too late for their good opinion anyway."

They had reached their parking space, and David's fingers drummed on the roof of his car. "Do you realize that to defend your honor I almost got into a fight back there with Lord Devereux, Viscount of Essex? Do you know that had I smashed his jaw, he could have had me thrown in jail for assault?"

Kate hung her head. "I hadn't really thought about it. I thought you were just jealous."

"Jealous?" David shook his head. "Well, I suppose on some level I am. After all, *he* has kissed you and God knows what else. But I was trying to protect you, both from his advances and his accusations. You know, Kate, I hate to say this, but these arguments you are throwing at me—that we should go ahead and sin because people think we are anyway—really, they sound like the sort of nonsense Old Screwtape tries to dish out. I'm afraid you're missing the whole point. God's principles are for our good. If we're obedient to what He has called us to, then we will be blessed. If we disobey, we are opening ourselves to a lot of heartache. It's that simple."

Kate was silent for a moment, then said, "Okay, I'm sorry."

David lifted her chin. "Do you know what your name means, Miss Katherine?"

Kate shook her head.

"It means 'pure.' I want to present you on our wedding day as my pure bride."

"What does 'David' mean?"

"Beloved."

Kate smiled. "Well, that fits."

David smiled back. "Thank you."

Kate gingerly pushed back in place a stray lock of his dark hair. "I don't even know what your middle name is."

"Lawrence. I was named for both my grandfathers."

"What does Lawrence mean?"

"It probably derives from the laurel tree. Remember the Greeks crowned victors with laurel leaves. 'To gain the laurels' or 'resting on his laurels' denotes obtaining victory and honor."

"Hmmm...that fits you too, doesn't, it? Your zeal for honor and all."

"I suppose so." He grinned. "I usually thought of it in terms of being the victor at the next football match. But maybe God in his foreknowledge knew I would be fighting a battle for purity and that He would enable me to be the victor. With His help and your help I can win this battle, Kate."

"Okay, beloved victor."

"Okay, pure little meadow."

"Meadow?" Kate crinkled her nose.

"Lee, or *leigh,* is Anglo-Saxon for meadow."

Kate laughed. "Well, we're a pair, aren't we? A tree and a meadow."

He opened the car door for her, smiling. "We're a perfect match."

David and Kate spent the rest of the afternoon browsing the shops of Oxford and comparing their tastes in household furnishings and décor, and then enjoyed a quiet dinner in the Mitre, discussing plans for their future together. The first challenge of their betrothal had been met and overcome. David left Kate with a sense of contentment and joyous expectation for sharing their good news with his family the next morning at church.

As he unlocked the door to his flat on Holywell Street, he heard the telephone ringing on the first-floor landing. He bounded up the stairs to answer it before Mrs. Bingley would be disturbed.

"Hello, MacKenzie speaking."

"Oh, David, thank God it's you!"

Although the voice on the other end was breathy and weak, he immediately recognized it.

"Charlotte? What is it?"

"David, I'm having another one of those spells. My head is killing me and I feel so faint. I…I think maybe you were right—I should see a doctor. I'm sorry to bother you. But I don't know anyone else to turn to. Oh…I feel so dreadful…it's horrible. I'm scared. Please…" her voice caught in a sob. "Could you please take me to the infirmary?"

"Yes, yes, of course." David answered. "Now stay calm. Just lie down and put your feet up. I'll be over right away."

Sixth Week, Early Sunday A.M.

David parked his car on Walton Street near the back entrance to Somerville College. Hitting the intercom button at the postern gate, he stated his identity and purpose for calling. The door buzzed opened, and he stepped into the hushed quiet of the college grounds.

Founded in the late nineteenth century, Somerville was a new college by Oxford standards and was exclusively for women. The architecture, an eclectic mix of traditional and contemporary designs, reflected the college's pride in the past and pursuit of the future. David walked quickly towards Penrose, a large neo-Georgian brick building that suited his personal taste more than the modern residence halls. The building had a graceful arcade that opened onto the small lawn of the Fellows' Garden. Penrose housed Fellows as well as undergraduates, and it was there, on the ground floor overlooking the garden, that Charlotte was staying. David hurried through an opening in the garden hedge and knocked quietly on her door.

"Charlotte, it's David."

He heard her voice faintly through the door. "Come in, it's unlocked."

He entered the apartment and found her stretched out on the couch. Her fair skin looked even paler than usual in sharp contrast to the freckles sprinkled across her nose. She was still dressed in the short skirt and fishnet stockings she had sported at Eights. Her feet were propped up on the arm of the sofa. David averted his eyes.

"Thank you for coming. I'm sorry to bother you so late." She rubbed her forehead and her eyes filled with tears. "I feel dreadful. I must look dreadful too."

"Don't be silly. Let's get you to the infirmary. You know the Radcliffe is practically right next door. Can you manage walking over, or shall I call for a stretcher?"

"I think I can manage...with your help." She struggled to sit up and then slumped over, her head in her hands. "Sorry," she whispered, "I'm so dizzy."

David put his arm around her shoulders. "It's all right, take it slowly. There's no hurry. Let your head clear. I'm right here with you." He waited a few minutes and then asked, "Ready?"

Charlotte nodded and leaning into him, stood unsteadily. She took a deep breath. "All right," she said. "I'm ready. Just take it easy."

"You set the pace. I won't let you fall." With his arm around her, they shuffled slowly out of the door, down the path, past the postern gate, and out onto Walton Street.

"Any idea what could be wrong?" David finally spoke as they approached the bright lights of the Radcliffe Infirmary.

"No." Charlotte gasped for breath. "My word, I am so short of air after this little walk. Wait a second and let me catch my breath." They stopped and Charlotte breathed heavily. "Okay," she sighed. "Let's go. Almost there."

As they started up the stairs, Charlotte suddenly swooned and collapsed into David's arms. He carried her up the steps and into the infirmary.

"She's fainted. She needs help!" David called out to the clerk behind the reception desk.

Their dramatic entrance caused a stir. Responding quickly, orderlies wheeled in a stretcher and whisked Charlotte off to an examining room.

The receptionist spoke to David. "Is she your wife?"

"Sorry?" he walked over to the desk. "No, no. She's not my wife—she's just a friend."

"Patient's name?"

"Charlotte Mansfield."

"Age?"

"Twenty-five."

"Symptoms?"

"Umm...dizziness, fainting spells, weakness, headache, shortness of breath...I...I...think that's all."

"All right, sir, have a seat here in the waiting room."

"Yes, thank you." David sat down heavily. He remembered all too vividly the last time he had been to the infirmary—after Kate's accident. He had been so distraught over the thought that he could lose her. He felt none of that panic for Charlotte, but he did feel compassion. He hated to see anyone suffering, especially someone smaller and weaker than he. He bowed his head and prayed for Charlotte and for wisdom for the doctors attending her. Then he took his New Testament out of his inside jacket pocket and settled in to reading and waiting.

After about an hour, Charlotte emerged, pale and wan, on the arm of an orderly.

David stood up quickly. "You're all right? You can go home?"

Charlotte nodded. "They're running some blood tests. It may just be anemia. I've got some pain medication for my head and orders to go home to rest until they get the lab report back."

"Do you want a wheelchair or something?"

"No, I'll be fine." Charlotte smiled. "I've got you."

By the time David settled Charlotte back in her rooms, the night was far advanced; and he caught only a few hours of sleep before escorting Kate to the Sunday morning service at St. Aldate's. They slipped into the pew with the MacKenzie family only minutes before the worship music began. Kate noticed with surprise, and David with pleasure, that his sisters Ginny and Natalie had joined them. David correctly surmised that his parents, knowing of the impending engagement, had invited the girls home from their university for the weekend. The sisters leaned over and smiled and waved down the pew, straining for a glimpse of Kate's hand. Kate liked David's sisters and admired their loving relationship with their older brother. Although strikingly different in appearance, both girls were vivacious, affectionate, and even-tempered.

As soon as the service was over, they crowded around Kate and David.

"So, did you propose? Is it official? Oh, let me see the ring!" The girls giggled and fussed over Kate and then warmly hugged her and David. "We're so happy," they babbled on. "We knew you and David were right for each other and told him so back at Thanksgiving."

"Really?" Kate blushed with pleasure. "But I had just met you then."

"One look at you two—" Natalie said laughing, "we knew, dear, we knew. David couldn't keep his eyes off you, for all his attempts to keep his distance as your tutor and all."

"And we're so happy he gave you the MacKenzie ring," Ginny added. "It's just right for you. We're very glad to have you in the family."

"Thank you," Kate smiled happily. "You're very kind."

Annie MacKenzie embraced Kate tightly. "Oh, Kate, we are very pleased indeed. There's no one I'd rather have marry my David." She released Kate, and her eyes glistened with tears. "God is so good. I know He has brought you two together."

Kate couldn't trust herself to speak and merely nodded in happy agreement. Then she felt a tug on her skirt. Looking down, she noticed little Hannah.

Kate knelt beside her. "Yes, Hannah, what is it?"

The little girl's rosebud lips drew into a pout. "Are you going to marry David?"

"Yes, honey. I am."

"But *I'm* going to marry David."

"Oh, yes, I remember." Kate gently took her hand. "Hannah, David loves you very much and you are his favorite little sister in all the world. We would like you to be in the wedding as our flower girl. Would you like that?"

Hannah's cornflower-blue eyes grew wide. "Do I get to wear a pretty dress?"

Kate nodded. "Yes. A very pretty dress, and you'll carry a basket of flowers."

Hannah looked up excitedly, "Mummy, Kate says I can be a flower girl and wear a pretty dress!"

"Wonderful, darling." Annie stroked Hannah's blond ringlets and smiled at Kate.

"What's this all about, sweetheart?" David scooped Hannah up into his arms.

"I'm a flower girl!" Hannah crowed.

"Are you now? Well, won't you be a pretty sight?" He winked approvingly at Kate. "You know, we are causing quite a stir here in the sanctuary. Maybe we should head back to the house and carry on there."

"You're not going to the college luncheon?" Annie asked.

"If you have enough for us, I think we'll skip it and eat with the family. I understand the girls have to catch the coach back this afternoon."

"Yes, that'd be fine. You all go on and take Hannah with you. There are some people I need to speak to first."

"All right, Mum." David kissed his mother's cheek. "We'll see you in a bit."

The rectory soon filled with laughter and chatter as the MacKenzie children gathered in the kitchen and prepared their noonday meal.

Natalie triumphantly brought in a tray filled with dishes from the student luncheon in the Rectory Hall next door.

"Those ladies love me," she announced, "and gave me all this good stuff to bring over. Now Mummy won't have to cook supper either."

As David gave thanks for the food, they bowed their heads, and then they began serving each other. The boys maintained a polite but shy distance from Kate until David announced their engagement.

"Will," David addressed the oldest of his brothers, "I'd like you to stand up with me as a groomsman. Would you?"

William was pleased. "Yes, of course. I'd be honored."

"What about me and Richard?" ten-year-old Mark broke in. "Are we going to do anything?"

"Well, I'd like you to be the ushers," David replied.

Richard groaned. "Does that mean we have to wear DJ's?"

"DJ's?" Kate asked.

"Dinner jackets." David clarified. "No, this is going to be a very small wedding. Your Sunday suits will do fine."

"Good," Richard chimed in. "I hate fancy affairs."

William playfully shoved Richard. "Who asked you, anyway? By the way..." he turned to Kate. "We're glad to welcome you into the family. I know you'll make David very happy."

"Thanks, Will." Kate smiled. "I hope so."

"Did the ladies send over the food?" Annie breezed in, and removing her hatpin and hat, shook out her shoulder-length hair. "That was thoughtful of them," she replied to the grunts of assent. "You boys washed your hands? Did someone say a blessing?" When she was satisfied all was in order, Annie sank into her chair at the large kitchen table and pulled off her high heels. "Ooh, that feels better," she said, rubbing her stocking feet.

"Hello, everyone!" Eric MacKenzie sang out as he entered the kitchen.

"Hello, Dad!" his children chorused back.

He gave Annie a peck on the cheek and asked in a low voice. "How was the sermon?"

"Well done, honey. I heard lots of good comments. Sit down and eat some lunch. The women of the church sent over this huge platter from the student luncheon. Wasn't that nice?"

"Yes, indeed." Eric pulled up his chair and served himself. "Did you say a blessing? Dinner napkins in laps, lads!"

The younger boys sheepishly grabbed their cloth napkins to comply.

"Now, Kate," Eric addressed her in gentler tone. "I'd like to express to you our great pleasure at your engagement to David. Annie and I couldn't be happier."

"Thank you, Reverend MacKenzie. I'm very happy too."

"Dad," David spoke up. "We discussed this before, but Kate and I would like to ask you properly to officiate at the wedding."

"You know I'd be honored. But we will have to start the premarital counseling right away to get in all the sessions. Should we just keep our Sunday afternoon get-togethers for that?"

"Sure, that would be fine."

"When is the wedding?" Natalie piped up.

"Right after term, I hope." David answered.

Ginny hopped up and checked the wall calendar. "Let's see. Eighth week ends on the nineteenth of June, so the next Saturday after that is the twenty-sixth."

"That's my birthday," Kate spoke up.

"So it is." David reached over and toyed with a lock of her hair. "Would you like to get married on your birthday?"

"That would be a wonderful gift." Kate could not help smiling.

"Well, you wouldn't be likely to forget her birthday or your anniversary since they'd be the same day." That astute observation came from Mark.

"David!" Natalie protested. "That's less than a month away. How can you plan a wedding in such a short time, and how can Kate's family get here with such short notice?"

"Perhaps we'd better reserve the church for the next weekend as well, until we know for certain," Eric suggested.

"Of course. That'd be fine, Dad." David answered. "But, Nat, we're not planning a huge fancy affair. Kate's parents may want to do something like that back in Virginia. We plan to take the Grand Tour over the Long Vacation and then go over to the States in September when her family can have the kind of wedding reception they want. I don't even care if they want to do the ceremony again. But here I'd like to have a simple, quiet wedding with just a few friends and our families. We don't need months of planning for that."

"But, you are going to buy a new gown, aren't you, Kate?" Natalie asked.

"I'd like to, but I haven't a clue where to look."

"We'll help you!" Ginny responded enthusiastically. "If it's all right with you, of course. You and Mum can come down to London on Saturday and meet us and we can all go shopping together on Oxford Street and at Harrods. I mean, if you want to, of course."

"I'd love to!" Kate felt relieved to have some feminine guidance and companionship for this important purchase. "That would be really great."

"Oh, this will be fun!" Then Natalie added conspiratorially, "And maybe we can pick out some new dresses while we're at it."

"And I get a pretty new dress too! Kate said so." Hannah had not missed the tenor of the conversation.

"Don't get carried away, girls," Annie warned. "You may see something you like and have to let me make it for you. We're always on a tight budget, you know."

"That'd be all right, Mummy," Ginny soothed. "Mum is an excellent seamstress and sews most of our clothes," she explained to Kate. "You could never tell the difference between hers and store-bought."

Eric stood up and excused himself. "Come along, David. Let's look in the office and check those dates to reserve the church. Let the women talk about wedding clothes and make their plans. I always tell my prospective grooms to stay out of it."

"All right. But girls"—David looked significantly at his sisters—"remember that this is going to be a small and simple wedding. You can make your grandiose plans when you have your own weddings and have to invite the entire parish. But this is going to be less than thirty people."

"Why, our family alone is half of that!" exclaimed Ginny.

"Exactly. Family and a few very close friends. This is a wedding, not a production."

"Got it." Natalie made a shooing motion with her hand. "Now run along, big brother, and don't spoil our fun."

The rest of the boys excused themselves and headed upstairs to change out of their Sunday clothes. David and his father walked down the corridor to the front of the house, where a small office lay next to the entrance. Eric checked the church schedule and penciled in a reservation for both potential dates.

"Everything going all right, David?"

"Yes, Dad. Thanks. I proposed at the Fellows' Dinner Dance as I had hoped, down by Addison's Walk. And as you know, she accepted. So everything is splendid. I just hope things don't get carried away in terms of plans and we lose our focus on what's truly important."

Eric chuckled. "Women love to plan weddings, lad, even small ones. So just stay out of it and let them have their fun. You get to worry about the honeymoon and little things like providing a home and income for your wife."

"Right. Well, I've got that covered. I do enjoy planning trips, and I am looking forward to showing her about Paris and all."

"Are you leaving for the continent right away, or will you take some time here in the UK first?"

"I have thought about staying over here for the first week. Maybe taking her up to Scotland for the honeymoon—and I'm really keen to spend the wedding night in a castle somewhere. Kate would love the romance of all that."

"Aye, and Scotland is a bonnie idea, lad. '*My heart is in the highlands; my heart is not here...*'" Eric's Scottish burr grew stronger. "Maybe if we get your auntie to come doon for the weddin', ye can stay in her cottage at Anstruthers."

"Bonnie idea, Dad." David echoed, smiling.

"And is everything else all right, lad? You've seemed a wee bit troubled about something."

David sighed in resignation. "You know me too well, Dad. There *is* something."

"Sit down, son."

David did, taking a deep breath and exhaling slowly. "You know, Dad, Charlotte is here for the term as a guest lecturer at Somerville."

"No, I didn't know that." Eric took out his pipe and tapped the old tobacco into an ashtray.

"Yes. I've seen her a bit around town. She nearly fainted about a fortnight ago at Blackwell's. Then last night, she called me asking for help to take her to the infirmary. She's had these spells with headaches, dizziness, and faintness. In fact, she fainted on the way to the infirmary. Anyway, it may be just anemia. They took some blood, and I suppose she'll get the results back tomorrow."

"You're saying you went over there last night?"

"Yes. It was quite late before I got back, what with getting her to and from the infirmary and waiting for the doctors to attend her and all."

"How did Kate feel about you going over to Charlotte's?"

"Well, that's one thing that's bothering me. I haven't wanted to tell her about it, because I think she would just blow it up into something it wasn't and get all hurt and jealous."

"Does she have reason to be jealous?"

"No, not at all. I don't have feelings for Charlotte anymore."

"What about Charlotte? Does she have feelings for you?"

David hesitated. "I'm not sure. Charlotte is hard to understand. But I suppose she might."

Eric slowly packed new tobacco into his pipe. "I think I understand your desire to help Charlotte since she rang you up with a real need. But I don't think it's wise for you to be alone with any woman, especially an ex-fiancée."

"Yes, you're right, Dad. But it was just the emergency circumstances and I didn't stay long. I just got her to the infirmary and back."

"You be the judge on how much you should say to Kate." Eric lit his pipe and began puffing slowly. "Sounds like you did the right thing, responding to the need, but the going alone is the sticky part. If Charlotte calls you again, you may want to take Kate with you. Or perhaps your mother could go."

"Oh, Kate would never go and Charlotte wouldn't want her to. Charlotte's a fairly private person and doesn't like people around when she's not feeling well or looking her best. And I think she's intimidated by Mum."

"Your mother, intimidating?"

"Well, I think Charlotte feels inadequate compared to Mum. So she tries to make herself look better by putting Mum down. Anyway, hopefully, she just has a simple case of anemia and this won't come up again."

"Yes," Eric agreed. "Let's hope you're right."

18

Sixth week, Tuesday

David and one of his students were completing a tutorial on George Herbert when Charlotte knocked lightly on the open door and stepped into his rooms in the New Building.

"So sorry to interrupt," she apologized breathlessly as the two young men rose at her entrance. "I can wait outside until you are done."

"No problem." David answered. "We're just finishing…Simon, we're reading Donne for next time. You have the reading list?"

"Yes, sir. I'll see you next week, Mr. MacKenzie. Good evening to you, miss." He nodded to Charlotte as he gathered up his books and left.

Charlotte waited until he was out of the door and then spoke. "May I talk to you for a few minutes?"

"Certainly. Please be seated." David gestured to the sofa and pulled up a chair. "What is it? Did you get the test results back?"

"Yes." Charlotte pushed her red hair back from her forehead.

"Is it anemia?" David prodded.

"Yes."

"That's not so bad, is it? I mean, can't you readily remedy it with iron supplements and proper rest?"

"Yes, but the doctor didn't like the look of it and wanted a more definite diagnosis as to the type of anemia. So yesterday, I had to go in for a bone marrow test—a biopsy." Her face reddened as if she were holding back tears.

"That sounds serious," David remarked sympathetically. "What was it like?"

"It was ghastly. The spot where they went in hurt all last night."

"When do you get the results back?"

"I did this afternoon. I just saw the doctor and came right over here." Her eyes brimmed with tears. "I'm sorry to bother you, but I needed to talk to someone."

David pulled his chair closer. "Tell me, Charlotte," he spoke gently. "What did he say?"

"He said…he said…I have acute aplastic anemia."

"I'm sorry. I'm completely ignorant. What does that mean?"

"It's a rare type of anemia and…in the acute stage, it's…"

"Yes?"

"It's frequently fatal," she whispered and broke into sobs.

David sat in stunned silence.

"Oh, Charlotte…I can't believe it," he finally stammered. "There must be some sort of treatment for this. You're a young woman. Surely they can do something. What did the doctor say?"

Shaking her head, Charlotte wept.

Compassion welled up in David, and he moved beside Charlotte on the sofa and put his arm around her. Leaning her head onto his chest, she began to heave with sobs.

David sat quietly and let her cry herself out while he rubbed and patted her shoulder and rocked her gently. At last her sobs subsided, and taking a handkerchief out of her handbag, she dabbed her eyes.

"They'll first try blood transfusions," she sniffed. "The last resort would be to attempt a transplant of bone marrow. But it's a very experimental procedure, and it's never been done successfully before. That would be ironic, wouldn't it? I guess with my demise I could still contribute to scientific research."

"Now, don't despair. You can beat this. I can donate blood for you. We're both A-positive, aren't we? And if it comes to this transplant, then perhaps I could be a candidate for that."

She squeezed his hand gratefully. "You're a darling, David. But much more has to match than just blood type. They would look first to someone closely related—like my brother."

"There you go. I'm sure he'd do it. Have you told your family yet?"

"No. You're the first person I've told. Please don't go spreading it around, David. I don't want it to affect my job."

"Surely, you're going to let your family know. They may be able to help."

"You remember, my father left when I was only four. He may be dead for all I know, and just as well if he is," she said bitterly. "Mother has a new boyfriend up in Leeds. She won't want to come if she doesn't have to. I'd rather not tell her, but she may know where John is."

"You don't know where he is?"

"No. He's gone off to find himself and the true meaning of life." Her tone held a note of sarcasm. "He and a mate are backpacking somewhere in the Orient. He's been gone for months." She dug into her handbag and pulled out a pack of cigarettes.

David sighed deeply. "Your mother must have some way to contact him. An embassy, perhaps?"

"I don't know. I will just have to hope he contacts her sometime and she can pass on the message to him. Meanwhile…" She fumbled with her lighter. "I'll get the blood transfusion and hope for the best."

David took the lighter from her and flicked it to light her cigarette. "When are you going in for that?"

"Tomorrow morning." Her hands trembled as she took a long drag and slowly blew out the smoke.

David nodded. "How can I help you, Charlotte?"

Her eyes glistened with tears. "Just be here for me, David."

"I will."

"May I ring you if I need to talk or something?"

"Of course. And if you need help getting to the infirmary tomorrow...oh, blast! I have a lecture in the morning. When are you scheduled?"

Charlotte shook her head. "No, no. I'll be fine. It's right next door. And I could ask my scout to help if I need to." She patted his knee. "Thanks, though."

"Sure. Just let me know how I can help. How did you get here? Do you have a way back to college?"

"I'll get a taxi."

"I can give you a ride. I'm heading over that way to the Bird and Baby for the Inklings meeting."

Charlotte smiled. "Well, all right. That would be very nice of you."

Turning out the lights and locking the door, they started down the staircase. Charlotte took David's arm on the steps, and he shortened his stride to match hers.

"Sorry," she said breathlessly. "I have to take it easy."

"No, I'm sorry. I wasn't thinking. Forgive me. You set the pace."

She leaned slightly on his shoulder as they slowly walked across the lawn. Suddenly David stopped.

"What is it?"

"I forgot I'm supposed to pick up Kate. She's joining us for supper before the meeting."

Charlotte laughed lightly. "I don't think that MG of yours will hold the three of us. Nor will Kate appreciate my company. Just walk me up to the Porters' Lodge and I'll get a taxi there."

"I'm sorry, Charlotte."

"No problem, darling. Probably best not to even mention this to her. We don't want to make your little fiancée unnecessarily jealous. Congratulations by the way. I'm sure you two will be very happy."

"Thanks."

When he had hailed a taxi and seen her safely settled in, David said, "I'll ring you later to see how you're doing. And I'll be praying for you, Charlotte. You don't mind, do you?"

"No." She smiled faintly. "I need all the prayers I can get."

Over dinner, David, Austen, and Yvette planned out the Inklings' meetings remaining in the term. They concluded that with the preparations for his upcoming marriage, David might find continuing to host the meetings too much of a burden. Yvette volunteered to present some of Joy Gresham Lewis's poetry, and Austen agreed to take on more of Tolkien, hoping to convince the venerable author to return for another reading.

On this particular evening, David had planned to discuss Lewis's sermon "The Weight of Glory." Its theme—that every person we meet is an immortal and that by our actions we are helping them on their journey to either heaven or hell—truly resonated with him. He felt particularly a weight of responsibility towards Charlotte and was unusually subdued during their dinner conversation.

Concerned, Kate finally addressed him. "David, is something the matter?"

David toyed with his spoon before replying. "Yes, I suppose there is."

"Do you want to tell us about it?" Yvette asked.

"Yes. But it has to stay confidential." He looked at each of them, and when they had nodded their agreement, he forged ahead. "Charlotte came by my rooms this afternoon." Kate's mouth dropped open in disbelief. He held up his hand. "Now, hold on. It's not what you think. She's been ill lately, having these dizzy spells, headaches, and such. Sunday night I took her to the infirmary because she was having a particularly bad spell and—"

"You never told me that!" Kate interrupted.

"No, I'm sorry. I didn't think you'd understand and I wasn't sure there was any reason to tell you. Anyway, they did some blood tests and determined she has anemia. But the doctor wanted more information and yesterday she had her bone marrow tested. He told her today she has acute aplastic anemia."

"Oh, Lord, have mercy," Austen whispered.

"What's that?" Kate asked.

"It's a blood disorder, and in the acute phase is frequently fatal."

There was shocked silence.

"How's she taking it?" Yvette finally ventured.

"How'd you think? Not well. She's completely shattered…and so am I. She's only twenty-five, and she doesn't know the Lord from the man in the moon."

Tempering her personal indignation with compassion, Kate slipped her hand into David's and squeezed it sympathetically.

"Surely, there are treatments?" Austen asked with an optimism that he did not feel.

"Yes. She's having a transfusion tomorrow. But for the worst cases, the only hope—and it's still very experimental—is a transplant of bone marrow, and apparently they look for someone related by blood. Her brother would be a candidate but he's off in the Orient somewhere and she doesn't know how to locate him."

"How dreadful," said Yvette.

"Yes. It is. I asked her if I could pray for her and she said she could use all the prayers she could get. So that's something positive anyway."

"Well, of course, we'll be praying for her." Yvette reassured him. "And maybe the transfusion will be the cure."

Austen noted that since students were arriving, it was time to move to the back of the pub for the meeting. As the evening got underway, David's professional demeanor took command. He began with a dramatic reading of Lewis's sermon and then led the group in a lively and probing discussion of the text and how it applied to their personal lives. When David announced the upcoming meetings and topics, Kate waited expectantly for him to mention their engagement. But he neglected to—and as the gathering dispersed, Kate couldn't help but be disappointed. Having already shown the ring to Connie, she proudly displayed it to Nigel, Colin, and Twila and accepted their congratulations. David, however, seemed preoccupied and aloof as he bade his good-byes.

When most of the students had left, Kate almost shyly asked David, "Are you mad at me or something?"

"Of course not. Why would you think that?"

"Well, you've been ignoring me or avoiding me, I'm not sure which."

"Why, neither, Kate. That's silly." He stuffed his notes and papers into a book satchel. "We've had a meeting going on and a number of people to talk to."

"But you didn't think to announce our engagement."

Chagrined, he stopped packing and looked up. "I'm so sorry. You're quite right. I should have. Did you tell anyone?"

"Well, Connie knew, of course, and she had told Nigel. And I showed some of them the ring. Still, I was hoping you would say something."

David picked up her left hand and kissed it. "I will next week, my love. I promise. And maybe it will be better anyway after we get your parents' official blessing. I'm sorry. I must have been thinking about the meeting and this business with Charlotte." He swung the satchel over his shoulder. "You know, I should probably go check on her since Somerville is right down the street. Will you come with me?"

"No, David, I won't!"

"What?" David was surprised at the vehemence in her tone.

"Look, I'm sorry she's sick and I know you're worried about her, but there is absolutely no way you are going to get me over to see Charlotte—not that she would want me to anyway. And I certainly don't want you going over there now by yourself."

"Kate, I'm disappointed in you." David spoke as if to a recalcitrant child. "Here's a young woman with a potentially fatal illness who needs comfort, and you're being self-centered and immature."

"What kind of comfort does she want, David?" Kate's voice rose enough to turn some heads. "If you think I'm being selfish and immature not to want my fiancé holding the hand of another woman, then I guess I am."

"Sshh! Don't make a scene, Kate," he warned in a whisper, taking her firmly by the elbow and leading her out of the pub's front door.

When they were standing outside, Kate fumed, "I'm not going to pretend I'm not upset, David. You English with all your proper rules of etiquette. 'Don't talk too loudly. Don't make a scene.' You're just hypocritical."

"It's not hypocrisy, Kate. It's called self-control."

"Don't get all holier-than-thou with me. Didn't you make a scene with Stuart Devereux at The Head of the River?"

David rubbed his forehead in exasperation. "Kate, what does this have to do with anything? What are we arguing about here?"

"I don't want you to go to see Charlotte!" she cried.

"All right," he answered in a measured tone. "I won't. I'll take you home now. Let's go."

They rode back to St. Hilda's in silence. When he let her out of the car, Kate turned to him and asked, "Will I see you tomorrow?"

David thought for a moment. "If you come to my lecture. But you know I have a tutorial afterwards. And the football team is playing Marjons, so I won't be back until late and will have to miss the Bible study at St. Aldate's. I guess I'll see you Thursday at our tutorial."

He stroked her cheek with the back of his hand. "Kate, I love you. I will always love you. You have no reason to feel threatened by Charlotte. I'm not happy about the words we had tonight, but that doesn't change the fact that I love you. Understand?" He gently kissed her cheek.

Kate nodded, her eyes brimming with tears. She felt intuitively that although she had won her way, she had lost something indefinable but crucially more important.

19

Sixth Week, Tuesday evening and Wednesday night

David parked his car at Magdalen and walked back to his flat, kicking pebbles as if they were soccer balls as he mulled over what he should do about Charlotte. He knew Kate would object to his telephoning her, but hadn't he promised Charlotte he would check on her? And shouldn't he honor his word as a gentleman?

After overcoming his anxieties about calling, he found to his consternation that Charlotte didn't answer. Slowly hanging up, he wondered what this could mean and decided she must have gone to bed early and turned the ringer off. He didn't want to entertain the thought that she could have gone back to the infirmary, for fear of the resentment he might feel towards Kate if something had gone amiss and he hadn't been there to help. He resolved to try again in the morning.

Try again he did, several times throughout the next day—before and after his lecture and in between tutorials—but each time there was no answer, and he began to worry.

After coaching the University football match, David returned to his flat to shower and change. Mrs. Bingley rapped on his door as he was getting dressed. He zipped up his jeans, pulled a T-shirt over his head, and opened the door.

"Yes, Mrs. Bingley?"

"Oh, David, dearie, I'm sorry to bother you, but that young woman, Charlotte, rang up several times tonight."

"Did she leave a message?"

"She says she's feeling very badly and won't you please come to see 'er. She sounded mighty ill, indeed she did."

"All right, thank you, Mrs. Bingley. I'll give her a ring now."

Mrs. Bingley moved aside her generous girth from the doorway so that David could slip by and climb the stairs to the telephone. This time Charlotte answered.

"Charlotte? David here. Are you all right?"

"Oh, David. Thank God. I've been trying to ring you all day. You didn't phone me."

"Yes, I did, Charlotte. I tried several times, but there was no answer."

There was a moment's silence on the other end. "Oh, I must have been at the infirmary. Well, anyway. At least I've got you now. David"—her voice quavered—"could you please come over? I feel so terrible. The transfusion was dreadful. I'm…I'm so scared…there's nobody I trust…please…will you come?"

David hesitated and then decided. "I'll be there in a few minutes."

David hurried over to Somerville College and found Charlotte lying listlessly on her sofa. Her lacy blue nylon negligée clung to her body, clearly defining its contours. As his eyes flicked over her figure, David reproached himself for recognizing her attire from their days at Cambridge. He tried to concentrate instead on observing her face. Her naturally fair complexion looked translucent, like porcelain. Charlotte's pale eyelashes completely disappeared without mascara, and for this reason, David had never seen her without makeup. The fact that she was wearing some even now made no impression on him. He was too intent on studying her expression for signs of discomfort or distress.

Charlotte held out her hand to grasp David's. "Thanks for coming, darling. I'm sorry to be such a bother."

"What can I do for you?" he asked anxiously. "Can I get you something?"

"A glass of cold water would be divine. The glasses are right above the sink."

David was happy to be of some use and promptly returned with the water.

Charlotte struggled to sit up and allowed David to support her shoulders as she took a sip. "Thank you," she whispered, managing a grateful smile before sinking back onto the cushions.

"Tell me what's going on," David prodded. "Won't the transfusion help?"

"My hematologist, Dr. Gardiner, is hopeful—but today was ghastly and I feel worse than ever."

"Will you have to have another one?"

"He'll check my blood over the next few weeks and give me more transfusions if necessary. If there's no improvement, we'll decide whether or not to contact the specialists about a transplant."

"Have you found your brother?"

Charlotte sighed. "No. I did ring mother and let her know, but it will take her a while to track him down." She placed her hand on David's arm. "Tonight it was so quiet that I started becoming obsessed over what could happen...that I could possibly die...and I was frightened to be alone. That's why I rang you, David. I know I need to go to sleep, but I worry that I might never wake up if I do. The doctor gave me some sleeping pills and I thought about taking them all at once and getting it over with—but then I realized I really would fall asleep and never wake up, and I got scared again. Oh!" Tears filled her eyes. "It's such a vicious cycle." She squeezed his arm more tightly. "I'm so afraid!"

His own eyes filled with tears of compassion, and he covered her hand with his. "Charlotte, I'm sure the doctors will be able to help you. I know you don't believe in God the way I do, but I wish you did. I think He would be a great comfort to you."

"It's partly *Him* I'm afraid of. I start to worry that maybe there is a God—and if there is, He won't be too happy with me. I think that if I'm right and there is no God, well, then it would be hard to die so young, but it won't matter in the end. But if you're right about Christianity and I'm wrong, then I have a lot to be worried about. If there is a hell, I certainly don't want to end up there. So perhaps I should let you tell me more about what you believe."

David inwardly rejoiced. "I'd be happy to share with you anytime."

She caressed his hand. "I just may take you up on it if things get serious, but not tonight, please. I'm feeling very tired and don't really think I'll be leaving quite this soon."

"I certainly hope not." David wasn't sure how hard to pursue this slight spiritual openness from Charlotte. "Perhaps I could leave you my pocket New Testament, and then you could read some of it whenever you feel up to it."

"That would be fine. Thank you, that's most kind of you. I'm beginning to feel like I could use some outside help." Yawning, she covered her mouth. "David, darling, I'm so exhausted. Would you be a love and help me to bed?"

"Of course." He stood up and put his arm behind her shoulders to try to help her to stand. She struggled to pull herself up and then fell back onto the cushions.

"Sorry," she whispered.

"No problem," he replied and scooping her up in his arms as if she were a child, he carried her into her bedroom and gently laid her on the bed.

"Thanks," Charlotte said weakly.

"You know, David..." She spoke wistfully, her eyes filling with tears. "Sometimes when I think about dying, I think about all the research I want to do but won't get the chance to. Or things I may miss out on with my family and friends. But more and more often, I've been thinking about what a fool I was to ever let you go." Clutching his hand with sudden urgency, she pled, "David, I'm so sorry. I was such an idiot. Will you forgive me?"

"Of course, Charlotte. I forgave you long ago."

"Well then, can't we let bygones be bygones and go back to the way we were?"

Suddenly David had the sensation that he was struggling, as if underwater. He felt desperate for air, and the clutch of Charlotte's hand was pulling him deeper and deeper down.

"Charlotte, I...I...I," he stammered. "I really have to be going now."

Her grip tightened. "Please don't leave me, darling. Can't you stay with me until I fall asleep?"

David pulled his hand away and backed out of her room. "I'm so sorry. I have to run. Do get some sleep, Charlotte."

As he closed her apartment door, he called over his shoulder without waiting for a reply, "Good night!"

Leaning against the colonnade to the Fellows' gardens, David fairly gulped down the cool night air. He shook his head in bewilderment and thought, *What was going on in there?*

20

Sixth Week, Thursday

A steady spring rain was falling, fitting Kate's mood exactly. She brushed the tears off her cheeks, kept her head under her umbrella, and forged across Magdalen Bridge towards the New Building and her tutorial with David.

She was late. She had barely finished her essay when she had received the phone call from her parents. And since that call she had been unable to stop crying. She was angry with herself for being so emotional, but that frustration only made her cry harder.

Why am I crying all the time? It must be that time of the month and that's why I feel so lousy. My emotions are spinning out of control. And these are supposed to be some of the happiest times of my life…I'm engaged to the most wonderful man in the world and…

Then the recollection of her parents' call incited a new flow of tears. She passed through the Porters' Gate, had a respite from the rain under the shelter of the cloisters, then hurried back again into the elements as she crossed the grass to the New Building. Leaving her umbrella at the foot of the stairwell, she tried to compose herself. She took a deep breath, mounted the stairs, knocked lightly on David's open door, and entered.

Nigel was in mid-sentence, reading his essay on *A Midsummer Night's Dream*, but he stopped and arose with David as Kate hurriedly hung her mackintosh on the coat rack and settled into her customary spot on the old green sofa.

"I'm very sorry I'm late," Kate apologized breathlessly as the men sat back down. "Something came up just as I was getting ready to leave. Sorry to interrupt, Nigel. Please go on."

David nodded to Nigel to continue and then studied Kate's flustered face with concern. He surmised it had more to do with the cause of her tardiness than the fact of it. Her large brown eyes were puffy, and her mascara was most definitely smudged. The rain could account for it, but he guessed she had been crying. He tried to give his attention to Nigel and his paper—however, he was utterly distracted as Kate began sniffling and wiping her eyes.

Finally he couldn't bear the artificial formality of the tutorial another moment and blurted out, "For goodness' sake, Kate, what is the matter?"

Nigel shifted uncomfortably in his chair and then placed his essay on the coffee table, pantomiming to David that he would go. David nodded.

"I'm sorry, Nigel," Kate gasped through her tears.

"No problem." Nigel stood and flung his trademark scarf around his neck. "I'll come by tomorrow after lectures?"

"Certainly," David replied. "That would be fine."

Nigel slipped quietly out of the room. David sat watching Kate for a few moments and then repeated his question more gently. "Kate, what is it?"

She shook her head as if she didn't yet trust herself to speak.

"Come here," he coaxed.

She rushed to him, and he drew her onto his lap and held her tightly as if she were a small child. He stroked her hair until she could compose herself.

"My parents called," she finally managed to sob. "They don't want us to get married."

David felt as if he had been punched in the gut. "What did they say?"

"They said they don't want me to get married so soon. They don't want to lose me and have me live forever in England. And that they don't even know you, so how could they entrust me to you? And that...that..."

"What?"

"That you're not good enough for me."

David couldn't help smiling. "Well, they're right about that."

"No, really, they mean it. My dad always says nobody is good enough for me, but..."

"Kate, of course he feels that way. I know my dad will say the same about any of my sisters' suitors and so will I."

"No, but my mother...you don't know her. She's from an FFV...First Family of Virginia...the Lees, you know, like Robert E. Lee. That's where I get my middle name. She's all into the high-society thing and the country-club set. It's like she thinks marrying a college professor would be beneath me or something."

"You can't be serious."

Kate's eyes filled up again.

David shifted Kate off his lap and into the chair, then walked over to the fireplace. "I must say I'm astounded. Now, if you were the daughter of an English peer, I would expect these class distinctions, but for an American family to worry about my lineage..."

"You know, I think if you were a lord or something, my mother would be absolutely thrilled."

"Oh, good grief, I'm a MacKenzie! Tell her that I'm descended from King Kenneth, one of the finest Scottish kings of all time and a Christian too. And moreover, I'm half-American. I think we're related somehow to George Washington through his aunt. Doesn't that make me superior to the Lees? Kate, I can't believe your parents would care about such nonsense."

"Well, my mother does, anyway. And my father asked all these questions about your income that I couldn't answer. He couldn't see how I could be happy living on a professor's salary and wanted to know where we were going to live and if I had seen your apartment and if I could truly be happy there."

David's hands gripped the mantel, and he looked at her. "Kate, do you wonder about that?"

"I hadn't thought of it before," she answered honestly. "I just know I love you and want to marry you, but I hadn't thought about money."

"When I wrote to your father asking for your hand, I gave him my income. Obviously a don's compensation will never be at the level of a successful solicitor in the States. But I can supplement my income with publications—and although we will never be wealthy, we can live quite comfortably here in Oxford. It's up to you, if you can be happy with that. And by the way, we can walk over and see my flat now, if you like. And if you object to it, we can always look for someplace else to live."

"But, my parents aren't going to let me marry you!" Kate wailed.

David rubbed his forehead. "Kate, please. Would you try to stop crying?"

"I can't," she sobbed. "I'm sorry! When I started crying on the phone, Daddy said I wasn't old enough to get married anyway. Maybe he's right."

"Oh, for goodness sake, women cry as well as girls. Now, was there anything else your parents objected to?"

"They want me to finish school."

"Well, of course. Didn't you tell them St. Hilda's has agreed to keep you on and that we had written to William and Mary about accepting your credits here towards graduation?"

"Yes. But my mother was most upset about our getting married so soon. I told you she would want all this time to plan a big wedding."

David shook his head. "I thought you said they don't want us to get married at all. Then why is your mother talking about planning a big wedding?"

"Oh, I know it doesn't make sense. But this came later after I had tried to explain some things. She got all upset when I told her that I was going to go to London on Saturday with your sisters to pick out a gown. She wants to go with me. Mother of the bride and all that."

"I thought she didn't want a wedding."

"She doesn't. But if there is going to be one after all, she wants to have her say."

"And so she shall. If all she's worried about is picking out your wedding dress, let her do it. You can wear a burlap sack for all I care. I just want to get married and soon. It's the other stuff that troubles me more. When can I talk to your parents?"

"I don't know. The whole thing ended in a mess. I was crying and was late for my tutorial and then the connection got bad. So they just said they'd call again soon."

"And tell me"—he sat down next to her and took her small hands in his large ones—"did any of their concerns put doubts in your own mind?"

"Maybe, a little"

"What?"

"I want my parents' blessing."

"So do I. But, what else are you worried about?"

"Well, I hadn't thought much about not going back home again ever. I mean to come here for a term is not quite the same as living here forever, is it? When I was back in Richmond, all I could think of was coming back here to be with you. But, now this is all a little scary. David, don't you ever have any doubts?" She looked down at his hands holding hers. She loved his hands. They were large and strong and reminded her of Michelangelo's *David.*

"No. Not since I made up my mind. I've been praying about this almost since I met you, and have earnestly sought the Lord for His will. I believe we are supposed to be together. But you have to be convinced in your own heart, Kate."

"But my parents?"

"We should pray and trust that their hearts will change, and you know, my parents"—the phone began ringing and David finished his sentence as he strode over to his desk—"are in full agreement."

He picked up the phone in mid-ring. "Hello, MacKenzie here...Hi, there. How are you?...Oh. I'm sorry. No...no, I can't. I'm in the middle of a tutorial, actually. May I ring you later?...All right. Take care...'bye." Deep in thought, he returned the telephone to its cradle. "So, what was I saying?"

"Who was that?" Kate asked.

David swallowed. "Just a colleague."

"It was Charlotte, wasn't it?"

He hesitated.

"Yes."

"Why didn't you say so, then? Why did you try to hide who it was?"

"Because I didn't want you to get more upset."

"And you told her you would call her later?"

"Yes. She's ill and scared. She needs someone to talk to."

"She doesn't need to talk to you, David!"

"Kate, she doesn't know very many people here. And besides, she doesn't want it getting out that she's sick. So there aren't many people she can talk to."

"Have you been over to see her?"

He took a big breath. "She called pretty late last night because she couldn't sleep. She was frightened and in a lot of discomfort and asked me to come over."

"And you went?"

"Yes."

"Alone?"

"Yes. It was too late to go with anyone else. Kate, why are you asking me all these questions? We were talking about your parents."

"Don't you see the hypocrisy, David? You won't be alone with me unless we're in a public setting. You want to avoid even the appearance of evil with me. But you'll go over to her rooms, late at night, *alone!*

And you hid this from me! Why didn't you tell me?"

"Well, I haven't had a chance."

"You wouldn't have told me, would you—if she hadn't called just now?"

"I don't know. I haven't known what to tell you. You've been so emotional lately, and I didn't want you to get all upset with everything else going on. Kate, I didn't intend to go alone. It just worked out that way because it was so late. And besides, I asked you to go with me Tuesday night and you refused. Look, she's really, really ill. I just can't let her suffer alone."

Kate met this statement with withering silence. Then she stood up, her eyes flashing. "You know, maybe I have doubts because of her too. Maybe I shouldn't be wearing this."

She yanked off her engagement ring and slid it across the desk. "Here, take it back."

21

Sixth Week, Thursday Evening

David stared at the ring on his desk. Then he looked up at Kate. "What are you doing?" he asked in disbelief.

Tears streamed down Kate's face. "It's not right for me to have it."

"It's not right for you to give it back to me. I won't have it!" He picked the ring up and held it out to her. She shook her head. He walked around the desk and stood over her. His jaw tightened with indignation, but when he looked down on her— she who was so small and vulnerable and whom he loved so deeply— his manner softened. He took a deep breath.

"Kate, I'm sorry about this business with Charlotte. It was a bad decision for me to go over there alone, and I promise I won't do it again. But, Kate…" His voice cracked with emotion. "This ring is a token of my commitment to marry you. That commitment hasn't changed despite what your parents say or what you're feeling. And it will not change unless you decide you absolutely do not want to marry me. I don't want this back unless or until you make that decision. I want you to keep it as my pledge to you. If you don't feel right wearing it, I understand, but please take it."

Her long, thick hair hid her face from him, but she nodded. "All right," she whispered.

He slipped the ring back on her finger. Then cupping her face in his hands, he wiped her tears. "You know, once when Mum was scolding Hannah, Hannah said to her, 'God gave you a nice face and you've messed it all up.' She might say that now to you—such a pretty girl in all these tears."

A laugh stifled Kate's sob. "I must look awful."

"Well, I think I'm supposed to fib here and say you've never been more beautiful...but...I won't fib...you're always beautiful to me." David pulled her into his arms. "Oh, Kate, I love you so much! I believe we can work these things out with God's help. Will you spend some time in prayer and try to hear what He is saying to you? I want you to be as certain as I am."

"I do too—of course I'll pray."

"I have an idea—let's go to the Turf Tavern for supper and then I'll take you to see my flat. Funny, I never thought to have you see it before. Would that be all right?"

Kate nodded.

"Let's go then." He released her and strode over to the coat rack for their mackintoshes. "Oh, blast. I completely forgot about your tutorial. Did you bring your essay?"

"Yes. It's on the coffee table with Nigel's."

"Well, bring it along and we'll read it over dinner. What did you write about anyway?"

Kate smiled wryly. "Shakespeare's views on love and marriage as portrayed in *A Midsummer Night's Dream.* But boy, when I think about it now, it's ironic, isn't it, that we read this play? I mean, when Hermia and Lysander don't get her father's blessing to wed, they run off into the forest."

"You're not suggesting we elope, are you?" David asked as he held her coat for her and gently pulled her long hair out from the collar.

"No, but I wish we had an Oberon and his magic so that it would all work out for the young lovers in the end."

"We have someone better than that," David answered with a smile. "We have God."

In typical English fashion, the clouds had blown away and left a freshly scrubbed spring sky. David and Kate decided to stop by his apartment before dinner since it was on the way to the pub and Kate needed to remedy her appearance. Holywell Street, a narrow medieval lane passing between the old city wall and the grounds of several colleges, was quiet and quaint. The afternoon sun slanted over the rooftops lighting the pastel row houses in a soft glow. As many tourists and students before her, Kate was struck by the hushed charm of this little lane nestled so close to the bustle and choking automobile fumes of High and Broad Streets. Although David had promised Kate they could look elsewhere should his flat not suit her, he anxiously hoped it would. Its proximity to Magdalen, the University Club Sports Grounds on Mansfield Road, the Bodleian Library, and even Blackwell's Bookstore made it the center of his universe.

"That house, number 99"—David pointed to a long stone house with red trim—"was Professor Tolkien's house until a few years ago when he moved out to Headington. It's owned by Merton College, as are several other houses on this street. And that's the entrance to New College, which is naturally not new at all but one of the oldest colleges in Oxford. You can see some of the old city wall from inside, just like you can at the Turf Tavern. I love this street because it's so central to everything. The only disadvantage is that it's a bit narrow for parking, so I leave my car at the Fellows' car park up at Magdalen." David unlocked the front door to a soft yellow row house trimmed in white. "I use my bicycle a lot from here or just walk as everything is so close."

They stepped into a tiny foyer that faced a narrow flight of stairs and an even narrower passageway to the back door. They heard a muffled chorus of dogs barking from the apartment upstairs.

"Those are Mrs. Bingley's corgis," David explained. "I hope you like little dogs because she has three. She's my landlady and a widow—a bit nosy but very motherly and kind. We share the telephone up there on the first-floor landing. I'll take you up there to meet her after you freshen up."

David swung open the interior door to his apartment. "Well, here it is, although I'm sorry I haven't cleaned it up for company," he said apologetically as he hurriedly straightened some books and newspapers that were spread out on his couch. Kate wasn't surprised that one wall of the room was lined with bookcases, but the working fireplace was a welcome anomaly in a town where many were being walled up in favor of electric heaters. A small breakfast table with two chairs was set in the alcove of the front bay window overlooking the street. The afternoon sun cooperated at that moment by shining through the large window, suffusing the entire room with bright warmth.

"It's not fancy," David said. "I'm not particular about furniture and such, so these are castoffs from the rectory." He motioned to the sofa, a worn wingback chair, and a scarred-up coffee table. "But we can fix it up however you like."

"It's charming!" Kate pronounced to David's immense relief.

"The kitchen is here," David gestured to a galley-like kitchenette off the short hallway. "It's small, I'll grant you, but I confess I don't cook at all. I hope it will be adequate for two. And here's the bathroom ...complete with toilet," he added with a smile. "Why don't you pop in here to freshen up while I make sure my bedroom isn't a disaster?"

He opened his bedroom door and quickly picked up some discarded clothing and smoothed out the bedspread. David liked order and neatness, but was often in a hurry; and living alone had given him the luxury of shedding socks and trousers where he pleased. As he stuffed his soiled clothes into the laundry hamper, he reflected that he would have to alter his casual habits to keep his bride happy. *A small price to pay,* he thought with a grin, *for sharing my lonely bed.*

Her toilette accomplished, Kate stood in the doorway surveying the room. It was furnished in Spartan fashion with a double bed, chest of drawers, and desk. She noted with amusement the piles of books stacked in and under the bed table. Walking over to look out the large paned window, she found it opened over the back garden, a tiny walled lot bursting with flowers.

"You didn't tell me you had a garden. You know I love gardens!" Kate was excited about this unexpected boon.

David stood beside her looking out the window. Then he gingerly reached out to smooth back a strand of her hair. "So, how do you like it? My flat, I mean. Would you be happy here?"

Kate smiled up at him. "Oh, yes! I love it!" she look around. "It is small. But it's cozy and cheery."

"And you know if you do feel cramped, right down the street is the Magdalen Deer Park, and you'll have full access to it anytime you want."

"I know. It's in a perfect location, David. Don't worry. If my parents agree to it, I know I'll be very happy here."

He took her in his arms and buried his face in her hair. It's sweet herbal scent filled him with longing. "You know," David said hoarsely, forcing himself to let her go, "we'd better get out of here. I don't trust myself alone with you in here." He glanced at his bed. "This is too tempting."

Kate followed his look and reluctantly backed away from him. "You're right."

"Well, then...perhaps I should introduce you to Mrs. Bingley now," David suggested.

Kate nodded. "Okay."

They hurried back to the hallway, and David bounded up the stairs to rap on his landlady's door. The answering chorus of barking crescendoed as Mrs. Bingley cracked open the door.

"Hush, darlin's," she clucked at her dogs. "It's your big brother David! Bless my soul. Com'in, com'in." She opened the door wider, and the fat little dogs squeezed out, snuffling around David's shoes and wagging their tails in greeting.

"I don't want to intrude on you, mum. I was just heading out for supper, but I wanted you to meet a very special young lady." He motioned for Kate to come up the stairs. She followed, and the dogs swarmed around her feet, sniffing.

"Mrs. Bingley, this is Kate Hughes."

"Hello." Kate held out her hand in greeting.

The landlady's plump hand engulfed Kate's. " 'Ello, dearie. Pleased to meet you. Oh, aren't ye a pretty li'le thing?"

"Nice to meet you, Mrs. Bingley."

"You're the one who 'ad the terrible accident, aren't ye?"

"Yes, ma'am."

"Oh, my word," the older woman patted her bountiful bosom as if she were still in shock from the event. "I got the phone message from Mrs. MacKenzie saying you 'ad been taken to 'ospital and I 'ad to tell David when he got 'ome. Oh, my word, 'e looked white as a sheet—thought you were dead, I'll warrant. 'E about died 'isself. Well, I'm glad to see you're doin' all right and yer such a pretty li'le thing. I can see why David 'as taken a fancy to ye."

Kate smiled. "Thank you, ma'am."

"Can I offer ye a cuppa tea, then?"

"No, thank you, mum." David answered quickly. "As I said, we were going out to supper, but I wanted to bring Kate by to meet you."

"Oh, I'm glad ye did." She patted Kate's hand again. "Come by anytime, dearie. Oh—didnya ring up just a li'le bit ago for David?"

Kate withdrew her hand. "No."

"Must 'a been that other young lady of yers, David. All the girls love 'im, you know." She winked knowingly at Kate.

"Thank you, Mrs. Bingley," David said quickly. "We'd best be going."

"Oh, I remember now! It was Charlotte. Yes. Charlotte! I thought she was in Cambridge. But anyway, she said she was feeling very badly and would like you to ring 'er as soon as possible."

"Right." David began to pull Kate towards the stairs. "Cheers, Mrs. Bingley!"

Kate was too emotionally exhausted to fight anymore. She decided to pretend she hadn't heard Mrs. Bingley's comments about Charlotte's phone call—for the time being, anyway.

Taking his cue from her, David was only too happy to skirt another confrontation over his old fiancée. The last one had nearly ended their engagement, and he sensed Kate's feelings were still too fragile to endure another round. As they walked down Holywell Street, their conversation was uncharacteristically guarded, and each danced delicately around any topic that might lead to more discord. When they had settled in for their supper at the Turf Tavern, David remembered Kate's tutorial essay, and they both eagerly seized on this neutral ground for conversation. Shakespeare, a shared love, was always safe.

22

Sixth Week, Friday Evening

David was able to banish all anxieties from his mind on the football pitch as he played for the Mansfield Road University staff team against Oxford University Press. The cool, clear evening, the perfectly rolled green grass, the adrenaline rush of the athletic contest, all delighted him. David thought that heaven must consist of vast libraries and level playing fields since these were two of his favorite places on earth. Fiercely competitive at all times, David's awareness of Kate sitting in the stands gave him even more incentive to play his best. Like a knight in a jousting tournament, he wanted to impress his ladylove. After making an assist and scoring a hat trick, his colleagues on the opposing team chided him good-naturedly.

"Hey, MacKenzie," one called, "lay off or we won't publish that book of yours!"

David laughed. "All right, lads! We'll take it easy on ye." He switched himself from center half to the defensive midfield, or stopper, position and tried to maintain possession of the ball without humiliating the other team with more goals. With only minutes remaining, one of his forwards slipped another goal past the keeper to the groans of the outmatched Oxford Press team. Mansfield Road whooped with victory and patted each others' backs as they left the field.

"Good game, Mac," a number of the men called out to David. "Coming to the club?"

"No, thanks," he answered with a grin. "I have better looking company here than you blokes." He nodded towards Kate. "I'll catch you at our next training. Good game, mates."

Smiling, he walked over to Kate. "Now this is a perfect evening: beautiful weather, beautiful game, and a beautiful girl. Thanks for coming, sweetheart. I'd give you a hug, but I'm all sweaty." He took her hand and brought it to his lips. Then he frowned. She wasn't wearing his ring. Kate noticed the change in his expression and pulled her hand back as if to hide it.

David tried to adopt a teasing tone. "Don't tell me you've gone and lost it."

"No. I...I have it, safe in my jewelry box." Kate couldn't meet his eyes.

He sighed and dropped the pretense of teasing. "Why?"

"You said that it was your pledge to me, but that I didn't have to wear it if I didn't feel right about it." She didn't look up.

"Right. Well, I want to hear more of this, but we should walk. It's getting chilly out here." He helped her down from the stands and put his jacket over her shoulders. "Have you had supper?"

"Yes."

"I should take a shower, but would you like to go out with me after that?"

"I need to study. I was planning to go from here to the Bodleian."

"On a Friday night?"

"I have a lot of work to do, and I don't want to get behind."

"All right. I'll walk you over." David slung his soccer bag over his shoulder, and they started down Mansfield Road toward the library. "Now, tell me about the ring."

Kate steadied herself by looking up at the sky. "My parents called me again this afternoon."

"Did you ask your father when I may speak to him?"

"Yes. He said he would answer you by letter."

"Good grief! That will take forever. We can't discuss this by mail. We won't be able to read the banns and it'll put the wedding off too long."

"What do you mean? What are the 'banns'?"

"For a couple to be married in the Anglican church, the banns—the public announcement of their intention to be married—must be published or read for three consecutive weeks in their parish church. If someone knows just cause why they shouldn't be married, he has notice to come forward with the information. I was hoping Dad would read our banns this week so we could be married on your birthday."

"How can he read the banns if my parents don't want us to get married?"

"Well, that's why I want to talk to your father."

Kate stopped walking and looked up at David in anguish. "David, you're not getting this. He doesn't want to talk to you! They don't want us to get married. They called to say they are flying over next week and bringing my little brother Timmy and his nanny."

David quietly took this in, but he stubbornly held to his position. "Well, that's good then, isn't it? Because I can talk to them all the sooner."

"But that's not why they're coming. They're coming to take me home—and that means I'll have even less time to be with you!" She had tried to hold back the tears, but now they spilled down her cheeks. "I can't go back home. I can't leave you again. I can't..."

"Hey...it'll be all right." David dropped his bag and, enfolding her in his arms, laid his cheek on the top of her head. "So, did you decide you can live with me here in England after all?"

Kate nodded and whispered, "Yes."

"And you don't mind not being rich?"

"I don't care about the money or even where we live. I just know I want to be with you."

"Are you convinced in your own heart that it's God's will for us to be together?"

Kate pulled back and looked up at him. "Last night when I got back from dinner, I did as you asked me to. I got alone in my room and knelt beside my bed. Then I prayed and I asked the Lord to forgive me for my sins—for my selfishness and anger and jealousy—and to speak to me, that not my will but His be done. And a Scripture verse came to my mind. It was Psalm 45:10."

"Well, what does it say?"

"I remember it, but there was more after that. You don't have a Bible with you, do you?"

"I may have a pocket New Testament, but it has the Psalms too." He zipped open his bag and dug around until he found a small green Gideon New Testament and handed it to her.

Kate flipped through the pages. "Here it is. It says, '*Hear, O daughter, consider, and incline your ear; forget your people and your father's house; and the king will desire your beauty.*'" She looked up. "I felt like God was speaking right to me, calling me 'daughter.' And your name—'David'—is the name of a king."

"Well." David sighed and smiled. "This king definitely desires your beauty. So, you took this as the word of the Lord to you?"

"Oh, yes. It so specifically fit. And it goes on to describe a wedding. Listen—'*Since he is your lord, bow to him; the people will sue your favor with gifts, the richest of the people with all kinds of wealth. The princess is decked in her chamber with gold-woven robes; in many-colored robes she is led to the king, with her virgin companions, her escort, in her train. With joy and gladness they are led along as they enter the palace of the king. Instead of your fathers shall be your sons; you will make them princes in all the earth. I will cause your name to be celebrated in all generations…*'"

Kate looked up expectantly at David for his affirmation.

"Amen!" he declared, and they both laughed. "That's wonderful, Kate." He grasped her arms. "You do take it as a confirmation, don't you?"

"Yes, I do. I mean I did, but then I got that terrible call from my parents and now I don't know what to think. The verse says 'to forget your people and your father's house.' I know we should be married and I'm willing to leave the States and live here, but I don't want to elope. I do so want a wedding and my parents' blessing."

The tears still glistened on her cheeks. David cupped her face in his hands and gently kissed them away. He longed to kiss her on the mouth, but merely brushed his lips across hers. Then he spoke. "I think we should believe God gave you the scripture as a promise. It does go on to describe a wedding. I think we should continue to pray that the Lord will change your parents' hearts and that we will be able to have a proper wedding."

"Me, too." Joy and relief crowded the sorrow and anxiety from Kate's countenance.

David picked up his bag and slung it back over his shoulder. "Well then, let's stop moping about and have some fun."

Kate took his arm as they resumed walking. "You know, that's another thing that's been bothering me. I always thought that being engaged would be a fun and happy time. But so far it's been extremely stressful and an emotional roller coaster."

"My parents always talk about that to newly engaged couples," David replied thoughtfully. "We have all these heightened romantic expectations that don't match up with reality. They say that engagement is a good preparation time for marriage because we don't just get hitched and live happily ever after. There are the day-to-day pressures of life that have to be faced. My mum says that engagement is a bit like a pregnancy. After the initial thrill of announcing it and getting congratulated, you have to go through the stress of making plans and waiting and not feeling all that well in the meantime. But the prize in the end makes it all worthwhile."

"Yes, I suppose so. But I do wish it were more fun. I wish it could be an endless round of parties and showers without the worries and trials."

"Don't we wish all of life were like that?" David squeezed her hand. "Well, my love—I think we appreciate the good times all the more for the bad. Now, wouldn't you like to do something fun tonight? The cinema, perhaps?"

"I still need to go to the library. With my parents coming next week, I want to get ahead on my essays."

"How about tomorrow, then? Are you still going up to London to go shopping?"

"No, I called your mother to cancel yesterday after my mom complained about me not buying my bridal gown with her. So, I think I should just slog away on my papers tomorrow."

"You're not going to work all tonight and all tomorrow too. As your tutor, I won't allow it. I have a mind to take you up to Stratford tomorrow evening...it's only an hour away...we can have dinner and catch the RSC."

"The RSC—is that a train?"

"No, silly. The Royal Shakespeare Company. Whatever play I can get tickets for will be the one you write your final essay on. How does that sound?"

"It sounds wonderful!"

"Excellent. We have a date then."

When they arrived at the Bodleian Library, David reached down and caressed Kate's cheek. "Don't work too hard, my princess. This has been an emotionally exhausting time for you. I want you to get some rest tonight, all right?"

Kate smiled slyly. "Yes, my lord."

David grinned. "You know I like that. I like the part of the psalm that said 'since he is your lord, bow to him.' That's a good verse for you to remember."

Kate smirked and playfully pushed his hand away. "You're not my lord, yet."

"Not yet," David smiled. "But soon. *À bientôt.*" He kissed her forehead. *"Bon soir, mon amour. À demain."*

Kate kissed her fingers and pressed them to his lips. "*À demain.* Till tomorrow," she repeated.

23

Stratford-upon-Avon
Sixth Week, Saturday Night

It was a perfect summer evening: the midnight-blue sky, the warm gentle breeze, the view of swans swimming gracefully on the River Avon. David and Kate were finishing their dinner as they sat on the outdoor terrace of the Dirty Duck pub across the street from the Royal Shakespeare Theatre. David sported white trousers and his Oxford Blues blazer and tie, and Kate looked radiant in a chic cocktail dress in raspberry silk, accented with a strand of pearls and low white stiletto heels. He was pleased to see that, in deference to him, she was wearing his engagement ring as well as her abundant dark hair down long and held back with a large bow. Periodically, as they talked, he would reach over and affectionately toy with a thick strand that fell invitingly over her shoulder.

David decided not to talk to Kate about his concerns for Charlotte, at least for this magical evening. She likewise decided not to point out Stuart Devereux sitting behind him across the terrace, at least until it became unavoidable.

David pushed his plate back contentedly. "Well, I can't believe how blessed we are to have gotten tickets on such short notice to *Hamlet*, of all plays—and with David Warner as Hamlet and Glenda Jackson as Ophelia. It's received brilliant notices. I'm sorry not to have thought about getting a group up from the Inklings." He smiled as he reached over to take her hand in his. "Although I am glad to have you all to myself."

"A group is coming from Christ Church," she said, hoping to telegraph a subconscious warning about Stuart. "Nigel and Connie are coming up with some kids on the bus."

"The *coach,* darling," he corrected, grinning. "You must learn to speak as a proper English woman."

"Does that mean I have to speak with an English accent?"

"Heavens, no! Your southern drawl is most charming."

Kate smiled. She was certain she found his British accent even more so. But she pursued the word choice issue. "I thought in Oxford, it was called the bus."

"Right. Within the city, it's a bus. Intercity, it's a coach. Harkens back to the old days of the stagecoach, I warrant. 'Coach' sounds rather more romantic and civilized than 'bus,' don't you think?"

"Like 'restroom' or 'bathroom' as opposed to 'toilet'?" Kate replied archly. "I thought you Brits didn't use euphemisms."

"Touché!" He laughed. "Anyway, I'm glad Nigel is coming up. He can write about *Hamlet* as well."

"We did *Hamlet* in the fall term," Kate reminded him.

"Yes, so we did—in the *autumn* term. But there are plenty of themes to explore. It's such a rich play—my favorite, anyway. I wrote my master's thesis on it."

"Oh, great," Kate sighed. "Nothing like a little pressure to come up with something brilliant."

"You write well, Miss Katherine," David reassured her. "If memory serves me, your Michaelmas *Hamlet* paper was excellent and was on 'appearance versus reality.' I asked you to do that to get you to think about how not everything is at it seems. I was hoping you would consider the idea that maybe even though you had *seen* me with Charlotte, it did not mean I still cared for her."

Kate's smiled in surprise. "That was sneaky of you! But it didn't work. I'm not that astute, I guess."

"I was also hoping you'd realize that Lord Devereux wasn't the knight in shining armor he appeared to be."

"Well, I did—but too late," Kate replied, trying not to look over to Stuart's table. "Certainly not while I was reading *Hamlet.* So I guess if you want me to apply my reading to my life you'll have to be less subtle in your approach."

A barkeeper suddenly appeared at their table with a bottle of Mums champagne and two glasses, interrupting their exchange. As he uncorked the bottle, David exclaimed, "I'm dreadfully sorry, but I didn't order this."

The man deftly filled the glasses. "Compliments of Lord Devereux, sir."

'Oh, blast, is he here?" David muttered. "Well...thank you," he said more politely to the barkeeper. "Well." He clinked his glass against Kate's. "Here's to us!" Then turning around to search for Stuart, he caught his eye and held the glass aloft in a toast of grateful acknowledgment. Turning back to Kate, he sipped his champagne. "And here's to Lord Devereux," he added grimly.

"And here he comes," Kate whispered.

David sighed. "Lovely!"

Kate watched Stuart saunter towards them carrying two half-empty champagne glasses. Like David, he was wearing white trousers and a navy college blazer. On his arm hung a tall slender girl with straight, blonde, shoulder-length hair. She had the long angular features of a British aristocrat, attractive but not beautiful. Kate recognized her as one of the girls from Somerville College who had been at the Clifton Manor house party. *Lydia...or is it Lucy?*

As soon as the couple reached their table, David stood up. "Lord Devereux."

"Mr. MacKenzie," Stuart responded smoothly. "May I introduce Lady Lucille Bertram?"

David bowed his head courteously. "Lady Bertram."

"Lucy," Stuart continued the introductions, "you remember Kate Hughes?"

"Hello, Kate." Her ladyship greeted her graciously.

"Hello, Lucy."

"Lord Devereux." David spoke next. "I understand we have you to thank for the champagne. That was most generous of you."

"A small gift of congratulations on your engagement."

"Thank you."

"And also," Stuart added, "a peace offering. It comes with my humblest apologies for my beastly behavior towards Miss Hughes at Eights." He looked at her apologetically. "I am sorry, Kate. I do and say the most dreadful things when I'm tanked."

Kate nodded her forgiveness.

"And, Mr. MacKenzie," Stuart continued. "I've challenged your Christian charity more than once, and I hope you will accept my sincere apology."

"Apology accepted, Lord Devereux." David became aware that except for Kate, they were still standing. "Would you care to join us?"

Stuart smiled, put down the champagne glasses, and pulled out a chair for Lucy. "Delighted."

David shot a glance of desperation at Kate. She stifled a smile. *So now his impeccable British manners backfire on him,* she thought. *That's what he gets for doing the proper thing. Reminds me of my mother, who, with her ingrained Southern hospitality, magnanimously invites people in to dinner when she has no expectation of them accepting.*

"So, Lord Devereux," David was saying in an attempt at civil conversation, "Are you here to see *Hamlet*?"

"'Stuart,' if you please, Mr. MacKenzie. Yes, *Hamlet* is one of my favorites. The language is so rich."

This time Kate couldn't help but smile at this echo of David's sentiments.

"We put it on at Eton," Stuart continued with enthusiasm. "I played Laertes. I'm a big fan of the Bard's, Mr. MacKenzie, and yours as well. You may have noticed that I rarely miss your lectures."

David was rather astonished. He had noticed Stuart at his lectures, but had surmised his attendance had more to do with his interest in Kate than in Shakespeare. "Are you reading English at Oxford?" he asked.

"Wish I were. I started out to, but thought I'd better switch to economics and management so I could be of some use to my father in handling the estates and his businesses. It means, though, that I won't graduate for another year."

Oh, jolly, thought David. *He'll be back again next year.* He turned his questions to Stuart's date. "And you, Lady Bertram, are you reading English?"

"Oh, I enjoy Shakespeare," she replied amiably. "But actually I'm reading biology at Somerville."

Stuart jumped in. "Lucy has studied with Miss Mansfield this term."

He directed his next comment to Lucy. "Mr. MacKenzie's an intimate friend of hers."

"Ah, right," Lucy answered as if remembering something. She turned to David. "You're *David* MacKenzie, then? Well, I've heard a lot about you actually. Charlotte Mansfield has been a fabulous asset to us at Somerville. She's a good lecturer, but even better in the lab. I'll hate for her to go back to Cambridge after the term. Perhaps you can talk her into staying."

David cleared his throat. "I don't think so." He glanced at Kate and noticed her growing discomfort with the conversation. "Well, now. Looks like people are gathering to go in the theatre. We'd better get going too. Thanks so much for the champagne." He stood and helped Kate up from her chair.

"Where are your seats?" Stuart asked as he rose with Lucy.

"Oh, up in the nosebleed section, I'm afraid," David answered cheerfully. "I only rang up this morning and feel quite lucky there was anything left."

As they walked across the street to the theatre, Lucy put her arm through Kate's so that she could examine her engagement ring. Stuart and David followed silently.

"I say," Stuart exclaimed suddenly. "Let's exchange tickets! I have seats in the stalls. My old man gets season tickets every year. Lucy and I will sit up in the crow's nest and you and Kate down front."

"I wouldn't think of it," David protested.

"Why not? It will be my engagement gift."

"No, I couldn't."

"Well, for Kate, then. I insist. She deserves the best."

David looked up sharply. *What was that supposed to mean?*

"Don't misunderstand me, Mr. MacKenzie," Stuart said meeting his eyes. "I mean it. She deserves the best, and you are a far better man than I. I'm genuinely glad for you both. I know you will make each other very happy." He extended his hand.

David hesitated while he read the sincerity in Stuart's eyes. Then he clasped his hand warmly. "Thank you, Stuart. I appreciate that." Then he smiled broadly. "And I will take you up on those seats."

Seventh Week

After happily reconciling with Stuart Devereux and thoroughly enjoying their evening in Stratford at the theatre, Kate and David had to devote their time to readying themselves for the impending arrival of Kate's parents and the end of the term. To complete as much of her work as possible, Kate sequestered herself in the reading room of the Radcliffe Camera, except when the balmy weather beckoned her outdoors to study.

David joined her when his duties as lecturer and tutor permitted, and he furiously attacked the pile of papers on his desk waiting to be marked. Austen and Yvette stepped in as promised to assume charge of the Inklings Society meetings, which relieved him of that preparation. However, his greatest stress came not from his responsibilities, which he enjoyed and had learned to balance reasonably, but from the frequent telephone calls he received from Charlotte. She was often distressed, and that in turn distressed him.

One night she had called in a panic, describing symptoms similar to a heart attack. From her nurse's training, David's mother, Annie, had warned him that patients with acute anemia could have such sensations. David had pleaded with Charlotte to go with him to the infirmary, but she had refused, claiming she would go in the morning if the symptoms persisted. She had called again that night, begging him to come over and sit with her so she could sleep. He couldn't betray Kate's trust by going over alone, but he had offered to come with Yvette or his mother. Charlotte had insisted she did not want others to see her or to know of her condition.

Whenever he thought of her, he felt an incredible turmoil of pity and fear, and that indefinable sensation of drowning—of being dragged under and unable to breathe. *Is this how Charlotte feels? And isn't there anything more I can do for her? Something has to be done! Perhaps she should try this experimental transplant. She is so young and gifted and has so much to offer the world. Please, God, heal her. Please, God, bring her to know You. Save her, Lord. Have mercy on her and give her the gift of eternal life. And use me as You will.*

Thus he prayed for her often. But he was conflicted about how much time and thought he should be giving to Charlotte, as well as his reluctance to share those concerns with Kate. Wrapped up in her own pressures, Kate seemed oblivious to his; and if the thought did cross her mind that something was bothering him, she attributed it to the same stress she was under—her parents' arrival and her desperate desire for their approval of her marriage.

The Hughes flew in early Thursday morning with Kate's brother Timmy and his nanny, Kitty, and hired a car to drive to Oxford. Kate was to meet her parents at the Randolph Hotel for lunch with Connie while Timmy napped. Although genuinely glad to see her parents again, Kate was unhappy with the tenor of their conversation in the elegant hotel dining room. It rapidly became an interrogation of Connie about David. Having known the Hughes for some time, Connie, to her credit, was not intimidated by the barrage of questions. She took it all in stride and spoke highly of David, putting him in the best possible light to these concerned but critical parents.

"So, Connie," Helen Hughes prodded further, "you seem to really like this David MacKenzie."

"Yes, ma'am, I really do, as do all the students. He's quite a popular lecturer and highly sought out as a tutor."

"What makes him so popular?"

"Well..." Connie thought for a minute. "Probably that he's such a good teacher. He really knows his material and makes it interesting and even funny, and he truly inspires the students to do their best work. Now, I don't actually have him since I'm studying history, but I've sat in on a few tutorials with Kate and my boyfriend, Nigel. And I can understand why they like him so much. Besides, he's not that much older than us, so he really relates well to the students and seems to really care for them."

"Do the other professors regard him as highly as the students?" This question came from Kate's father.

"I really wouldn't know that, Mr. Hughes, except to say that for a man so young to have earned his degree from Cambridge and then his masters from Oxford and already be lecturing as well as tutoring, must say something about their estimation of him."

Satisfied with her response, Tom Hughes nodded.

"What do you think of the way he treats Kate?" Helen Hughes asked. "Do you think she could be happy with him?"

Kate opened her mouth to answer, but her mother interrupted her. "I want to hear what Connie thinks, Katherine."

"Mrs. Hughes, I think any girl would be happy married to David MacKenzie," Connie answered honestly. "And believe me, there are plenty who wish they were in Kate's shoes. He treats her wonderfully. He adores her, he protects her, he's sensitive to her needs, he's concerned about her spiritual growth, and..." she hesitated, "...he's very romantic."

Tom Hughes snorted. "Sounds like some sort of pansy."

"Daddy!" Kate protested.

He shrugged. "Does he play any sports? Football?"

"English football—both rugby and soccer," Kate answered proudly. "He's captained both the Cambridge and Oxford soccer teams and helped each of them win the coveted 'blues.' And now he's assistant coach for the Oxford varsity team and is the captain of the University staff team. Daddy, I know you'll like him." She added coyly, "He loves American football too."

Tom Hughes grinned at his daughter. He knew her wiles, but she had always been able to melt his heart and get her way in the end. Her mother, on the other hand, was of a different mettle and not susceptible to Kate's charms.

"Even if all you say is true, Katherine," Helen Hughes interjected, "and this David MacKenzie of yours is God's gift to women, as you and Connie seem to be claiming, it still doesn't change the fact that he's only a college professor and will never make much money, and that his father is a rector with a ridiculously large family, which means they'll always be poor. This is England, remember, and there's still a very rigid class structure. I mean, obviously, with him you will not mix with the best society, as you did with that viscount you were dating. Now, *he* introduced you to the Prince of Wales!"

"For your information, mother, Lord Devereux thinks very highly of David and told him just the other night that he regards him as the much better man."

"Well, we'll see about that. When do we meet your Mr. MacKenzie, anyway? Your father and I thought perhaps you could bring him to dinner here tonight."

"That would be great," Kate answered. "And if you like, you could first come by Magdalen College after my tutorial and David could show you around."

"I don't know," her mother replied skeptically. "We're really tired from the flight and would like to take a nap. What time is your tutorial over?"

"Usually by four, but if it runs over or if you come early or late, you can just stop at the Porters' Lodge, and they'll either give you directions to David's rooms or you can phone him and we'll come down to meet you."

Helen sighed and looked at her husband.

"I think we should go over there," he responded. "We shouldn't take too long of a nap anyway or we won't ever go to sleep tonight. It's only fair we see where the boy works, and I've always wanted to see Magdalen College anyway." He turned to his daughter. "This may surprise you, honey, but I've always liked C.S. Lewis's books too—and it would be a real thrill to see where he lived and taught."

"Really, Daddy? Then I can't wait for you to see it. It's incredibly beautiful. And David knows so much about it. He's a fabulous tour guide."

"Yes, yes…it seems this David is fabulous at everything. He's all you can talk about. What about your old Pops? Don't you remember you're Daddy's little girl? I mean, you hardly know this boy! I'm the one who's taken care of you your whole life. I walked you all night long when you were a baby and wouldn't sleep. I taught you how to ride your bike, and how to play tennis. I listened to your prayers and your piano recitals and choral concerts—and I paid for your education…am still paying for your education, for that matter." His tone was lighthearted, but Kate knew he also was speaking his heart. "And who is this guy who thinks he can just come along and steal my little girl away from me and keep her over here thousands of miles from home in some little apartment? And leave me forgotten, like some piece of used Kleenex?"

"Daddy." Kate stood up and put her arms around her father's neck. "You know I love you. I appreciate all you and Mom have done for me and I will always be your girl. But," she added, "I have to grow up and leave home sometime."

"Yes, Sugar, I suppose so." Tom gave her a kiss on the cheek. "But I'm just not ready for it yet."

He assumed a more jocular tone. "All right, you girls go on and let us take our naps. We'll try to get over to Magdalen College about four o'clock. Thanks for coming by for lunch and, Connie"—he stood up to shake her hand—"thanks for putting up with our cross-examination. The jury is still out on this young man, but you were a good character witness for him."

"Thanks, Mr. Hughes," Connie answered. "And Mrs. Hughes. Thanks for lunch. It's good to see you again. Hope you enjoy your stay here in Oxford." She whispered to Kate as they left, "And let's hope they enjoy it enough to let you stay."

A few hours later, Kate and Nigel wrapped up their tutorial with David on *King Lear,* and Nigel took his leave of them. Preoccupied with her apprehensions about David's introduction to her parents, Kate had been unusually quiet in their discussion. She had been surprised at first to see that under his academic robe, David wore a coat and tie, until she realized he would have anticipated the possibility of her inviting her parents to his rooms. She looked around and noted with satisfaction that he and Watson must have spent some time sprucing up the old place. Even the windows sparkled as they stood open to the warm summer breeze and welcomed in the sweet scent of the wisteria climbing in profusion over the ancient yellow walls.

Before Kate had an opportunity to recount much of her lunch with her parents, the conversation was interrupted by Watson.

"Mr. MacKenzie?" The scout knocked lightly on the open door and came in. "Miss Hughes' parents are coming up the stairwell now and sent me on ahead to inform you."

"Right." David stood up and straightened his robe and tie. "Watson, would you please go in the bedroom and tidy things up a bit?"

"Yes, sir. But we just tidied up the bedroom."

"Yes, yes, I know. But I would like you to be about for a few minutes, in case they accept my invitation to dine in Hall."

"Right you are, Mr. MacKenzie. I'll just putter about for a bit."

"But David," Kate objected, "they've invited you to dinner at the hotel."

"It's all right, darling. Tonight's a guest night, and if they'll come, it will give them a good first impression of things."

Then the Hughes were standing in the doorway.

"Ah, Mr. and Mrs. Hughes!" David strode over to the door. "Please come in. I'm David MacKenzie." He shook their hands firmly. "I'm so glad you came up. It's very nice to meet you at last."

It pleased Kate that David and her father stood at exactly eye level with each other. Just shy of six feet tall, her father liked to round his height up to an even six. David had laughingly told her that he too was six feet tall, but for only a few minutes when he first got out of bed in the morning.

A former collegian football player, Tom Hughes' natural burliness had thickened with middle age. Still a handsome man, his sandy hair was sprinkled with white, and his hazel eyes were flecked with green and gold. His skin had the healthy amber sheen of a year-round tan. He was an avid sportsman—hunting, golf, and tennis—and he carried himself with the supreme confidence of a successful lawyer and politician.

David noticed that Helen Hughes had the same petite bone structure as Kate and his own mother but stood a few inches taller than both. Her dark chin-length hair was perfectly coifed in the style of Jackie Kennedy, and she wore a simple pink linen suit with white pillbox hat, pumps, and gloves that were reminiscent of the former First Lady as well. Her large dark eyes framed by thick lashes, her high cheekbones, small nose, and full lips, all echoed Kate's. But although she was a lovely woman, her fine features were now pinched with worry and peevishness. David quickly discerned that Mrs. Hughes was much like her violin, the beautiful instrument she played in the Richmond Symphony Orchestra. She was finely tuned and if tightened too much or mishandled, her strings could easily snap.

David welcomed them into his rooms and exchanged pleasantries about their flight and hotel, which segued into their invitation to David to join them for dinner.

"Thank you. That's most kind of you." David answered. "I would, however, like to ask you instead to do me the honor of dining in Hall tonight with me. It just so happens to be one of our guest nights, and it would give you the opportunity to dine in one of the loveliest refectories in Oxford, as well as to meet some of my colleagues."

Helen exchanged an uneasy glance with her husband. "Are we dressed properly?" Tom was wearing a navy blue sports coat and khaki slacks.

"Perfectly," David declared.

"Well, thanks," Tom decided. "That would be right nice."

"Excellent. I'll inform my man." Then David called out, "Watson?"

His deferential middle-aged scout promptly appeared from the bedroom. "Yes, Mr. MacKenzie?"

"Please convey to the cook that I'll have three guests for dinner tonight."

"Very good, sir. Anything else I can do for you before I go down, sir?"

"No, thank you, Watson. That will be all."

"Righto. Good evening." He gave a slight bow to the assemblage and left.

Kate nearly burst out laughing at David's cleverness. Having a personal manservant would definitely impress her mother. She was right.

"Was that man your valet?" Helen asked.

David winked at Kate before turning to her mother to answer. "Not exactly, ma'am. Watson is what we call a scout. He cleans up, runs errands, and even brings up food. In the old days, the University men usually had their own personal servants, but these days, our scouts serve several dons or a larger number of students."

"What exactly is a don?"

"Why, that's what I am: a university tutor or lecturer. In the States you would call me a professor."

"But you *are* a professor, aren't you?"

"Well, here, ma'am, a professorship is a very elite position. They are elected by the faculty and hold endowed chairs."

"Do you aspire to be a professor?"

"Certainly. But that won't happen for many years. Even C.S. Lewis was not awarded a professorship after more than twenty years as a Fellow here at Oxford. He finally left because he was offered a chair at Cambridge."

"Really? I see. And what about these rooms? Do you rent them? Is this where you live?"

"No, ma'am, I don't rent the rooms. They are given to me along with whatever meals I want as a part of my stipend. I could live here if I liked. If you want to look around, you'll see there is a bedroom. In fact, I did live in these rooms my first year as a Fellow, but they're rather drafty in the winter and never very private, so I let a flat a few blocks away. You are welcome to come by to see that too if you like."

Helen gave a look at her husband. He cleared his throat and then spoke.

"To be honest with you, son, there's something we'd like to ask before we do any more looking around. I don't know any graceful way around this, so I'm just going to ask you straight up."

"Please," David answered. "I'd be happy to answer anything."

"You know, I have to tell you frankly that we were quite shocked to get your letter asking to marry Kate. We had no idea your relationship was that serious. Now, I know Kate seemed to be sweet on you, but we thought it was only a schoolgirl crush. And then to have you want to get married before she's even graduated—and so soon—it made us wonder if you have to get married."

"I'm not sure what you mean."

"What I mean is—do you *have* to get married. Is Kate pregnant?"

"Daddy!" Kate gasped.

"Now, Sugar, your mother and I have talked about this for days, and we want you to know that no matter what you have done, we will always love you. But you don't *have* to get married. We can work something out." He almost glowered at David.

"Mr. Hughes." David stiffened. "You are most mistaken. Kate is *not* pregnant. In fact, it would be most impossible. Mr. Hughes, Mrs. Hughes, you must understand that I am a committed Christian, as is your daughter, and we determined at the beginning of our relationship that we would conduct ourselves with the utmost purity. In short, Mr. Hughes, I have not ever inappropriately touched your daughter and, moreover, we have not even kissed yet."

"Oh, come now," Tom Hughes scoffed. "I wasn't born yesterday. I know what goes on at these college campuses. And you expect me to believe you two haven't even kissed?"

"We haven't, Daddy." Kate's voice shook with emotion. "We decided to save our first kiss until our wedding day."

Now it was the Hughes' turn to be incredulous. "What?"

"That's right," Kate affirmed. "Our first kiss will be at the altar."

"Then there may not be a first kiss. Look, I'm thrilled and relieved that you're not pregnant, as I'm sure your mother is. But that doesn't mean that we are going to let you two get married. And if you're not pregnant, what's the rush?"

"Mr. Hughes, allow me to say how much I truly love your daughter." David spoke now with earnest passion. "And I don't merely love her—I admire, esteem, and adore her. I can't possibly convey to you the depths of my feelings. Sadly, the English language is inadequate. In Greek, there are four words for love: *phileo, storge, eros,* and *agape.* Combined, even these words only begin to express my love for Kate. I would, without a moment's hesitation, give my life for her, and I don't say that lightly or as a cliché. She is the most beautiful woman I have ever known, and I'm not speaking only of her physical beauty. That's a mere reflection of her inward beauty. As you know, she's a remarkable young woman, and I'm sure much of who she is can be attributed to your parenting.

"I'm certain you believe there is not a man in the world good enough for her, and I quite agree with you. If I thought it was really in her best interest *not* to marry me, then I love her enough to give her up. But I do believe God has brought us together, and I know that with His help, I will do and be everything I can to love her, provide for her, and make her happy. My commitment to Kate is for as long as we both shall live. I appeal to you and Mrs. Hughes to give us your blessing to be married. Our hope is to be married soon, and we have kept ourselves pure in that hope."

David glanced at Kate and saw her beaming with approval at his boldness.

Tom Hughes cleared his throat. "Well spoken, son. I don't think a father could ask for more for his daughter than to find a good husband who truly loves her and has her best interests at heart. However, we are not ready to give our blessing yet. We can not be moved simply by an eloquent address. We would like to have some time to get to know you better, see your circumstances firsthand, and meet your family."

"Quite right." David answered. "And that reminds me, my parents are most keen to meet you as well, and my mother asked if you might like to come over tomorrow evening after dinner for some coffee and dessert. I'm sorry it can't be for dinner, but I have a football match, which—by the way—I would be honored for you to attend, if you have the interest."

"You play football?"

"Sorry. Soccer. But, Mr. Hughes, as a sports fan I'm sure you would enjoy the match. We're on to a winning season, but this match promises to be a close one. Should be quite exciting."

"No soccer for me, thanks." Helen spoke up. "But, Tom, you should go if you want to. You can pick me up at the hotel afterwards. I do think we should accept your mother's invitation, David. She was so good to Kate after the accident and very thoughtful to call me to keep me informed of what was happening over here. I would like to meet her and your father very much...and all your brothers and sisters as well, I suppose."

David chose to overlook this last little insensitive comment. "We would also like to meet Kate's brother Timmy. Would you please bring him too?"

An awkward silence fell while the Hughes exchanged looks.

Tom Hughes answered. "Thanks for the invitation, but we don't want to impose on your family."

"Mr. Hughes, I assure you that he would not be an imposition. I have three younger brothers and a three-year-old sister. I'm sure Timmy would enjoy himself."

Tom cleared his throat. "I'm sure he would too, but Tim is a...special child."

"Really, it's not a problem," David insisted. "Children are always welcome at our house, and every child is considered special."

"He would be fine," Kate affirmed. "Please let him come. I haven't had much time with him."

Tom glanced at Helen, who reluctantly nodded. "All right."

"Excellent!" David smiled reassuringly. "Shall we make it eight o'clock then? And Mr. Hughes, if you decide you want to come to the match, Kate can give you directions."

"Sounds good," Tom Hughes concluded. "Now how about that tour?"

"Right." David first showed his guests about his rooms, making certain they caught the beautiful view from his window over the Deer Park, where a large herd grazed peacefully among a profusion of wildflowers. Then he took them on his customary tour of Magdalen's extensive property as he explained some of the history of the college and information about the University and its life. David had many strengths, but speaking was one of his greatest, and he kept the Hughes entertained and enthralled by his personalized tour.

By the time they arrived at dinner, they had reluctantly grown impressed both by their surroundings and by this young man who wanted to marry their daughter. These favorable impressions grew as they sat down to dine in Magdalen's magnificent Hall with its sixteenth-century linen-fold paneling. It was clear from the banter and conversation in the Hall that Connie's assessment of David's popularity with students and the respect he enjoyed among other dons was a correct one. And Dr. Palmer, the President of Magdalen, after being introduced, confirmed how highly David was esteemed in the University.

Since there were very few women present, Kate and her mother spoke little during the meal. Yet Kate was pleased to overhear David affably and knowledgeably discussing with her father his two favorite topics: American politics and football.

Pleading fatigue, her parents declined a visit to David's flat after dinner and waited by the Porters' Lodge while he secured a taxi to convey them back to the hotel. David discerned that the Hughes family might want some time alone together, and he took his leave of them. While they waited, Kate couldn't resist asking her parents for their impressions.

"Well?" she asked apprehensively.

"Well, what?" her father rejoined.

"Well, what do you think of David?"

"Quite honestly, Kate," Tom replied. "I like him. I like him very much. Maybe he just knows how to make a good first impression, but he certainly appears to be a fine young man." He grinned. "Anyway, a Brit who knows so much about the Washington Redskins can't be all bad."

"Mom?"

"Oh, honey." Helen sighed. "I'm so tired I can't think straight. Do you know we've been up all night on a plane?"

"Yes, Mom, I know—but how do you like David?"

Helen sighed again. "He is very handsome, I'll give you that, and his manners are as handsome as he is. I can understand why you've fallen for him. But that still doesn't mean I think he'd make a suitable husband for you. Oh, Kate, I was hoping you would marry someone from our set. Why couldn't you have fallen in love with some nice young Virginian gentleman from William and Mary?"

"Or how about UVA?" Tom added.

Kate knew her father set great store by his alma mater, the University of Virginia, and she had a sudden inspiration. "Daddy, David's grandfather was a professor at UVA!"

Tom grunted. "Really? Why didn't you mention that before?"

"I don't know. I forgot about it—and since you didn't seem too impressed with David being a professor, I thought it wouldn't make much difference to you."

Tom's curiosity was piqued. "What's his grandfather's name? Maybe I knew him."

"Granddad." Kate grimaced in chagrin. "I don't remember his real name. David always calls him 'granddad.' I think he said he taught English—or maybe it was religion—but anyway, I guess you can ask him about it tomorrow."

Tom Hughes looked thoughtful. "A professor at the University of Virginia…Huh! Whaddaya know? Helen, maybe this young man is from good stock after all."

25

Seventh Week, Friday

The Hughes spent the morning touring Oxford on the Guide Friday Bus and joined Kate for lunch at St. Hilda's. In the evening, Tom Hughes decided to attend David's football game, a closely contested match between the Mansfield Road University Staff team and AFC Jericho. With only minutes to spare, the Oxford staff won by a goal off David's assist. Although it had been his first English football match, Tom Hughes had quickly become an enthusiastic fan and cheered loudly for the home team and its captain, his prejudices brushed aside by his grudging regard for David's athletic prowess. Kate fairly glowed with pride. After the game, she and her father returned to the Randolph for her mother and brother. David showered and changed, then drove straight to the rectory to meet them there.

When he walked in, David noticed that his family's home was especially clean and orderly. Fresh flowers from the garden brightened the hallway, and he heard classical music playing softly from the record player in the parlor. Striding back towards the kitchen, he spied little Hannah dressed in a blue smocked dress, crinoline petticoat, and white patent-leather shoes. A blue satin bow adorned her blonde ringlets.

"Now, don't you look pretty tonight?" David complimented Hannah and his mother's handiwork as he picked up his sister and kissed both her cheeks. Still holding her in his arms, he went to his mother, who was preparing the coffee and tea, and kissed her as well.

"Hullo, Mum. Everything looks fabulous. Thanks for having them over tonight and for all your hard work."

"You're welcome, honey. Have you had any dinner?"

"No—frankly, I'm starving. May I raid the fridge?"

"I saved you a plate. It's warming in the oven."

"What a marvelous mummy you are! Hannah, do you know we have the best mummy in the whole world?"

Hannah nodded solemnly. David kissed her again and put her down. "Now, be a good girl and be sweet to Kate's brother Timmy, all right?"

"Okeydokey!" she sang and skipped off down the hall.

" 'Okeydokey'? What are you teaching that child, Mum?" David took some potholders and pulled his plate from the oven.

Annie smiled. "Good ol' American English. How was your game, honey?"

"Brilliant. Very close match, but of course we completely dominated them." He grinned.

"Of course." Annie's smile broadened. "That's what you always say."

"No, seriously. It was close. Jericho has a good team, but we triumphed one–nil with just minutes left on the clock." David gave this account as he shoveled in his dinner.

"Did you score the goal?"

David swallowed. "The assist. Oh, it was sweet. A little dribbling, a feint, and then I served it up to Gerrard, who slid it right in the corner of the net."

"Well done! And was Mr. Hughes there to enjoy your victory?"

"Indeed he was. And Kate as well. I think he did rather enjoy himself."

"How do Kate's parents seem to like you?"

David carried his empty plate to the sink and rinsed it off. "I think her father's warming up to me. Mrs. Hughes is another story, though. In her mind, Kate is '*a star out of my sphere*,' to quote the Bard. I don't know what it will take with her, except a miracle."

"Well, I hope the children behave and we don't ruin things for you."

"Mother," David remonstrated playfully. "Everyone adores you and Dad, and as for the boys, we'll just pretend they're wards of the state or something."

Annie laughed. "Get out of here!"

"I need to. They'll be here soon."

"Where's Kate?"

"She's riding with them to show them the way. Where are Dad and the boys?"

"Upstairs. Your father is in his study, and the boys are in the family room under strict orders not to make a mess."

Just then the doorbell rang, and Hannah shouted, "They're here! They're here!"

"I guess they're here," David said dryly. "Well, here we go. Lord help us!"

By the time he reached the end of the hall, the house had been sufficiently alerted to the arrival of company. William, who had been tasked with answering the door, performed that function in a friendly, polite manner, while Eric MacKenzie emerged from his study and the younger boys clattered down the stairs.

Annie could hear introductions being made in the parlor as she carried the tea tray into the dining room. She prayed silently that her family would be a blessing to the Hughes and that the Hughes would subsequently bless the marriage. She fretted that her own family might be the cause of their disapprobation and fervently hoped that the evening would successfully amend any apprehensions Kate's parents might have on their account. All was as ready and as proper as she could make it.

She smoothed out her dress, took a deep breath, and stepped into the parlor. Surveying the room, she saw that her husband and Mr. Hughes were still engaged in conversation near the hallway entrance. Mrs. Hughes and her young son stood with Kate and David by the fireplace, where Hannah was presenting Kate's mother with some flowers from their garden.

Nice touch, David, Annie thought approvingly. Hannah then took Timmy's hand and led him over to her brothers. Short and plump, Timmy had the sandy hair of his father. Annie immediately recognized the sweet round face and slanted eyes characteristic of a child with Down syndrome.

She walked up to Kate's mother and extended her hand. "Hello, Helen." She smiled warmly. "I'm Annie, David's mom. I'm so glad to meet you after all those telephone conversations last December."

Helen took her hand and gushed in her southern drawl, "Annie. I'm so glad to meet you at last! I want to thank you again for being so wonderful to Kate. I don't know what we would have done during that terrible time if y'all hadn't looked out for her. We're so grateful."

"It was our pleasure, really."

"And these flowers are gorgeous! That little Hannah of yours is adorable. Why, she's just the sweetest little thing I ever did see."

"Thank you." The two women watched their children interacting for a moment. Then Annie turned and looked steadily at Helen. "Your Timmy is very sweet too." Helen read in Annie's eyes the sincere compassion only another mother could share. "Thank you," she said quietly. "He really is."

Eric brought Tom Hughes into the parlor to complete his introductions. The boys nodded their greetings as they stood uncomfortably on the edge of the room, waiting for their chance to escape. "Tom, would it be all right if the boys take Timmy upstairs for a few minutes and show him some of their toys?"

Tom looked to Helen for guidance. Kate observed their reluctance. "I'll go up with him and get him settled," she volunteered.

"Okay, honey," Tom agreed.

"Excellent," Eric approved. "Go on, lads. Have fun, and we'll call you down for cake." The boys readily accepted this reprieve and clambered up the stairs with Timmy, Hannah, and Kate in pursuit. "Tom, I think you've met everyone now but my wife, Annie."

Annie walked toward Kate's father and offered her hand.

"Hi, Tom. It's nice to meet you." She awkwardly dropped her hand when he failed to take it.

Tom was staring at her stupidly. "Annie?" He repeated slowly. "Annie? 'Little Annie'?"

Mystified, she smiled. "No one has called me that in years. How did you know that was my nickname?"

Tom shook his head incredulously. "Annie Little! Kate said David's grandfather was a professor at UVA. Your father was Lawrence Little, professor of religion, wasn't he?"

"Yes."

"And you lived in the second pavilion on the right side of the lawn, facing the rotunda." This was a statement, not a question.

"Yes. Pavilion IV." Annie was perplexed. "I still don't understand. How do you know all this?"

"I took Old and New Testament Surveys from your father and was one of the myriad young Virginia gentlemen who came to his weekly soirées. Coffee or hot chocolate in the parlor in the winter, and lemonade and iced tea out back in the gardens in the spring. And always Mrs. Little's famed black velvet cake and chocolate-chip cookies."

"Oh, my word!" breathed Annie.

"We thought your father didn't suspect that all those young men weren't there for his vast store of knowledge, but for a glimpse of his three pretty daughters and especially little Annie, the youngest and prettiest. Now I think maybe he did know, but was glad for any means to share his faith with the students. My goodness, Annie, you don't look a day older than you did in high school!"

Annie couldn't so easily place Tom Hughes among the young collegiate men who had paraded through her parents' house.

"You probably don't remember me. I played football but was a lot slimmer than I am now."

Then the memory clicked. "You're Tommy Hughes! I don't believe it!"

Tom laughed. "Small world, isn't it? Helen, this is Professor Little's daughter."

"Well, I'll be!" Helen exclaimed.

The Hughes and Annie began reminiscing while Eric and David served coffee and cake. Kate, slipping quietly back into their company and hearing the tenor of their talk, exchanged hopeful glances with David.

Suddenly their animated conversation was cut short by a wail.

Helen stiffened. "That sounds like Timmy."

David stood up quickly. "Please don't get up. I'll go check. Kate, why don't you come with me?"

With Kate following, he bounded up the stairs and was met by a worried William.

"Timmy cut his foot on the train set. It's bleeding a lot."

"How did he cut his foot?" David asked as they climbed rapidly to the top-floor sitting room.

"He insisted on taking off his shoes and socks and then stepped on it. I'm sorry. I was doing my homework and not paying attention."

"It's all right, Will." David tried to reassure his brother but was confronted with the increasingly loud cries of a frightened Timmy, who was sitting on the floor holding his bleeding foot. Hannah joined the wails in sympathy.

"All right, everybody. No need to panic." David spoke calmly. "Hey, buddy. It will be all right. Here's Kate," he said as they both dropped to their knees beside Timmy. "Let me take a look at that, big guy."

"It's okay, Timmy," Kate soothed. "David will take care of you."

David gingerly looked at the sole of the boy's foot and then whipped a clean handkerchief out of his pocket and wrapped it gently but tightly around the wound to stop the bleeding. "It's a lot of blood but just a small gash," he told Kate. "I don't think it will need stitches. We'll let Mum look at it. Please go get her and get some hot water and towels ready in the kitchen." He smiled at Timmy. "Okay, buddy, we're going to take you downstairs and clean this up." David raised the little boy and tried to support him with his arm around his waist, but Timmy stubbornly refused to budge.

"Right." David sighed. "All right, big guy, since you don't want to hobble downstairs, how about a horsey-back ride? Does that sound like more fun?"

Timmy smiled through his tears. David squatted down and pulled the boy onto his back.

"Will, please walk down behind us so I don't drop him." The MacKenzie children filed down three flights of stairs behind their big brother and his Tiny Tim burden. On the first landing, David said, "Timmy, my boy, I hope you will remember not to take off your shoes next time." Then he began singing in his strong baritone, *"I got shoes. You got shoes, all God's children got shoes. When I get to heaven, gonna put on my shoes—gonna walk all over God's heaven..."*

Timmy joined in—"*...heaven, heaven...heaven, gonna put...shoes and gonna walk... heaven!*"

Halfway up the staircase, the Hughes encountered the astonishing spectacle of their small son clinging to David's back and dangling a handkerchief-wrapped foot while smiling broadly and singing lustily off-key.

"Gracious sakes!" Helen exclaimed anxiously. "Timmy, are you all right?"

"Gonna put shoes, Mama!"

"He's okay, Mrs. Hughes," David assured her. "It's just a little gash. Let's go down to the kitchen and clean it up."

Kate and Annie had already gathered towels and a basin of warm water in the kitchen. David carefully lowered his lively burden into a chair and carefully unwrapped his bloodied handkerchief, placed Timmy's foot in the basin, and gently washed away the blood and dirt.

"David's right," Annie said as she checked it, applied peroxide, and bandaged it. "No need for stitches, but he'll want to keep off it because it will be sore for a few days. So have him keep it elevated as much as possible—and he'll probably want some aspirin for pain."

Tom Hughes stood with his hand on his wife's shoulder as they watched the tender ministrations to their son. This family had taken care of their daughter in dire circumstances and was now treating their handicapped son with equal solicitude.

Helen felt strangely humbled and touched. "Thank you…so much," she murmured with tears glistening in her eyes. Tom squeezed her shoulder. She looked up at him and nodded.

"We're just so sorry Timmy was hurt and it happened here," Annie answered as she dried her hands. "But thankfully, it's nothing serious."

David stood at the sink washing his hands. Helen could see there were blood stains on the back of his trousers. "Oh, I'm sorry, David, he's ruined your slacks. We'll buy you another pair."

"Don't worry about it. They'll come clean. They've been through a lot worse." He smiled at Timmy. "How you doin', buddy? All better?"

Timmy nodded.

"How about some cake? Would you like that?"

"Yep!"

"All right. Would you like another ride?" David squatted down, and Timmy put his arms around his neck.

"Giddyup!" Timmy cried gleefully.

David loped into the parlor with his laughing rider and lowered him gently on the sofa.

Timmy clung to his neck. "I like you," he said.

David smiled. "I like you too, Timmy."

"Be my brother?"

David chuckled and replied quietly, "I'd love to be, buddy."

Guileless, Timmy appealed loudly to his parents. "Mama, Daddy, he be—my brother?"

The sight of their son, his chubby arms wrapped around David's neck in trusting affection, and David, returning his embrace with loving acceptance, pierced their hearts.

"Timmy, would you like that?" Helen asked. "Do you want David to be your brother?"

Timmy's smile broadened. "Yep! I do!"

Helen smiled through tears. "You know, honey, I believe I do too."

"Yippee!" Timmy shouted.

Laughing, David hugged him more tightly. *Yippee!* his heart echoed.

Tom Hughes took his wife's hand in his. He then looked kindly at David. "Young man, I know we've been hard on you and I hope you won't hold that against us. One day, I think you'll understand how difficult it is to let your children go. You know we had our reservations, but the more we've seen of you and gotten to know you and your wonderful family—well, we'd be honored to have you for our son-in-law."

David disentangled himself from Timmy's arms and warmly shook Tom's hand. "Thank you, sir. The honor is mine. I promise I'll take great care of your daughter."

"Oh, Daddy! Mom! Thank you!" Kate cried happily as she hugged them and then was caught up in David's embrace.

"Yippee!" shouted Timmy again, and everyone laughed with joy.

26

Eighth Week

The atmosphere at the MacKenzies' immediately shed cautious social niceties in favor of warm familial excitement. Once Helen Hughes had embraced the idea that her daughter was to be married to this young Oxford professor, it took little to convince her of the efficacy of proceeding with the wedding on British soil as soon as possible. After all, wasn't half the family there already, and weren't Kate's sister and other brother flying over to join them for the summer holidays? So long as she could be on the scene to plan the wedding, Helen was content.

It was agreed that the banns would be read on the next three consecutive Sundays, and the men went into the church secretary's small office by the front door to confirm the reservation for the church on the third of July. Annie walked Helen through the rectory garden and into the Rectory Hall, and Helen promptly decided on an afternoon wedding at two o'clock followed by a garden reception, weather permitting. If it rained, the reception could easily move into the Hall.

Helen began planning the guest list. *And how many guests did they foresee inviting? Let's see...our family makes six, yours is how many? Yes, nine, ten with your great-aunt MacKenzie, that makes fifteen so far. Connie and her boyfriend Nigel, sixteen, seventeen. Austen and Yvette. Who are they? Oh, yes. Let's see, that makes nineteen. President and Mrs. Palmer of Magdalen College, twenty, twenty-one. Mrs. Bingley? Who?*

Oh, David's landlady? Twenty-two. Kevin Ryan, his college... "suite-mate," did you say? And those Inkling Society students still in town, plus a few of the young men from the soccer team. So about thirty? Thirty-five? That should be easy enough to accommodate. I should think that in Richmond, we'll have to invite about three hundred. Oh, do remind me, Tom, to call home tomorrow to reserve the Country Club of Virginia for September. And Annie, what about you and Eric? Don't you have friends here you would like to invite? Yes, I know David wants to keep it small. Yes, I can understand that if you invite a few friends you'd have to invite the whole church. Your friends are going to help you with the rehearsal dinner in the Rectory Hall? How sweet. A Scottish "kay-lee"? Never heard the term before. How do you spell it? C-e-i-l-i-d-h. Sounds like a charming idea to bring in the MacKenzie Scottish heritage as well. Now, Annie, tell me which caterers are well-respected in town. You must have worked with hundreds of weddings at the church and would know the best of everything. Could you give me a list? Wonderful!

On Saturday morning, the Hughes took Kate up to London. Acquiescing to David's sisters' request to join them, they wasted no time in selecting a wedding gown at Harrods. Kate liked the full-skirted gowns because they made her feel like a princess, but her more practical mother convinced her to chose the straighter sheath style since it would be easier to pack and transport home; and moreover, the straight look was the most fashionable at the moment. Kate was satisfied when she determined that the silk sheath with its three-deep horizontal pleats across the flared hem could be worn on its own as a strapless evening gown. For the wedding, a short-sleeved bolero jacket of Venetian lace with tiny seed pearls covered the top of the gown, and they ordered a silk tulle fingertip veil attached to a wide hair band covered in matching lace.

After eating lunch on Oxford Street, Helen Hughes selected her own mother-of-the-bride suit—also silk, in a robin's-egg blue coordinated with a hat and handbag. She ordered her shoes dyed to match and to be delivered to the Randolph Hotel in Oxford. Then she took the girls to look at china and silver patterns. Tom Hughes joined them at four o'clock for tea at the Ritz. He had prudently separated from the women, seeking refuge in the National Gallery nearby. His dark raw-silk suit would do just fine, thank you, for the wedding.

On Sunday, Eric MacKenzie proudly read the wedding banns at St. Aldate's. On Monday afternoon, Helen made an appointment for David to meet them in London at Harrods to make a final decision on their patterns for Royal Doulton china, Waterford crystal, and Gorham sterling. David, who cared little for such things, obediently complied—anything to keep his fiancée and his future mother-in-law happy. Annie's good friend Jennifer had offered to make the wedding cake as her gift. When Helen was convinced that her work was quite as beautiful as any professional's and would, in fact, taste ever so much better, she agreed. After all, it would be a small cake. By Wednesday, Helen Hughes had secured the services of a caterer, florist, photographer, and engraver in Oxford, and had called her housekeeper in Richmond with a list of vendors to contract for September as well. Once Helen Hughes set her mind to something, she was a paragon of efficiency.

Kate spent the rest of her time finishing her final essays for the term. On Thursday, she had her last tutorial with David and Nigel on *Hamlet.* Since the afternoon was clear and warm, David suggested they hold their session across the street from Magdalen in the Botanic Gardens. A slight sadness and sense of nostalgia clung to the three as they discussed this greatest of plays. The end of term acutely highlighted the inevitability of the passage of time and the changes borne with it. Although by no means Kate's last literary discussion with David, it certainly would be her last official tutorial with him.

When their comments were concluded, Nigel stood and offered his hand to David.

"It's been a real pleasure, Mr. MacKenzie. I look forward to studying with you again next Michaelmas."

"Thank you, Nigel. What are your plans for the summer? Will you be able to make it to the wedding?"

"July third, is it? Absolutely. I'll be staying in Oxford this summer working with Mr. Lewis's secretary, as you suggested. I appreciate the recommendation, by the way. My family will be on holiday at Brighton next week, so I'm taking Connie down to the seaside to meet them, but we'll definitely be back in time for the wedding. Wouldn't miss it for the world." He flashed his big toothy grin.

"Fabulous," David said, returning his smile. "We'll look forward to seeing you."

"Righto. I'll catch you two later." Nigel strode off, whistling.

"Excellent fellow, that Nigel," remarked David to Kate. "Keen mind, affable personality. He'd make a good don. What's going to happen with him and Connie? She is returning to the States, isn't she?"

"Yes. It's been the source of a lot of tears. She's quite envious of me getting married," Kate replied. "But Nigel has another year to go, as does she. Before going home, she plans to knock about over here with some of the other American girls. Then in September, Nigel will visit her in the States. He'll probably attend our reception there. Wouldn't it be wonderful if they got married too? Then I could have a good friend over here."

"Yes, darling," David said gently, "that would be very nice. Do you think you'll be terribly lonely here?"

"No." Taking his hand in hers, she smiled. "After all, I'll be living with my best friend."

David kissed her hand, his blue eyes reflecting their shared joy. Suddenly, his face clouded with concern.

"Kate, there's something I need to talk to you about." He glanced at his watch. "Unfortunately, I don't have much time for discussion right now because I'm due at a faculty meeting soon."

"Oh no, you don't, David MacKenzie. You've gotten my curiosity up so you'd better tell me now. What is it?"

He took a deep breath. "It's about Charlotte."

Kate frowned and pulled her hand away.

"Now, just listen, Kate—please. She's still quite ill. In fact, she's much worse."

"I thought she had a blood transfusion."

"She did. It seemed to work for a bit. But now she's going downhill fast. It's really rather frightening. Anyway, the doctors want her to try an experimental treatment—a transplant of bone marrow—as soon as possible."

Kate's suspicions arose. "How do you know all this? Have you been talking to her?"

"Yes," David answered cautiously. "She rings me up sometimes."

"How often?"

"Oh, I don't know."

"How often?" Kate insisted.

David thought for a minute. "I guess fairly often."

"Have you been seeing her?"

"No, not since the time I told you about."

He checked his watch again.

"I only have a few minutes. What I want to talk to you about is the experimental treatment. They still have not been able to reach her brother, who is the most likely person to get bone marrow from. If they can't do this transplant, the doctors don't give her long to live, barring a miracle. Kate, I want to be tested as a possible donor, as they call it. Charlotte and I have the same blood type, so I may match."

"But if you are a match, when would they do this 'transplant'? What does it entail? What danger is it to you? And how can we get married if you're laid up in hospital?"

"I don't know how it works. I need to talk to the doctors."

"But why you? Why do you have to be the big hero… and for *her!*"

"Kate, I just want to look into it. I can't sit back passively and watch a woman die. I don't think I could live with myself if I could have helped, but didn't."

"So she's that important to you? Would you do the same thing for someone else? For me?"

"Kate," David took her hand in his and locked his eyes on hers. "I would die for you."

"And for Charlotte?"

"The Bible says, *Greater love has no man than this, that a man lay down his life for his friends.*"

"David, you don't have to be the savior of the world!"

"Of course not, darling. I don't presume to be, and I certainly hope that laying down my life literally won't be required of me. But laying it down figuratively may be—and at the very least, I want to make myself available. Can you understand that?"

"Yes, I guess so. Look, I really feel badly for Charlotte…and of course, I don't want her to die. I just wish her brother would show up or someone else could give the marrow." Kate sighed. "But I suppose it wouldn't hurt for you to talk to the doctor."

"That's my girl." He kissed her gently on the forehead and stood to leave. "I love you, Kate. I'll ring you tonight after dinner."

She nodded in reply and then watched him walk through the stone arch of the gardens out to the High Street. She sat staring at the massive stone tower of Magdalen as her thoughts and feelings tumbled about disconnectedly.

"Well, hello, Gorgeous!" An aristocratic accent commanded her attention. "The sight of you makes this lovely day even lovelier."

"Oh hello, Stuart," Kate answered glumly.

"Sorry, am I that distasteful to you?"

"No, I'm sorry. I was thinking about something else. Here, have a seat." Kate moved her books and Stuart complied, stretching out his long legs.

Kate tried to be more cheerful. "How are you? Are you finished for the term?"

"One more tutorial to go. I'm doing fine, thank you, considering that the most beautiful girl of my acquaintance is shortly to be married to another man."

"Oh, Stuart!"

"No, no. Really, I'm fine. I can still admire your beauty from afar. But what about you? You don't look too happy. You're not having the wedding-bell blues, are you?"

"No, not at all."

"Well, what is it, then? You can tell old Stu all about it."

Kate thought for a moment, then answered with a question. "Stuart, may I ask you something? And will you promise to tell me the truth?"

He sat up straight. "I've never lied to you, have I?"

She looked at him skeptically.

"Well, I may have dissembled a bit, but never outright lied." He smiled good-naturedly. "I am a gentleman, you know, and have some sense of honor. Of course I'll tell you the truth. Fire away."

"Okay." Kate took a deep breath. "You know back at Eights at the Head of the River when you accused David of making an honest woman of me?"

Stuart groaned. "Kate, I apologized for that already. I am truly sorry."

"No, it's not that. But, why did you say that?"

"I told you, I was drunk. I'm sorry."

"No—I mean, where did you get the idea we were sleeping together? Where did you hear that?"

Stuart shrugged. "I don't know. Rumors. J.C.R. gossip, I suppose."

"Stuart, did you start those rumors?" Kate asked pointedly.

"Heavens, no! Why would I do such a thing? I may be a cad, but I'm not malicious."

His answer satisfied Kate as to his innocence in the affair, but she had other suspicions. "Okay. But remember that day you picked me up on Magdalen Bridge and I told you I was going to Cambridge with David? Did you tell anyone else we were going?"

"Well, let me see...I was feeling rather put out about it, so I may have." Stuart thought for a moment. "Ah...yes...I did go over to Somerville that night and complained to Lucy and Lydia."

"Somerville." Kate's suspicions grew. "Now, think hard. Do you remember anyone else there at the time?"

Stuart's brow furrowed in concentration. "Ah...yes...I do remember. Miss Mansfield was there. I thought it a little odd she should be hanging about the J.C.R. rather than the S.C.R., but she and Lucy get on quite well." He looked at Kate closely. "What? You don't think she started the rumors, do you?"

"I don't know. But I wouldn't put it past her."

"Well! *Hell hath no fury like a woman scorned.* Pretty low nonetheless, I should say. So, is that what's been bothering you?"

"There's more than that. Did you know she's been really sick?"

"Charlotte Mansfield?" Stuart asked incredulously.

"Yes. She's been keeping it a secret, but if you won't spread it about, I'll tell you. She's been diagnosed with a severe type of anemia called aplastic anemia, and it could be fatal. She needs a transplant of bone marrow—it's an experimental treatment—and her brother, who is the best possible match for the transplant, is in the Orient somewhere and can't be reached. Anyway, she's been calling David a lot, and now he's thinking of being tested to see if he can give the marrow—and right before we're supposed to be married."

"Well, I can see why you're not too happy. But are you sure about all this? This aplastic anemia bit? I haven't heard a word."

"I told you, she wants to keep it quiet. She doesn't want to lose her job."

"I see." Stuart was thoughtful. "Well, this is rather dreadful, isn't it? I'm sure it must be most distressing to all of you. I wish there was something I could do to help."

"No, of course there's nothing. But thanks just for listening."

Stuart stood up. "Well, I'm sorry, darling, but I must be off. I do hope all this sorts out for the best."

He took her hand and kissed it chivalrously. "Good-bye, Gorgeous. You will make a stunning bride. Don't fret your pretty little head about all this. It will all work out in the end. I'm sure the Big Man Upstairs will see to it."

Kate sighed and then smiled. "I'm sure you're right. Thanks. Good-bye, Stuart."

~

Later that evening after dinner, David sat at his desk in the New Building working through a stack of essays. He fidgeted in his seat and chewed on the end of his pen. He loathed marking papers and was thankful when a knock at the door interrupted him. But the tall, lanky figure standing in the hallway took him by surprise. David stood up.

"Lord Devereux! Please come in."

"Sorry to bother you, sir. I know you're busy, but if I could have just a few minutes of your time."

"Certainly. Please have a seat." David indicated a chair across from his desk. "I say, Lord Devereux, that was awfully kind of you to give up your seats at Stratford."

"No problem," answered Stuart as he sat down. "And please call me Stuart."

"Right. Stuart. What may I do for you?"

"Mr. MacKenzie, I ran into Kate in the Botanic Gardens, and she confided to me that Miss Mansfield is quite ill."

David frowned. "That's supposed to be confidential. Miss Mansfield doesn't want it spread about."

"Yes. I quite understand—and you have my word it won't go any further. But out of my respect for you and my regard for Kate, I would like to...I feel compelled to say..."

"Well, what is it, man?"

"Mr. MacKenzie, I don't quite know how to say this, but I don't believe Charlotte Mansfield is truly sick."

"But of course she is. She just hasn't told many people. She's a very private person—and as a single woman in what is predominantly a man's field, she is very anxious not to appear to be weak in any way. Rightly or wrongly, she is concerned about job security."

"But sir, what proof do you have that she's ill?"

"Proof? Why, my own eyes! I took her to the infirmary myself one night when she could hardly walk. And I've seen her in tremendous pain. It's been most distressing."

Stuart stroked his chin thoughtfully. "Mr. MacKenzie, I've listened to a lot of your lectures on Shakespeare. One theme you particularly like to illuminate is 'appearance versus reality.' In *Othello, Macbeth, Hamlet,* and certainly many of the comedies, you've said that Shakespeare demonstrates things are not always what they seem."

"What are you saying, Stuart?"

"Well, *'since brevity is the soul of wit, I will be brief.'* To wit: You have seen Charlotte Mansfield very ill. I have equally seen her very healthy—in fact, I've seen her partying away at Somerville and numerous pubs and clubs about town. My friend Lucy Bertram has become quite an intimate of Charlotte's, and I've been quite often in the company of both. I believe one of us is seeing the 'appearance' and one of us is seeing the 'reality' of Miss Charlotte Mansfield. In short, one of us is deceived. I think you follow me?"

"Yes, quite." Perplexed, David shook his head. "But, I don't understand. I would imagine she must be putting up a good front for the people at Somerville."

"Nobody is that good an actress," Stuart declared flatly. "Not if she's as ill as you say. Kate said she could die if she doesn't get this marrow transplant. No one who is dying of this aplastic anemia could stay up all hours dancing."

"But, I saw her at Blackwell's. She nearly fainted. I don't believe it was a charade."

"You know, you're right. Early in the term, she did have some fainting spells, and she said you'd taken her to the infirmary. She did have anemia. But just a mild case, is what Lucy reported. Certainly, not anything serious."

David rubbed his forehead tiredly. "I just can't believe it. If she doesn't have it, why would she say so, why would she...I just don't understand it."

"I know you and Charlotte were once engaged. From the way she talks about you, I am certain she regrets having broken your engagement. In fact, I would hazard a guess that she is obsessed with you. This sickness of hers has gotten her a lot of attention from you, hasn't it?"

"Yes."

"Mr. MacKenzie, I believe Charlotte Mansfield is a sick woman, but not in the way you have supposed."

"But where's your proof, man? If you are right, how would we know?"

"Kate said you want to be tested to see if you can give bone marrow to Charlotte. Here's my suggestion. Go ahead and inquire at the infirmary tomorrow. Talk to Charlotte's doctor and see what he says. If I'm wrong, I'll most humbly eat crow with all the attendant apologies."

"And if you're right?"

Stuart smiled. "If I'm right, then I'll expect an invitation to the wedding."

David looked at him quizzically. "Why are you doing this? Why should you get involved?"

Stuart looked down at his polished boots then back at David. "Atoning for my sins, perhaps? Really, I'm not all bad, Mr. MacKenzie. I'm generally a good sport, and if I must lose, I try to lose like a gentleman. I do think Kate is a capital girl and I have the highest respect for you. I'd hate to see this business spoil your happiness."

"All right, Stuart. Nothing ventured, nothing gained. I was planning to speak to the doctor anyway, so I'll go to the Radcliffe Infirmary tomorrow and we'll see what he says."

"Excellent, Mr. MacKenzie. Would you mind giving me a ring at Christ Church afterwards? I'll be very interested to hear one way or the other." Stuart stood to leave and extended his hand.

David grasped it firmly. "Right, Stuart. I will. And call me David."

27

Eighth Week, Friday Afternoon

David sipped his tea thoughtfully as he struggled internally with how to reveal to Austen and Yvette the reason he had summoned them to the Eagle and Child on the last Friday afternoon of the term. That question was foremost in his colleagues' minds as they bantered back and forth about examinations and essays.

Finally Yvette spoke up. "All right. What's going on? Did you invite me here to talk about my singing in the wedding?"

"No." David shook his head. "Kate did ask you, then? I told her what a lovely contralto voice you have. So, will you sing?"

"Yes, of course." Yvette flashed her wide smile. "I'd be honored. But what *do* you want to talk about, then?"

"Well, I know it's not about *me* singing. Out with it, old boy," Austen prodded. "I can tell something is amiss."

David sighed. "Right. But the whole thing is so surreal, I doubt you'll believe me."

Austen put down his cup. "Try us."

"All right. I've told you how deathly ill Charlotte has been. She's been ringing me quite a bit late at night, either in acute pain or just dreadfully frightened. I had decided to volunteer to see if I could give bone marrow for this experimental transplant. Kate was none too happy about it—nor to learn that I've had anything to do with Charlotte again. Apparently, Kate confided her misgivings to another student, who unexpectedly gave me a heads up. He told me he didn't believe Charlotte was sick at all. He had seen her quite a bit at parties and dances and didn't think it could be possible for her to have aplastic anemia.

"So today I went over to the Radcliffe Infirmary and asked for a consultation with Dr. Gardiner in order to volunteer to be tested for a match. He hadn't the foggiest idea what I was talking about and called for Charlotte's charts. Horrified that his diagnosis could have been misunderstood, he informed me that she had been treated for a mild form of anemia, given iron pills, told to rest up, and then had been retested two weeks later. Her blood count was perfectly normal. We're not talking about a miraculous recovery here, you understand. There *never was* any aplastic anemia. It seems Charlotte fabricated the entire story."

Austen and Yvette sat in shocked silence. Finally Yvette exclaimed, "I can't believe anyone would do such a thing!"

Austen spoke quietly. "Charlotte wants David any way she can have him, and I believe she would do anything to prevent him from marrying another woman. Actually, I'm not surprised. To my mind, Charlotte always seemed rather unstable. I'm sorry that you fell for this, David. It must have taken a tremendous emotional toll on you."

"Yes, it has," David agreed. "Not to mention, it could have cost me my marriage. Kate was understandably very unhappy about the time I spent with Charlotte."

"Do you mean you went over to see her?" Yvette chided him. "Are you *mad?* You said she was a seductress, and yet you were batty enough to go over there? Certainly not *alone?*"

"Yes, I did go alone twice," David admitted sheepishly. "I am a complete idiot. I can't believe I was so duped."

"My, my—when are you men ever going to learn?" Yvette looked like she was about to launch into a lecture.

David held his hands up in surrender. "*Mea culpa, mea culpa!* Please, Yvette, I feel badly enough."

"Well, I should think so," Yvette clucked disapprovingly. "Why didn't you ring me up or ask for my help? I could have seen through her wiles."

"I'm asking for your help now," replied David. "I want to confront her as soon as possible. This has been eating me up. I dread facing her, but I want to get it over with and get on with my life. The wedding is only two weeks from tomorrow. I know I shouldn't go alone this time. I think I should have a witness, but I didn't think it would be fair to ask the student, as it could jeopardize his friendships."

"Right you are," Austen said thoughtfully. "Then I'm your man."

"No, I don't think you should go, Austen." Yvette spoke up. "I think two men would be too threatening. *I'll* go with you, David."

The two young men exchanged glances. Austen nodded. "She's probably right. I'll be your prayer cover."

"Thanks." David looked at Yvette. "Could you go with me now? She's right down the street at Somerville and we could catch her before dinner."

"*Carpe diem.* It won't get any easier if we wait."

David took a deep breath and slowly exhaled. "Right. Let's go."

They stopped to check in at the Somerville Porters' Lodge. The porter greeted David on sight.

"Ah, Mr. MacKenzie! Here to see Miss Mansfield?" He looked at his watch and winked. "Bit early, what?"

David cleared his throat. "I'm here to introduce my colleague, Miss Goodman. May we go in?"

"Certainly. Shall I ring Miss Mansfield and tell her you're on your way?"

"No! No...I'd like to surprise her."

The porter peered out from under his bowler. "Right you are, Mr. MacKenzie. Go on in. You know the way, don't you, sir?" He winked again.

David grabbed Yvette's elbow and pulled her through the doorway.

"Good grief!" he muttered. "Here I thought I was doing my Christian duty by ministering to the sick, and look what kind of an example I've been. This is absolutely dreadful."

"I told you you shouldn't have come here alone," Yvette whispered.

"I know. I know."

David led Yvette through the grounds of Somerville to the serene Fellows' garden that was graced by the Georgian arcade of Penrose. The outer door to Charlotte's set of rooms was open. They could hear female voices punctuated by girlish giggling.

"No sporting the oak here," David said, referring to the Oxford custom of shutting the outer door when privacy was desired. He knocked on the inner door, which was slightly ajar.

"Come in!" Charlotte's husky voice called out. "Door's open."

David took a deep breath and pushed open the door, allowing Yvette to enter first. Two young women sat on the sofa. David recognized Lucy Bertram, Stuart's date in Stratford. Charlotte, wearing a typically short skirt and stiletto heels, came out of the kitchenette carrying a cocktail glass. The girls' laughter died down when David and Yvette entered.

Charlotte visibly paled. "David! What a surprise. What are you doing here?"

"Uh, I wanted to introduce my friend and colleague, Yvette Goodman. She's the Fellow in English Lit at St. Hilda's I told you about. Yvette, this is Charlotte Mansfield and Lady Lucille Bertram."

The women all nodded to one another.

"And this is Lydia Price," Lucy added, gesturing to the other young woman. "How are you, Mr. MacKenzie? It's nice to see you again."

"You've met before?" Charlotte asked.

"Yes, remember? I told you we'd met at Stratford a fortnight ago," Lucy answered.

Charlotte looked annoyed. "Oh, right." Then to David, "Do come in and sit down. May I get you something to drink?"

David shook his head. "Not for me, thanks. Yvette?"

"No, thanks, I'm fine."

The group awkwardly traded pleasantries.

"You know," David said, "Maybe this is a bad time and we should come back later."

"No, we're the ones that have to go." Lucy stood up.

A look of desperation crossed Charlotte's face. "Don't go!"

"No, really, we should get dressed for dinner. We'll see you in Hall. Come on, Lydia. Nice to see you again, Mr. MacKenzie, and to meet you, Miss Goodman."

Giggling, the two girls sailed out.

Sighing heavily, Charlotte sank into a chair. "Oh, thank God they've gone. I trust I can speak plainly with Miss…Goodman, did you say?" She lit a cigarette and took a deep drag. David noticed that her hands trembled.

"It's getting so hard to keep up this pretense that everything's all right. I'm glad the term is ending and I can just rest and not have to pretend anymore that I'm not ill."

"It won't do, Charlotte." David spoke quietly.

"Oh, you're right." She puffed nervously on her cigarette. "I should probably just quit this charade."

"Yes, you should. You should quit this charade that you are ill."

Charlotte blew out a cloud of smoke. "Sorry?"

David leaned forward. "Charlotte, I decided to be tested to see if I could give bone marrow for the transplant."

"Really?" Charlotte took a swig from her glass as she considered this.

"Oh, David," she finally said, "you are so wonderful! That's fabulous of you, and I really, really appreciate your even considering it so close to your wedding and all. But, you know, your prayers were answered. My mother finally got in touch with John, and he's on his way home. Hopefully, he will be here soon and will make the perfect match. I still have a lot to go through, but thank you so very, very much for considering it. You are such a dear, but you won't need to help."

"You're right. I won't need to help, but not because of John. I made an appointment with Dr. Gardiner this morning to be tested. Odd thing was, he had absolutely no blooming idea what I was talking about."

Charlotte laughed uneasily. "Of course not. I switched doctors, didn't I tell you?"

"No, you didn't. Dr. Gardiner called for your records. He's your doctor all right. The one you saw when I took you to the infirmary the night you were feeling faint. He said he treated you for simple anemia and your last blood count was perfectly normal. Charlotte, you've never had aplastic anemia. You've never had a blood transfusion, and neither is a bone-marrow transplant under consideration, because you don't need one. You have fabricated this entire illness."

"I have not! That's outrageous. That old doctor didn't know what he was doing—which is why I got a new one. I am very, very sick!"

"Yes," David answered quietly. "I suppose you are."

"What's that supposed to mean?" snapped Charlotte.

"It means that this whole elaborate deception is really rather bizarre behavior, and perhaps you should see a professional counselor."

"I resent that!"

"I resent what you've done to me! Maybe you thought it was a great joke, but I took it all very seriously. You've cost me many sleepless nights, caused me a great deal of anxiety on your account, and threatened my relationship with Kate."

Charlotte smiled.

"Oh, you find that amusing, do you?" David angrily raised his voice. "Was that your purpose all along?"

Charlotte jabbed her cigarette into an ashtray. "You needn't start shouting, darling. I've appreciated your sacrifices, but think of me. After all, I'm the one who has the fatal disease."

"It's a lie, Charlotte!"

"I told you, you've got the wrong doctor."

"I haven't. And besides, people have seen you out at all hours dancing and partying. There is no way you could have aplastic anemia and be out clubbing. You are lying!"

Suddenly Charlotte looked frightened. "Who told you that?"

"It doesn't matter. Just stop the charade," David pleaded.

"Miss Mansfield," Yvette intervened. "I must warn you that if you keep up this pretense, we will be compelled to report your unethical and unorthodox behavior to the Principal at Somerville as well as to your superiors at Cambridge."

Charlotte's eyes narrowed like a cat's. "Who asked you into this, you half-caste?"

"Charlotte!" David remonstrated.

Yvette's eyes locked on to her adversary's. "As a member of the Oxford faculty, I volunteered, and I will certainly act in the best interests of the University."

"You wouldn't dare report me."

"Oh, yes, I would."

"Why should anyone believe his story? I'll say it's all a mistake and David misunderstood."

"You forget he has a witness now. I heard your claims to be ill."

"Well, I am!"

"You can't have it both ways."

"I think this conversation is finished. I think you'd better leave now."

"Miss Mansfield," Yvette answered serenely. "I assure you that no report will be made so long as you drop the charade and leave David alone."

"Charlotte," David tried to adopt Yvette's calm demeanor. "Just come clean."

Charlotte glared fiercely at him. "Get out *now!*"

David walked with Yvette towards the door.

"No, wait! Get this bloody thing out of here." Charlotte snatched his New Testament off the coffee table and hurled it at him.

"Now get out!" she shrieked. *"Get out!"*

28

Saturday, July 3, 1965

Helen Hughes straightened her daughter's veil and kissed her on the cheek.

"You look beautiful, Sugar," she whispered, her eyes glistening with tears.

"Thanks, Mom." Kate smiled at her mother. "So do you."

Kate smoothed her gown and glanced happily around the paneled Oak Room of St. Aldate's. Everyone was here. Her family. David's. Their friends. All her life she had waited for this day. All her life she had waited and dreamed and planned. Once it had seemed to her that her wedding day would never come...and now it seemed, so suddenly, to have arrived.

Two weeks earlier, David had come to her and begged her forgiveness for his involvement with Charlotte and his blindness to the truth. He shared how he had been deceived, and Yvette had reported that Charlotte had returned quietly to Cambridge. Kate felt fury and immense relief, and then compassion for David's emotional turmoil. She also felt strangely satisfied that Stuart Devereux had redeemed himself by coming so gallantly to their rescue. He had more than earned his invitation to their wedding.

Kate had been fêted with a whirlwind of bridal showers and parties, after all. Yvette and the girls at St. Hilda's had embarrassed her with a trunkful of scanty lingerie. The matrons of St. Aldate's had given her a more practical shower of everyday gifts for the kitchen and bath. The church college-age fellowship had taken up a collection for a shopping spree at Marks and Spencer. As for David, the Inklings Society had surprised their gratified faculty sponsor with a hefty gift certificate to Blackwell's Bookstore, and the Magdalen Senior Common Room had contributed a generous check for the honeymoon.

Kate's brother and sister had arrived from the United States and pleased Kate by rapidly making friends with their MacKenzie "siblings-in-law." David had quickly won over Debbie and Scott, and thus Kate had only had to contend with her sister's obvious crush on her handsome bridegroom. Before long, however, Debbie had been clamoring to be introduced to the "dashing Lord Devereux"—or any available nobleman, for that matter. Kate had not obliged her and had been relieved when her father planned a family holiday to Bath for the weekend of Kate's twenty-first birthday. David had taken the train down to join them for high tea in the Pump Room and her birthday dinner at Sally Lunn's House, but he had insisted on returning to Oxford to allow the Hughes to enjoy their last family vacation alone together. Although she had longed to be with him, Kate appreciated David's sensitivity toward her parents.

Now at St. Aldate's, the Mistress of Ceremonies, Mrs. White, signaled to Ginny and Natalie to close the guest book as she hastened to herd family members into line to process into the sanctuary. The organist began playing "Jesu, Joy of Man's Desiring," since Helen Hughes had insisted on being seated to the strains of Bach. Ginny, in ice blue, and Natalie, in pale green, blew kisses to Kate as they took their brothers' arms and floated down the aisle in clouds of chiffon. William, dapper and quite serious in his role as a groomsman, returned to escort his mother.

The young MacKenzie men looked quite different today in their suits than they had the previous night at the Rehearsal Dinner. At their festive Scottish ceilidh, they had sported kilts in the MacKenzie tartan.

Kate and Debbie had giggled earlier together about the oddity of men in skirts, but the actual appearance of these proud, handsome Scots belied their preconceptions.

After the evening rehearsal and a fine feast prepared by the women of the church, Eric MacKenzie had welcomed Kate into the MacKenzie clan by presenting her with a sash of their dress tartan and a beautiful brooch with the family crest: *"Luceo non uro—I shine, not burn."* Then the festivities had broken loose with highland dancing and the "crack," or singing and storytelling—many of the tales roasting the good-natured groom. The boisterous mood had softened with Kevin Ryan's rendition of "Danny Boy" in his pure, sweet Irish tenor, which had brought tears to many an eye. Next, Eric MacKenzie had brought out his bagpipes and regaled them with "Amazing Grace." The combined families had mingled their voices in this hymn of praise and gathered around the bridal couple to conclude the evening with prayer.

From the church doors, Kate now watched as Annie took William's arm to walk down the aisle. Annie glanced back and gave Kate a serene, reassuring smile. Like Helen, Annie wore a suit, but hers was made of peach linen. A wide-brimmed cream-colored hat framed her youthful face. If Kate had not been told, she would never have guessed that Annie herself had sewn her ensemble.

Then Kate watched her brother Scott offer his arm to his mother and escort her to the front of the church. The organ paused.

Kate glanced at her father, who was nervously pressing his thumbs together, and gave his arm a squeeze.

"I love you, Daddy," she whispered.

Tom Hughes blinked at her in surprise. "I love you too, Sugar." Then his eyes brimmed with tears.

The organ burst forth with John Stanley's *Trumpet Voluntary,* and Mrs. White, deferring to American custom, signaled Debbie, as Kate's maid of honor, to proceed. Debbie's long, straight, pink chiffon gown and bolero jacket complimented the bride's. A large pink bow with a short net veil pinned back Debbie's sandy shoulder-length hair. Right on her heels toddled Hannah, also pretty in pink, her chiffon dress puffed up by her stiff crinoline petticoat, like a swirl of cotton candy. A wreath of baby's breath crowned her golden ringlets. Accustomed to commanding the center of attention, Hannah demurely dropped a trail of rose petals from a tiny wicker basket. Beside her walked Timmy, smiling broadly and proudly bearing a pillow with the wedding rings tightly tied in place. At the sight of the children, the congregation collectively smiled and sighed.

The assembly rose as the organ solemnly swelled with a glorious theme from Handel's *Rinaldo.* Kate clutched her father's arm. *This is it, I want to remember every person's face. I want to remember every moment.* She tried to smile at her friends standing along the aisle. She looked up to the front of the church, took in the Reverend Eric MacKenzie and Austen, the best man...and then—David.

Suddenly, Kate had eyes for no one else. David beamed at her. She smiled back, thinking that if her heart grew any fuller it would surely burst.

She heard Eric MacKenzie reading the words of the liturgy, but she felt almost as if she and her husband-to-be were in a fog. For a few moments, everything seemed to be moving in slow motion. She and David answered, "I will," to the betrothal vows...and then her father was giving her away, kissing her gently on the cheek as her hand was placed in David's.

David. My beloved husband.

Her betrothed squeezed her hand, and her attention returned to the present as her father-in-law and pastor began to read from Ecclesiastes 4:9-12:

> *Two are better than one, because they have a good reward for their toil. For if they fall, one will lift up his fellow; but woe to him who is alone when he falls and has not another to lift him up. Again, if two lie together, they are warm; but how can one be warm alone? And though a man might prevail against one who is alone, two will withstand him. A threefold cord is not quickly broken.*

Eric went on to give a short homily that illustrated how the third strand of the cord that binds together a marriage is God Himself. He exhorted David and Kate to keep their Lord, Jesus Christ, as the center of their lives and their marriage. Then he asked them to take each other's right hand, as if they were shaking hands on a contract, as they repeated their covenant vows.

David's voice boomed in confident affirmation, "I, David, take thee, Katherine, to be my wedded wife, to have and to hold from this day forward: for better, for worse; for richer, for poorer; in sickness and in health; to love and to cherish, 'til death us do part, according to God's holy ordinance; and thereto I plight thee my troth."

Kate swallowed, and with tears in her eyes repeated her vows. Then they exchanged rings as the token of their pledge.

They knelt while Yvette stood to sing "The Lord's Prayer." As her rich contralto filled the ancient sanctuary, Kate recalled her mother's initial objection to having Yvette sing after she had discovered the young woman's racial heritage. They had convinced Helen that it would be impolite to withdraw the request made of Kate's tutor, and she had relented. When Yvette's voice soared with "For Thine is the kingdom and the power and the glory, forever," Kate knew her mother would be pleased with their decision.

As the ceremony neared its close, Eric MacKenzie prayed a blessing: "O Almighty God, Creator of mankind, who only art the wellspring of life; bestow upon these Thy servants, if it be Thy will, the gift and heritage of children; and grant that they may see their children brought up in Thy faith and fear, to the honor and glory of Thy Name; through Jesus Christ our Lord. Amen."

David squeezed Kate's hand again and wiped a final tear from his cheek. Then he grinned at her as he helped her to her feet. Joining their hands, Eric pronounced, "Those whom God hath joined together let no man put asunder. Forasmuch as David and Katherine have consented together in holy wedlock, and have witnessed the same before God and this company, and thereto have given and pledged their troth, each to the other, and have declared the same by giving and receiving rings, and by joining hands; I pronounce that they are Man and Wife. In the name of the Father, and of the Son, and of the Holy Ghost. Amen."

The congregation stood to sing together "Be Thou My Vision" while the bride and groom and their honor attendants signed the church registry. Kate and David's voices rose with the others on the verse,

Riches I heed not, nor man's empty praise,
Thou mine inheritance, now and always:
Thou and Thou only, first in my heart,
High King of heaven, my Treasure Thou art.

Eric MacKenzie added this final blessing: "God the Holy Trinity make you strong in faith and love, defend you on every side, and guide you in truth and peace; and the blessing of God Almighty, the Father, Son, and Holy Ghost, be among you and remain with you always. Amen."

Arm in arm, David and Kate turned to face their loved ones as their father joyfully announced, "Members of the household of faith, Ladies and Gentlemen, I now present to you Mr. and Mrs. David Lawrence MacKenzie." He leaned over and added, "You may kiss the bride."

Kate, expectant and smiling, looked up at David. He lifted her chin and brushed her lips with his. Then he kissed her gently, almost chastely. Kate felt a touch of bewilderment as cheers and applause erupted from the congregation and a peal of change bells joyfully proclaimed their union. Then Debbie thrust Kate's bouquet back into her hands, and David swept her down the aisle past the smiling faces of their friends and family.

When they reached the Oak Room, David pulled her behind the great doors. He gathered her in his arms and looked at her longingly. "That kiss was for the public," he whispered. "Now for us." He smiled broadly. *"Come on and kiss me, Kate."* His lips eagerly found hers, and her mouth yielded to his. This time, Kate felt a rush of desire. They clung tightly together, yearning to be one.

Releasing her breathlessly, David buried his face in her hair. "Oh, my darling, I love you so much it hurts," he said. His lips brushed her hair and forehead. He bent to kiss her again, when he felt someone tugging on his trousers. David and Kate looked down in surprise to see Hannah and Timmy watching them expectantly. They both laughed, giddy with love.

"Sorry, you two," David said, smiling. "You'll have to wait. I'm busy kissing my wife." He turned to Kate and asked, "Was it worth it, Mrs. MacKenzie?"

"Worth waiting for?"

He nodded.

"Oh, yes!" she cried happily, throwing her arms around his neck.

And they kissed again.

Anglo-Oxford/American Glossary

bird: slang term for a young woman, as in the American term "chick"

Bird and Baby: nickname for the Eagle and Child, the pub frequented by C.S. Lewis and the Inklings

biscuit: cookie

Blackwell's: the largest bookshop in Oxford, located on Broad Street

bloke: a guy

Blue: award of colors for representing the University in a sport. Oxford Blues are a dark blue; Cambridge Blues are light blue.

boater: hard, flat-topped straw hat worn in summer, especially when boating and during "Eights"

the Bod, or Bodleian: main library at Oxford University; receives a copy of every book published in England.

boot: car trunk

Carfax: the center of the city of Oxford where Cornmarket, The High Street, St. Aldate's and Queen Street meet. The tower there affords a great view.

ceilidh: (kay-lee) informal evening of song and fun

cheerio: good-bye

the Cherwell (pronounced "charwell"): one of two rivers in Oxford (see Isis)

chips: French fries

Christ Church: the largest and perhaps richest and most prestigious college at Oxford (nicknamed: "The House"). The college chapel is Oxford's cathedral.

coach: long-distance bus

college: one of about forty institutions that make up the University of Oxford

come up: to arrive as a student at Oxford, as in, "Has he come up yet?"

crack or *craic*: (Irish) talk, conversation, gossip, chat; a tale, a good story or joke

cuppa: cup of tea

daft: crazy

dear: expensive

dinner: lunch or dinner

dinner jacket, or D.J. : tuxedo or dark suit with black bow tie and fancy shirt worn for formal dinners and college balls

don: college tutor, from the Latin *"dominus,"* or lord

the Eagle and Child: pub on St. Giles St. that was the meeting place for the Inklings

eight: rowing boat with eight oarsman and a coxswain to steer

Eights Week: intercollegiate rowing regatta held in Fifth Week of the Trinity, or summer term

Exam Schools, or Examination Schools: building on High Street where exams and some lectures are held

Fellow: member of the governing board of a college; many of the college tutors are Fellows

first floor: second floor

flat: apartment

football: soccer

fortnight: two weeks

fresher: first-year student

Fresher's Fair: stalls for all the University clubs and societies held at the beginning of each academic year in the Exam Schools

go down: leave as a student at Oxford either temporarily or permanently

ground floor: first floor

hall: communal eating place in (a) college. One eats "in hall" and lives "in college."

Head of the River: winning crew or college in Eights Week. Also the name of the pub near the finishing line at Folly Bridge.

Hilary Term: Oxford's spring term. Americans would call it a winter term, as the eight-week term lasts from mid-January to mid-March.

holiday: vacation

The House: another name for Christ Church

The Inklings: Perhaps the most important literary club of the twentieth century, which met informally for more than thirty years on Thursday evenings in C.S. Lewis's Magdalen rooms and Tuesday mornings in the Eagle and Child pub. When Lewis commuted from Cambridge on weekends, they continued to meet on Monday mornings at the Lamb and Flag until Lewis's death in 1963. One had to be invited, normally by C.S. ("Jack") Lewis; members included his brother, Major Warren ("Warnie") Lewis; J.R.R. Tolkien; Charles Williams; Owen Barfield; Hugo Dyson; Dr. Robert (Humphrey) Havard; and Nevill Coghill. The friends read aloud their works in progress (including Tolkien's The Lord of the Rings and Lewis's The Chronicles of Narnia) for the others to critique and discuss, but the meetings often had no agenda other than good conversation and rich fellowship.

interval: intermission

Isis: a tributary of the Thames River in Oxford

Jack: the name with which C.S. Lewis christened himself when he was four

J.C.R., or Junior Common Room: club and lounge for Oxford undergraduates

the King's Arms, or the K.A.: possibly the pub most frequented by Oxford students, at the corner of Parks Road and Holywell Street

let: rent

loo: toilet, or bathroom

mackintosh, or mac: raincoat

Magdalen College (pronounced "maudlin"): the College in Oxford where C.S. Lewis was a Fellow from 1925 to 1954. When Lewis took a Chair in Medieval and Renaissance Literature at Cambridge in 1955, his rooms there were in **Magdalene College** (also pronounced "maudlin").

mate: friend (girl or boy)

May Morning: May 1st. A carol is sung at sunrise from the top of Magdalen Tower and students welcome May with all manner of frivolity.

M.C.R., or Middle Common Room: club and lounge for Oxford graduate students

Merton College: where J.R.R. Tolkien was Merton Professor of English

Michaelmas: the eight-week autumn term, October–December

nappies: diapers

nought: zero. Nought Week is the week before the term officially begins.

the other place: Cambridge. At Cambridge, "the other place" is Oxford.

Oxbridge: Oxford and Cambridge Universities

paralytic: drunk

porter: guard at the front gate of each college. The porters serve as concierges, confidants, and bulldogs (policemen)

Porters' Lodge: building for the porters by the front gate that also serves as the mailroom for students

the pond: the Atlantic Ocean. The "other side of the pond" is the U.S.A.

pitch: playing field

punt: flat-bottomed boat

quad: short for **quadrangle,** a rectangular courtyard inside a college. Only dons are allowed to walk on the grass. Called "courts" at "the other place."

queue: line

queue up: line up

Radcliffe Camera, or Rad Cam: distinctive domed library in Oxford

ring up: call, telephone

St. Hilda's College: a women's college in Oxford, located along the Cherwell River. Home of the Jacqueline du Pré Music Building.

scout: person who cleans college rooms, more like a servant in Lewis's times

S.C.R, or Senior Common Room: club for Oxford Fellows

sent down: expelled

the Sheldonian: the Sheldonian Theatre, where matriculation and degree ceremonies, as well as concerts, are held

solicitor: lawyer

Somerville College: formerly a women's college (now co-ed) at Oxford. College of Margaret Thatcher and unofficial Inkling Dorothy L. Sayers.

sporting the oak: In college rooms with two doors, if the outer door is open the occupant is receiving visitors. If the outer door is closed, the occupant does not wish to be disturbed and is "sporting the oak."

stalls: Orchestra section of a theatre

toff: someone with money or from the upper class

Trinity Term: eight-week "summer" term, from April to June

tube: subway

tutor: college teacher. In term time, a student meets with his tutor at least once a week for a tutorial, or "tut," to read aloud and discuss an eight-page essay on the subject he is "reading" or studying.

underground: subway

Wellingtons, wellies: boots

Compiled with assistance from Rick Steve's *Great Britain and Ireland 2001*, Emeryville, California; Avalon Travel Publishing by John Muir Publications; and the University of Oxford web site's "Glossary of Terms" (Jonathan.Bowen@comlab.ox.ac.uk., 1994).

Acknowledgments

This book was written with the help and encouragement of many people to whom I am extremely grateful, but I would like to publicly thank the following:

My husband, Bill, and my children: Katherine Ryan (Craddock), Christen Marie (Young), Cheryl Anne, William Brett, Richard Aaron, Mark Devereux, David Scott, Brendan Michael, and Kevin Morey for their ideas and love and patience as I spent time away in the UK and long nights on the computer. Particular thanks to Katherine for sharing her journal of her experiences as a student at Oxford in the Michaelmas term of 1999, for allowing me to print her sonnet "Matthew 6:26" ("The Pigeon-Lady"), and most of all for being the inspiration for the story by saving her first kiss until her wedding day; also to her husband Chris, who honored that commitment; and to both of them for demonstrating by their lives that purity is indeed possible.

My parents, Earl and Betty Morey, for their prayerful encouragement of this project and for my mother's invaluable editorial assistance. My sister Debbie Holden, sister in-law Erika Morey, my mother-in-law Kathleen Jeschke, and sister-in-law Anne Jeschke for their suggestions and encouragement of my first writing ventures.

My church family at The King's Chapel in Fairfax, Virginia, for their wonderful love and support of me and my family. In particular, Marilyn White for her editorial help and for sharing the vision from the very beginning and praying it through to completion. Inece Bryant for her indefatigable enthusiasm, support, and prayers. Elizabeth Sheridan, her mother Dr. Tessa Hare, and Karen Walker for keeping my British English straight; and Karen's father, Martin Wilton, who helped us track down details from British phrases to fragrances. Patrick and Barbara Kavanaugh, who brought me pictures and paraphernalia from St. Hilda's College, loaned me books and a videotape of Jacqueline du Pré, and graciously gave me an impromptu piano-and-cello concert of "The Girl with the Flaxen Hair" in their living room. Jacque Dietrichson for formatting my manuscript. Chuck Beasley, Diane DeMark, Stacey Ipsan, Ed and Nora Phelps, Alastair and Jacqui Thomson, Virginia Walden, Sharon Wells, Dianna White and Molly Wooddell, for their encouragement, comments, and readings of early drafts. All my UK traveling companions. Andrew White for his magnificent map of Oxford. Tom and Elizabeth Bevans for their faithful love and prayers.

Dr. Stan Mattson and the C.S. Lewis Foundation for making it possible for me and my daughters Katherine and Cheryl to attend the Oxbridge '98 and 2002 conferences, which inspired me to pursue my interest in Lewis, begin writing again, and fulfill a lifelong dream to study at Oxford and Cambridge. Jodi Johnson, former Head Resident at the Kilns, for her hospitality. The Reverend Simon Ponsonby and the staff at St. Aldate's for welcoming Katherine and pilgrims from the USA into their fellowship and for answering all my questions. Tom Hall, Secretary to the Student Work at St. Aldate's, who took the time to research and e-mail answers and who even unearthed drawings of the rectory as it was in the 1960s. Andrew Cuneo, Doctor of Philosophy and tutor at Merton College, for answering my queries, being an excellent tutor of Renaissance Poetry for Katherine, and inspiring a new generation of Inklings as the President of the Oxford University C.S. Lewis Society. Grant and Rachel Vallance, for opening their Oxford home to us and guiding us across Port Meadow to the Perch and the Trout Inn. George Johnston, Merton Porter, and Kim Cameron, Conference Manager, for being such wonderful hosts at Merton College. Simon Bailey, Keeper of the Archives at the University of Oxford Bodleian Library; Sue Waldman, Sheldonian Custodian; Philippa Ouvry, Assistant, Jacqueline du Pré Music Building; and Anne Wilson, I.T. Manager, St. Hilda's College, Oxford, for answering e-mail queries. Eileen Roberts, St. Hilda's Alumnae Relations Officer, for meeting with me and showing me about St. Hilda's. Alistair McEwan, Mansfield Road Football Club, who not only provided info on the University staff club, but also warmly welcomed my fictional hero, David MacKenzie, to join their club team!

Joyce Hart for acting as my literary agent. My writers' club, The Capital Christian Writers, who provided speakers and seminars just as I needed them and put me in contact with prolific author Loree Lough, whose critique was invaluable. Joanie Tooley for background story. The women in my book clubs (We Love Jesus and Books, Oakton Glen, and Vienna Soccer Moms) for their encouragement. The Journal Newspapers for giving me my first professional break as a free-lance travel writer. Dr. Sharon Decker (wherever you are), my University of Virginia English 101 writing instructor, for inspiring me to major in English literature and teaching.

My new publishing family at Harvest House and editors Terry Glaspey, Nick Harrison, and Paul Gossard for their vision and inestimable critical expertise, which brought this new edition to your hands.

And finally—but really firstly—my first edition publisher, Tom Freiling, and his lovely wife, Nancy, of Xulon Press. It was Tom who came to me with the idea of setting a novel around the Inklings and the Eagle and Child pub—and without whom this book may never have been written.

I owe you all an incredible debt of gratitude.

List of References

Books on C.S. Lewis

Carpenter, Humphrey. *The Inklings: C.S. Lewis, J.R.R. Tolkien, Charles Williams, and Their Friends.* London: Allen & Unwin, 1979.

Como, James T., ed. *C.S. Lewis at the Breakfast Table and Other Reminiscences.* New York: Macmillan, 1979. Contains Walter Hooper's exhaustive bibliography.

Dorsett, Lyle. *A Love Observed.* Wheaton, Illinois: Harold Shaw, 1983.

Duncan, John Ryan. *The Magic Never Ends: The Life and Work of C.S. Lewis.* Nashville, TN: W Publishing Group, a Division of Thomas Nelson, Inc., 2001.

Duriez, Colin. *The C.S. Lewis Encyclopedia.* Wheaton, Illinois: Crossway Books, 2000.

Duriez, Collin, and David Porter. *The Inklings Handbook.* St. Louis, MO: Chalice Press, 2001.

Glaspey, Terry. *The Spiritual Legacy of C.S. Lewis.* Nashville, TN: Cumberland House,1996.

Green, Roger Lancelyn, and Walter Hooper. *C.S. Lewis: A Biography.* London: Collins, 1974; New York: Harcourt Brace Jovanovich, 1974. Revised British edition: HarperCollins, 2002.

Gresham, Douglas. *Lentenlands.* New York: Macmillan, 1988.

Hooper, Walter. *Through Joy and Beyond: A Pictorial Biography of C.S. Lewis.* New York: Macmillan, 1982.

Lewis, C.S. *Surprised by Joy: The Shape of My Early Life.* London: Geoffrey Bles, 1955.

Sayer, George. *Jack: A Life of C.S. Lewis.* Wheaton, Illinois: Crossway Books, 1994. First edition titled *Jack: C.S. Lewis and His Times,* Harper & Row, 1988.

Sibley, Brian. *C.S. Lewis Through the Shadowlands: The Story of his Life with Joy Davidman.* Grand Rapids, MI: Baker Books, 1994; Spire Books,1999.

Vanauken, Sheldon. *A Severe Mercy.* New York: Harper & Row, 1977. London: Hodder and Stoughton, 1979.

Books on J.R.R. Tolkien

Carpenter, Humphrey. *Tolkien: A Biography.* Boston: Houghton Mifflin Company, 1977.

Coren, Michael. *J.R.R. Tolkien: The Man who Created The Lord of the Rings.* New York: Scholastic, Inc., 2001.

Duriez, Colin. *The J.R.R. Tolkien Handbook.* Grand Rapids, MI: Baker Books, 1992, reprinted 2002.

Pearce, Joseph. *Tolkien: Man and Myth, A Literary Life.* Harper Collins/Ignatius Press,1998.

Books on Jacqueline du Pré

Du Pré, Hilary and Piers. *Hilary and Jackie,* previously titled *A Genius in the Family.* New York: Ballantine Books, 1997.

Easton, Carol. *Jacqueline du Pré: A Biography.* Summit Books/Simon and Schuster, 1989.

Wilson, Elizabeth. *Jacqueline du Pré: Her Life, Her Music, Her Legend.* New York: Arcade Publishing, Inc., First USA edition, 1999.

More Fine Fiction from Harvest House Publishers

Austen Series

First Impressions

Debra White Smith

Loosely based on the beloved *Pride and Prejudice*, Debra White Smith's *First Impressions* weaves a spell-binding, modern-day tale on the challenges and rewards of love. Eddi Boswick has just settled in Texas to establish her law practice. Joining a local theater group, she is thrilled when she is given the role of Elizabeth in *Pride and Prejudice.* William "Dave" Davidson III amassed a fortune in the computer industry but leads a quiet life on his ranch. On a dare he tries out for the play and lands the role of Darcy. Sparks fly each time the lawyer meets the rancher. When Eddi uncovers Dave's secret will her heart soften? Will Dave's fear of "being tamed" keep him from discovering love?

ISBN: 0-7369-0872-2 • U.S. $10.99 Can $17.50

Growing Up on the Edge of the World

Phil Callaway

In this tender coming–of–age story, a young boy discovers a hidden stash of money—and more trouble than he thought possible. As he unravels the mystery of its origin, he discovers an even greater mystery—the mystery of the grace of God as it is expressed through a small community of believers. With a cast of characters worthy of a Mark Twain novel, a mysterious illness, an astounding confession, and a lump–in–the–throat climax, this story is sure to bring laughter and tears as it entertains and enriches a wide range of readers.

ISBN: 0-7369-0730-0 • U.S. $10.99 Can $17.50

The Gate Seldom Found

Raymond Reid

First self–published by the author in 2001, *The Gate Seldom Found* dramatizes the true story of a little known Christian fellowship that flowered late in 19th century Canada. The saga opens in southern Ontario in January, 1898. Alistair Stanhope is shaken by the untimely death of his best friend, causing him to question his faith. Unable to find the depth of spirituality he is seeking within his church, he and his wife, Priscilla, begin to meet with a close circle of friends for support. From these intimate gatherings comes an awakening that touches many lives with the simplicity of following Jesus Christ. A novel that will impact readers for years to come.

ISBN: 0-7369-1369-6 • U.S. $13.99 Can $22.99

About the Author

Melanie Morey Jeschke is a pastor's wife, home-schooling mother of nine children, and former high school English teacher, who writes travel articles and fiction. She graduated with an honors degree in English literature from the University of Virginia, where she also studied European and English History. Melanie has made a number of trips to England and Oxford, where she has attended two conferences on C.S. Lewis. She resides in northern Virginia with her children and husband, Bill Jeschke, Senior Pastor of The King's Chapel.

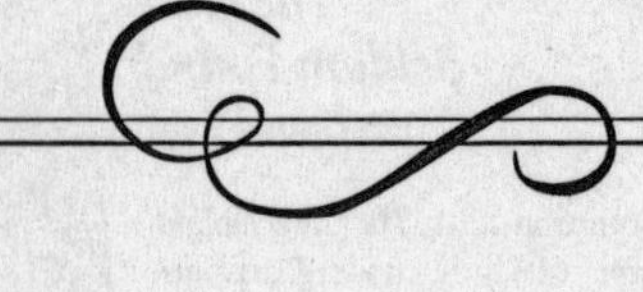